EINSTEIN'S DESK

EINSTEIN'S DESK

DR. ROBERT MELILLO
AND DOMENIC MELILLO

Phase Publishing, LLC
Seattle, WA

Cover art by Tugboat Design
http://www.tugboatdesign.net

Phase Publishing, LLC first paperback edition
March 2020

ISBN 978-1-952103-04-9
Library of Congress Control Number 2020903160
Cataloging-in-Publication Data on file.

DEDICATIONS

This book is dedicated to those who bring light into my heart and my home, the love of my life, Susan, and our children; Joseph, Alexandra, Olivia, and Nicholas.

~ DJM

First, this book is dedicated to my family, who inspire me every day in everything I do, my brilliant and beautiful wife, Carolyn, and our three children; Robert, Ellis, and Ty.

Next, this book is also dedicated to the two people who first lit the spark of curiosity and passion for science, health, and literature in me; my parents, Catherine and Joseph Melillo.

Lastly, I dedicate this book to the memory of the two greatest minds that have ever lived, Albert Einstein and Nikola Tesla. Their work has changed mankind forever.

~ RJM

PROLOGUE

Hotel New Yorker, Suite 3327
January 7, 1943

The old man sat at his desk; the same worn, mahogany desk where he had worked for a decade. He looked up and stared blankly at the hazy window, not seeing anything beyond. Slowly, as it had so many times before, an image of his younger self was reflected in the glass.

"Ah, my young self," the old man half-smiled, "you have returned yet again."

The image nodded but didn't return the old man's smile. "You are sad," it observed.

"I'm thinking about the past."

"That makes you sad?" the young image queried.

"The past ten years do," he replied. "It has been a brutal decade for me. I have dreamed many dreams and have seen every one of them die."

"That's not true, is it?"

After a moment of thought, the old man agreed. "You're right. Some of them have been stolen. I am a failure and they, the ones with influence, think I am a fraud. But do you know the worst feeling? It's the abject disappointment I feel in myself. I was supposed to be the light. I was supposed to bring the power; unlimited, free, and forever. I was going to save mankind and show them the way. But here I sit in the fading sunlight of yet another evening alone, and all I feel is the weight of the deepening darkness inside me."

The image frowned. "It's not as if you haven't accomplished anything at all. You have."

Nodding with a frown, the old man sighed. "But those accomplishments were the least of my dreams. Those were the easy things, the low-hanging fruit. The really impactful dreams, the truly revolutionary ones, have been laughed at and dismissed. The narcissistic and mercenary minds of powerful men will not accept that change is coming. All they think about is their own oxen which will be gored by the strength of my understanding and the changes wrought by my inventions. Thomas Edison, J.P. Morgan, George Westinghouse, even Roosevelt, have marginalized me and made me a laughing-stock."

"Then, perhaps," his younger self suggested, "you should just take all your dreams and the paper they are written on and burn them. The world is not ready for them. The world does not deserve them."

Cocking his head, the old man thought for a moment. "That's not completely true. The men of power do not deserve them, but the rest of the world, the humble and struggling people of the world, they do deserve them."

With a sigh, the old man remembered watching the faces of the simple, hard-working multitude as his power lit up the White City at the 1893 World's Fair in Chicago. "Remember the World's Fair, my young self?"

With a small smile, the image nodded. "I remember. Your heart was filled as you saw the wonderment and adoration on the faces of the crowds witnessing such a dazzling sight for the first time."

"Yes! That proved that my concept worked. The

world was astounded, and I made Edison look like a fool."

"Many described it as 'seeing a vision of heaven'," the image added.

"It was then that I knew my dreams could change the world; that I could reshape it."

"A heady feeling indeed," the image acknowledged. "Afterward, all the newspapers around the world proclaimed you the most famous person on Earth."

The old man frowned. "Now, fifty years later, I am forgotten. Over time, I have grown weary of the lesser minds that cannot understand my vision."

"But there is one man with the intellect and vision to rival yours, is there not?"

With a sad smile, the old man replied, "Yes, I am glad that I have preserved my dreams and entrusted the most important of them to this man of integrity. He, above all others, will know what to do with the last discovery and with the key. And with the last dream."

He nodded to himself, then looked up to see the image had vanished, as it usually did when he finally settled on a course of action. He looked at his watch; 8:00 p.m. Time to go to dinner. It was only a short walk to the restaurant at the Waldorf. He would be on time to eat at 8:10, as he had been for the past decade. His table, and his meal of assorted steamed vegetables and a glass of milk and honey, would be waiting for him, along with the eighteen starched napkins that the head waiter knew he required.

He put on his coat and hat and headed to the elevator. As the elevator doors opened, he saw two men. They were familiar, but not entirely welcome.

"Good evening, sir," the taller one greeted him. "May we join you for dinner? We have a message for you."

"Perhaps another time, gentlemen," he replied,

stepping around them.

"Now is better," the shorter man insisted, placing his hand on the old man's arm. "You must hear it now."

Looking back and forth between them, the old man reluctantly agreed.

Walking together to the Waldorf, they were silent, giving the old man time to think, and remember. When they first approached him a year or so ago, he had been flattered by their attention. They had given him lavish compliments and listened attentively to his stories. No one listened to his stories anymore. Everyone thought he was a feeble, crazy old man. But not these two. They had treated him with respect. Maybe he had said too much back then, maybe he told them too many secrets, but the attention was as intoxicating as the whiskey they fed him.

They arrived at the Waldorf and were seated immediately. The old man slid his slender six-foot-two frame into the seat held for him by the waiter and invited his "guests" to do the same. The waiter offered menus to the guests, but they refused and ordered coffee.

After the waiter left, the taller man leaned forward and spoke in a hushed tone. "You know why we are here." It was more statement than question.

Nodding, the old man put on the white cotton gloves he always wore for dinner. He already knew what they wanted.

"It is past time," the shorter man whispered. "You were supposed to deliver it last month."

Again, the old man nodded. He had agreed to give them the secret, but now…

"We will not leave without it," the taller man hissed.

Looking at them, the old man knew that their calm demeanor was only a mask. Inside, they were predators just waiting for a chance to get the secret, and they would stop at nothing to achieve that end. They were just like all the rest. They didn't really care about his dreams or his stories; they just wanted his secrets for themselves. And the man they served was the worst; the others paled in comparison. He was the most dangerous one of all. The old man's only reason for agreeing to work with these animals was to see one of his grandest dreams fulfilled.

When it had become clear who they really were, something changed in him. He laughed to himself. His mistake was clear, now. He had no need for their recognition, appreciation, or their money anymore, and he cared not for their praise. He had seen the darkness in them and in himself and wanted no part of it. His only interest was in the light, and the light had been passed along to another where it would be safe and would someday shine brightly.

The waiter delivered his meal and their coffee. Once he again retreated, the old man began to eat. After a few bites, he looked up. He pasted a smile on his face.

"Gentlemen, I respectfully decline your request. The secret is no longer available."

Seeing the glare on their faces, he leaned forward and whispered, "You might as well give up. I will take it to my grave."

Without hesitation, he went back to his meal.

Fury on their faces, the taller man whispered, "You will regret that decision, old man. There will be consequences."

He watched them go, grateful that they left without drawing too much attention to themselves. They will need the anonymity later, I suppose, he thought. Even knowing the possibilities of the potential consequences mentioned, he didn't care. He understood the way the world and the universe worked. Equal and opposite reactions, yin and yang, darkness and light. He finished his meal, said goodnight to the staff, and headed back to the New Yorker hotel to continue his work.

His key made its usual scraping sound in the old, worn lock. It was familiar and comforting. As he opened the door, he was hit from behind and pushed roughly into the room. All he understood at this point was that he was face down on the bed and that there was unbearable weight pressing down on him. Although his heart pounded hard, he did not feel afraid.

For some reason, his mind was filled with images, theories, inventions, visions, and the face of his rival, the man of integrity. The keeper of his last and greatest dream.

He thought about gravity; he thought about electricity; he thought about time and space. Finally, he thought about the light, and he was at peace. All would be well.

Then all became darkness, and he flew into the light.

CHAPTER ONE

Petrie home, 2004

Carol lay on her bed, exhausted. She closed her eyes, once again remembering her beautiful wedding and the dreams that seemed to have faded with the years.

The snow had fallen fiercely as they said their vows beside the glowing fireplace in the great hall of the mansion. There had not been a dry eye in the house for Roger and Carol Petrie's wedding. It was that beautiful.

As they'd begun their first dance as husband and wife, a classic jazz band was playing their song. The ensemble was made up of older black gentlemen and one younger female singer who had played with Count Basie and Duke Ellington. For the rest of the evening, they had thrilled the guests with old romantic standards by Gershwin, Sinatra, and Cole Porter.

What was more, it seemed that everyone there wanted to dance. Roger's mother sang "I Wish You Love" with the band. It was her signature song and her wedding gift to them. Her still-incredible voice left everyone stunned, just as it had fifty years ago. She'd been only thirteen years old when she sang at Carnegie Hall. Everyone agreed that she had a rare gift and that she could have been one of the greats, but she was shy and always dreamed of being a mother and a wife. It was a perfect gift at what was a fairytale wedding for this perfect young couple.

A few months later, Carol was pregnant. It was such an incredible experience to hear that she would soon be a mother for the first time. She and Roger were so excited to begin having children, to become the perfect family they knew it was their destiny to be. They were so certain that all the hopes and dreams of a young, intelligent, and accomplished couple were about to be realized.

Opening her eyes, she observed her third child, Ian, sitting silently in thought on the floor of the bedroom. Suddenly, he was lit by a sunbeam from the skylight above. As the bright light surrounded him, she remembered the fateful day in the doctor's office. His words would forever be burned into her psyche.

"I'm sorry Dr. and Mrs. Petrie, your son has autism," he'd said.

Carol's mind had been enveloped with a sense of numbness, just as Ian was enveloped in the light now. She remembered hearing something about an institution at some point in Ian's life. She recalled feeling defensive, telling him in no uncertain terms that she would never let that happen. That was out of the question.

But sometimes, she feared what would happen to him if they were gone. Would he be able to survive alone? Who would take care of him? Would he ever fall in love or be loved? So many questions, so many fears, so many regrets. Once again, she wondered if it was her fault in some way. Had she waited too long? She had known that he was not progressing typically and had hoped he would catch up, but that had not happened. She'd mentioned it several times to her pediatrician, but he always told her not to worry, that kids all develop at different times in different ways.

She had asked him, "Then why did you give us this document that has all of these developmental milestones on it if it doesn't matter?"

Now, at three years old, he was still not speaking, and this, she was told, was the big red flag. Ian struggled with all the typical age-appropriate milestones, and she knew he was falling further behind every day. But there were flashes of brilliance in him. His drawing was remarkable for his age, and he already drew with perspective. His eye contact was excellent. Sometimes she felt as if he could read her mind.

He was very empathetic and could feel her pain. He would come over and soothe her when he sensed that she felt sad or anxious. She didn't understand how he could be so exceptional in some ways, yet so far behind in others.

Carol just wanted Ian to be happy, and she wondered now if that was even a possibility. It often made her weep. As she lay there on the bed watching him on the floor, her heart broke once again. She loved him so much that her heart actually ached. They say a mother is only as happy as her least happy child, so she prayed for a miracle.

The pain she felt was overwhelming and was taking a toll on the family. His brother and sister, Roger Jr. and Ella, did not really understand the struggles Ian had, but they still treated him with love and gentleness. Carol was sure they felt the sadness seeping into their home, and it challenged them.

Of course, her pain was shared by Roger, but it was different for him. His pain manifested as frustration, denial, and sometimes anger, which was not his true nature. Many times, she'd heard him bemoan the fact that even as a specialist in developmental functional neurology, he still didn't have the ability to help his own son.

This was changing him, changing them. She wondered where the happy, vibrant, talented, and intelligent couple went. Where had they fled? Would they ever return? Could they ever be happy again knowing that their youngest son would never experience all the hopes and dreams they had planned for him?

As she rose from the bed and gathered up the toys that Ian once again refused to play with, she heard Roger's car pull into the driveway. Ella squealed with delight, realizing her daddy was home. She picked up Ian and headed downstairs for dinner. Roger Jr. ran past her down the stairs and leaped into his dad's waiting arms from the last step.

After the dinner dishes were washed and put away and the children were finally asleep, Roger and Carol sat at the kitchen table, exhausted, just staring at each other. There was a dullness, a deadness that had descended on their lives. It could only be described as a heaviness that had nothing to do with the actual work of life, or family duties, or even their love for one another. Rather, it had to do with lost dreams and unexpected reality.

"Did you see any progress in Ian today?" asked Roger.

"No, he was the same today as yesterday, and the day before, and the day before that," Carol replied. "It's the same every day. I hope for a sign of improvement, anything to give me the sense that all the work we're doing is having a positive effect. I guess we just have to keep trying and hope he'll improve."

"Hope is not a strategy!" exclaimed Roger. "I'm tired of hoping. I'm tired of dealing with this! It is consuming us, it is consuming *you*! You work with him all day and then spend all night on the computer searching for answers. We've discussed the fact that most of what is on the internet is nonsense, and you know it. You know none of this is your fault, right? None of it is my fault, either. That's what every specialist has told us. There's no way we could have known, and there's nothing we could have done to prevent his autism. I think we just need to accept that if he's going to improve, it will be at his own pace and eventually he will be fine. We have to stop dwelling on it and accept it. He is what he is, and we can't change it. I'm done."

"Really, Roger?" Carol questioned with a frown. "Done? Done with what? Trying? Dreaming? Believing? I know you better than that, Roger. One of the things that made me fall in love with you was your dreams. Your faith in our future. The picture you painted of our life together. You always talked in terms of possibilities and destiny.

"Will you so easily abandon all of that when the first real battle of our life comes? I'm bone-tired all the time. The weariness and hopelessness often overwhelm me, too, but then I remember your dreams, and I believe that somehow, someway, we will make them real. You need to do the same."

Roger stared into her eyes. How many times had he told her that it was her eyes he had loved from the first moment he saw them? She knew he saw the desperation and disappointment in them now. She closed her eyes for a moment.

When she opened them again, she saw he had put his head down. Finally, he quietly admitted, "I have forgotten those dreams, Carol. Can you remind me? Can you make me believe them again, too? Please?"

Her eyes filled with tears as she looked at the man she loved, so in pain, so disheartened, so in need of her strength, and she asked him, "Do you remember that patient of yours? JoAnne? Do you remember what she told you? The prophecy?"

"Yes, I remember," responded Roger. "I also remember that I was foolish enough to believe her nonsense."

"It was not nonsense," said Carol reaching across the table and grabbing his hand. "She was right about so much. She predicted the birth of each of our children with incredible accuracy. She predicted the gender of each child correctly, as well as the months they would be born. She was right about all of that, so why not the rest?"

"You mean that drivel about all of our children being 'special'?" replied Roger, finally looking up and meeting her eyes.

"Yes!" replied Carol. "She said that they were *all* special and that if we raised them with love, and believed in their uniqueness, that one of them would one day change the world. She did not say Roger Jr. would do that, or Ella, or Ian. She said *one* of them would do it. We don't know which one it could be. We must give them all the chances they deserve to fulfill that prophecy. We can't give up on Ian. He could be the one."

"You still believe that, after all we have been through with him? After so much struggle and disappointment?" asked Roger, searching her face for the slightest trace of doubt.

"I do," said Carol firmly, "without a doubt. All I ask of you, Roger, is that you believe with me. I can't do it alone. I don't want to do it alone. I need you to believe with me. Can you do that for me? For us? For Ian?"

Roger sat with his head in his hands for a while, then rose from his chair. He walked around to Carol's side of the table and hugged her from behind. "I can do that, my love."

Then he kissed the top of her head gently, and they stayed like that for a very long time. Hugging. Believing. Together.

Petrie home, 2006

Five-year-old Ian dreamed once again of playing in the light. Not the sunlight or the firelight, but *the* light. The light was his friend. It lifted him up, warmed him, and tickled him. Just like his daddy always did when he came home from work. In his dream, he was laughing and smiling. He was weightless and free. He was brave.

The light gently laid him back down on his bed and then exploded into every color. It put on a show for him in his dreams. First, it became a rainbow frowning at him, then it turned upside down and smiled a multicolor, radiant smile. Then, it morphed into fireworks, exploding and streaking and bursting across the nighttime sky. Then, the fireworks became stars and galaxies spinning and shining, sparkling and glistening.

Ian laughed and clapped as the light returned from the heavens and enveloped him. He felt comforted by its warmth as he sensed its vibrations filling every part of him.

He heard it whisper to him, "Time to wake up my little one, we have a big day ahead of us."

Ian opened his eyes as his mother kissed his cheek. He did not want to get up. He wanted to go back to sleep and play with the light. But he couldn't tell his mother what he wanted, because the words hadn't yet come, so he just buried his head in his pillow hoping the light would find him there in the darkness.

His mother gathered Ian from his bed and hugged him tightly as she carried him downstairs for the breakfast that waited for him on the table. Carol knew exactly what it would be every day, because he would not eat anything else; bananas and Cream of Wheat. That was it. Nothing else.

As Ian sleepily picked up his spoon, played with the food, and yawned, his mother opened the kitchen blinds to let in the early morning sun.

A single bright shaft of sunlight sliced through the room and landed on Ian's breakfast. He suddenly smiled, giggled, and clapped his hands with delight as the light made his Cream of Wheat glisten and sparkle.

He turned to his mother while pointing at his food and said, "Mama, I eat light!"

Startled, his mother dropped the dish she was drying and stood there staring at Ian in shock. Ian had never spoken before. Ever. Nothing, not a word, and here he had just said an entire meaningful and funny sentence.

She rushed to him and hugged him desperately. "Yes, sweetie, you are eating the light! Mama loves you so much! Keep eating, sweetie, and keep telling Mama about it." She sat there with him at the kitchen table crying, as they talked about the food and the light.

It was the most beautiful conversation any two people had ever had.

CHAPTER TWO

2008

Belief is very powerful. It is not scientific. It is not tangible. It is not physical. But it can definitely move a mother. From the day Ian was first diagnosed with autism, she was a mother on a mission. She searched, she worked, and she read. She read everything she could about it. Everything she had found on the internet and in books made it appear hopeless.

She'd met with doctors, therapists, and specialists. They all told her that Ian was never going to get better. They said the best she could hope for was to manage his situation and to prepare for a life of dependency, maybe even an institution down the road. That made her mad; that made her cry; that made her determined to never give up searching for her own answers.

Then, when Ian spoke his first words, she doubled her efforts, no longer believing that autism was the right diagnosis. No longer believing that there was no hope. She believed that Ian was special, and that he had a rare gift. She knew that the doctors were wrong. She knew it deep down to the inside of her bones.

Two years had passed since she heard those sweet words. There had been others, but not frequently and not consistently. She still had no answers and she was at the end of her rope.

Today, Carol sat in a big-chain bookstore at a table piled with more books about autism and ADHD. Looking at that pile, she didn't know where to start. Feeling overwhelmed, she started to cry. She prayed.

"Dear God, you made Ian what he is. I know you love him and want the best for him. Help me! Help me to help him! Help me to figure out how to let his light shine so that he can utilize the wonderful gifts you have given him. Show me the answer, please. PLEASE!"

She put her head down on the pile of books and allowed the tears to fall. When she eventually calmed herself down, her eyes fell on one particular book. The cover was different from the others. It had a sense of hope to it. She picked it up and read the back cover. It said that there was hope and healing for what Ian had.

Carol began to read further and was immediately drawn in. Not only did the author describe Ian's symptoms and his behaviors, he seemed to understand her struggles, too!

It was like the author was describing Ian to a T. It was as if he knew everything about her son. He seemed to know things about Ian that only she and Roger knew. No one else understood or could explain Ian, yet here was a man whom they had never met, who explained it all. She began to read, not stopping until a clerk tapped her on the shoulder.

"I'm sorry, ma'am," he said kindly. "We're getting ready to close. Is there a book you'd like to buy before I close the till?"

Carol nodded, a little irritated at the interruption.

Quickly, she paid for the book, left the store, and made her way to the car. Her mind was racing. There was hope!

When she reached the car, she unlocked it and climbed in, setting her purse and purchase on the passenger seat. Opening the bag, she pulled out the book and finished reading it. As she read the last line and closed the cover, she sat with tears streaming down her face.

"Thank you, God," she whispered. "Thank you for guiding me to the hope I've been seeking."

So excited by the information she had read in the book, she drove home and immediately went to the bedroom and woke Roger.

"Hm? What?" he mumbled sleepily.

"Wake up!" Carol shook him again. "You have to read this!"

Roger shook his head. "Read what? What time is it?"

"A little after ten," she answered. "I found the most amazing book. It's by a Dr. Robert Mills, and he has the answers we've been looking for about Ian. You have to read it!"

"Really? That's great. I'll look at it first thing tomorrow, I promise." He patted her hand, closed his eyes, and pulled the blanket up over his shoulder.

Carol shook him again. "No, Roger. This is too important. You have to read this right here, right now!"

Roger opened one eye and studied her for a moment. Then, with a sigh, he sat up, pulling the pillow to support his back.

"All right. Where's this miracle book you're talking about?"

Carol watched him as he read the back of the book. When he was done, he looked at her, raised one eyebrow, then opened to the first chapter. Carol settled herself on her side of the bed, opened a magazine from her bedside table, and tried to read. But she didn't see anything on the pages as she flipped through them.

Finally, at one in the morning, her husband finished. He looked at her with tears in his eyes.

"This is amazing!" he exclaimed. "This is the help and hope we've been praying for."

"I know," Carol smiled, wiping tears from her own eyes. "I know."

The next morning, they called Dr. Robert Mills and made an appointment to meet with him at his office in Manhattan.

A few weeks later, Roger and Carol waited anxiously while Dr. Mills and his team assessed Ian. Finally, a perky young woman came into the waiting room and motioned for them to follow her.

"Hi, I'm Beverly. I'll be one of Ian's coaches," she said over her shoulder as she led them down the hall.

"Where's Ian?" Carol asked.

"He's still going through the assessments," Beverly answered. "Dr. Mills wants to chat with you two for a few minutes, if you'll just wait in here. Can I get you anything? Coffee? Water? A snack?"

"Nothing, thank you," Carol answered after seeing Roger shake his head.

"All right, then. Dr. Mills should be here shortly. Just make yourselves comfortable." She indicated two wing-back chairs sitting in front of an oversized desk, then stepped out, closing the door behind her.

Carol turned to her husband. "I'm so nervous! What if they find they can't help him? What if they blame us? What if we've done…"

Roger took her hand and patted it softly. "Shh. Don't overthink this. I'm nervous, too, but if we speculate without facts, we'll get ourselves upset for nothing."

"You're right," she sighed. "It's just so hard to wait!"

She moved to one of the chairs and sat, pulling a tissue out of her purse. She looked up when the door opened, and Dr. Mills entered.

"Dr. and Mrs. Petrie, I'm Dr. Robert Mills." He stuck his hand out and shook each of theirs. "I'm so glad you've brought Ian to us. From what you said on his intake forms, I believe we can help him."

Carol looked at Roger, relief written all over her face.

"I'd like to get to know you and your family situation a bit better," Dr. Mills continued. "Would you mind if I asked a few questions?"

"Not at all," Roger answered.

"First, how did you two meet?" he asked. "Tell me your love story."

Carol and Roger took turns answering Dr. Mills's questions. He wanted to know everything; what they did for a living, what their life was like before they were married, and even what they ate and how they took care of themselves.

Carol told him their history, education, jobs, passions, and interests. Roger shared how he had been a division one quarterback in college, how Carol had been a world-class fashion model, and that they both had exceptional IQs.

Carol finished by telling him that after many years of marriage, they were still passionately in love and how they had worked to create a warm and loving home environment for their three children, of whom Ian was the youngest.

"Tell me about Ian's siblings," Dr. Mills invited.

"Neither of them shows any signs of the struggles Ian's had," Roger replied. "They are smart and creative, and they make friends easily."

"What about nutrition and exercise?" the doctor asked.

"We're very careful about that," Carol said, "both for ourselves and the children. I've never understood why Ian was born with his issues. It doesn't make any sense to me."

Dr. Mills smiled knowingly. "Ian's problems aren't your fault, so you can stop blaming yourselves."

There was a knock at the door and Beverly stuck her head in at Dr. Mills's invitation.

"Ian's finished, doctor," she said, then left quietly.

"We'll analyze the data we've collected and be in touch in a couple of weeks," Dr. Mills said. "Meanwhile, just do what you've been doing and try not to worry."

"Easier said than done," Roger sighed.

Dr. Mills stood and came around the desk. He took Roger's hand, put his free hand on Roger's shoulder, and squeezed it lightly.

"I know. But as a wise man once said, 'Worry is a waste of whatever it is you waste when you worry, so why bother?'"

Roger and Carol laughed, feeling the tension draining away thanks to Dr. Mills's wit and friendliness. As they left the office with their seven-year-old son in tow, Carol felt relief and hope building inside her once again.

Two weeks later, Carol and Roger met with Dr. Mills again. Without preamble, he spoke the words they'd been hoping for.

"Dr. and Mrs. Petrie, your son is not autistic. In fact, from a neurological point of view, he is the exact opposite."

Carol bit back a sob as she squeezed Roger's hand. "I knew it," she whispered.

Dr. Mills smiled. "Furthermore, there is nothing

'broken' in his brain and no brain damage."

"Then what's wrong with him?" Roger asked.

"Ian has a neurological immaturity in his left hemisphere which manifests in the behaviors you've observed in him. In fact, Ian has incredible right-brain skills."

He went on to explain that almost all children who are delayed in speech at three to five years of age receive the autistic label, but in many cases, as in Ian's, it was not the correct diagnosis. Additionally, his research showed that autism, similar to ADHD, is a delay in development of the right hemisphere with often exceptional left-brain skills.

"But Ian has a delay in his left hemisphere with remarkable right-brain skills," he said. "In all my years of research and work with children on the spectrum, I have never encountered a child with Ian's spatial and creative reasoning abilities. They're off the charts."

"What does that mean for Ian?" Carol asked. "If he has such abilities, how can he use them if he can't talk well, or read, or…" her voice broke.

"Mrs. Petrie, in time, and with the proper care and encouragement, Ian could very well be the next Albert Einstein," Dr. Mills said.

"Einstein?" Roger asked, incredulous.

Dr. Mills nodded and explained that Einstein exhibited many of the traits and challenges that Ian was grappling with when he was a child. He had delayed speech. He struggled in school. He was easily distracted and was often reprimanded for daydreaming. This was all due to his very strong right-hemisphere skills. The same skills that Ian possessed.

"I believe that with my nine-month program, and a few years of ongoing follow-up, we will be able to balance

Ian's hemispheric processing speeds so that the left hemisphere will be as strong as the right. When that happens for Ian, the world will open up for him. Not only will he retain his incredible right-hemisphere skills, but he will acquire new left-hemisphere ones. The issues that plagued him will dissipate, and he will be free to utilize his amazing brain for anything he chooses. In fact, I wouldn't be surprised if, over time, he develops some extra-sensory perception abilities."

"You mean like clairvoyance or mind-reading?" Roger asked, sounding doubtful. "That seems pretty far-fetched to me."

"Not as far-fetched as you might think," Dr. Mills replied. "More than likely, he'll develop an ability to perceive details in the world around him to the point that he'll see and understand things we don't even notice. It might seem almost magical."

"Oh, Dr. Mills," Carol breathed, tears in her eyes. "This is more than I ever hoped for!"

Roger agreed. "This news is the answer to our prayers. It confirms our belief that Ian is special, not broken."

Dr. Mills nodded. "I believe that the kids I work with are truly gifted, possessing areas of their brains that are naturally stronger than most kids. If one side of their brain is exceptional and the other side is delayed even just a bit, it can lead to significant disabilities if left unbalanced. If corrected, however, these kids often have unusual skills and abilities. I also believe that it is the incredible right-brain gifts you two have that have been passed on to Ian and all your kids. That doesn't mean you are at all responsible for Ian's struggles. In fact, the genetics you've passed on to him will be instrumental in helping us to help him."

After enrolling Ian in Dr. Mills's program, Carol and

Roger left the office, feeling much better than they had just a few weeks ago. The world suddenly seemed filled with hope, unlimited possibilities, and light.

"Ian! How many times have I told you to clean up this mess? Your room and desk look like a disaster area. Get up here and clean it now!" ordered Carol Petrie as she stood in the middle of a room that looked as if a tornado had just blown through. Clothes, books, and toys were scattered everywhere.

"How does this happen so fast?" she asked Ian as he came in behind her. "I just cleaned in here yesterday."

Ian just shrugged and grinned. "A messy desk is a sign of a genius mind?" he suggested hopefully, pointing to the picture of Einstein's desk hanging on his wall.

She laughed. "Well, Ian, if a messy desk is the sign of a genius, then you most certainly are one!"

Carol reminded herself that Ian was not even eight years old yet. Keeping a tidy room wasn't a top priority for him. But Dr. Mills said that Ian could do this now, and she pushed down the frustration. She took a deep breath and reminded herself that Ian was better; much better. Before she and Roger found Dr. Mills, Ian would not have even acknowledged the mess. Today, at least he knew that it ought not to be this way.

Carol smiled and asked, "Were you looking at that picture again instead of tidying up? Don't you ever get tired of looking at a picture of a messy desk?"

Ian replied, "It's not just a messy desk, Mom, that's the thing. It's so full of interesting stuff that I could look at it all day!"

"But it looks so messy," said Carol.

Ian looked at the picture and smiled. "I like Dr. Einstein, and I like that he was messy. Just like me! So, messy can't be all bad, right?"

Carol returned Ian's smile and hugged him. "I know you do, but let's just get going so we don't get caught in traffic. You can finish straightening up later. Today is a big day. Dr. Mills is going to give us your final assessment." She gave him a kiss, and they headed downstairs.

Dr. Roger Petrie, Carol, and Ian were sitting in Dr. Mills's waiting room as he walked out of his office to greet them. He had a huge smile on his face.

"My favorite family!" he exclaimed as they greeted him with a round of hugs. They headed into his office and took their seats.

"So, time for our final assessment," said Dr. Mills. "It is so hard to believe that nine months have gone by so quickly. It seems like only last week that you brought Ian here for the first time."

Ian said, "Sure, that's because I was doing all the work!"

The adults laughed, and Carol observed that Ian's comment was something he would never have said before. The humor and self-awareness were refreshing after so many years of silence and sullenness.

"Okay, let's get Ian set up with the coaches for his assessment, and I will be back in a few minutes to talk with both of you." Dr. Mills left Carol and Roger alone in his office.

Carol looked at Roger. "Isn't it so different now? Remember when we thought it was our fault? That somehow we were responsible for his challenges?"

Roger nodded. "I know. It was so hard to accept. Everything we had been told before seemed to be putting the blame on us. It is such a relief to know that we're not the cause of his struggles. And that there's hope!"

"So," said Dr. Mills returning to the office, "let's talk about where we go from here. I am confident that Ian's final assessment will show that we have far exceeded everything we set out to accomplish. His right and left hemispheres will be in balance, and his innate abilities will have not only improved but have been enhanced by the neurological changes. However, that doesn't mean our work is done. There are still some problems that, if dealt with properly, should resolve over time so Ian can realize his full potential. Handling these problems correctly will be critical. You'll need to work together to ensure his continued progress and do all you can to maximize his potential. Have you been supporting his interest in Einstein, as I suggested?"

"Yes, we have," replied Carol. "Ever since you told him about his similarity to Einstein at the same age, he has been driven to learn everything he can about him. He's asked for books about his life and work. We've given him all the ones that have been written for his reading level and a bit beyond. He watches every television show that has anything to do with physics or time and space and has even tried to get through a couple of Einstein's published papers. Last week, he dressed up as Einstein for the Halloween festivities at his school."

Roger added, "In one of the books, there was a picture of Einstein's desk, which was taken just after his passing. He's studied that picture every day since then. He even asked us to make him an enlarged physical copy of it, so he could study it more closely and in greater detail."

Carol laughed. "He uses that picture to try and justify having a messy desk and room. He's really taken your comments to heart."

Dr. Mills grinned. "You're not letting him get away with that, are you?"

Carol shook her head. "No, but I'm afraid it's a losing battle."

"Try not to worry about that too much. There are worse things than a messy room. I want to share a little of Einstein's childhood, so you'll understand what Ian could face in the next few years.

"Einstein's parents loved him, but they did not understand him. His father was extremely overbearing and made him feel like a failure. In fact, when Einstein wasn't accepted for a teaching job at a university, he felt terrible for disappointing his father, who had even written many letters on his behalf. His father died soon after, and he died thinking Albert was the failure of the family. Einstein was so distraught that he told his sister in a letter that 'it would have been better if I had never been born'. He contemplated suicide. Usually, it's right-brain dominant people who actually follow through with suicide. I believe that if Einstein hadn't had a wife and hadn't landed that job in the Swiss patent office, he very well may have taken his own life. The world would have lost his genius and all his theories.

"You have a much better understanding of how Ian's mind works than Einstein's parents. You can nurture him in a way that Einstein wasn't."

Roger reached over and took Carol's hand, squeezing it lightly. "That's certainly our intention, Dr. Mills."

"I know it is," the doctor smiled. "I've seen nothing but love and gentleness as you've worked with Ian. However, there are a few things you should watch for. Right-brain geniuses tend to be hyper-aware of what others think of them. Additionally, Ian may be extra sensitive to his own emotions. As he becomes upset, that may upset him more, starting an emotional spiral that can quickly get out of control."

Carol nodded, her expression serious. "We've seen evidence of that already. He throws…" she hesitated, choosing her words carefully, "…well, they're not exactly temper tantrums, because he's not usually angry. But he seems to lose control, like he can't express what he's feeling."

"That's not unusual," Dr. Mills reassured her. "The best thing you can do in those cases is to remain calm, speak soothingly, and make sure he doesn't hurt himself. When he's calmer, you can talk about what set him off, and teach him better ways to handle the overwhelming emotions."

Roger looked uncomfortable, shifting in his seat. He released Carol's hand, pursed his lips, then admitted, "I'm afraid I'm not as patient as my wife when dealing with Ian's outbursts. I don't know how to calm him down."

Dr. Mills looked Roger in the eye and spoke earnestly. "How do you usually calm yourself when you're upset or angry?"

"I go for a run," Roger said without hesitation.

"Good. Teach Ian to run, or play basketball with him, or football, or anything that gets his body moving. Physical exertion will help him learn to calm himself," Dr. Mills suggested.

"What about martial arts?" Carol asked. "I've heard that teaches kids discipline, as well as how to protect themselves."

Dr. Mills nodded. "Good idea. I think Ian could benefit from that kind of training. The discipline will be a wonderful tool for him, but learning to defend himself will give him more confidence. How is he doing in school? He's in second grade, right?"

"Yes," Carol answered. "That's one of the things we wanted to talk with you about. If his right and left brains are balanced, why is he struggling? He seems to have such a hard time learning and remembering. He still has trouble reading books that are written at his grade level. Arithmetic is hard for him. Nothing seems to come easy for him, and I think it embarrasses him. When I've asked him about it, he says the teacher gives instructions, and he gets confused. He feels like he is the only one who doesn't understand. The other kids start to work right away, but he's embarrassed to ask her to explain."

Dr. Mills sighed. "I was afraid of that. One of the worst things that can happen to a right-brain-dominant kid is to be embarrassed. Ian knows he's smart, but when he doesn't understand something, he feels stupid, and that's incredibly embarrassing for him. This could lead to self-esteem issues. Watch for signs that he's withdrawing."

Roger cocked his head. "Was that the reason he didn't talk for so long?"

"Partly," Dr. Mills nodded. "There were some neurological issues with the imbalance in the hemispheres of his brain which kept him from learning to speak. His left hemisphere and verbal language areas were delayed and quite immature. That's the main reason he didn't speak. We've corrected that, but there are secondary emotional scars that will take a while to heal. When he gets frustrated or upset about school and learning, remind him that learning takes time. He needs to believe he is smart and work hard. He will soon catch up to the other kids.

"Ian spent seven years in a delayed learning mode. Once he started working with us, he improved and progressed at a phenomenal rate. But because he started school before our work began, it's going to take time for him to catch up. He simply missed much of the information the teachers tried to give him."

Roger looked concerned. "How much do you estimate he missed?"

"If I had to put a number to it, I'd say he absorbed only about twenty-five percent of the information he was exposed to in his first five years of life. Perhaps a bit more, once he started interacting with the world."

"That little?" Roger sat back, looking discouraged.

Dr. Mills smiled. "Don't worry. Now that his brain is in balance, he has the ability to catch up in his academics. He will need tutoring, but because his brain is working so well now, he will absorb the information he missed very quickly, perhaps two hundred percent faster than other kids. Within a year or two, he should not only be caught up, but should start to excel beyond other kids his age in some areas. As long as his confidence continues to increase with his skill, Ian will be able to reach his full potential.

"That's why I encouraged you to give Ian a positive role model in Dr. Einstein. If he can understand that the world's greatest genius started out life in the same way, struggling and being told he wasn't smart and that he wouldn't amount to anything, then Ian can overcome his doubts and other people's expectations of him."

Roger laughed. "Well, he's certainly taken that to heart! He talks about him all the time! Especially since Carol bought that book about him."

"He looks at the pictures mostly right now, but he carries that book with him everywhere!" Carol added.

"That's also typical of right-brain-dominant children," Dr. Mills confirmed. "They struggle to read, but they love looking for the meaning in pictures."

"That's the truth!" Roger added, growing excited. "That picture of Einstein's office is a perfect example."

Carol jumped in. "And he talks about *you* all the time. You really have become such an incredible influence on him. With all the talk of Einstein and Dr. Mills in our house, we feel like we have gained two more members of the family!"

"Well, that is truly an honor," Dr. Mills replied. "You know how I feel about Ian and about both of you. I will always be here for you, and I want to stay involved with Ian as he progresses. After all, I want to be there when he accepts the Nobel Prize someday! Until then, keep him challenged. Feed his brain everything it can handle."

"That is such a relief to hear, Dr. Mills," said Carol. "Ian is finally happy, and that's all I really ever wanted. I just prayed for the special child I knew was trapped inside to one day be free." Carol started to cry, rushed to Dr. Mills, and hugged him. She noticed that Roger had tears welling up, too.

As Carol pulled away, she added, "We thought he might never be able to accomplish all that we dreamed for him. You have changed all that. Thank you."

"Not only that, Dr. Mills," Roger added, "but you also may have just begun the fulfillment of a prophecy!"

"Really?" asked Dr. Mills. "Explain that one to me."

Roger and Carol looked at each other, and Carol smiled. "Roger, you tell the story. After all, she was your patient."

Roger agreed and recounted the story of his patient JoAnne and her predictions. When he was finished, he said, "I am a man of science like you, Dr. Mills, but how do you explain that? She appeared one day like an angel and then vanished. Life is strange but wonderful, isn't it? Today, you have just given us back our hope, our dreams, our prophecy, and our Ian."

Dr. Mills smiled. "Thank you for sharing that. I'm touched by your story and the sentiment. Just follow Ian's lead. He knows where he wants and needs to go. Beyond that, just keep him healthy and loved. It seems that the world might someday very well owe you both a great debt of gratitude."

CHAPTER THREE

Einstein's home, Princeton, New Jersey
April 16, 1955

Albert Einstein sat at his desk. He had recently finished what he believed to be his greatest accomplishment, but he was not happy. In fact, it had turned his world upside down. What he thought would bring the world into a new dawn of peace, security, understanding, and new horizons, had turned out to be his greatest nightmare.

His rival was right. The world was not ready for this discovery. He thought back to the day in 1943 when he'd received the package of documents from him. It had arrived one day after the news of his death. He opened it immediately, reviewed the information, but did not understand.

It had taken him months of private study to break it down into formulas that he could work with. His rival's brain worked differently than his, and that had been the primary cause of the friction between them. Although they had great respect for each other, they saw the universe differently. They were trying to accomplish similar things from two widely divergent viewpoints.

With time and hard work, he had achieved a better understanding of his rival's theories, and surprisingly, they were not so different from his own. In fact, seeing things in this new light triggered ideas that had never crossed his mind. Had the old man been on to something? He believed so, and from that day in 1943, he'd begun to work on his Unified Field Theory in a different way.

Einstein began to see things with new eyes. It would take years, more than a decade would pass, before it finally all came together. Here before him were all the answers, but he knew he could tell no one. There were some missing pieces that became apparent upon the completion of the work. The implications of this discovery led to one final question, and only the old man had known the answer to that final question. Einstein knew he had purposefully left it out of the documents, knowing that Einstein would find it only after he understood the first part of the information.

He took out a piece of stationery and began to write.

Dear Clarence,

You have been a true source of strength for me over the past two years. I have valued finally having someone to confide in, someone worthy of the work I am doing and trustworthy enough to keep it secret. While you have been away on your vacation, I have found the answer!

Yes, I know this will be a source of great disappointment for you, but please do not worry. I know how much you have contributed and assure you that someday, your name will be next to mine when it is revealed to the world. I know that you will return in a week, but I strongly believe that you need to hear this right away.

Although I have resolved all the conflicts and been able to craft a final formulaic solution, we cannot reveal it to the world. You need to know that the answer was not what we were expecting, and it has created a new problem. We cannot open this door until we know how to close it. You know how I felt about the Manhattan Project, the conflict I had between my mind and my soul. This is worse.

I am going to make one copy of the equations and all my work and then destroy the originals. It will remain where it was born. When you get back, I will reveal its location to you, but ONLY you. Then, we will spend the rest of our years trying to resolve the remaining question. If we never find the answer together, then you will need to carry on. I know that someday, a mind greater than mine or yours will surface.

When that happens, make sure you train him or her to understand. It may be that we must wait for this person. But until then, I must say, Nikola was right. We cannot reveal this. The world is not ready. We have more work to do, and I need your help with the key.

Hurry home,
Albert

Einstein laid the letter aside, intending to mail it after making the copy of all his and his rival's documents and concealing them.

He stood up from his desk to get the special kit he'd bought a few weeks ago. It was made for just this type of secrecy. He moved to his file cabinet to get the Zapp outfit. It would take some time, but this was the best way to keep this information secret. When Clarence returned, he would show him how to use the camera and the technique for concealment. Bringing the documents to his desk, he began the process.

By the next morning, everything was complete. The documents had been copied and concealed, and Einstein had hidden the odd, metal key included with the package in a safe place where it would not be discovered easily. He felt tired and had a tremendous headache. Assuming it was from the worry and stress, he decided to lay down and rest. He could mail the letter to Clarence the next day.

Little did he know that he would never return to his desk.

Dr. Mills's Office, New York City, 2018

"Thanks, Dr. Mills," said Ian. "I would never have gotten into Princeton without your work with me over the past ten years. You've helped me make my dreams come true."

Dr. Mills replied, "Ian, I had very little to do with this. You are an extraordinary young man, and what you have achieved is mind-boggling! I am happy that I was able to give you the tools to develop your mind, but the raw material was there already. You have done the work, and you have made the sacrifices. This is all you. My goodness, think of what you have done! The PhotoEx app you created alone would be enough for any lifetime. But you accomplished that before your eighteenth birthday. Not to mention the thirty-three million dollars you now have in the bank because of it. I guess there will be no student loan debt for you."

Ian laughed. "Thanks! I'm happy about all of that, but

you know what I really want to do. That's why I chose Princeton over all the other schools that were after me. I really need to follow in Einstein's steps and learn more about him. I feel a real connection with him, and every time I step onto Princeton's campus, I can feel his presence. I want to see what he saw and live where he lived. I need to understand how he saw the world and what drove him. And it's all because you told my parents to introduce me to him. You saw something in me that no one else saw. That's why I came here today… to tell you myself and thank you."

"Well, Ian, I am proud to have had a part in it," replied Dr. Mills. "You have a long road ahead of you, but the whole world is your oyster. Always know that I will be here for you. I have been your doctor for more than ten years now, and I want you to think of me as your friend from this moment on. Whatever you need, you can count on me. Now, go out and ask your parents to join us. I want to say hello to them, too."

Outside the office, Ian signaled his parents, who were busy chatting with the staff that they had grown to love over the years. Everyone in the center had been expressing their pride and excitement for Ian and his parents. Ian noted that each one of them had shared a part in his success over the years.

When his mother saw him, she took his father's arm, urging him to excuse himself. Together, the happy family re-entered Dr. Mills's office.

"Roger! Carol!" Dr. Mills exclaimed. "How proud you must be of this boy! I am so happy you decided to make a detour on your way to Princeton to share the news with me. What a day!"

They both hugged him and sat down. "We wouldn't have missed this opportunity for the world. You have been such a huge part of this, and we needed to express our thanks for all your help. From the day I found your book, you have been our lifeline and our guardian angel." Carol's voice hitched a little.

"I agree," added Roger. "You helped us see Ian's challenges in a whole new light. Because of that, we were able to plan for the future and feed his need for information. Your belief in his gifts was a gift to us. All that he has already accomplished flows from those gifts. I especially remember the impact you had on us when you explained your theories of the mind and how they related to physics. The idea that consciousness, relativity, quantum theory, and the workings of the mind could all be connected somehow was fascinating and eye-opening. I hope you get the chance to pursue that line of research. Maybe you and Ian can work on it together!"

Dr. Mills laughed. "I will pursue it, but I doubt I could work with Ian; he would quickly become frustrated with my inferior intellect! Although I won't hesitate to ask for his help when I need it. I hope I can say the same for him."

"Always," replied Ian. "Always."

"We should get going," said Carol. "Once again, Dr. Mills, thank you for everything."

"You're welcome," replied Dr. Mills, "but before you guys head out, I wonder if I could have about twenty minutes of Ian's time to discuss with him some of my most recent findings. I believe they will help him in his work at Princeton. You two can head downstairs for some coffee, and I'll send him down when we're done. Would that be okay?"

"Certainly," responded Roger. "We appreciate you sharing your expertise with Ian anytime." Roger and Carol hugged Dr. Mills and headed to the coffee shop.

Dr. Mills sat at his desk and invited Ian to have a seat across from him.

Dr. Mills looked at Ian with an urgency that Ian didn't quite understand. "Ian, the last time we spoke, we talked about the importance of knowing your outcome in advance, that before you go into a situation, you must have a vision of what you want the ending to look like. If you also remember, I asked you to tell me what outcome you wanted from college and why you decided to attend Princeton. I remember the look on your face when I asked you that, but you didn't hesitate. You said you wanted to do what Einstein hadn't. You want to discover a Unified Theory of everything. You also asked me if I believed in destiny, if everyone has a purpose. I told you that I do. You seemed a little troubled. Do you remember?"

Ian nodded, recalling that day.

Dr. Mills continued. "You weren't sure why you had struggled as a kid with a disability. You felt bad that your parents had to endure that. You weren't sure what that was all about and what that had to do with your purpose and your destiny. You asked me if I could tell you what it all meant. How did these pieces all fit together with your past, present, and future self? I couldn't answer you then. I am not sure why, but I didn't know if you were ready. I've thought a lot about your questions since then, and I'd like to try to answer them for you now, before you leave for college. Is that okay?"

Ian sat forward in his chair and nodded again. Finally! Perhaps now he'd understand what these struggles were all about. He couldn't wait to hear the what Dr. Mills had to say.

"Ian, I wanted to chat with you for a moment about an area of my research that I believe will add to your understanding of physics, and really transform your studies."

A little puzzled by this turn of the discussion, Ian decided to rely on his trust in this man who had helped free his mind.

"That would be great, Dr. Mills," said Ian. "What's your research about?"

Dr. Mills began to explain the focus of his research, understanding the nature of consciousness and how it emerges from the brain. He told Ian that current research was showing more of a connection between Einstein's work in relativity, modern concepts of neuroscience and consciousness, and how even gravity was believed to play a significant role in human consciousness.

Ian stopped him. "Dr. Mills, I don't understand the connection between the brain, consciousness, and Einstein's theories. Can you explain that more?"

Dr. Mills nodded. "Sure. Knowing you as I do, my guess is that you are probably the only teenager on the planet that will actually understand these concepts. They are some of the most sophisticated theories in science, and very few people in the world understand them. Before I begin, let me ask you, what is the one thing in the theory of relativity that, at the most basic level, changed everything we understood about the universe?"

Ian thought about it for a moment, then answered, "The concept of space-time."

"Exactly!" Dr. Mills exclaimed. "Before Einstein, it was believed that bodies in space, the planets, galaxies, solar systems, moons, etc., were all separate bodies that were not connected to one another in any way. They were believed to be completely independent with no interaction.

"Also, it was believed that time was a separate and

distinct concept that linearly measured the past, present, and future and that it was fixed and unchangeable. Einstein, with his incredible theories, showed that space and time were not separate things, but rather interconnected, and together essentially create the fabric of the universe. They were two sides of one coin woven together to form space-time. These concepts were no longer separate; these two distinct concepts became one, and this changed everything. Time was the bridge that connected all of space.

"Furthermore, space-time was interconnected with gravity, and gravitational forces could curve and bend space, and this could alter our perception of time. Time could be perceived to speed up or slow down, and perhaps even go backward, based on the influence of gravity, speed, and the shape of space. I am sorry if I am speaking too simply for you, Ian. I know you know this very well, but I needed to articulate it so that I can then relate this to consciousness."

"No, go on, doc," Ian said, "I love the way you just simplified his theories and really clarified them, that's tough to do. I love listening and can't wait to hear where you're going with this."

"You know, Ian," Dr. Mills replied, "that Einstein himself said that the ultimate sophistication is simplicity. He also said that if you can't explain something in simple terms, it means you don't understand it very well. So, thank you.

"So, what does this all have to do with consciousness? In the old days, we used to think of the brain as a fixed organ, and within this organ lay areas that control or process different types of information, and that these zones were essentially separate and distinct bodies in space. It was viewed the same way that we used to think of celestial bodies. We thought the different regions of the brain all acted pretty much independently from one another, doing their own individual jobs. However, with the advent of more sophisticated brain imaging tools, we started to understand that the brain was a much more dynamic organ than we previously thought.

"It became apparent that there wasn't any way to really describe memory and thinking in these old terms of isolated bodies in space. Also, we understood that although the brain was localized, meaning that there were areas that were somewhat specialized in function like areas for vision, hearing, touch, movement, motor control, and executive function, etc., it still wasn't clear how all this information came together in the brain. There was no one place where all these areas would bind together.

"So, the question was, how do we bring all these separate areas or bodies in space together to form one thought or memory or experience as we do? We don't experience the world one modality at a time in sequence; we experience everything at once, blended together into one perception of reality. The answer to this question became known as the binding problem.

"It was one of the primary things neuroscientists struggled with in the mid-'80s and '90s, because they knew that this had something to do with human consciousness and self-awareness, which is what makes humans unique. The answer came when scientists discovered the glue, or bridge, for all these separate areas of the brain that work together and coordinate their information. That bridge was *time*!"

"Wow!" exclaimed Ian. "That's exactly the same discovery that Einstein made about the bodies in space!"

"Correct," said Dr. Mills, "and it was discovered that

there was a timing mechanism in the brain and nervous system that acted like a metronome or a conductor to bind separate areas of the brain and blend them all together to give us our perception of reality at any given moment. They discovered that it was this combining of space and time in the brain that creates consciousness. It was further revealed that there was a pacemaker for the brain that created this timing mechanism in the form of frequency waves or oscillations.

"So, just as we might have a pacemaker in our heart that helps to coordinate the contraction of all the muscles in our heart to fire at the same time, we have a pacemaker in our brain known as the thalamus. It allows for different areas of our brain to fire simultaneously.

"This explained another mystery of the brain. Scientists knew that we needed all these areas of the brain involved in perception connected together to peak at the exact same instant. This ensures that what we see, hear, feel, and think all connect in a single moment in time. Previously, we believed that this happened only through physical connections in the brain and between the hemispheres. It was thought that through the synapses, the brain communicated with itself. However, there was a problem. If all these separate areas needed to fire simultaneously with one another, then physical connections could not work. There would always be some delay in sending information through these wires to other areas of the brain. It would therefore essentially be impossible for all these different areas of the brain to fire at precisely the same time. Yet we know that simultaneity is a unique feature of our brain.

"Furthermore, and adding to the confusion, was the fact that the most advanced areas of the human brain are the furthest apart from one another. That makes physical communication between them even more challenging. Although the human brain is the largest brain of all animals relative to body size, we are the only ones with a high level of consciousness and self-awareness. This all seemed confusing until the solution of time was understood. The human brain had become more dependent on timing connections than physical connections over the course of evolution. Therefore, we could activate areas of the brain that were far away from one another, and they could all be connected temporally rather than physically. They all fire at the exact same moment of time, and everything gets frozen in that moment of time, creating a thought or a memory.

"This also meant that we could link more areas, brain cells, and networks together, because there weren't any physical limitations. The more areas of the brain we link together, the smarter we can become, because we can process and bring more and more information together at the same time."

Dr. Mills took a moment to make sure Ian was following, "Do you understand this, Ian? Is the connection becoming clearer?"

Ian was very excited. "Absolutely, Dr. Mills, this is so awesome. I never understood any of this before, and I couldn't envision the connection. I guess like most of the world, I don't really know anything about the brain. You have explained it so well, and in my language, physics, which is mind-blowing!"

"Yes," Dr. Mills said, "everyone thinks in terms of neuroanatomy, neurophysiology, or neurochemistry, but the real answers and the future of brain research is in neurophysics. There is even a name for it: systems neuroscience. My research partners and I have written papers on what we call a neural continuum. It really has to do with unseen forces of nature that are involved in brain function. It is also about how these unseen forces can go awry in various psychological and developmental conditions like ADHD, autism, dyslexia, OCD, and even schizophrenia."

Ian nodded his understanding. "So that's how you helped me and so many others. The thing I'm not seeing yet is how this leads to consciousness, and what does this all have to do with gravity?"

"Great question, Ian," responded Dr. Mills. "Now I will bring it all together for you, and here is where it all comes together and gets *really* cool," said Dr. Mills. "The story of human evolution is also the story of how our brains grew and developed. But how? The answer is stimulation. As an infant, we have only about twenty-five percent of our brain mass, but when we exit the womb and are exposed to the outside world and all its stimulation, this turns on genes that make our brain cells grow.

"From that point on, the brain grows larger and forms trillions of connections with other brain cells so that by age three, the child's brain is ninety percent of the adult size. However, not all stimulation is equal. Light, sound, temperature, and touch are all variable stimuli, meaning they are not always there at the same level. There is only one form of stimulus that is constant in our universe, and that is *gravity*! It is *always* there.

"Light is sensed by our eyes and sound by our ears, but where do we sense gravity? The answer is in our muscles, especially in our postural muscles. They allow us to stand upright by defying gravity and fighting its effort to push us back down on all fours. Bipedalism, or standing upright, allowed us to harness the power of gravity because our muscles, especially the ones along our spine, are constantly fighting and straining against gravity. In turn, it is constantly stimulating them, and therefore constantly stimulating our brain even when we are lying down and sleeping."

"Fascinating," Ian murmured, completely enthralled with this new information.

Dr. Mills continued. "This gravitational stimulation is so great that over a couple of million years, it caused our brain to grow much larger. This stimulation, along with some minor epigenetic adjustments to the expression of our genes, like our body producing brain cells twenty-five days longer than other primates, led to the large human brain. This eventually led to us developing the intellect to use all this extra brain space.

"So again, Ian, what you see is that all of this wouldn't be possible without time and its ability to connect things separated in space. The brain, especially the human brain and consciousness, are all as dependent on space-time as is the universe! In fact, just as we know that there is dark matter and energy in the universe that seems to somehow connect it all, there is also a form of dark matter and energy in the brain. It is believed to be related to this ten-hertz rhythm and movement."

Ian took a moment to process, then asked, "Dr. Mills, are you saying that because the same principles that govern the universe are also involved in the brain, that it's possible that our minds can extend outside of our head and interact with the universe? That we can transcend space and time?"

"Ah," Dr. Mills replied, "now you're really getting to the big question, and the short answer is yes. There is some excellent research to suggest that the mind is capable of extending outside of our brain to interact with other people and machines. It may even be able to predict the future and see the past. If we understood how time really works, and how the universe, time, and gravity all interact on a large and small scale, then perhaps we could also understand how the mind interacts with the universe. This is all part of the Unified Theory of the universe that scientists have been searching for, and what Einstein was still looking for when he died."

He leaned forward, again fixing an intent gaze at Ian. "Perhaps, Ian, *you* will be the person who will finally be able to answer that question and unlock the most ancient riddles of the universe! That is why I wanted to have this discussion with you now before you go off to Princeton. Promise me that you'll remember this and keep looking for the answers."

Ian didn't know how, but somehow, he had an eerie feeling that all this information was going to be critically important to him and to the world. His thoughts raced as he began to catch the vision of his destiny.

"I promise, Dr. Mills," he replied solemnly.

Dr. Mills rose from his chair and walked around his desk to give Ian a hug. "Remember who you are and what you are capable of, Ian," encouraged Dr. Mills.

During the long drive to Princeton, Ian was very talkative. After his discussion with Dr. Mills, he felt very excited about the next four years and all that he would experience.

At one point, his father asked, "Ian, what is it that you really want to accomplish at school?"

Ian, with barely controllable excitement, replied, "Dad, you know that the world of physics is always finding new and amazing aspects of the universe. Well, I want to answer all the questions out there regarding the things that are now a mystery. For example, no one has yet answered the questions about dark matter and dark energy. Physicists have determined that up to seventy percent of the matter in the universe is dark matter and cannot be seen. They have no idea why this is or what this matter is composed of. The same for the dark energy. But it's there, and it must play an incredibly significant role in the workings of space, time, and reality. We can infer its existence from its impact on forces like gravity, but it is still a mystery. I want to know what it is.

"Also, the wave and particle duality of light. Experiments have shown that light behaves both as a particle and as a wave. Since the days of Einstein, scientists have been trying to directly observe both aspects of light at the same time. This is a huge mystery! How can anything, especially an actual particle which is supposed to have mass, behave like a wave, which does not have mass? I need to understand that, and I will.

"Then, there is the idea that time as we know it and observe it only moves in one direction: forward. Why is that? Why isn't it possible for time to move outward in many directions like the ripples on the surface of the water when you throw a rock into it? I believe it may be possible for us to observe time moving omni-directionally. I want to work on that and resolve the issue.

"Finally, the last two that really interest me are the supposed speed limit of light and the Unified Field Theory. Einstein's theories extrapolated that nothing can travel faster than the speed of light, because at the speed of light, the mass of the traveling object approaches infinity. Since it would take an infinite amount of energy and velocity to surpass that barrier, it has been deemed impossible. But recently there has been speculation that there are quantum particles that may *always* travel faster than the speed of light. If that is true, then I need to understand that and figure it out.

"I think Einstein may have been close to resolving this. He worked on the Unified Field Theory right up until his death in 1955. He was always frustrated by the fact that relativity, which deals with the physics of large bodies like stars and black holes and universes, was contradicted by quantum physics, which deals with small things like sub-atomic particles and the building blocks of all matter.

"They are, in many ways, opposing views of reality. Both have been proven to be mostly correct in independent experiments, but they cannot both be true at the same time, at least as we understand them today. Einstein was committed to reconciling the differences with an overarching theory which would explain the observations of the large bodies and the small bodies. He was searching for the one theory that would unite both disciplines of physics. To the best of our knowledge, he was not successful, and since his death, no one else has even come close.

"I think that it is possible that Einstein was closer to achieving this than we know. I believe that it is possible that he actually had the answer but died before he could tell the world, *or* that what he found was so revolutionary that he did not want to reveal it to the world.

"In everything I have studied about Einstein, it is clear to me that the solution to this problem was within his capabilities. It really should have just been a matter of understanding what the bridge was between the two and working backward from there. I believe he found that bridge and either discovered the solution, or was very close."

"Why do you believe that, Ian?" asked his dad. "What

evidence do you have?"

"I don't really have any hard evidence yet, Dad, and that's one of the reasons I chose Princeton. I am hoping that during my time there, I can find some of those answers," Ian responded.

"Okay," his dad replied, "but don't let this distract you from your main studies and getting your degree. We know you can get lost in your thoughts, and your imagination can run wild. This is an Ivy League university, and you won't have time for daydreaming and following your crazy imagination. You have to stay focused."

For the rest of the drive to Princeton, Ian just looked out the window and remained silent. He did not want to tell his parents about what he'd found a few days ago using the upgraded version of his PhotoEx app. He wasn't sure why, but he knew that it would make them worry even more about him. They were right when they said that his imagination was a bit vivid, and he knew he could see things that others couldn't. That made people, including his parents, a bit nervous. But he *had* found something fascinating while experimenting with his PhotoEx in a new way.

He'd been examining the picture of Einstein's desk that his parents had given him years ago. He had always had the feeling that there was more on that desk than anyone knew about. Einstein had died suddenly from an aneurysm, and Ian believed that whatever he was working on at that time was somewhere on that desk.

He was so convinced that he developed additional experimental capabilities for his PhotoEx app to help him search the documents on the desk more closely. The new upgrade combined what can only be described as an X-ray capability, with the microanalysis capability of the original app, to take it to a whole new level. It had allowed him to be able to see what was behind or underneath something else in a picture. In essence, it allowed him to be able to examine the picture of Einstein's desk in layers. He could read every document on that desk even if it was covered over by another document or object. What he found just a few days ago had confirmed his suspicions.

Underneath a few other papers on the desk, he had found a letter that Einstein had written to a person named Clarence back in 1955. It seemed that this fellow, Clarence, knew Einstein, and was on vacation at the time the letter was written. Einstein was writing to inform him that he had solved a major problem and had discovered the final solution to whatever it was they were working on together.

Ian scanned the rest and felt instinctively that it would be best to keep all this information a secret from his parents until he knew more and could prove it.

Finally, they arrived at the main campus of Princeton University and headed to the orientation site. Ian got out of the car. "I will meet you back at my dorm when we're done. Have fun, you two," he said to his parents, then slammed the door and hustled off to orientation.

A few hours later when Ian returned from his orientation, his parents helped him move into his dorm room. His new roommate, Peter Wu, was already there when they came in. Ian dropped his backpack and shook Peter's extended hand.

"So, what's your major, Ian?" asked Peter.

"Physics, and yours?" Ian replied.

Without hesitation, Peter answered, "I have a double major; computer programing and electrical engineering. I plan to get a Ph.D. in electrical engineering, I think, or maybe both." Ian just smiled and thought, this dude seems cool. I think we will get along.

Just then, another student popped his head into the room. He was dressed very fashionably and looked way too cool for an Ivy League school.

"Hey, guys, I'm Dylan, from across the hall. Nice to meet you!"

Ian detected a bit of a Southern accent, so he asked, "Where're you from, Dylan?"

"I'm from just outside of Atlanta," Dylan replied. "Home of the Braves, the Falcons, and the most beautiful girls in the world."

"What's your major?" Ian asked.

"Well, besides women, I'm deciding between literature and history, especially World War II history and immediately after the war. I have been fascinated with that period since I was a kid. My grandpa was in World War II, and he would tell me tons of great stories. He was in a tank division with General Patton. How cool is that?"

Then Dylan went up to Ian and whispered in his ear, "Get rid of your parents. There are some great parties happening tonight. I've already seen about ten girls I want to meet, and I am going to need a couple of wingmen."

Ian smiled and gave a small nod. He turned to his parents. "Okay, Mom and Dad, looks like I'm all set here. Thanks for the help. I'll call you tomorrow." His parents offered to take them all to dinner, but the boys politely refused, saying they would just like to go to the cafeteria and eat.

Carol looked puzzled, but Roger laughed. "Okay, fellas. I get your not-so-subtle hint."

Carol's eyes widened for a moment, then she laughed, too. They kissed and hugged Ian, told him they were proud of him, and urged him to work hard.

Ian loved his parents, but he couldn't wait for them to leave. Once they drove away and were out of sight, he ran up to his room, where Peter and Dylan were talking and laughing. Ian high-fived both of them, then Dylan ran to his room and returned with something tucked under his arm. He closed the door and pulled out three beers.

Peter immediately said, "Dylan, we can't have those here! If our resident assistant sees, they'll kick us right out."

"Don't be such a baby, Peter," Dylan laughed. "The RAs are up to their eyeballs in new residents, the door is locked, it's just us, and no one will find out. We have to celebrate this day! Years from now we will look back and remember the first day we met, so let's toast to our future!"

Ian felt like he had just come home. He couldn't help smiling.

"We need some music," Dylan commented as he connected his phone to the Bluetooth speaker in the room. Immediately, music started blasting. "I love classic rock and roll, so I hope you're not into that house music crap! I really like my classics!" Dylan screamed over the music.

Ian focused on the music and heard a very familiar song and words. "Hey, you like the Ramones! That's awesome!"

Ian smiled and thought of his parents, who also played all these classic songs. How many times had his dad told them the story of the summer he spent working at the Malibu Dance Club when the Ramones played there? His father had helped them set up their equipment. Now, he would have his own Ramones story to tell his kids someday… a long time from now. He leaned back on his bed, closed his eyes, and thought about how great this all was, how much fun he was going to have.

CHAPTER FOUR

"Come on, Ian!" called Peter. "We're going to be late if you don't get your butt out of bed right now!"

Ian roused himself one more time as he finally responded to Peter's urging. They were both heading to the same freshman physics class and were running late. Ian dressed and grabbed his books and a protein bar as they headed to the class. They found their seats just as the professor was starting the lecture.

"Thank you all for being on time," he said sarcastically, looking directly at Ian, who still felt half-asleep. "I am Professor C.J. Kearney. I will be outlining the coursework for the year, but the course will be taught by another professor. She has not yet arrived from Sweden, so I am filling in for her today. I have just retired from teaching here for the last fifty years and will be taking an advisory position in the physics department going forward. After doing this for so many years, this first day of class is still fun for me.

"Before we begin, I want to challenge you a bit. I have done this on the first day of class for fifty years and feel it is an effective way to illustrate the kind of thought processes that you will need to develop if you desire to be successful, groundbreaking physicists someday."

He then turned to the blackboard and drew nine dots in a square grid pattern, three rows of three dots each. Turning, he looked at the class. "The problem is this: how can you connect all nine dots that I have drawn, with just one straight line? The rules are that you cannot lift your pen off the paper, and you cannot go back over a line. Remember, it must be *one straight line.*" Then he added, "I know all of you can calculate equations, but I want to see if you can think outside of the box and solve this problem without the use of mathematics, equations, or calculations of any sort. Physics is much more than math and equations. It's about true creativity, seeing things that no one else can see; seeing familiar things in a brand-new way."

As he finished describing the challenge, Ian sleepily mumbled under his breath, "One big, fat line."

Professor Kearney turned to Ian. "What did you say?"

"One big, fat line," Ian mumbled again.

Professor Kearney then said, "Speak up, boy, say it again."

Ian, completely embarrassed by being singled out, said meekly, "The answer, sir, is that one big, fat line would connect all nine dots."

The professor looked stunned and seemed unable to speak. Finally, he asked, "What's your name, son?"

Ian replied, "Ian Petrie, sir."

The professor raised one eyebrow. "Are you the same Ian Petrie who won the Intel competition with that invention of that photograph analyzing application?"

"Yes, sir," Ian responded with a slightly embarrassed smile.

The professor nodded. "I read about that in the paper. I'm impressed by the thought process you utilized to create your innovative application. Well done, young man. Your answer to the challenge tells me that you have an incredibly creative mind. Please meet me after class in my office. We have a number of things to discuss."

Ian was proud, excited, and a little embarrassed being singled out this way on the first day of class.

As soon as he got out of class, he called his parents and told them the story. After the call, he headed for Professor C.J. Kearney's office. He couldn't help but smile.

Professor C.J. Kearney stared out the window without seeing what lay beyond the glass. Only one other person had ever come up with the correct answer that quickly. He thought back to his first day at Princeton.

One student read this question aloud to his fellow students at the start of the semester. They all tried to figure it out, and they made a bet on who could figure it out within twenty-four hours. Most of them spent the day running through numbers and calculations and angles. They had come up with many elaborate equations, but none of them could identify a reasonable solution.

The following day, the students were discussing the apparent insolvability of the problem when Professor Einstein walked into the room to start the day's lecture. They all fell silent for a moment. Then, one smart-aleck student in the class figured he would try to stump the famous professor. Pointing to the image of the dots on the blackboard, he asked Einstein the question they had all been struggling with. Einstein looked at it for just a moment, smiled, and simply stated, "One big, fat line."

The students sat in stunned silence. They had no response to Einstein's quick and simple solution to a supposedly unsolvable problem.

All but one. He just smiled and kept his secret to himself. Young and cocky, he felt proud that he had figured it out within the allotted time, when no one else had.

The professor was pulled from his reverie by a meek knock on his office door. Stepping quickly to the door, he opened it and grabbed Ian by the shoulder, hustling him into the room.

"Welcome, Ian, please sit." Then he pushed him down into the old, worn, Victorian chair across from his enormous desk.

"So, Mr. Petrie, my first question for you is what made you develop your PhotoEx application? What was the impetus? Scientific leaps like yours usually have a way of deriving from an unmet need of society. What was that driving need?"

Ian replied, "There was an old photo of something that I've been obsessed with since I was a kid, but it was blurry, and I couldn't see all the details. I tried traditional enlargement techniques, but they only made it blurrier. I found this frustrating. So, one day while I was playing my violin, the idea popped into my head. I suddenly knew… actually, I saw how it was possible to create an application that could expand the size of anything in the picture and even make it clearer as it got bigger. I spent a few months working on the prototype, and when I tested it, it really helped.

"Recently, I realized that there was a document in the photo that was partially hidden because it lay under another sheet of paper. I wanted to be able to look closely at that document, as well.

"I theorized that since the document I wanted to view actually existed, and it was there in the picture, then even though it was covered by that other piece of paper, which seemed to be fairly thin, I should be able to enhance what showed through and reveal what was underneath. Again, I got a vision of how I could improve the application by adding a filter that would allow me to see through the layer of paper and enhance images and words that were previously completely obscured. It worked! Sort of. I was able to extract some of the darker words, enough to do a Google search. With Google's help, and some sleuthing in some not-for-public-eyes databases, I was able to piece together the paper underneath.

"As you may know, I sold the original application for thirty-three million dollars to Google. But I have not yet rolled out the upgraded version. I think I can probably get a few more million from Google for it, but that will have to wait, as I have more testing to do."

The professor smiled. "Boy, that was some thirty-three million-dollar picture! May I ask what the photo was that motivated you so powerfully?"

Ian replied, "It was a picture of Dr. Einstein's desk taken on the day he died, right here at Princeton, sir."

Startled, the professor sat back in his chair. He instantly recalled being in Einstein's office on the day that photo was taken.

He had just returned from his vacation, which he had cut short upon hearing the news of Dr. Einstein's death. He'd missed the brief and simple memorial service and was feeling very lost. Einstein had been his mentor and friend. He decided to go to his office to be around the last remaining familiar and comforting reminders of this great man.

Using his key to enter the office when no one else was around, he stepped inside, closed the door behind him, and rested against it for a moment. Then, he sat at his mentor's desk and just drank in all the sights and smells of that familiar place.

As he sat there, he started to sort through all the papers, books, and documents on the desk and noticed a letter addressed to him under a few other documents.

Just as he started to read it, a crew of journalists from Life *magazine burst into the room. They announced that they were there to take some pictures of Einstein's office that they were planning to use for an article about him for the next month's issue. He'd quickly shoved the letter under the only thing within reach, a thin sheet of onionskin paper which he frequently used to trace technical drawings. Hoping it would be enough to obscure the document from the photographers, he jumped up from the chair and left the room.*

He'd stayed in the kitchen adjoining the office until they were done. When they had gone, he hustled back into the office, grabbed the letter, shoved it into his coat, and left. That was the last time he was in that office, and it remained a seminal day in his life. He had never revealed the contents of that letter to anyone.

Watching the young man in front of him, the professor wondered if this boy could possibly have read that letter. He could very well be an answer to a prophecy of sorts. He had almost given up that anyone would ever come along as Einstein had predicted in that letter. He never thought he would see the day that the one that Einstein alluded to would appear. It was very possible that the one he had been searching for all these years was sitting right in front of him.

Ian continued. "That is also why I am here at Princeton, sir. I wanted to be at the place where Einstein last worked. I have many personal reasons for feeling so connected to him. I feel that in a strange way, he saved my life. He was a bright, shining star throughout my youth, and that got me through some difficult times. I want to honor his memory and his work, and I believe that people are getting it all wrong. I don't think they understand what he was thinking, and I don't think they fully understand what he was seeing. I have come to believe that he was much further along with the solution to the Unified Field Theory than people give him credit for."

"Really?" Professor Kearney raised one eyebrow. "Why do you believe this?"

Ian looked around, leaned forward, and hesitantly confided, "Pardon me, sir, but I have never told anyone this before, not even my parents. I have always been desperate to talk to someone who may have known him, who worked closely with him, knew how he thought and what he was doing at the end of his career. I am hoping that you may be that person, or that you know someone who knew him. Did you know Einstein well? Did you have a working relationship with him? You have been here at Princeton so long. Perhaps you can help me understand him better."

"Yes! I knew him," replied the professor, smiling. "He often talked about the different projects he was working on during his last two years. I was devastated by his death. I believe that I knew him as well as anyone on earth at that time. Feel free to ask me whatever you want, and I will answer as best I can."

Ian's face lit up. "Thank you! I've been hoping I'd find someone to confide in here. Okay, here goes. During my most recent analysis of the picture of Einstein's desk, I found something that I think could be a breakthrough. I believe he found the solution to the Unified Field Theory, and he was about to publish it, but then had second thoughts and pulled it back.

"I think he came up with the ultimate understanding of the universe and of space-time itself. The implications are incredible! It would have been the greatest discovery of all time. I believe this because I found a note addressed to someone named Clarence. In it, Einstein talked about this final paper, and he mentioned someone named Nikola. This Nikola person had told him that 'the world wasn't ready', whatever that means.

"I don't understand any of it. Why would he hold back the greatest discovery of all time? People are always saying that he never figured it out, that he was too feeble and old at the end to put it all together, that he was intimidated by younger scientists and quantum theory.

"Excuse me, sir, but I think that is nonsense! This was Einstein, the greatest mind the world has ever known, and I believe that he figured it all out. I want to know if I'm crazy or not. I feel connected to him. I feel like I know his mind and how he thought about things. The only person that can tell me if I am crazy or not is you."

Ian's expression was a mixture of desperate longing for an answer while, at the same time, fearful of what those answers might be.

The professor recognized that look. It mirrored what he was feeling at this very moment. He considered all that Ian had told him and knew what he had to do. Even though it might be dangerous for him to reveal who he was and what he knew to Ian, he was reasonably convinced that Ian was bright and sincere, perhaps even the "greater mind" that Einstein predicted would show up. It was too early to tell; he'd just met the boy. However, his time was running out.

But he wasn't sure if Ian was the one he'd been instructed to "train up and make understand". He had waited for this young man his entire life, and now, perhaps, here he was, sitting across from him. The professor couldn't wait any longer. He had to take a chance.

After a moment, the professor smiled. "Ian, first let me tell you about the challenge you just solved in class. You are the first person I know since Einstein to have figured out the correct answer to that challenge instantly. That tells me that you have a mind that works similar to Einstein's. I don't think you are crazy. I think that there may be a real, undefinable, and incredible connection between you and Einstein. In fact, I believe that he predicted you would come here someday.

"To quote Dr. Einstein, 'I believe there are no accidents in the universe and that everything happens for a reason. God does not play dice with the universe'. You, my boy, are no accident. You were born with a purpose, and everything you have gone through has made you who you are today. It has prepared you for what you must do. Everything your parents did, all your teachers, good and bad, friends, enemies, everything has brought you to this time and place. There is much I must share with you. The very first thing I will share with you is that I am Clarence."

Ian stared at him wide-eyed and stammered, "Excuse me? Did you just say that *you* are Clarence? The same Clarence that the letter on his desk was addressed to?"

"Yes," replied the professor, "that is me, one and the same. My full name is Clarence James Kearney. Most people know me as C.J. I never really liked the name Clarence, but Dr. Einstein thought it was funny, so that is what he called me. Strangely, it made me feel closer to him."

"So, that letter was written to you!" exclaimed Ian. "You were the one that he was going to fill in on the great discovery. You were the one that he was going to share the glory with. You were the one that he was going to share the location of the…" Ian stopped talking abruptly, suddenly looking wary.

The professor jumped in. "Yes, I am he. I was in the office the day the picture was taken. I was the one who shoved it under the other documents on the desk so it could not be seen by the photographers. I waited until they left and then retrieved it. After all, it was for me, it was my possession. I took it back to my room and read it over and over, trying to understand. I have it to this day.

"The fact that you were able to see it under all the other documents in that picture has confirmed for me that you, Ian, may be the one that Dr. Einstein was referring to in the note. To be honest, I never believed that there would ever be anyone with a 'greater mind' than Einstein, destined to complete the work. But he believed it; he was counting on it. I don't know how, and I don't know when, but maybe, with my help, we can do this.

"But we don't have much time. Things are happening now around us related to all this that are sensitive and dangerous. Also, I personally don't have much time left. I am dying of cancer. The university has been very supportive of my employment, even after I passed the traditional age of retirement so many years ago. They value my reputation and influence in the world of physics and often leveraged my relationship with Dr. Einstein for large donations to the school. But because of the cancer and the fact that I'm 81 years old, it has become obvious that I need to retire from the job I love."

The professor paused, took a deep breath, and tried to curb his excitement. After a moment, he continued, "But right now, young man, I think we have done enough. This has been a big day for both of us, and I am tired. Here is what I propose. We will meet every day in this office, and I will tell you everything I know, and you will tell me everything you know, and together, we will figure out the secrets of the universe."

"Figure out what secrets, exactly?" Ian asked.

The professor responded, "It's exactly what you thought. Einstein did have the final answer! I have determined from the letter and the work we had done together that he had found the answer. But as the letter states, he never had the chance to explain to me what he found or why he felt it was too dangerous for a world not ready to receive it.

"In his letter to me, he stated that he made a copy of the answer and that it would 'remain where it was born' until someone would come along that could understand his thought processes and figure out the answer to the great dilemma raised by the solution. I hope he was talking about you, Ian."

Ian looked incredulous.

The professor continued and cautioned, "But, Ian, this may be very dangerous. Powerful people want to get their hands on the secret. This is one of the things Einstein feared the most. He feared that the fruit of his work might be used by people with bad intentions. He was tortured by the loss of life initiated by his discoveries, which had led to the Manhattan Project. He vowed that never again would he allow his work to be used for destructive purposes. You mustn't tell anyone about this, even your parents or best friends. Anyone you tell would be in grave danger, do you understand?"

"Yes, professor," Ian said.

The professor straightened, and dismissed him formally, "I will see you tomorrow, then, Mr. Petrie."

Before Ian left, he turned back. "Professor, in all the years you have been studying the note, have you figured out where Einstein hid the copy of the equations? He said it would 'remain where it was born'. Do you know what that means?"

Shaking his head, the professor replied, "Sadly, Ian, I do not. I have looked for it everywhere. It is my hope that maybe your unusual connection to Einstein, plus your visualization skills, might help me uncover its hiding place."

As Ian left the office, he committed himself to work on that solution. He was so lost in thought that he failed to notice the two men in sunglasses and business suits sitting on the bench across from the professor's office.

They watched him pass. One of them spoke into his cell phone as they stood and returned to their car.

New York City, 1943

The New Yorker hotel staff was in a panic. Walter, the elevator operator, was just coming on shift and noticed the emotional charge in the air the moment he walked into the lobby. After clocking-in, he caught one of the upstairs maids, Josephine.

"What gives?" he asked. "Everyone's so nervous!"

Josephine pulled him aside and whispered, looking around nervously. "Haven't you heard? One of our long-term guests was found dead this morning."

"What?" Walter was incredulous. "Who? How?"

"The guest in 3327. You know, the quiet, tall, elderly gentleman with the slicked-back white hair?"

Eyes wide, Walter started to say his name, but two bellboys approached them, chattering in hushed tones.

When they had passed, he leaned towards the maid and whispered. "How did he die? Who found him?"

"Two maids found him. They said he was on his bed, fully dressed, with his arms crossed over his chest. The official story is that he died peacefully in his sleep."

"Official story?" Walter caught her look. "I take it you don't believe that."

"Not one bit!" she exclaimed, keeping her voice low. "I knew the man. He was meticulous. He never took a nap or lay on the bed with his shoes on. But no one ever asked me for my observations, nor anyone else, either. Not that I've heard."

"You said 'official story'. What officials?" Walter was beside himself with curiosity.

Josephine looked disgusted. "Well, the FBI came and surveyed the scene, if you can call it a survey. They were awfully quick about it and departed after only a few minutes. What's more, the old man had a safe in his room, and the FBI took a few papers from it, but from what I saw, it wasn't much. The old man always had huge piles of paper on his desk, and many times, I've seen documents and strange objects lined up along the walls and on his bed. The FBI left with none of that. Where did it all go?"

Walter looked thoughtful. "Last night, I saw two men approach him as he exited the elevator. As usual, he was on his way to dinner at the Waldorf…" He hesitated, his expression growing concerned. "They had German accents. That seems suspicious, don't you think?"

Josephine nodded, then caught a look from a supervisor entering the hallway. She ducked her head and moved quickly to the stairs.

Walter, too, moved to his station in the elevator. Strange that no one asked the staff about the old man, he thought. He would have told them everything, and he knew the other staff members would have, too. But no one asked.

As the first guests entered his elevator, he shrugged a mental shrug, deciding that if it wasn't important enough for the FBI to bother asking about, then he'd just mind his own business and go about his job as usual.

The crew from the New Yorker cleanup operation arrived at the FBI office in Manhattan. They returned with only a few documents, and the bureau chief was not happy.

"How is it possible that this is all you guys recovered?" he asked the senior agent.

"I don't know, boss," he responded. "When we got to the scene, the safe was already open. This is all there was. Either someone got there before us, or the old man got rid of the papers himself."

Enraged, the FBI director slammed his hand on the desk and shouted, "Well, FIND THEM! We cannot have sensitive information like that floating around out there. You-know-who is anxious to get his grubby Nazi hands on that information. If it falls into his hands, it will cost you your jobs. Not to mention possibly your liberty. Find them."

The crew left his office, going back to the conference

room they were using as a staging room to put their heads together. This would be a very long night.

CHAPTER FIVE

Dr. Kearney's office, Princeton, 2018

Dr. Kearney's plan was to meet with Ian every day over the next few weeks. Their discussions would focus on Einstein, the man he was, what his motivations and drives were, what he feared, and what was behind his great theories. He hoped to open Ian's mind to the man in every possible way. If they were successful, Ian might perhaps discover the answers to Einstein's mystery before it was too late.

As they started on that first day, Dr. Kearney said to Ian, "To know any man, you must go beyond what is written in any book, and Einstein was not like any other man; he was so much more than people know. But what you need to know, first and foremost, is that he was not born a genius, and he hated that people thought that. He worked incredibly hard to become the great man of science, and it wasn't easy.

"As I know you understand, he started out with people thinking he was learning disabled. Some people today even think he would have been labelled autistic. So, for you to truly understand how he thought, you have to understand the struggles he went through and the challenges he conquered to eventually come up with this final solution at the end of his life. You must walk in his footsteps, so to speak. You must follow the same path to get to the same end. As you know, we don't have much time. I feel there are forces around us that are closing in and that events that have taken decades to develop will soon start to converge."

Ian interrupted. "Wait, Dr. Kearney. What forces? What events?"

Dr. Kearney shook his head, "There's not time to go into all that. So, I will give you the abridged version, and I will stick to the most important and significant events in Einstein's life as he revealed them to me.

"The first thing you need to understand if you are going to be a researcher someday is that most people believe that when Einstein wrote those three amazing papers in 1905, the scientific community and the world immediately accepted his theories as fact and that they opened their arms wide to him. Nothing could be further from the truth.

"Your first lesson, Ian, is that any great scientific theory only becomes great for two reasons. First, it is a great leap forward that ultimately will be proven correct. The second is the most important. The researcher or creator of the theory must fight with all their strength to make sure that it *is* eventually proven correct. They never give up.

"There are many viable theories out there, proposed by brilliant young scientists, that no one has ever heard of because they were not willing to fight for their theories. They give up too soon, and because of that, their work is forgotten, and their names are lost to history. So many discoveries never made it because the researcher could not stand the heat. Einstein was not one of those men. He was a fighter.

"If you think that people in the science world are just going to say, 'Hey, there is Ian Petrie the multimillionaire', and accept whatever you say, think again. The fact that you invented that PhotoEx application, and sold it for all that money, will be viewed by many people as a negative. They might believe that you were lucky, that you are not a serious scientist. It may actually make it harder for you to gain acceptance in the scientific community.

"This was true for Einstein. The fact that he came out with three papers at such a young age, with no academic credentials or academic positions, made it harder for him to be taken seriously. But people did not understand what had led up to Einstein writing those papers, what drove him to that point. He was a very emotional and sensitive person, again, unique among scientists."

The professor paused to pick up a pipe and light it, then continued, "As you may know, when Einstein was around your age, he wasn't very serious about life or his classes. No one really understood what was going on in his head. He was, however, very serious about his personal studies. He wanted to explore what he found interesting, regardless of what he was supposed to be learning. He loved the ladies, and he loved to go to the pub with his friends. He was actually a great romantic and had an incredible sense of humor.

"After he gained notoriety, he was invited to take a position as a full professor at the University of Berlin. This was a tremendous honor, and in June of 1913, Max Planck, the most famous physicist in the world, and Walther Nernst, a famous chemist, were sent by Kaiser Wilhelm to recruit the best scientists in the world to come to Berlin. The two men took the train to Zurich,

Switzerland, to convince Einstein to take the job.

"It was really his dream job. He would be a full professor with few teaching duties, so could focus on his research. He would become a member of the Prussian Academy of Science, one of the most prestigious organizations in the world.

"However, when the two men presented the offer to him, Einstein just smiled and said, 'Give me a few hours to walk in the mountains. I must walk and think about this. I will meet you back here at the train station at three o'clock, and I will be carrying white flowers or red flowers. If I have red flowers, I will accept your offer, if I have white flowers, I will not accept your offer to come to Berlin with you.'

"Imagine the scene, Ian," the professor said. "Here are two of the greatest scientists that have ever lived, at the train station in Switzerland, waiting for Einstein to make his decision, standing under the clock as it strikes three. There is steam from the trains coming off the tracks. Then, walking through the steam, Einstein emerges. The two scientists can see him and that he is carrying something, but the steam is partially blocking their view. Suddenly, wind blows away the steam, and they see Einstein walking toward them with no socks on. In his hand is a bunch of red flowers. He is going to accept their offer.

"How different would history be if he had listened to his wife, who loved that city and their apartment there and didn't want to leave Zurich?

"I want you to get this, Ian, the side of Einstein that the world and the history books do not know. The sense of drama that was Einstein. He saw the importance and grandiosity of the universe, but at the same time, he also saw the humor and irony in it. He saw everything at once, both sides of it all. It was miraculous to him."

The professor paused. He stood and turned his back, facing the window. Taking out a handkerchief, he wiped his eyes. It always choked him up a bit to think about his mentor in such a personal way.

After a moment, he turned back to face Ian and continued. "Backing up to earlier in his life, after barely qualifying for his Ph.D. by graduating fourth in a class of five, Einstein tried to get a job teaching at a university or even high schools. He applied to many schools, but no one ever hired him. They didn't see his potential; they only saw his grades. Einstein's father died when he was twenty-two, and he went to his grave believing that Albert was the failure of the family. His friend got him a job in a patent office reviewing patents and inventions.

"Then in 1905, at the age of twenty-six, out of literally nowhere, in one year he wrote three of the most significant scientific papers that have ever been written. I asked him one time where that burst of creativity came from, and how was he able to do it. He said that he didn't take life seriously until his father died. It devastated him, and he went into a deep depression. He even wrote his sister saying it would have been better if he had never been born, and he wanted to kill himself.

"The job helped him get out of his depression and helped him learn how to organize his thoughts, but his pain was his primary motivation. He wanted to make his father proud. As soon as it became emotionally important for him, it all just happened.

"He said he had always been able to have these ideas, visions, and 'thought experiments' in his head, but in 1905, he finally got serious. He decided that he would no longer be a failure. This was when his full genius kicked in, and it just flowed out of his head on to paper."

"As I said before, you must understand that if you make any great discoveries like this, they will not be met with instant acceptance. In fact, the opposite will happen. Many in the scientific community will attack you. It may take years to prove you are right. In your case, there will be other dangers. There will be those that will want to use this information for their own ends. To do that, they may have to discredit you, attack you, or worse. Einstein was strong in his convictions. He had many who attacked and vilified him. He was a Jew who lived in Nazi Germany where they wanted to imprison him. He had devastating setbacks, and people tried to steal his theories, but he prevailed."

The professor approached Ian and grabbed him by the lapels. "Ian, I need to know you understand how hard this journey will be! You are so young. Are you strong enough to do this, boy?"

"I don't know, professor," Ian blurted out. "I mean, I'm not sure."

Letting him go, the professor returned to his chair behind the desk. "Well, Ian, Einstein didn't do it alone; he was helped along the way. When Einstein first wrote his papers, he sent them out to many scientific journals. They all turned him down or completely ignored him, and he heard absolutely nothing for months. They all said 'who is this kid?' He wasn't connected to any major university, he had never written anything before, and now he was proposing some crazy, completely new theory that would turn the world of physics upside down.

"However, Max Planck, the editor of one of the best scientific journals in the world, *Arnalen Der Physik,* saw Einstein's paper come across his desk. When he read it, he instantly realized its genius and published it. He became a mentor and a friend to Einstein. If it wasn't for

Planck reading that paper and helping Einstein, it might have never been published.

"If Planck had not been Einstein's mentor, he may have given up his fight, because there were many in the physics community that wanted to destroy Einstein. His theories completely overturned Isaac Newton's theories, who for almost two hundred and fifty years was the god of physics."

The professor stopped again and looked at Ian. "The point, Ian, is that I want to help and protect you in the same way. Einstein said, 'Everything happens for a reason, and some things and some discoveries are destined to happen, but only at the right time'. Your being here at this place and time is no accident, son. This was all meant to be, and Professor Einstein knew it."

"How did he know it?" Ian asked anxiously. "How could he know?"

The professor glanced at his watch, smiled, and said, "Enough for today. Each time we meet, I will give you examples of how Einstein fought for his theory to be accepted. You will find it to be a fascinating story filled with great drama, suspense, and romance. We will continue tomorrow. Now, go study, go to the pub, and chase girls just like Einstein would have done at your age."

Ian had taken the professor's advice. He'd gone to the library and studied. Then, when he got back to his dorm room, his roommate, Peter, and his other friend, Dylan, were waiting for him. Before he knew it, they were sitting in a pub drinking beer. Apparently, Peter's hacking ability and his computer skills allowed him to make incredibly realistic fake IDs, because they got in with surprising ease. Everyone in the pub was older, and there were many pretty girls.

The night was a bit of a blur, but he remembered several conversations with several girls. All he knew when he awoke was that he had a serious hangover and was getting texts from girls he didn't remember meeting. It was time for class, and then off to meet with the professor again.

As he walked out of his dorm, he couldn't help noticing a big black Escalade parked nearby with two guys inside. Ian had a great memory for faces. He was terrible with names but almost never forgot a face. Through his fogginess, he suddenly remembered that he had seen those two men in the pub last night and had felt like they were watching him. Maybe he was just being paranoid. Probably just a coincidence, he thought to himself as he hurried on to class.

When he finally met with Professor Kearney, he told him about the car, the men, and the pub. Professor Kearney looked concerned. "So, I see you took me literally yesterday about the pub and women. That was meant to be a joke. But all joking aside, Ian, time is running short, and I must get you up to speed quickly. So today will be a long session.

"I need to explain to you how and why Einstein fought so hard to get his theories accepted, and how sometimes what looks like your greatest defeat can end up leading to your greatest victory. Also, what sometimes looks like a mistake may actually be the answer to all your questions.

"As I've told you, even after Einstein's theories of relativity were published, most people in the scientific community did not agree with Einstein's conclusions or even understand what he was writing about and wanted more proof. In his first paper on the Theory of Special Relativity, Einstein came up with the famous equation, $E=MC^2$, basically saying that energy can be created from or released from any mass. He also realized that when traveling at the speed of light, you would perceive the passage of time differently. This is when he proposed that space and time are interwoven into one structure called space-time.

"This was revolutionary, but very specific to one set of circumstances. Einstein wanted to have a theory that applied to everything, and he wanted it to include an explanation of gravity. In the 1600s, it's said that Isaac Newton observed an apple falling from a tree and came up with the conclusion that the apple was pulled to earth by an unseen force that he called gravity. However, even Newton never felt that was a great explanation, because, in general, things are not pulled in the universe… they're pushed. So, rather than thinking of the earth pulling on something, Einstein imagined that somehow something was pushing down on the earth.

"Two years after his first paper was published, still working as a patent clerk with no recognition at all, he published his most famous paper. It was at that time that he came to understand that what was doing the pushing was space, and that planets and other large bodies would warp space around them like a ball laying on a piece of fabric. This curved space would push objects toward the planet.

"Einstein was not only completely overturning the theories of Newton; he was saying that space-time was bendable and malleable, which was something that most scientists could not even conceive of. This was his paper on the Theory of General Relativity published in 1907.

Once again, it was met with criticism. First, because no one could understand it, and second, because it needed to be proven, and no one believed it was possible to prove his theories.

"Einstein hoped others would rally behind him and try to confirm his theories, but no one did. It was up to Einstein to come up with a way to prove his own theories. But this was much harder than it seemed. It was 1911, and most of Einstein's concepts were way beyond the science of the times.

"Einstein himself hadn't fully worked out all the details of his theory, and he had struggled for four more years to come up with the right equations and answers. He eventually came up with the idea that if someone could take a photograph of the sun during a total solar eclipse, the stars that would be visible around the sun could be seen and photographed.

"His theories on space-time and gravity predicted that as the light waves traveled to earth and went through the sun's gravitational fields, the gravity would be so strong that it would warp space around it and the light would be bent slightly as it passed by the sun. The photograph that would be taken on earth would be able to document that bending of the light.

"This could only be done when the sun was completely covered by the moon, otherwise the light of the sun would be too bright to photograph the light that the stars emitted. If he could convince someone to photograph a total solar eclipse, he believed it would prove his theories.

"So, the first thing to note here, Ian, is that Einstein came up with this idea himself. No one else had any idea how to prove his theories, only he could come up with the solution. If he had relied on others to validate his theory, it would have never happened."

The professor lit his pipe, then continued. "Einstein's next step was to convince someone to go and take this picture. So, he published a paper in 1912 about light being bent around the sun, and he encouraged the astronomy community to go out and confirm his theories.

"Eventually, he caught the eye of a young assistant at the Berlin observatory named Erwin Finlay-Fruendlich, who eventually wrote a letter to the famous Lick Observatory in California. The head of the observatory was William Wallace Campbell, the foremost expert and pioneer in eclipse photography. Campbell eventually agreed to go, and he and Finlay-Fruendlich made plans in the summer of 1914 to go to Russia.

"In early June, they left from Berlin to go to Russia. Einstein was there to wish them luck and was obviously anxious. He knew that his whole career depended on the results of this trip. To increase the chances of their success, the group decided to split up. Finlay-Freundlich went to Southern Crimea, while Campbell and his group went to Kiev.

"What they didn't know at this time was that on June 28, 1914, the Archduke of Austria, Franz Ferdinand, was assassinated, Kaiser Wilhelm declared war against Russia, and World War I began. Finlay-Freundlich was in the middle of nowhere in southern Crimea setting up his telescope and camera equipment. The conditions looked great, and he was sure he would get a clear picture. But before he could finish setting up, Russian soldiers showed up.

"They saw a German scientist with a telescope and a camera, and they accused him of espionage, immediately arrested him, and confiscated his equipment. Campbell, who was in Kiev, was also approached by Russian soldiers, but because he was American and since the U.S. was still neutral, he was allowed to photograph. But just as he was set up and ready, a bank of clouds covered the sky. The eclipse happened, but he could not get a clear photograph. He failed and had to leave his state-of-the-art equipment in Russia.

"This was a total disaster for Einstein, and when he heard the news, he was devastated. He felt that this was his greatest defeat. Here he had two opportunities with the best experts in the world, and they had both failed. Who else would try?

"Over the next couple of years, Einstein found himself isolated from many of his friends who supported the war. His marriage was also falling apart. Einstein was depressed, but he immersed himself in his work. He went back to trying to find a final solution to his theory on general relativity and the gravity problem.

"To do this, he went back to his calculations on the bending of light. It was then that he realized that his initial calculations were wrong! He also realized that if Finlay-Fruendlich or Campbell had been able to make photographs of the eclipse that day using his incorrect calculations, they would have proven his theory wrong, thus discrediting him and his work. What looked like his most epic failure may have saved his career and ultimately led to his greatest triumph."

The professor stopped at this point. "Ian, this is the second, and perhaps most important, lesson that you must remember. There may come a time when you feel like you are defeated, and all is lost. Remember this story and realize that everything happens for a reason. You may not understand it at the time, but if you are doing the right thing for the right reason, the universe will ultimately give you the answers you seek, but not always in the way you expect. During these darkest of times, you must not quit. You must have faith and fight like Einstein did. Fight for what you believe!"

Ian was almost in a trance listening to the professor. His incredible visualization skills allowed him to see the images of the solar eclipse in his mind. He could feel what Einstein felt; it was like he became a part of Einstein's story, while the rest of the world faded away.

The next day, when he was back in the professor's office, Ian greeted the professor and right away said, "I saw those guys in the black car again, and I'm positive they're following me."

The professor wrinkled his brow. "I'm not surprised. Time is running short, and this may be our last long session. So, let's finish this story. Einstein now believed he had the final equation for the Theory of General Relativity solved. He just needed someone to prove it.

"Eventually, word of Einstein's discovery made its way to England to a man named Arthur Edington. He was the head of the Oxford University Observatory and one of the most respected astronomers in the world. He was also very religious and was against the war. When he found out that Einstein was also a pacifist, and that he had written an antiwar manifesto, Edington committed himself to trying to help him prove his theory even though England and Germany were at war. The next full eclipse was in June of 1918. It was nowhere near Edington, and although he wanted to go, he couldn't.

"The 1918 eclipse was in Washington state, close to William Wallace Campbell, so Campbell decided to try to photograph it again. There was one problem; his equipment, which had been state-of-the-art four years before, was still in Russia. Although he would have to use substandard equipment, he decided to take the risk.

"The day of the eclipse, June 8, 1918, was a very cloudy day. But as the eclipse started, the clouds parted, and Campbell took the pictures. He felt certain that he'd gotten good photographs. His assistant did the painstaking calculations of the photos, and unfortunately, the preliminary data seemed to prove Einstein's theory was wrong.

"Meanwhile, World War I finally ended. Just in time, too, because there was another full eclipse visible in Africa in May of 1919. Edington was committed to being there to film it. It took him a couple of months to get there, and he went to Africa at the height of malaria season. He had one assistant, and they had to hack their way through the jungle for days, lugging huge and heavy equipment to get to the right spot. They spent a full month building a photographic telescope.

"On the day of the eclipse, it was pouring rain, and all looked lost, but just as the critical time approached, the rain stopped, and the clouds miraculously parted. Edington looked up and saw that the moon was now directly in front of the sun. He raced to take the pictures. Remember, taking pictures was a painstaking and difficult process back then. So many things could have gone wrong. After it was over, Edington developed the film and realized that almost all the film was useless except for the last few pictures. He believed that he could get enough data out of those photographs to reach a conclusion.

"In the middle of the Congo, by candlelight, he did the painstaking calculations himself and eventually got his answer. He headed back to England at the same time

Campbell arrived there to reveal the secret results of the Einstein experiment. He was going to address the Royal Astronomical Society, which was partly created and founded by Sir Isaac Newton himself. Campbell stood up to address the audience and announced that Einstein was wrong. But simultaneously, there arrived a cable from Edington revealing his preliminary findings, which proved just the opposite; Einstein was correct.

"Four months later, on November 6, 1919, Edington addressed the Royal Astronomical Society with what he felt were his final, irrefutable results. He began his comments by pointing to the large portrait of the founder of the society, Sir Isaac Newton and said, 'Forgive us, Sir Isaac Newton, your universe has been overturned'. Edington then went on to tell the audience that the predictions of Einstein were exactly correct, and that his photographs of the eclipse prove it.

"Overnight Albert Einstein became the most famous man in the world, and the newspapers said that everything anyone had believed about the world and the universe was wrong. Most people believe that this was when Einstein and his theory were finally accepted by the scientific world, but that wasn't true. There were still extremely vocal critics who said Edington and Einstein were wrong. It wasn't until 1922 that Einstein's theory was finally unequivocally proven and accepted.

"Einstein had to fight every step of the way, from the age of twenty-six until he was forty-three to finally prove his theories. There were so many things that went wrong, and many more that could have gone wrong, but I believe that the universe or God directed his journey. Can you imagine the world today if Einstein's theories weren't validated?

"Almost nothing we have today could have been

invented or even conceived. Yet his Theory of General Relativity will pale in comparison to the discovery of the Unified Theory of everything. It will be the greatest accomplishment in human history and will change the world and the universe for all time. This could be the greatest thing to ever happen to mankind... or it could be the worst. I believe that this is your path, and that the universe will guide your way.

"Nothing worthwhile comes easy, Ian. There is always a fight, and you have to be willing to endure and believe. Einstein once said that 'Only those who can see the invisible can do the impossible'. I believe you can see the invisible as well as anyone who ever lived. But when you can see things that almost no one else can, you must understand that almost no one will believe you. People ridicule what they don't understand. You are not going to be able to do this alone.

"Einstein could not have proven his theory without a host of other players who fought jungles, world war, malaria, jail, and months of travel to prove him right. If you are right and just, the universe will bring others to you who will rise up to help and protect you. But there will also be enemies that will rise up to stop you. Worse yet, some enemies will look like friends. Remember, it all revolves around you, and you must trust your gut. I have told you this story so you will understand what Einstein went through and to prepare you for what is to come.

"Not many people know this, Ian. Most people don't think Einstein and Tesla had any connection. All anyone really knows is that they didn't seem to get along, but Einstein and Tesla once worked together on a secret project for the government. That project resulted in one of Einstein's greatest successes, and also one of his greatest failures, and it shook him to his core. I also know that it gave him great respect and admiration for Nikola Tesla, because he told me so. He considered Tesla to be the greatest of all the minds he had ever met, and that is saying a lot.

"I believe Tesla had information that ultimately helped Einstein come to his final answers. The two greatest minds of the 19th and 20th centuries collaborated to solve the ultimate mysteries of the universe. I don't think either one of them could have done it alone. I think you will need to look more into this key connection."

Again, Ian had slid into a near-trance while listening to the professor. Again, he could see the images in his mind. Again, he could feel what Einstein felt. It was as though he was in Einstein's story, while the rest of the world faded away. The professor's voice, combined with the story he was telling, put him in a state where he felt totally connected to Einstein.

He felt himself connect with this man who had died decades before. He needed to know even more. He wanted to hear the whole story. Somehow, he knew it would be important, although he didn't know why. He just felt it would make all the difference.

Ian reflected on the session, grateful that the professor allowed for a few moments to process his thoughts and feelings. He was amazed by all the things that had fallen into place, and all the difficulties that had to be overcome for Einstein to have his theories accepted. He wondered if he would have been as strong and persistent as Einstein, whose resolve was incredible. Ian had no idea about all that. Before, he would have said Einstein was a genius whom the world instantly loved and embraced.

Now, he had even more respect for Einstein. Ian felt overwhelmed, intimidated, and pretty scared, but he was also excited. He believed he was about to start his own journey. He thought that people would talk about it someday, and he hoped it would be filled with drama, suspense, excitement, and maybe a pretty girl or two.

Ian wondered if his problems as a child, being diagnosed with autism, struggling with dyslexia and learning disabilities, were all part of helping him prepare for some later challenges he would have to endure. He hoped he was ready. It was scary and exciting at the same time.

"Now, Ian, go home and think about what I've told you and get some rest," advised the professor.

"Thank you, professor," he said. "Like Einstein, I believe that everything happens for a reason, and I believe that about you and me. I have learned more from you in our sessions than I have from any teacher I've ever had. Because of you, I feel I am ready."

Ian stood up and gave Clarence a big hug. He noticed how frail the professor had become, and he felt a sense of sadness. I won't let this man down, no matter what, he thought to himself.

This was not the end, though. They had many more short sessions, fitting them in where and when they could. Ian found them all fascinating. He and the professor became closer and closer as Ian's understanding of Einstein and his theories grew.

CHAPTER SIX

Dr. Kearney's office, Princeton, 2018

"Ian, can you give it a rest, please?" shouted Peter Wu. "I'm trying to hack into the cafeteria computers to change the menu for next week. I can't focus on what I'm doing with your awful violin playing!"

Ian didn't respond. When he played the violin, it took him to other places in his mind. Right then, he was in Bern, Switzerland. He was visualizing the view from Einstein's apartment where he lived when he perfected his Theory of Relativity. He had studied the man and his history for so long that even though it was just a visualization exercise, it felt very real to him.

Ian had been meeting with Professor Kearney for a few weeks now. They had discussed many things about Einstein and his theories, and Ian understood so much more, but they had not come any closer to understanding what it was that Einstein had discovered before his death.

They had figured out that Einstein was probably referring to Nikola Tesla in his note. The two men had had many interactions. They rarely saw eye to eye on most issues but had great respect for one another. The professor had told Ian about a comment that Einstein had made regarding Tesla. He was once asked by a reporter how it felt to be the smartest man in the world. Einstein reportedly replied, "I don't know, you'll have to ask Nikola Tesla."

Ian and the professor had searched everywhere for written evidence that Tesla and Einstein communicated over the years. They had found many references to general communications, but nothing earth-shattering. Still, they must have communicated. Evidently, there was something that they both agreed was too sensitive for the world to know about. It couldn't be Einstein's theories of relativity, since the world knew all about those.

Everyone also knew Einstein was working on the Unified Field Theory, so it couldn't be that, either. It had to be something that connected the two men, and which they shared with each other. Maybe two sides of the same coin. Maybe a new way to see an old problem. Maybe a combination of their life's work.

"Ian! Seriously, dude, enough!" shouted Peter Wu into his ear.

Ian, startled out of his visions, responded, "I'm sorry, Peter. I'm working on some important stuff, and I need my visualization time. Go back to hacking the lunch menu and all that other important stuff you do. I have to go see the professor, anyway."

Ian cased his violin and headed over to the professor's office. The door was open. He took his seat and waited for the professor to arrive. Five minutes later, the professor entered and seemed agitated.

"Clarence, what's going on? You're never late, and you look really upset."

Ian had recently taken to calling the professor Clarence. They both thought it was funny that Ian was doing what Einstein used to do.

Clarence replied, "Nothing really. I just keep thinking I see government types lurking about. They don't seem to be watching, but they are always there. Nothing tells me someone is watching me like someone who looks like they're not watching me. You know what I mean?"

"Not sure I am tracking with you, Clarence," replied Ian, "but, hey, you're the boss. Let's forget about them for a while and get back to business."

The professor settled into his chair and took a deep breath. He motioned for Ian to proceed.

Ian hesitated for only a moment, then resumed where they'd left off the day before. "I've been thinking about the whole Tesla/Einstein connection. I think that may be the key. Let's talk about that some more. You mentioned that there was a project that the two of them worked on together? I have never found one in any of the generally available research. What was it?"

The professor nodded. "Yes, as I told you before, there was a secret government project that involved both of them, but it's not generally known or acknowledged and is almost impossible to verify. In 1943, the navy conducted an experiment on the *USS Elderidge.* It was called Project Rainbow. The work on this project had been progressing for a few years.

"It's said that both Tesla and Einstein contributed to the development of the technology used in the early 1930s. The navy was supposedly trying to develop an early version of stealth technology. The cover story the navy told was that they were trying to make their ships invisible to radar. It would be reasonable to assume that they enlisted the help of the two greatest minds available.

"Tesla was dead by the time they conducted the test in July of 1943, but it's very possible he worked in concert with Einstein on this project in the years before his death. Dr. Einstein never talked about this project much, but one time, he acknowledged to me that it was one of the most difficult and harrowing experiences he'd ever had. I believe it set his research on the Unified Field Theory back years and solidified his desire to carefully control the dissemination of his work from then on."

"Did he ever mention Tesla? What was it about the project that frightened him so much?" asked Ian.

"He only made vague references to Tesla, but I have done a lot of research. Project Rainbow is now referred to as the Philadelphia Experiment. From what I can gather, the true intent of the experiment seemed to involve the warping of space-time to enable the navy to teleport their ships anywhere in the world instantly.

"Think about that, Ian! What kind of advantage would that have been for us in World War II? Instead of taking weeks to get our navy in position, we could respond instantaneously to any threat. We could have a whole fleet show up on the enemy's doorstep before they knew we were coming. From the scraps of information out there, it seems that the experiment was a partial success.

"According to eyewitnesses, what actually happened was that by using an exceptionally large Tesla coil, they created an electromagnetic field around the ship, which they hoped would shield it from radar. It seems when they turned the coil on, it created this weird energy field and eventually, a green mist of some sort started to engulf the ship. Eyewitnesses have testified that the ship disappeared, or just vanished into thin air, and then supposedly disappeared from the Philadelphia Navy Shipyard and reappeared in Norfolk, Virginia, reappearing in Philadelphia a while later. According to secret reports, when the ship was inspected after it returned to Philadelphia, the crew was in bad shape. Many of them were found imbedded in the hull and beams of the ship. Apparently, it was horrific. The navy has always officially denied it, but this is the rumor.

"The project was classified, and most of the documentation on it has been heavily redacted or has completely disappeared over the years. There are even some rumors that the ship traveled in time unexpectedly, but that has not been confirmed. All I know is that it shook Einstein to his core.

"From that moment on, he seemed to have gained a much greater respect for Tesla and talked about him in much kinder terms. So, it is very possible that they collaborated on this project and maybe even shared their ideas. They may have combined their theories to develop the technology. No one knows for sure, but it is possible.

"That is why finding what Einstein left for me is critical. It could very well be the final result of their combined efforts. We must find it!"

"I agree," said Ian. "In fact, I've really been focusing on this whole thing. I have been thinking and visualizing while playing my violin, and I think I have come up with some ideas."

"Your violin?" asked the professor.

"Yes," replied Ian. "Early on, I learned that many of Einstein's greatest breakthroughs came while he was playing the violin. So, I took lessons. I'm not very good, but that's not why I do it. I visualize the problem I'm working on while I play, and it helps clarify things for me. That's how I came up with the PhotoEx app."

"That's astounding, Ian. It's so very like Einstein himself!" observed the professor. "He loved to play 'Lina', his violin, and I sat with him often while he did just that. Bach, Beethoven, and Mozart were his favorites. He often said that while he was playing the violin and ruminating on his ideas, it seemed like he was giving birth. I remember him saying, 'I live my daydreams in music. I see my life in terms of music'. He confessed to thinking about science in terms of images and intuitions, often drawn directly from his experiences as a musician, only later converting these into logic, words, and mathematics. Einstein used as many parts of his mind as he could to experience and interpret the world, to create knowledge. Far more than a diversion or hobby, music was such a part of the man that it seems to have played a role in his scientific working processes. It sounds as if the same might be said of you!

"In fact, his old violin is still here on campus. It's in the Exhibit Hall warehouse. All his things are in storage right now, waiting for the preparations for the next Einstein exhibition scheduled to open on campus next week. They're going to restage his home, which the university now owns, to look exactly like it did when he died.

"Right now, it's just filled with replicas and representative pieces, but after next week, it will be just as it was in 1955. I was waiting to tell you about that as I thought it would be a nice surprise for you. But now that you know, we can look forward to viewing it together."

"That's amazing, Clarence! That's exactly what I wanted to talk with you about," said Ian excitedly. "I have this idea. Dr. Einstein said that he had hidden the copy of the documents, and that it would remain where it was born. Knowing that you were on vacation just before he wrote the note to you, and knowing that he had not discovered the final answer before you left, he must have found the answer while you were away. Where was he during the time you were on vacation?"

"He was here on campus. He had no trips scheduled during that time," answered the professor.

"So, if he was here, then this is where the solution was born. Did he ever work anywhere else but his office while he was here?" asked Ian.

"No," responded the professor. "His office was the only place he did his real work."

"*Great!*" Ian declared. "That's just what I was hoping. It's my belief that he most likely hid the answer in the desk where he was working when he made his discovery. Where is that desk, Clarence? Do you know?"

"Of course, I know. It's as I said; it's in the warehouse with his other items. I would never allow myself to lose track of that desk. It was an important part of my life," replied the professor.

Ian smiled and winked at the professor. "Clarence, I have a plan."

After laying out his plan for the professor and answering all his objections about how dangerous it was and how careful they were going to have to be, Ian went back to his dorm room to implement the next step. He waited until his roommate Peter arrived.

"Peter, I'm sorry about disturbing your work before. I get so caught up in my own head sometimes I just zone out and forget that there are other people in the room. Can you forgive me?" Ian asked.

Peter looked at Ian like he had two heads. "Sure, dude, no worries. What's gotten into you? Why all the formality? You never apologize for anything. Why now?"

"I need your help," Ian said. "You are one of the best hackers in the country, and I have a job I need your help with. Are you in?"

"Maybe," replied Peter. "What are we talking about here? Concert tickets? Grades? Offshore bank accounts?"

"No, nothing like that," responded Ian. "Something much bigger. I need you to hack into the computers of the FBI. Can you handle it?"

"Seriously, bro? The FBI? What could you possibly need from them that you would risk getting us both a life sentence?" asked Peter.

"Just the future of the world as we know it. Nothing big. Seriously, can you do it?" Ian replied, looking dead serious.

Peter looked at Ian for a moment, then nodded. "I can. But it will cost you some of those millions sitting in your bank account."

"Sure," Ian agreed. "If you're successful, Princeton is on me. Let's get down to details."

Ian spent the next hour filling Peter in on what he needed to know. He didn't tell him the specifics of what he and the professor were working on, only that he needed to have all of the FBI files on both Tesla and Einstein downloaded and printed out. He also told him that he was going to need schematics of the security system and layouts of Einstein's old house.

Peter took it all down and got right to work.

Ian was satisfied. The wheels were in motion. Now, he had to scope out the area around Einstein's Princeton home. He grabbed his coat and headed out.

He went to 112 Mercer Street in Princeton. It was dark, but the house was well-lit. It was a small, white, cottage-style home with a nice front porch, surrounded by three-foot-high, well-trimmed hedges. A small, wrought-iron gate guarded the entrance to the walkway leading to the front door. There was what appeared to be an addition on the right side of the house; that was where Einstein's office was. The adjoining homes were close, but the properties were shielded from view on both sides by huge hedges about ten feet high.

Piece of cake, Ian thought. Once we deal with the security system, this will be easy.

Satisfied with what he saw, he headed back to campus. He failed to notice the black SUV tailing him back to campus, however.

Berlin, 1943

The two agents arrived to present to their leader with what they took from the old man's hotel room. After lugging in the crate of documents and devices, they stood by it and waited.

"I think we've succeeded this time," the taller one remarked, his tone filled with pride.

"I'm sure we have," the shorter one agreed. "It has to be in here. The *Führer* will be pleased."

Frowning, the taller one looked down at the crate. "But what if the *Führer* is angry that we killed him?"

"It does not matter," the shorter one scoffed. "He refused to give us what he promised, but we took it anyway. We warned him that's what would happen."

"*Wahr*, true."

"Besides," the shorter one continued, "We searched every inch of his hotel room, broke into the safe, and took all the documents from there…"

"We even searched his body," the taller one interjected.

"And re-dressed him and positioned him in a restful pose on the bed," the shorter one added, then pointed at the crate. "It has to be in here. There is nowhere else possible!"

Suddenly, the door opened. They snapped to attention as the *Führer* entered the room with his entourage of physicists.

"*Heil*, Hitler!" they exclaimed in unison.

"Take your seats, gentlemen," Hitler replied. "I understand you have a crate that will make me very happy. Please, show it to me."

Two soldiers lifted the crate to the conference table, opened it, and dumped the contents in a pile on the table. The pile contained an array of documents, small devices, and some personal odds and ends. Without preamble, the physicists begin to sort through it.

Dr. Werner Heisenberg, the man in charge of this group of physicists, had been secretly driving his men toward the development of an atomic bomb. He believed that the information that they had contracted with Tesla to provide would be the key to finally creating that weapon and many more powerful ones currently under development.

Heisenberg spent the next twenty minutes sorting and categorizing the treasure trove. When he was done, he carefully reviewed three sets of documents. His face was unreadable.

Finally, the *Führer* became impatient. "Dr. Heisenberg, please tell us if we have what we need!"

Dr. Heisenberg removed his glasses, bowed his head, and replied, "*Mein Führer*, the information we have sought is not here. I would like more time to have our men dig through it all, but unless it is somehow secretly encoded here, I do not believe we have what we sought.

What we have here is a collection of dreams and illusions. The rambling last thoughts and creations of a madman. The tinkerings of a man-child occupying his last lonely hours, indulging his imagination with fantasy. The concept that we had hoped to be revealed to us was either just wishful thinking, or it has slipped through our hands. If it ever existed, it is not in this crate. There is no information here that will help us with *Die Glocke* for our time travel initiative, or our most urgent need, the death ray."

"Is it possible for you to surmise what his concepts would have looked like based on the information in the crate?" asked Hitler. "Tesla was quoted as saying, 'this death ray would send concentrated beams of particles through the free air of such tremendous energy that they would bring down a fleet of ten thousand enemy airplanes at a distance of two hundred and fifty miles'. Think of that, doctor! We could insulate ourselves from the Allies' attacks, buying ourselves more time to develop the uranium bomb and the bell. The death ray is critical to our efforts."

"I understand the concepts and implications regarding the death ray," Heisenberg replied. "At its most basic level, it is a charged particle beam weapon. I have an understanding of the science behind it, but the unique aspect of Tesla's concept was the open-ended vacuum tube that he developed. I have no idea how he was able to generate a vacuum without a closed tube. Additionally, only he knew how to propagate a beam through very long ranges in the atmosphere. He obviously knew much more than we do about how to make this a usable concept. Maybe the idea has died with him."

"That cannot be true!" the Führer exploded. "We know he was working on it right up until his death. We know he went nowhere except that hotel he lived in and the Waldorf for dinner. Is it possible that he hid the information elsewhere in the room?"

"No, *mein Führer*," the shorter agent replied. "We tore the room apart and found nothing other than what we brought here today."

"You know that we are experienced and professional, and that we have served you well for the past ten years and have never failed," the taller agent added. "I promise, *mein Führer*, we will return and track down that information. We will never give up. If it exists, we will find it, even if it takes us the rest of our lives."

The *Führer* fixed them with a serpent-like glare. "Find it quickly or the rest of your lives may be shorter than you hope."

The two most feared agents in all Nazi Germany left that room shaken but determined.

When they were out of earshot, the shorter one slapped his right fist into his left palm. "We must find it. Whoever has that information will wish they'd never laid eyes on it. We will track it down even if it takes two lifetimes."

Not speaking his doubts aloud, the taller agent simply nodded and followed his partner into the street.

CHAPTER SEVEN

Professor Kearney's home, 2018

The night before the opening of the Einstein exhibit, Professor Kearney, Ian, and Peter gathered at the professor's house, just two blocks from Einstein's old home. They planned to rehearse and review the plan for breaking into the exhibit to give Ian the opportunity to examine Einstein's desk.

"I know you two believe that you have accounted for all contingencies," Professor Kearney said. "I believe you when you say that your information is accurate and incontrovertible. However, as a physicist, I want to remind you of Chaos Theory. Are you familiar with it at this point in your education?"

Peter responded first. "Yes, sir, I have a basic understanding."

"But we would love to hear you explain it to us," Ian added, "and why you think it applies to us tonight."

"Chaos," the professor began, "is when the present determines the future, but the approximate present does not approximately determine the future. Do you see where I am going with this, boys?"

"No," said Ian. "Please continue."

"Basically," he replied, "we can plan for everything we think might happen, but we can't predict everything that could happen. Thus, we can't ever be truly prepared, so be ready for anything to change in an instant."

"In other words," Ian grinned, "we must be like chameleons and be ready to adapt to our environment and circumstances, right?"

The professor nodded, his expression serious. "Right, but it's not to be taken lightly, Ian. Anything you change could have a butterfly effect on the future."

"I'm not familiar with that effect, either, professor," Peter interjected.

"When you're dealing with time-related events, any change in the past can affect the future. For example, if you go back to the beginnings of earth's existence, and accidentally squash the first butterfly, it could have far-reaching consequences in our present."

Ian sobered. "You're saying that the situation we're going into will be impacted by the initial conditions we encounter upon entering. We are dealing with several variables such as the time we choose to break in, the weather at that time, the amount of time we spend inside, and the unreliability of dealing with an electronic and computer-based security system. You are also saying that even though we believe we have considered and calculated every move and believe we can and will stick to our plan and timetable, any small variation could have a butterfly effect on the final outcome. Is that correct, Clarence?"

"Yes, that is essentially correct," replied the professor, "but it's more complex than that. If you're successful... *especially* if you're successful... the impact of your actions tonight can and will have far-reaching effects. None of which can be predicted but will absolutely be determined by the sum of your actions. You are, in essence and in reality, determining your own futures tonight. Maybe for all of us. Maybe even for those you love. Think about that before you leave here, boys. Do your best to stick with the plan but realize that something unexpected *will* happen. Account for that in your calculations and choose wisely."

Ian looked into Clarence's intense eyes and nodded.

"It will only be me and Peter," he said, "so we are limiting the personal variables. We know how the security system works and can bypass it for a short period of time. Even if that doesn't work, I have visualized where all the sensors are and have figured out how to navigate around and under them. We know exactly where the furniture is placed and how it all lays out. We can navigate the rooms in the dark, if need be. Our main objective is Einstein's desk. I even know that the neighbor on the near side property has a dog which they bring in for the night after 10 p.m. We've got this. We'll get out of there and head back to your house as soon as we're done. How is that for a bullet- and butterfly-proof plan?" finished Ian.

"Sounds about as bulletproof as it can be, but nothing is immune from random butterflies. Be careful!" warned the professor.

At precisely 11 p.m. the next night, Ian and Peter left the professor's house and walked the two blocks to Einstein's home. They quickly leaped the front hedges and in seconds were at the side entrance to the house. They waited until their breathing slowed down and listened for any sounds indicating that they may have been seen. They heard nothing.

Ian took out the electronic device he'd manufactured with Peter's help during the past couple of days. They found the exterior electrical junction box and the security system.

He attached the device to the junction box and the security system, which would trick the system into thinking that the circuits remained unbroken even though they would be passing through the lasers as they walked around the house.

They had calculated that they needed forty-five minutes to successfully complete their search. Peter took out the lockpicking tools and began to work on the old side door. They were inside in under two minutes.

Princeton campus, 2018

Two German agents had checked the dorm room for the kid. He wasn't there. They'd canvassed a number of other likely locations and found no sign. Their next stop was the old professor's on-campus office. They knew that the professor and the kid sometimes met there.

"Why don't we just go right to the professor's home instead of his office, Axel?" the younger agent asked.

"We will, Rolf," replied the older agent. "We just needed to work our way there from campus. The professor's campus office was the next closest spot and the most likely place to find them together. If we can find them together, we can take care of two problems at once. Maybe even three, if that roommate happens to be with them. Remember priority one: the professor. Priority two: the kid; then, if possible, the roommate who did the hacking. He probably knows nothing and may very well be just a pawn in the game. He can't be too sophisticated, because our systems guys, who were already hacked into the FBI systems, were able to trace the security break immediately. He tried to cover his tracks, but with the limitations of working from campus, he did a piss poor job. Probably in a hurry, too."

They arrived at the professor's on-campus office around 11:10 p.m. They did a quick check and found no one there and nothing of interest. They headed to the professor's house, which they'd been watching for the last few years. The lights were on. They exited the black SUV and split up, making sure to take the device with them. This would be the first time they'd had the chance to use it and prove its value.

Rolf headed to the back door, while Axel went to the front. After a moment, the younger agent heard the bell ring, followed by movement inside. As the professor opened the front door, Rolf kicked the heel of his boot into the back door, splintering the wood and slamming it against the kitchen wall. At the same moment, Axel shoved the front door open, pushing the professor to the floor. The old man tried to scramble up, but the agents overpowered and subdued him. Dragging him into his home office, they handcuffed him to his office chair facing the television screen mounted on the wall.

They silently watched as he tested his bonds. When he finally quieted, Axel spoke. "So nice to finally meet face to face, professor. I feel like we are old friends after observing you for so many years."

"So, it was you following me all this time?" The professor queried. "I am so glad I wasn't imagining it. But wouldn't it have been better just to make an appointment and meet with me at a more convenient hour?"

"Wow, who would have thought, a physicist with a sense of humor!" observed Rolf. "Do you think when we use the thought camera on him, we'll see the Comedy Channel?"

"The thought camera?" the professor asked.

"Yes, one of our most prized devices. Thanks to stolen information and model devices, we have developed the ability to see into your mind. We don't even have to trouble you by asking you to cooperate, we will just take the information we need."

"Rolf, hook him up to the television monitor, so we can all enjoy the show," Axel instructed.

The younger agent placed the visor-like device on the professor's head, connected the HDMI cable to the television, turned it on, and pressed the button on his remote control. Immediately, the professor seized up in agony. The vibrations and resonances in his head would be unbearable from the start, Rolf had been told.

Rolf and Axel intently watched the television screen, seeing everything that transpired in the professor's mind. They watched as the boys met with the professor. They heard them discussing the plans. They now knew that the boys had gone to Einstein's house to retrieve something valuable.

"Well, that's convenient," Rolf remarked. "We won't even have to go find them."

"That's right," Axel agreed. "They'll come to us and bring their prize with them. All we have to do is wait and relieve them of their prize when they return."

"That will kill three birds with one stone," Rolf chortled. "Isn't the thought camera such a wonderful device?"

"Yes, it is, my old friend, simply *wunderbar*. If the *Führer'd* had this in the old days, it would have made torture so much more fun."

The professor slumped in his chair, shaking and gushing gibberish.

Einstein's home, 2018

"Ian!" Peter whispered loudly. "You've been sitting at that desk for ten minutes and haven't moved. What are you doing? Come on and start looking. We only have thirty minutes left."

"Shh, I'm gathering my thoughts and visualizing where Einstein might have hidden it. We don't even know what it might look like, so I need to get into a state of mind where I can feel what he felt and see what he might have seen when he was concealing the secret. I don't have my violin, so that makes it harder. Just give me time," said Ian.

"Okay, just a few more minutes. I'll keep looking around the rooms for clues and see if there is anything else here that might help," offered Peter.

As Ian drifted back into the visualization state Peter had just jerked him out of, his mind took him back to that day in 1955, when Einstein wrote the note to Clarence. Ian had memorized every word of the note and now visualized Einstein writing the words on the paper in that challenging handwriting of his. He tried to imagine what was going through his head when he wrote it. Then, he rose from the chair and walked slowly around the room.

Einstein had mentioned that he'd made a copy of the documents. But there were no copy machines in 1955, so the only way to make a copy was to take a picture or write it by hand. A picture would be faster and fairly easy to hide, but if there were multiple documents, there would need to be many pictures. That would become increasingly hard to conceal. Maybe he just hid the film? No, Ian decided. Film would degrade too fast and could be easily damaged.

Just as he was feeling close to the answer, Peter interrupted him again.

"Ian. IAN!" Peter loudly whispered.

"What is it now?" Ian snapped, irritated.

"If you need a violin, I just found two!" Proudly, Peter held them out for Ian to see.

Ian smiled.

"And here's an ancient and smelly case," Peter added.

This is probably Einstein's actual violin, Ian thought. Maybe it will help. He accepted the violin and bow that Peter offered and began to play softly. As he played, he sat back down at the desk. Peter continued his reconnaissance.

Ian was now solidly in the past. His thoughts were coalescing. He visualized Einstein taking pictures. But the camera he was seeing in his mind was very small and unusual. He visualized him finishing, and then removing the film. But it was not normal film. It was very odd. Then he saw him leave the room and go to the kitchen, where he shut off the lights. A while later, he returned and pushed his thumb down on the note to Clarence. He smiled and grabbed his coat, hat, violin, and bow, then left. Ian's eyes burst open! He knew where Einstein had hidden the copy.

"Peter, let's get out of here! We need to get back to the professor's house right away," Ian said, a little too loudly.

Startled, Peter tripped over an ottoman and fell backward into a window, smashing it. Alarms screamed.

There had been no indications in the schematics that the windows were alarmed separately from the rest of the house. The alarms were so loud the boys could not hear each other. Lights started to go on doors up and down the street. They ran out of the house and out into the street, heading for the professor's, while the house sirens continued blaring. Ian ran, holding the battered case and bow in his left hand with the violin tucked underneath his right arm.

As they approached the professor's house, they stopped. They could see a police cruiser about three blocks away heading in their direction. Ducking into a bunch of bushes at the next-door neighbor's house, they hunkered down. Just then, they saw two men run from Professor Kearney's house, jump into a black SUV, and take off just before the police passed by the house. The SUV made a right turn at the corner just before the police passed.

Ian and Peter headed straight for the professor's house. They rushed in and found him handcuffed and babbling.

"Professor! What happened? Are you all right?" asked Ian, rushing to his side. The professor just stared at them and continued babbling. "Ian, we have to call an ambulance for him. He's in really bad shape," observed Peter.

"I know!" replied Ian. "This is not good. Professor! I know where Einstein hid the documents. You must help me! Where is the note he left for you? Is it here? In your office? Please tell me!"

The professor just rolled his eyes and babbled. He tried to talk but it didn't sound like a real language. Ian listened closely to what the professor was saying, and it sounded like "offish". Then, the professor stopped making any sound at all and started shaking.

"Ian, seriously, dude, I've called the ambulance. They're on their way," warned Peter. "Let's get out of here!"

With one last look at the professor, he bolted out of the house. Ian quickly packed the violin and bow in the case and joined Peter in a mad dash across campus to the professor's office.

With each running step, all Ian could see in his head were butterflies. Thousands of them. Everywhere.

As they rounded the corner, they didn't see the black SUV pull up to the professor's house, park, and turn off its lights; its occupants waiting in the dark for the boys to return.

Ian and Peter made it back to campus in record time. They stopped in front of their dorm to catch their breath. "Do you think we should go in there? Do you think the guys who attacked the professor know where we live?" asked Peter.

"It's possible," said Ian. "Where did you hide all the paperwork you hacked from the FBI files?"

"It's all in my locker at the gym," responded Peter.

"Okay, let's go there and get it. Then we have to go to the professor's office and find Einstein's letter."

They headed to the gym, retrieved the hacked files, and took off toward the professor's on-campus office. They entered the darkened building and quietly crept down the hall to the office door. Peter used his lockpicking tools, and they gained entry.

"Now what?" asked Peter.

"We start looking for the note," replied Ian. "I'll

search his desk while you look through the files."

The two boys searched feverishly. After a few moments of futile hunting, Ian took the violin out and began to play softly to help him visualize where the note that Einstein wrote to Clarence might be.

Peter heard him and shook his head. "Dude, you are so going to get us caught!"

Ian ignored him and played on. After a few minutes, he stopped playing. He walked straight to the desk and lifted the blotter. Underneath was the note they had been looking for.

"Peter," Ian whispered, "let's go; I have it!"

"Wow!" remarked Peter. "You and that violin make an awesome team. Can it help you pick lottery numbers?"

They grabbed the note and ran out of the building.

"Where are we going now, if we can't go back to the dorm?" asked Peter as they ran.

"To the parking lot to get my car, then to Manhattan. I have a friend there who will help us," said Ian.

CHAPTER EIGHT

FBI, New York City Bureau

Simmons, the assistant director in charge at the New York City FBI headquarters, sat at his desk poring over documents related to the current case. A knock at the door interrupted him.

"Come in!" he called.

"Sir, I have evidence of two separate, but essentially simultaneous, hacking incidents that happened a few days ago," reported the timid and frightened head of IT, Cameron Johnson.

"Okay, spill it," he ordered. "I don't have all night."

"They both involve the same file and occurred within six hours of each other," replied Johnson. "We've traced the first intrusion to an IP address for a student at Princeton University, but the other intrusion is virtually untraceable. It seems to have originated somewhere in South America."

"What was the file that was compromised?" asked Simmons.

"It was a file on Einstein and his connections to Tesla. It contained all the intelligence we had on both men and their possible implications for national security. Names of friends, associates, relatives, and detailed descriptions of their theories and inventions," replied Johnson.

"Odd that an obscure file like that would draw so much attention in such a short period of time," the director observed. "Make a copy and bring it to me, along with every other scrap of information we have on them. Something is going on, and I want to know what it is."

Johnson hustled back to the computer center to begin downloading all they had on Einstein and Tesla.

There was another knock on the door.

"What is it now?" he responded irritably. "Come in!"

"Sorry to disturb you, sir, I just need a minute," said one of his agents.

"Oh, it's you, Armstrong, I thought it was Johnson again," said Simmons, waving him in. "Come in. What's up?"

"Just thought you should know, we had a very strange call from the Princeton University police. It seems that two separate incidents took place there tonight, so they notified us. They feel that there is more going on than they can understand and want some help," explained Agent Armstrong.

"Why would the FBI be contacted about a campus issue?" he asked.

Armstrong replied, "It seems that a renowned physics professor, who knew Einstein, was attacked tonight. He's in bad shape. If I didn't know better, I'd say his brain is scrambled. They found him tied to his desk chair in front of his television, babbling and shaking. He's alive, but there's definitely something wrong with his brain. We don't know if he had a stroke, or if this is a result of whatever his attackers did to him.

"Around the same time, there was a break-in at

Einstein's old house a few blocks away. The university was scheduled to open a new exhibit about Einstein and had moved all his original furniture and belongings back into the house. The only thing missing is his violin. But there are signs that people were in the house rummaging around."

"Was anything strategic or sensitive taken?" asked Simmons.

"Not that we are aware of, sir. There were copies of many of his papers and theories and all his books, but none of that seems to have been disturbed. However, a homemade device was found attached to the security system which bypassed it. It was very simple, but highly effective," finished Armstrong.

"This is the second report I have gotten tonight that involves Princeton and Einstein," stated the director. "Obviously, something is going on. IT just reported a breach of the system by two separate hacking incidents earlier in the week. One of them was traced back to a student at Princeton, and it involved a file with information about Einstein and Tesla. It all must be connected. Physicists, Einstein, Tesla, strange brain-scrambling torture devices… sounds like an *X-Files* episode.

"Pick two men and head down to IT. Get the file download from Johnson and whatever he has on Einstein and Tesla and sort through it. Call the campus police and find out if they have any security video. Then, gather all you can on known associates of that professor."

"Yes, sir," Armstrong nodded curtly, then left the office.

"Definitely odd coincidences going on here," Simmons mused to himself, "and I don't like odd coincidences."

"So, where are we going?" asked Peter as he stuffed his face with corn chips purchased at a rest stop on the New Jersey Turnpike. "Who is this friend you're so sure will help us?"

"Dr. Mills, a family friend," replied Ian. "I am going to call him now, so be quiet, and let me do the talking." Ian dialed Dr. Mills, who answered on the third ring.

"Ian! So glad you called. How are things at Princeton? Have you solved any of the mysteries of physics yet?"

"Hey, Dr. Mills. Look, I am calling for some help. I can't explain all of it over the phone, but I need a place to hide out for a while. Some really crazy things have happened, and I had to leave campus. Can a friend and I stay with you for a few days?" asked Ian.

"Why of course, Ian, absolutely, but have you told your parents what's going on? Why aren't you going to stay with them?" asked Dr. Mills.

"It's really hard to explain, but I want to keep them out of this for a while," replied Ian. "I need to understand a few things, and you have always been such a great help. I would appreciate it if you didn't contact my parents right now. We'll explain it all when we get there."

"Okay, Ian, I'm still at the office, but I'll meet you at my townhouse. You remember where it is, right?" asked Dr. Mills.

"Yes, we'll meet you there in about an hour. Thanks so much, Dr. Mills." Ian hung up with a satisfied nod.

"Sounds like a really cool guy. What's his deal?" asked Peter.

"Dr. Robert Mills is a world-renowned functional neurologist," replied Ian. "He helped me when I was a kid and sparked my interest in Einstein. We've stayed in touch over the years, and he's become a family friend. He is one of the most amazing guys I've ever met. I know we can get some good perspective and advice from him. With the professor out of commission, we're going to need someone to confide in."

"Sounds like a good choice," replied Peter.

"Take out the files you got from the FBI," Ian requested. "I want to know what you found. Tell me what's in there that's interesting."

Peter reached into the back seat and retrieved his backpack. He pulled out a file and opened it. "I haven't read it all, because we were so focused on the schematics and the break-in, but I did notice some really wild stuff when I was printing it all out. There's lots of information about Einstein and Tesla's personal life. For example, did you know that Einstein met with the Israeli Prime Minister David Ben-Gurion back in 1953?"

"Yes, I did," replied Ian. "Remember, I'm an Einstein junkie. I've read everything I could about him since I was nine."

"Okay, but did you know that the FBI bugged that meeting and that Ben-Gurion and Einstein discussed the possibility of Einstein building an atomic bomb for Israel so they could protect themselves from all the Arab states threatening them?" asked Peter.

"That I did not know," replied Ian. "Anything else?"

"Yes," replied Peter, "there is speculation that Ben-Gurion challenged Einstein to develop a formula that would prove the existence of God! Einstein reportedly said that he did not believe in a biblical God, but that he did believe in a controlling consciousness that designed the universe. Have you ever heard of Einstein working on a formula to prove the existence of God?"

"No, I haven't," Ian answered, "but maybe after we

are done with all of this, I'll work on that. Go on."

"The stuff on Tesla is *really* weird," continued Peter. "It seemed like they were afraid of him, like he was a loose cannon or something. They seemed to think that his ideas had military applications, but they kept pushing him away while keeping close tabs on him. As if they were waiting for him to develop something super powerful, and then planned to take it away from him. There was no cooperation on the part of either party. Mutual suspicion, I guess you could call it.

"They have details on most of his inventions and theories, and they seemed to have worked on developing a number of them, with mixed results. There is a notation that says that his ideas and inventions could not be completed without further advances in technology and physics. Like he was way ahead of his time. Over the years, they seemed to have lost interest in his stuff. There is really nothing much about him after 1945," Peter finished.

"Well, he died in 1943. Doesn't that make sense?" observed Ian.

"Yes, except that they also noted that they suspected he was murdered, but they kept it quiet and fed the press a load of crap," said Peter. "It says that when they searched his room at the New Yorker hotel, it was basically cleaned out. Someone had gotten there before them and taken all his papers and devices.

"The report stated that they were especially upset about the loss of information about the death ray. They speculated that the information had been obtained by the Nazis, and they were in a panic. I guess after the war ended, they didn't have to worry about that anymore, so they shelved the file. However, I did find something very interesting that you have to see." Peter rummaged through the file and pulled out a picture. He showed it to Ian.

"Who is that?" exclaimed Ian.

"That, my friend, is Tesla's great-grandniece," said Peter. "They apparently have been keeping tabs on his family over the years. There was a suspicion that maybe his family members had been the ones that took all his documents to either sell to the Nazis or to keep them out of the hands of our government.

"This picture is of Angelina Novak. It says that she is a real scientific whiz kid, about eighteen years old. She's won several awards for her inventions and research and even published a paper that was recognized by the Tesla Scientific Society of Croatia. She is currently in the running for this year's Nikola Tesla – Genius of the Future award, which will be presented at a conference in a few days in Zagreb. Look at her! She's hot, with brains *and* beauty. I would love to meet her someday!" observed Peter.

Ian noticed that Angelina looked like a punk rock star. Long, dark, wavy hair, large, dark eyes, nose ring, piercings, and the hint of a tattoo at the base of her neck. Ian was smitten immediately.

He re-focused on the road and said, "If that is the way all women physicists look in Croatia, maybe I'll transfer."

"Well, her address is here in the file, so we can look her up. After leaving school unannounced, we may have no choice but to transfer there. If we're gone too long, we're going to have a lot of explaining to do," said Peter.

"I know," said Ian, thinking about Clarence.

He was worried about the man who had been his friend and mentor. He couldn't call and ask about him, or he'd draw unwanted attention. He decided that he would ask Dr. Mills to check it out. After all, he was a world-renowned brain expert, and there was certainly something wrong with Clarence's brain. That might be a good cover.

"Peter, get back to the file," suggested Ian. "Anything else in there that I need to know about?"

Peter rifled through more pages and said, "Here is something about an experiment that Tesla and Einstein both worked on called Project Rainbow."

"Clarence told me about that a few days ago," offered Ian. "What does the file say?"

"Not much," replied Peter. "A lot of this is redacted, but whatever it was and whatever happened, it scared the crap out of the FBI and the navy. It was apparently a bloodbath, and they began to doubt the validity of much of the Tesla material they'd accumulated over the years. They almost lost faith in Einstein and his theories, as well. They had already informed Einstein about the Manhattan Project planning, so they couldn't bail on him, but Tesla's theories, they wrote off as the ramblings of an unreliable maniac."

"We're going to have to dig deeper into that one," said Ian. "I want to know what happened and what they were really trying to accomplish. Clarence said it was possible that they were working on teleportation or time travel, but officially, they said they were working on some form of early stealth technology to cloak the ships from radar. I need to know the truth. What do you think, Peter?"

When Peter did not reply Ian looked over at him. Peter was holding another paper and was staring at Ian. "You have to see this one, buddy, and you are not going to like it."

He held out the picture. It was of the professor and Ian talking together on campus. Written on the picture was *Ian Petrie, Intel award winner, protégé of Professor C.J. Kearney.*

Ian glanced at the picture, then jerked the wheel to the right, pulled onto the shoulder, and slammed on the brakes. He grabbed the picture from Peter's hand and stared at it in disbelief.

They had his picture and had been following him! They knew about him. They'll tie me to the professor's attack, he thought.

"We need to get to Dr. Mills's house right away," Ian said to Peter and stomped down hard on the accelerator, pulling quickly back onto the highway.

FBI offices, New York City

"Okay, what have you guys come up with on the Princeton case?" asked Director Simmons.

"It's really coming together, director," replied Agent Armstrong. "The campus police have sent us some security video from campus and from a neighbor's home security system across from the professor's house. The neighbor's video shows a black SUV, with two men pulling up in front of the professor's house around 11:05 p.m.

"We can't actually see the professor's house, but around 11:50, the same two guys came running out of the house, hopped into the SUV and hightailed it out of there. About a minute later, a police cruiser drives by with lights flashing. They were responding to the break-in at the Einstein house. So, we know the two guys in the SUV probably were the ones that messed up the professor's brain.

"Then, a minute or so after the police cruiser passes by, two kids are seen running toward the professor's house. Again, we can't see the house, but it looks like they go in, and then come out running about ten minutes later.

"Then, two minutes after that, the black SUV parks in front of the professor's house again and turns off its lights. Eventually, an ambulance arrives, and the SUV takes off. A lot of activity for one evening at a humble professor's house, if you ask me," he observed.

"Agreed," responded Simmons. "What did the other video from campus show?"

"It showed two students heading into the building where Professor Kearney's on-campus office is. They come out about fifteen minutes later. One of them had a piece of paper and a violin," replied Armstrong.

"A violin? Did they take that from the professor's office?" asked Simmons.

"Apparently not," replied Armstrong. "It seems the only thing missing from Einstein's house was one of his violins. His original violin. The one he used all the time. It was part of the exhibit."

"Okay, great work. Find out who those kids are, get me a plate number for that SUV, and run facial recognition on the two men," ordered Simmons. "Find out what they did to the professor to make his brain go wonky, and let's not assume the other stuff is just some college pledging prank. Make sure we cover our bases. With this stuff tied into the hacking incidents, we have a severe security problem. And tell Johnson that I want the IP address for the second hack. And I mean right away. No excuses!"

"Excuse me, director, but we already know who one of the boys is," offered Armstrong. "Johnson gave us the file, and there's a picture of him in it." He handed the picture to the director. "His name's Ian Petrie, Intel award winner, and a protégé of Professor C.J. Kearney."

"Well, that helps tremendously," said the director, "but why is his picture in a file on Einstein and Tesla, and why was it hacked, twice? Is someone running intel on a project I don't know about? There's way more going on here than meets the eye. I want answers! Find Ian Petrie, find out everything you can about him, and do it now!" ordered Director Simmons.

Dr. Mills's home, Manhattan

The boys pulled up to Dr. Mills's townhome on the upper east side of Manhattan. Dr. Mills was waiting for them on the front steps and pointed to the underground garage where the door was just opening. They drove in, parked behind his Porsche, then got out and greeted Dr. Mills as he opened the inside basement door to the house.

"Ian, so glad you made it," said Dr. Mills, "and in record time, I think. You must have flown."

"Thanks, doc," replied Ian. "It's great to see you, and thanks for agreeing to let us crash here."

"Get your stuff, and let's go upstairs and talk," instructed Dr. Mills.

The boys gathered the files and their backpacks and headed into the house. When they got upstairs, they met Dr. Mills in the kitchen.

"Can I get you boys anything? Food? Coffee? Bail money?" Dr. Mills asked.

They laughed, and Ian said, "Coffee would be great."

Peter agreed and added, "Nice place you have here, Dr. Mills. Really impressive. There must be a lot of money in functional neurology, whatever that is."

"Peter!" Ian objected.

"What?" Peter looked confused.

The doctor laughed. "It's okay, Ian. This was an old fixer upper, Peter. I've been redoing the whole place over the past several years, and now it's finally done. I'm going to need to work until I am eighty to pay it off, but it's a really great place, and so close to my office. But enough with the small talk. Why are you boys here? What's going on?"

"I'll try to make it as brief as possible," Ian began. "You know I was working with Professor C.J. Kearney as my mentor at Princeton, right? Well, we've been working on something strange. Back in 1955, he knew Einstein. While he was on vacation, Einstein wrote a letter to him a day or so before he, Einstein, died. In the letter, he said that he had solved a major problem he was working on, but that after finding the solution, he realized that he could not reveal it to the world. He said he needed to be able to 'close the door' before he revealed how to open it.

"He indicated that he was going to make a copy of the information about the discovery, destroy the originals, and then he would hide a copy of all of it 'where it was born', revealing the location to only Clarence when he returned from his vacation."

"Who's Clarence?" Dr. Mills interrupted.

"That's what Einstein called Professor Kearney," Ian replied. "He thought it was funny, since it was actually the professor's real first name. Anyway, Einstein died the next day and never mailed the letter. It remained there on his desk.

"After hearing of Einstein's death, Clarence rushed back from vacation and went to Einstein's office. While sitting at Einstein's desk, he saw the letter, read it, and realized the astounding importance of it. But just as he was trying to absorb it all, reporters and photographers from *Life* magazine came into the office to take pictures for a story they were doing on Einstein's life. He quickly hid the letter under a pile of other documents on the desk and waited in the kitchen. After they left, he went back in, got the letter and left.

"Since that day, he's been trying to figure out what Einstein's discovery was, and where he hid it."

"And has he had any success?" asked Dr. Mills while pouring the boys huge mugs of cinnamon-flavored coffee.

"Not really," answered Ian. "He believes that Einstein might have found the solution to the Unified Field Theory, but it had to be more than that. In the letter, Einstein referred to Nikola Tesla. He said that 'Nikola was right, the world is not ready'. And he also referenced a key; an actual metal key.

"Clarence speculates that Nikola Tesla secretly sent information to Einstein before Tesla died and entrusted that information to him for safekeeping. Then, Einstein used some or all that information to help him develop the solution to the Unified Field Theory. Clarence has no idea what the metal key could be or where it might be hidden. He assumes it's hidden with the documents. Whatever Einstein discovered shook him to his core. This is huge."

"Okay, I get all of that, but why are you here?" asked Dr. Mills. "I would think you would want to be there working on this with him. Explain."

"We're here because Clarence was attacked and had his brain fried while we were breaking into Einstein's home, looking for the letter, and stealing his violin," Everything Ian said came out in a huge rush of syllables and emotion. "Then, we broke into Clarence's on-campus office, took the letter, and now we are running for our lives, because the guys who attacked Clarence are looking for us, and they know who I am! I thought that this would be a safe place to hide, because no one knows about my relationship with you and could never figure out this is where we went. *And*, I really need a friend, mentor, and some good advice now that Clarence is out of the picture. How's that for an explanation?" Ian finished, breathless.

Dr. Mills just stared at them, looking from one young man to the other and back again, seeming to review all the information in his head. His perplexed look suggested that he thought this might be a joke, but the fear in their eyes seemed real.

Finally, appearing to have absorbed it all, he said, "Looks like this is going to be a long night. I am going to make more coffee. Go into the living room and settle in. I need much more detail."

They spent hours filling him in on why the guys were after them, the Einstein/Tesla connections, and all the information in the hacked file. Then they talked about the break-in, what Ian visualized, and about the letter that Ian took from the professor's office.

"So, as I was sitting at Einstein's desk," Ian explained, "I visualized what he was doing on that day he wrote the letter. I imagined him taking photos of the documents with what looked like an old miniature spy camera. But the film was weird. I don't even know if I can call it film. What I was visualizing was very small... tiny, really.

"Then I saw him head into the kitchen, turn off the lights, and when he came back a long time later, he pressed his thumb on the letter and smiled. All I know is that the letter is the linchpin, and I've not had time to examine it."

"Then let's take a look at it," suggested Dr. Mills.

Ian took the letter out of his backpack and laid it on

the coffee table. They all examined it closely, but no one could see anything unusual. Then, Ian had an idea.

"I'm going to use my PhotoEx app on it. Maybe we can see if there are layers here that we're not seeing."

He opened the experimental version of the application on his significantly modified and upgraded iPad. He trained the newly customized, camera-like lens on the document and held it over the page while the app scanned and copied it.

After ten seconds, he saved it and called it back up again. The clarity of the image was amazing. On the first review, they didn't see anything unusual. There were no notifications regarding layers or hidden information. Ian was disappointed.

He frowned, but then increased the magnification a hundredfold. Amazingly, the image became even sharper. They could see the fibers of the paper and the details of the ink. It was almost as if they were looking at a landscape of mountains, valleys, rivers, and trees. It was truly stunning. They reviewed the document from top to bottom.

Finally, at the bottom of the letter they noticed a dot next to Einstein's signature. When looking at the dot without magnification, it appeared to be just a large period next to the name "Albert". But under the magnification provided by the PhotoEx app, it looked like a raised structure with ridges and variations in color. Ian ran his finger over the dot and could feel that it was definitely not an ink-drawn period.

"I don't know what that is, but it's definitely not ink," said Ian. "Let's increase the magnification and take a closer look."

As he removed his finger from the dot, it slid to the side. It had become detached from the paper. He was horrified. Had he ruined it? Did he damage it?

Ian carefully withdrew his hand and increased the magnification to five hundred. He trained his camera on the dot and activated the application. After ten seconds, they reviewed the image.

Dr. Mills said, "Ian, that is no period. It's not even a dot. It's a microdot!"

"What is a microdot?" asked Peter.

"A microdot is made from special film and is almost exclusively used in spy operations. It was developed during World War II by the Germans. They would send messages and include the microdots in the letter to send secret information. The most popular and advanced version of this method was done by using something called a Zapp kit, named after the inventor.

"This microdot could definitely contain the information you are looking for. But there's a problem. The microdots must be viewed through a microscope by a special machine, and I don't think there are any around anymore. Of course, we could do an internet search, but that will leave electronic trails, which is not something we want right now. I don't know how you're going to access that information without one."

"Doc," said Ian, "think about who you are talking to here. This is what I do. I'm certain that if I increase the magnification enough, we can read this. If I have to activate the X-ray component, I can do that, too. And even if I have to modify the app to read this, it will work. Trust me, I got this."

He fiddled with his iPad awhile, trained the lens on the dot, and began the scanning and examination process.

After about thirty minutes of multiple shots from multiple angles and more fiddling with the iPad, he saved his work and said, "Okay, gentlemen, let's see what we have."

He called up the images and, as clear as day, there were the documents that Einstein had concealed; more than one hundred pages of crystal-clear documents and images. There were also formulas that made Ian's imagination take flight and diagrams which sent him over the moon. Finally, there was a whole separate section with the information that Tesla had sent Einstein in 1943, and on the last page, an image of the oddly shaped metal key that Tesla had sent with the documents.

The three of them were astounded. Right before their eyes was the information that had shaken Einstein to the core. What would it reveal? Would they be able to understand it without the insight of the professor? This was going to take time. Lots of time.

"I wish I had a time machine, so I could slow down time and spend all of it working on this right now!" exclaimed Ian. "Do you realize what we have here?" he asked the others. "What we have here is the roadmap to the future. A bright and shining roadmap with no limits. Thank you, Dr. Einstein. *I love you*!"

Dr. Mills carefully picked up the microdot. "We'd better make sure this is secure and stays undamaged. If your iPad explodes or gets lost, we're going to want to make another copy. I'm going to seal it in a container and put it in my safe room upstairs for added protection."

He left for a few minutes and then returned. They spent the rest of the night skimming through the documents and planning. By the time the sun rose, they had a solid plan for dealing with all of it.

"Then it is agreed," Dr. Mills said. "You two need to get out of the country. You cannot stay here. Until you finish working out all the formulas and decipher all the information in the documents, you must stay hidden. You also have to follow the clues and the cryptic information in the letters and documents that Tesla sent Einstein.

"In the documents we have read so far, Tesla alluded to important information that he had hidden that would also 'Remain where it was born'. That phrase caught my attention, because it must be where Einstein heard that phrase initially and then echoed it in this letter to Clarence. So, that tells me there is more critical information to find.

"From my knowledge about Tesla, I surmise that he hid the additional information in Croatia, since that was where Tesla grew up and where many of his first ideas were born," said Dr. Mills. "Go there and find the trail. Follow it and find your destiny. Are you both in? I'll buy the tickets. I will give you all the cash you need and make the hotel arrangements in Zagreb. All you will need is your passports and a toothbrush."

The boys looked at each other and Ian said, "That all sounds great, except the part about the passports. Mine's at home."

Peter chimed in. "I don't even have a passport. I'm from California, and I've never been out of the country. How long does it take to get a passport?"

Dr. Mills just put his head in his hands. For a moment, he'd forgotten he was dealing with boys. "Too long, Peter. Much longer than we have," was his deflated reply. "Okay, here is what we'll do. Ian, I need to get in touch with your parents somehow and fill them in. I will tell them to get your passport and some clothes and meet us here tomorrow."

"Is that a good idea?" Ian asked, concerned. "Maybe the FBI has bugged by parents' phone."

"I'm guessing they haven't had time to do that, yet," the professor reassured him. "I'll make your flight reservations for tomorrow evening. Peter, you're out of luck, buddy. You'll just have to stay here with me until things cool down. Then, we can figure out what to do next."

Ian interrupted. "Dr. Mills, flying on a public airline doesn't sound safe to me, either. I'm sure the FBI is tapped into TSA's database. Just tell my parents to charter a private jet in your name. They can use the money from my bank account to pay for it. Tell them also to take out as much cash as you think I'll need."

"I'm not sure that's such a good idea, either, Ian," said Dr. Mills. "Although you're an independently wealthy young man, I'm sure once the FBI figures out you're involved, and they will, they'll track your accounts, if they haven't frozen them already."

Ian frowned. "I hadn't thought of that."

"I'll let your parents know what you need. I have some cash here you can have in the meantime," Dr. Mills offered.

"Thank you. What about the professor?" Ian asked, worry in his tone. "Will you try to find out what happened to him and where he is? Do you think you can figure out a way to get the information about him without raising suspicion?"

"Absolutely," said Dr. Mills. "I have connections everywhere in the medical community. I've consulted for the FBI on some strange cases involving brain injury. They know me and trust me. I guarantee someone will know something. I would love to get a first-hand look at what is going on in his brain right now. I may even be able to help him reverse the damage; we'll see. Either way, don't worry about it, I'm on it. You just focus on getting to Croatia and figuring out the roadmap to the future!"

CHAPTER NINE

Roger closed the door, looking at the sealed envelope in his hand.

"Who was that, dear?" Carol asked.

"A courier," Roger answered. "Just dropped off this envelope."

"Well, aren't you going to open it?"

Roger carefully tore it open and pulled out the single sheet of paper. Glancing at the message, he suddenly blanched.

"What is it?" Carol's tone showed her concern.

"It's from Dr. Mills. He's asking us to gather Ian's passport, charter a private jet, gather some of Ian's clothes, and head to his house right away," Roger replied. He looked up at his wife.

"Why would Ian need those things? What kind of trouble is he in?" She looked shaken.

"I'm sure it'll be all right, honey," Roger tried comforting her. "Dr. Mills said they would give us more details when we get there. Let's not read too much into this before we hear the whole story, okay?"

"How can I not read more into it?" asked Carol. "Our son is apparently leaving the country, leaving school, and we have no idea why. Aren't you worried?"

Roger reached across the kitchen table and took her hand. "Look, Dr. Mills is a smart and reasonable man. I am glad Ian went to him with whatever problem he had. I trust him. If Ian couldn't tell us about it, there must be a very good reason. Let's just do as he asked as quickly as possible. Time is apparently of the essence."

Carol reluctantly agreed and headed up to Ian's room to gather some clothes and a travel kit. Roger went to his study to get Ian's passport, which was with his and Carol's in the safe. When he had it in his hand, he opened it up. He looked at all the stamps in it and remembered the family vacations they represented. He smiled a little. Some of those vacations hadn't been very relaxing.

When Ian was younger, his neurological issues really were a stress point for the family. They had learned lots of patience and were able to manage his behavior better each time they traveled. The greatest changes took place during and after the time Dr. Mills worked with Ian. They were finally able to truly enjoy him after that.

What a blessing Dr. Mills has been to the family! He hoped his opinion would still be the same after tonight. Despite his bravado with Carol, Roger *was* worried. This was so out of character for Ian, and the idea of him traveling alone to Croatia, of all places, really frightened him.

Carol came back down with a travel bag full of clothes, toiletries, and extra chargers for Ian's cell phone and iPad.

"Roger," she called out to her husband, "I think we need to give him lots of cash. Who knows what the ATMs or credit card systems are like in Croatia. I don't want him running out of money."

Roger opened the safe again, took out five thousand dollars, and put it in his pocket. Before he closed the safe again, his eyes fell on the silver .38 caliber handgun with its black onyx stock. He kept it for protection, but did they really need the Glock right now? He thought about it for a few moments and decided. It was silly to think he'd need a gun just to go to Dr. Mills's house. Everything was going to be fine. He shut the safe and twirled the dial.

They got their coats, hopped in the car, and sped away to their meeting.

As they got to the highway, Carol gasped. "Roger, did you set the alarm for the house?"

"No, honey, I didn't. I forgot. It'll be fine. We will only be gone for a few hours, and nothing ever happens around here, anyway. We have to get to the meeting. Don't worry."

Fifteen minutes later, a black SUV drove slowly by their house. It circled the block and parked down the street. Two men exited the vehicle and made their way to the backyard of the Petrie home. There was the muffled sound of breaking glass. No alarm sounded, so the men entered the property, unseen.

At the New York City FBI offices in Manhattan, Agent Armstrong sat at the desk of the assistant director in charge, waiting for him to return. When he returned, they resumed their interrupted conversation.

"So, what additional information have you got?" the director asked Armstrong as he took his seat.

"We have Ian Petrie's address on Long Island," the agent answered. "It seems that his dad, Roger, is a prominent nuerologist, and his mom, Carol, was a world-class fashion model back in the '80s. Pretty high-profile family."

"Any other background on the kid or the family which would explain his involvement with this case?"

"Nothing jumps out," replied Armstrong. "We already knew the kid was a brainiac. You don't win the Intel award as a seventeen-year-old if you're a dunce. He won the award for his invention of a new application called PhotoEx. Apparently, he figured out how to enlarge pictures and not only keep the quality of the enlargement high, but it even improves the clarity the larger it gets. And get this, the kid sold the app for thirty-three million! Can you believe it? Beyond an ongoing schoolboy interest in Einstein, which many intelligent kids have, I can't figure out what this kid's role is in all of this."

The director frowned. "Send a team out to Long Island. The kid might have gone there after he left campus. Apparently, he's missed a bunch of classes, and no one has seen him or his roommate in the dorm. If he's not there, talk to his parents, and get their help in finding out where he might have gone. Find out if they know anything about his involvement with the professor or the break-in. Anything more on the professor's condition? Has he been able to tell anyone what happened to him?"

Armstrong replied, "He's been taken to Bellevue. They're going to have a team of neurologists examine him tomorrow. Apparently, whatever his condition is, it's strange enough to warrant closer inspection. We're going to have a couple of agents there to get the results and listen in while they examine him, in case he starts remembering anything."

"Okay, and what about Tesla and Einstein? Any idea why all of this revolves around them?" the director asked.

"We have a few ideas, but we'll have to retrace some steps from old case files to be sure," replied Armstrong. "We saw in the file that it was originally thought that Tesla was murdered. When no workable clues were found, and the sweep of his hotel room didn't produce any documents, the investigation died. But the rumor about Nazi involvement did not die. There are still people here that believe they are the ones who cleaned out the safe in the hotel room and made off with some very sensitive and valuable information.

"As you probably know, we've been monitoring Nazi cells all around the world since the end of World War II, and we have never seen chatter like we're seeing now. There is something going on that seems to have been building for a while. We are going to follow that lead and see where it goes."

"Nazis?!" the director exclaimed. "In this day and age? Why are you going to waste time running down that rabbit trail? Focus on the boy."

"Just trust me on this, boss," said Armstrong. "If I don't come up with any Nazi connection in a week, we'll drop it and focus on the others exclusively. And about Einstein, we know that the professor was his friend. That was a unique thing, since Einstein didn't have many friends, and Professor Kearney was one of the few he talked to about his work.

"Given that unique relationship, he probably knew more about what Einstein was working on than anyone else in the world. He's the only one that might be able to tell us how Einstein figures into all of this. We must find someone who can help us get some information out of him. A real brain expert. Any ideas?"

"Yeah," said the director. "My kid had behavioral issues a few years ago, and we took him to Dr. Robert Mills, the best brain doctor we could find. He is a world-renowned functional neurologist and is right here in Manhattan. In fact, we've used him as a consultant before.

I'll text you his contact information as soon as I get it from my wife. Go and visit him tomorrow and see if you can get him to help us with the professor."

"Sounds like a plan, sir," said Armstrong as he rose from his chair. Before he was out the door, the director added, "And get the phone records for the kid. I want to see who he's talked to and where his phone has been."

The Petries arrived at Dr. Mills's home, and after meeting Peter and hugging Ian, they settled themselves in Dr. Mills's living room to hear the explanations.

"Thanks for the coffee, Dr. Mills," said Carol, "but maybe I need something stronger. I'm not sure I'm going to like what you all have to tell us."

"Carol, please, after all these years, call me Rob. How many times have we talked about this? It makes me uncomfortable."

Carol laughed. "I know, it's just so hard. We have so much respect for you. How about a compromise? Will Dr. Rob do?"

"Sure, that's fine, if that's the best you can do. I suppose I can live with that," Dr. Mills said with a grin.

"Ian, what's all this about? Why have you left school?" Roger asked impatiently.

"It is a long story, Dad," replied Ian. "We can circle back and fill in the details later, but the bottom line is that Peter and I are on the run from people who attacked Professor Kearney and know that I am his protégé. Whatever information they want from him, they might think I know about it. We're afraid they are coming after me next. Peter hacked into the FBI computers and downloaded a file that had a picture of me talking with

Professor Kearney, and it had my name on it. So, the FBI knows about me too. I don't know if it was the FBI that attacked the professor or some other people, but either way, we can't let them find me."

"You hacked into the FBI computers? For goodness' sake, why would you do such a thing?" exclaimed his dad.

"Again, Peter did the hacking, not me," replied Ian, "but regardless, we needed to get access to all the information they had on Einstein and Tesla."

"Why on earth would you need that information?" asked his mom. "Don't you already know everything there is to know about Einstein? You have been immersed in him since you were seven years old! And anyway, don't they have libraries at Princeton?"

"Yes, Mom, they have libraries at Princeton," Ian responded, obviously exasperated, "but we needed to know more than is generally available. After Einstein died in 1955, the professor found a letter in Einstein's office that he wrote to him. In it, he said that he had made a major discovery, but the results frightened him so much that he decided that the world was not ready for it. He decided to destroy the originals.

"But before he did, he made a microdot copy and hid it. He said that the professor was the only one he trusted to share what was in it and where it all was hidden. Einstein died before he could reveal it to the professor. It has haunted the professor all these years. He could never find the documents, and he had almost given up. Then he found something that gave him hope!"

"And that was?" asked his father.

Ian replied cheerfully, "He found me!"

"Okay," said his dad, "you are going to have to explain that one to us."

"The first day of class with the professor," Ian began,

"I answered a riddle that no one has ever answered as quickly as Einstein. After class, I went to the professor's office and we talked. He asked me about my app. I told him about my interest in Einstein and the picture of Einstein's desk and how I found a note to someone named Clarence and how I suspected that Einstein had solved the problem of the Unified Field Theory but died before he could reveal it. He got a real faraway look in this eye and then revealed to me that he, the professor, was the Clarence of the letter, and that he had known Einstein back in 1955.

"He also told me that he thought I was the one that Einstein referred to in his letter. Listen to what he said:

'I know that someday a mind greater than mine or yours will surface. When that happens, make sure you train him up and make him understand.'

"He then said that together he and I would try to figure out what Einstein had discovered and where he hid the secret. So, we agreed to meet after class every day, and he would fill me in on all he knew about Einstein."

"Okay, so he thinks you are this greater mind. I get that, and he wants to access your mind to help him figure out what he needs to know, but what does Tesla have to do with this, and why on Earth are you going to Croatia?" asked his mom. "Why not the Catskills or California? Why Croatia? And you still haven't sufficiently answered the question about the FBI file."

Dr. Rob jumped in at this point to give Ian a break from the parental interrogation. "Carol, in the letter Einstein wrote to Clarence, he referred to Tesla. It raised the question as to what kind of communication the two men had and what that communication contained. Over the years, Professor Kearney has surmised that Tesla sent documents with secret information to Einstein. The letter also made reference to a key, which the professor has determined came from Tesla, and Einstein hid it wherever he hid the documents.

"He suspected that Einstein eventually combined his own understanding of physics with Tesla's information and utilized a synthesis of both to complete his Unified Field Theory. This has been partially confirmed by the documents that Ian found when he and Peter broke into the Einstein exhibit on campus."

"Broke into the Einstein exhibit?!" Roger exclaimed. "FBI hacks, nefarious men chasing you, secret documents, break-ins, this is crazy! Dr. Rob, are you involved in all of this? How could you be enabling this type of behavior? We need to go to the police and stop all this right now. They will understand this was all the professor's fault and that he never should have involved a student in such a dangerous situation."

"I understand," said Dr. Rob trying to calm Roger. "Let me continue, and after I am done, we can decide what is best, together. Yes, the boys broke into Einstein's home, but just to see if they could confirm Ian's belief that the secret was hidden in Einstein's desk, which was on display for the first time in decades. While there, Ian realized that the information was actually hidden in the letter to Clarence.

"They left Einstein's house and went back to the professor's home and found him in bad shape, shaking and babbling. He had been attacked by whoever thought he had secret information about Einstein's discovery.

"The boys called the ambulance to get him some help, and then went to his on-campus office to get the letter. After they got it, they decided to come here to hide out and decide what to do next. When they got here, we talked and examined the letter with Ian's PhotoEx app. That revealed a microdot on the paper. Ian examined the microdot, and we discovered that the microdot was what Einstein had used to conceal his secrets.

"We then scanned through the hundreds of pages of documents and what we found was that Tesla had indeed entrusted Einstein with his most precious secrets and a physical metal key. Tesla made reference to having hidden other information 'where it was born'.

"We have since determined that that place is his homeland of Croatia. Since we must keep Ian safe and hidden until he figures this all out, and he needs to get the hidden information that Tesla left to complete the puzzle, he must to go to Croatia. The FBI file that Ian asked Peter to hack has lots of details on Tesla and his life in Croatia. They need that to understand his mind and figure out his part in all of this. It will serve him well while he is there searching for the hidden information.

"So," Dr. Rob continued, "you'll need to reserve a private jet for Ian so he can fly out first thing tomorrow. I've made hotel reservations for him under my name in Zagreb. I hope you can agree with the plan and give it your blessing." Dr. Rob finished.

"Can I get that stronger drink now, Dr. Rob?" said Carol. "I really need it."

"Make that one for me, too," added Roger. "This is all so overwhelming."

Dr. Rob left the room to fill their requests. While he was gone, Roger asked Ian, "Is there any other way? Can't you just hide out at home? Or go somewhere else?"

"No, Dad, I need to go to Croatia. I need to find the Tesla information. If there was any other way, we would do it." said Ian, smiling.

Roger just rolled his eyes and then looked at his wife. "Maybe I should go with him."

Carol looked hopeful. "That would make me feel better."

"No, Dad," Ian objected. "The fewer people involved here, the better. Don't worry, I can handle myself. I have a 'greater mind', remember?"

Roger shook his head, looking back at his wife. "Can we really agree to all this? It sounds so bizarre."

Carol was silent for a moment, staring down at her hands. Finally, she took a deep breath and looked up. Her jaw was set in that all-too-familiar expression of determination.

"Roger," she said, "we trust Ian, and we trust Dr. Rob. If they say it's necessary, I'm willing to let them try this. I'm not happy about it, but we'll stay in touch with Ian and check in on him every day. Then, we can try to sort all this out back here at home and maybe figure out another way. Until then, let's agree and pray that Ian stays safe."

Dr. Rob came back into the room, handed the parents their drinks, and sat down. "Do we have a consensus?" he asked.

"We do," replied Roger. "We are willing to let this crazy plan go forward, if you agree to pull him back from Croatia if we feel he is in danger. Agreed?"

Dr. Rob frowned a little. "At this point, I'm not sure being here in the states will be any safer for him. How about this? If coming back here is safer, we'll bring him home as soon as physically possible. Will that do?"

Roger looked at Carol and she nodded.

The rest of the evening was spent discussing details and time schedules. Dr. Rob suggested that the Petries stay overnight so they could bring Ian to the airport in the morning, while he'd go to his office to find out what he could about the condition of the professor.

When they had finalized all the plans, Dr. Rob showed them all to their rooms and they retired for the evening.

That night, Carol slept restlessly, her mind filled with worry, while in the next room, Ian dreamed of butterflies again. Beautiful, dark-eyed, Croatian, punk rock butterflies.

In the morning, the Petries gathered up Ian's belongings before they all came together to say their farewells.

"Thank you, Peter, for sticking your neck out for me. I really appreciate it. How great is it that I had a world class hacker as a roommate!" said Ian.

"We'll see how great it is after we both get out of this alive," replied Peter. "I'll be fine here, but you are taking a big risk."

"A risk, yes," replied Ian, "but if we can figure this all out, the upside is huge. Just stay alive long enough for me to solve this, and we can all share in the benefits. And don't forget, Princeton is on me!"

"Don't worry, I won't forget. Be safe and come back in one piece," finished Peter as he and Ian shook hands.

"Dr. Mills," said Ian turning to the doctor. "Thank you for your help and insight. You really are a great friend, and I am so lucky to have you to rely on in addition to my parents. Please call me and let me know what you find out about the professor."

"I will," replied Dr. Rob, "and stay in touch, Ian. Let us know if you need any help. After I figure out what the issue is with the professor, maybe I will come over there and try to help you. I'll fill you in when I have a timeframe."

"That would be great!" said Carol. "That would make me feel so much better about this. Thank you for caring so much about our family, Dr. Rob."

They all hugged, and the Petries headed out the door.

Dr. Mills turned to Peter and said, "Looks like it's just you and me, Peter. I am going to head to the office. Keep the blinds closed, don't answer the door or the phone, unless it's me, and limit your cell calls. Until we find out what the FBI knows, we need to keep a low profile. Understood?"

"Got it, Dr. Rob," replied Peter. "What do you have to eat?"

"The refrigerator is stocked, and so is the pantry. Have anything you want, just stay out of the liquor cabinet!" admonished Dr. Mills.

"Will do, doc," said Peter, and he headed off to the kitchen.

On the way to the private airport, the Petries were glad to have some time alone with Ian to talk about all of this. They knew this was something they had to let him do, but they still had a feeling of dread. Ian's dad was the first to break the silence.

"Ian, all joking aside, we know you're a responsible and intelligent kid, but this situation would be challenging for a person twice your age. You not only have to be intelligent, but you also must be smart. You know what I mean?"

"I do, Dad," replied Ian. "I get it, I really do. I'll be careful and cautious. I need to stay alive and free if I am going to solve all of this. I know that. I do my best not to endanger myself or you guys any further."

"Keep a low profile. Don't draw attention to yourself and don't interact with people you don't know are safe," cautioned his mom. "And use the cash; I hear they can track people by their credit card usage."

"Understood, Mom, I've heard that, too," agreed Ian.

When they arrived at the airport, Ian said, "Just drop me off here. We don't have time to park, and the plane is just over there. I'll call you when I arrive. Love you, guys!" He opened the door and took off before they could argue.

Ian jogged until he reached the gate for the tarmac, then he turned around and came back to the car.

"I forgot something," he said opening the back door.

"My kiss?" asked his mom, hopefully.

"No," said Ian, "I forgot Einstein's violin!" He reached into the back seat, grabbed the case, then leaned up and kissed his mom. As he headed into the terminal, he yelled back over his shoulder, "Love you!"

Roger looked at Carol and they both said at the same time, "Einstein's violin?"

Dr. Mills was in his office thinking about how he was going to get the information on the professor when his receptionist entered.

"Excuse me, Dr. Mills, there are two men in the waiting room who would like to speak with you. They don't have an appointment. Should I tell them you're busy?"

"No, Jenny, I've had a few appointments cancel today, so it's fine. Any idea what they want?" asked Dr. Mills.

"No," replied Jenny, "but they are pretty scary-looking. Like military men or something."

"Okay, no worries. Show them in," Dr. Mills instructed her.

The two men filled the doorway as they entered. Both were over six feet tall with cropped hair. One was a little more muscular than the other. They did, indeed, look intimidating.

"Come in, gentlemen, please sit. How may I help you?" Dr. Mills greeted them.

The men took their seats, introduced themselves as Agent Armstrong and Agent Collins, and produced identification which showed that they worked for the FBI.

"Dr. Mills, it is our understanding that you are recognized as one of the world's leading experts on the functioning of the brain, and that you've worked for the FBI before. We need your help with a case we are working on that involves an injury to the brain."

"I see," replied Dr. Mills. "Why would the FBI be involved in a case related to a brain injury?"

"All we can say," said Agent Armstrong, "is that it involves national security, and the patient has information that is critical to the case. We need you to help us figure out how to get the guy's brain working again so he can remember what happened."

"How did his brain stop working? What was the trauma?" asked Dr. Mills. The agents looked at each other and then back at Dr. Mills.

Armstrong said, "From our initial analysis, it appears that a device of some sort was attached to his head. Whatever it was, and whatever it did, it scrambled his brain. The guy does nothing but shake and babble. It looks like he is trying to talk, but nothing intelligible comes out."

"And his eyes have turned from blue to almost white," added the Agent Collins.

Dr. Mills listened to them, very intrigued by their description of the patient, then said, "I think I can help. But first, what is the patient's background? Do we know if he had any previous trauma?"

"All we know," said Armstrong, "is that he was about eighty years old and was a long-time professor at Princeton University. They found him a few nights ago in his home in this condition. Can we count on your help?"

Upon hearing the description of the patient, Dr. Mills went cold. He knew they were talking about Professor Kearney. He couldn't believe that this had just fallen into his lap, but he was also very worried. This was all too coincidental, too close to home. He would need to be very careful not to reveal anything he knew about this, but he also knew that this was his opportunity to help Professor Kearney.

"I see," he said. "It sounds like something we need to address right away. With brain trauma, it is critical to begin treatment immediately, or the damage could become permanent. Where is the patient?"

"He's at Bellevue," offered Agent Armstrong. "In fact, we're going there after we finish here with you. A team of neurologists will be examining him to evaluate the situation. We're going to be there in case they get something out of him. Do you want to come?"

Dr. Mills said yes and picked up his phone so Jenny would know to cancel all his appointments for the next two days. He grabbed his coat and left with the FBI agents.

CHAPTER NINE

The Petries arrived home after dropping off Ian. They entered the house, and Carol immediately knew something was wrong.

"Someone has been in the house," she said to Roger. "Things are moved, and I had just straightened everything up before we got the call from Dr. Mills. Roger, please check the house."

Roger began going from room to room. Downstairs, everything seemed fine, but just a little off. He went upstairs, and when he got to Ian's room, he shouted to Carol, "Carol! Come up here quickly! Ian's room, hurry!"

Carol bolted up the stairs and into Ian's room. The room was turned upside down. Everything was out of the drawers and thrown on the floor. Furniture had been upended and the closet was torn apart. There were even big square holes cut into the walls at various places. She stood there in shock taking it all in.

"Roger, someone was here!" she said, her voice quivering with fear.

"They were obviously looking for something they thought Ian had. This is the only room in the house in disarray. What are we going to do?"

"I know what we are not going to do," Roger said to Carol. "We are not calling the police. With all the stuff going on involving Ian, we need to keep this quiet until he is safe. The police would start digging into things, and then connect him with all the trouble at Princeton."

"Are you suggesting that we stay here and make believe nothing happened? We can't do that. Whoever did this might come back again! We need to go somewhere else. Where can we go?"

Roger pulled out his cell phone and dialed Dr. Mills's number. It went to voicemail and Roger shared the situation and asked if they could stay with him for a few days.

"Carol, pack our bags for a few days. Call the other kids at school and tell them we have to go out of town for a few days on an urgent matter, and that we will tell them more when we can. I am going to get our passports in case we need them."

Carol went to the bedroom and started throwing clothes into their overnight bags, while Roger went to his study and opened the safe. He grabbed their passports and some cash. Again, his eyes fell on his gun. This time, he didn't hesitate. He grabbed the gun and a box of ammo and slammed the door. He was angry. How dare they violate his home? He didn't care who it was, FBI or someone else. He was going to do everything in his power to protect his family.

While on the way to see Clarence in the FBI's Crown Victoria, Dr. Mills felt his phone buzzing in his pocket. He grabbed it and looked at the screen, which showed it was Roger Petrie calling. Quickly, he put it back in his coat pocket, let it go to voicemail, and started a line of conversation.

"So, Agent Armstrong, what else can you tell me about this case? If I am going to be working with you, I need to know what I'm getting involved with. It may help me better understand the circumstances around the injury to the professor and may help me to help him more effectively."

"What kind of stuff do you need to know?" asked Agent Armstrong.

"Well, first, you can start by telling me why the FBI is involved in a campus incident, and how this could possibly rise to the level of a national security threat." Dr. Mills told him.

Agent Armstrong looked thoughtful for a moment, then took a deep breath.

"Look, I don't usually divulge anything to civilians during an investigation, but this time, I need your help and your cooperation. The professor was apparently involved in something secret relating to Einstein and Tesla," Armstrong explained. "We have information in our files connecting all of them. The professor knew Einstein. Whoever did this to him must think he has something important that they need to know.

"Given that Einstein was so heavily involved in government projects, we must assume that there could be a threat to national security if whatever information the professor had falls into the wrong hands. Right now, we're just being cautious. It could very well be nothing, but we can't assume that."

"So, you have no idea who attacked the professor or why?" asked Dr. Mills.

"We have video footage which shows a black SUV and two men going into and out of the professor's house around the time of the incident, but we also saw on the same video two boys entering the home shortly after that. We don't know which of them attacked the professor, so we're working on that."

"Wow!" exclaimed Dr. Mills, "How fortunate that there were videos. That should help. With facial recognition technology, you should be able to identify all of them, right?"

Armstrong replied, "We know who the boys are, but not the two men. We also think that they are all tied in with hacks into our systems that took place a few days before, relating to the files we have on Einstein and Tesla.

It's all coming together. We'll have this figured out soon, then we'll arrest them all and bring them in for questioning. What does this have to do with the brain, doctor?"

"Nothing, really," said Dr. Mills. "I just wanted to get more background. You mentioned Tesla and you mentioned that the professor was attacked with some sort of device. What can you tell me about that?"

"Our forensic scientists examined the professor. They found strange burn marks around his forehead and face. They determined that the tiny burn marks were not made with hot metal, or flames, or anything common. They said that they appeared similar to the type of burn marks you find on a person that has been struck by lightning. The burns were also not just on the surface but went all the way through the skull and into the first layer of the brain. What's that called again, doctor?" asked Armstrong.

"The meninges," replied Dr. Mills. "That's the name for the three layers of tissue between the brain and the skull. It protects the brain from damage. The strong, outermost layer is called the dura mater. Let's hope the burns didn't penetrate the dura mater. If they did, we could have a big problem."

They arrived at Bellevue and entered the building. They took the elevator to the now-secure top floor. The agents flashed their identification to the security guard and led Dr. Mills to an examining room. In the room were four prominent neurologists, whom Dr. Mills recognized.

On the examination table, the professor was strapped down, writhing and babbling incoherently. Agent Armstrong introduced himself and his partner and then Dr. Mills.

"Gentlemen, we have brought another brainiac to join the party. Meet Dr. Robert Mills."

By their expressions, he knew they recognized him immediately. The one closest to him reached out and took his hand, shaking it vigorously.

"Welcome, Dr. Mills. We're thrilled you could join us. We were just about to begin."

"Wonderful," Dr. Mills replied, "but first, if you will excuse me, I need to use the restroom. We had an exciting trip here. I'll be back in a minute." He excused himself and entered the men's room. Taking out his phone, he listened to the message from Roger, then called Peter on his cell.

"Peter, it's Dr. Mills. The Petries are headed back to the house. Look for them. When they get there, tell them I will be there as soon as I can. Don't open the door for anyone but them. Tell them about the safe room and give them the code. Finally, tell them that I am with the FBI right now, examining the professor. I'll fill you all in when I get there. Understood?"

Peter replied around a mouthful of food, "Got it, doc. Will do."

"Good," said the doctor. "And stop eating!"

He hung up and hustled back to the examination room to begin the work on the professor.

CHAPTER TEN

It was Ian's first solo flight, but instead of feeling nervous, he felt so energized he could barely concentrate on his iPad. He'd looked forward to the thirteen-and-a-half-hour trip and planned to use all of it to dig into the files. Let's start with the Tesla documents, he thought. They seem to be what started this whole chain of events.

He opened the first document, a letter from Tesla to Einstein which looked like a cover letter.

Albert,

I know that we have had our differences over the years, but we have always respected each other personally, if not necessarily each other's work. That is a pity. I believe there is so much that we could have accomplished together if we had just put our differences and stubbornness aside. I regret the wasted time. I am now at the end of my life, and I am seeing things in a different light, you might say.

I know that our early collaboration on Project Rainbow was a low point for both of us and may have poisoned the water for future collaborations, but it made me more determined than ever to perfect my understanding of what we were working to accomplish. You moved on to other secret projects with Von Neumann, so I know that you have probably wiped the dust of Project Rainbow from your shoes. But I must tell you now that we were not completely wrong!

I have done the follow-up work, and I have understood where we went wrong. We had everything right except one thing, and unfortunately, it was foundational. We started with a flawed premise. We were working with the foundational formulas you had developed and then built from there. But I have found that the formulas did not apply to what we were trying to accomplish.

We assumed that the forces we were trying to unleash would behave like all other matter, and that seemed to be a reasonable assumption at the time. But we needed to go back further, back to the beginning. We needed a primal, more ancient understanding of matter. I will stop there.

I want you to look at the work I have sent you and draw your own conclusions. Then, when you have finished, we can meet, discuss it, and move forward together. I believe that I don't have much time, so I hope you will give this information priority.

Also, I have not given you all the information. I am being watched by very dangerous men, and I fear that if this information falls into their hands, they will use it to enslave mankind. So, I have divided up the information, and have only sent you a portion.

You have the doorway to tomorrow in your hands, but every door needs a key. The metal key in the package will lead to the rest of the story. After you examine the documents, follow the trail of the key. It will lead to where my ideas were born. If you do not read this and act quickly, all that I have worked on all my life will remain there also, where it was born.

I trust you, Albert. Do not disappoint me. Your light must shine brighter as my light diminishes. Be that light, Albert! Lead the world to a new dawn, a new beginning. A new age of Eden. Without your leadership and integrity as a guiding light, I tell you this, the world is not ready to receive this information. You will understand.

Nikola

Ian was enthralled by what he has just read; an historic, secret communication between two giants of science. Obviously, it took Einstein years to understand what Tesla was trying to tell him, so how could he, Ian Petrie, possibly understand it all with so much less time? He needed a plan. He needed a process. He needed to think outside the box and use what was already in the documents. Since Einstein said that he had found the solution to what he and the professor assumed was the Unified Field Theory, Ian would start there. But Einstein had also said that he could not open the door unless he found the way to close it. Apparently, he had not found that.

Maybe that was the information that the key was to lead to? Maybe that was what Einstein had intended for him and the professor to work on after Clarence returned from vacation? Maybe what the key led to was not a way to open the door, but a way to close it, and lock it against unauthorized entry? That was logical.

Tesla had said that the additional information was sent to where it was born. That was why Dr. Mills had sent him to Croatia. Tesla was born and grew up there. It made sense. So, Ian pulled up the picture of the key Tesla had included in the letter to Einstein.

It was small and made of what looked like brass. It did not have teeth. The shaft of the key was hollow and round. Very odd. It reminded Ian of an old skate key his parents had once shown him. Why would Tesla send Einstein a skate key? He wouldn't. It must be for something else.

Ian examined the bow of the key, the part you hold while inserting it and turning it. On one side, it had the number 369 engraved on it. Ian fired up the PhotoEx app and ran the picture through. When it was done, he examined the file closely. On the other side of the key was a word engraved very faintly. Zooming in, he could barely make out the word *Pošte*.

Ian didn't know what that could mean, so he Googled it, feeling grateful that the private jet had unrestricted internet access. His initial search came up with Spanish and French translations meaning "post". Like a fence post or a teaching post. That doesn't make sense, he thought. So, he started searching other language translations.

Finally, it hit him to try Croatian. The translation read, "*Pošte* = Post Office". This was a post office box key! A Croatian post office box key.

Okay, he knew what the key was for. Progress. Now, he just had to find the post office box. Where could it be, and could he get into it without the actual key in his possession? It would definitely take some thought.

He Googled the postal system in Croatia and found that the original main post office building was still standing in Zagreb. At least someone there might be able to tell him which post office it belonged to. That was a good start. He knew his first objective.

As he was changing screens, the picture of Tesla's great-grandniece, Angelina Novak, flashed across the screen. He stared at it again. Peter wasn't kidding! She was smoking hot! Peter had also said that she was in the running for the Nikola Tesla - Genius of the Future award and that the ceremony was going to be held in a few days. So, he Googled that, too.

TESLA & FRIENDS: Annual NIKOLA TESLA - GENIUS OF THE FUTURE Award, Hotel Esplanade, 10th of October, 2016, Zagreb

Marking of 160th birthday of Nikola Tesla with three days of science, technology, and innovation. The three-day event dedicated to Tesla's birth will begin October 9 with a conference, titled "Tesla in Zagreb", on the theme of "160 years from the birth of Nikola Tesla". It continues October 10 with the traditional laying of the wreath at the monument to Tesla. A special program will be held, followed by a festive celebration and the presenting of the annual Nikola Tesla - Genius of the Future award at the Hotel Esplanade in Zagreb. On the third day of the event, on October 11 at the museum, a talk about Nikola Tesla will be held by the senior museum curator along with demonstrations.

All events, except for the festive celebrations and annual award presentation at the Hotel Esplanade, are open and free to visitors.

Ian realized two things. First, the conference was being held at the same hotel where Dr. Mills had made reservations for his stay in Zagreb. And second, he would miss the first day of the conference, but he would be there for the second and third days. He saved the information regarding the place and time and thought, I definitely have a new first objective!

The black SUV was parked outside a seedy motel on the New Jersey Turnpike. Inside the motel room, Rolf and Axel were examining the information they'd gotten from their raid on the Petrie residence.

"We should've waited for the parents to come home," Rolf complained. "We could have used the thought camera on them and had all the information we needed. Now we're back to square one."

"We couldn't wait there for them," replied Axel. "We had no way of knowing how long they were going to be gone, and we can't let the trail of the kid grow cold. We also don't know if they actually know where the kid is. Let's just dig through the stuff we got from the kid's room. There must be something we can use."

They sifted through the piles of papers and notebooks and Einstein memorabilia.

"This kid was definitely obsessed with Einstein," Rolf remarked, "but there's another name that keeps coming up up over and over again, almost as many times as Einstein. Do you know a Dr. Robert Mills? It seems that Ian has some sort of connection with him."

"Maybe we should pay this guy a visit," Axel suggested. "He's some sort of brain expert and has an office and a home in Manhattan. If the kid has such a connection with this guy, maybe he knows something?"

Rolf furrowed his brow thoughtfully. "I'm not sure it would be a good idea to barge into his office and use the thought camera on him right there. Seems kind of messy to me. Find out where he lives, and we can fry his brain in the privacy of his own home."

The Petries arrived at Dr. Mills's home. They knocked multiple times and rang the doorbell. Finally, Peter answered the door and let them in.

"What took you so long to answer the door, Peter?" asked Roger as he struggled with the bags.

"I'm sorry, Dr. Petrie, but Dr. Mills told me to be careful. He told me to not open the door for anyone except you, so I had to be sure," said Peter.

"Where is Dr. Rob?" asked Carol, looking around.

"He said to tell you that he was at Bellevue with the FBI, examining the professor," said Peter.

"The FBI!" exclaimed Carol. "Why is he with the FBI? And examining the professor? I thought he didn't know where the professor was? This all sounds very dangerous."

"Yes, it does," agreed Roger. "Peter, what else did he say?"

"He said that he would fill us all in when he returned and to tell you guys about the safe room he has in the house. I guess he's pretty worried. Oh, and he also told me to stop eating," finished Peter.

"I can see you have ignored that last instruction," said Roger, eyeing the half-finished peanut butter sandwich in Peter's hand. "Tell us about the safe room."

Peter took them upstairs to Dr. Mills's bedroom closet and showed them the safe room. The exterior door looked like all the other closet doors. When Peter opened it, there was steel door behind it with a keypad in the center. Peter punched the four-digit code into the keypad, and the door slid open quickly, disappearing into the wall on the right.

Inside the safe room, which was about eight feet square, was a cot along one wall, a toilet, and a small sink across from the cot. The remaining space contained a table with an array of electronic communication devices and video screens showing pictures of the various rooms in the house, plus the three entryways into the residence. The electronics had a backup battery system to enable them to work even if the power was cut off.

Peter said, "Dr. Mills said this room was here when he bought the place, and he decided to leave it when he remodeled." He gave the Petries the code, and they headed back downstairs.

"I hope we don't have to use that room," said Carol, "but it's sure good to know it's there if we do. Roger, maybe after all this is done, we should have one built for us in our home?"

"Just what I was thinking," agreed Roger.

After the professor's examination was completed, the FBI agents returned Dr. Mills to his office. They agreed to meet again the next day, after Dr. Mills had a chance to review the test results and come up with a treatment plan.

The doctor waited for them to leave and then headed for home. It was only a three-block walk to his townhome from the office, but today, it felt like thirty. He could not get there fast enough. When he arrived, he found the Petries and Peter safe and sound and in deep conversation.

"Glad you guys arrived safely," he said. "I was so worried about you. Are you all right?"

"Yes," replied Carol, "worried and concerned and a little shaken up, but all right. Thank you for allowing us to impose on you again. We thought this was the safest place for us. This way, we can all work together to support Ian while he's in Croatia. We can coordinate better, with fewer phone calls for people to trace."

"I agree," said Dr. Rob.

"Tell us about the FBI stuff and the examination of the professor," requested Roger. "What is all that about, and why did you contact the FBI? Isn't that a little dangerous, given what they know about Ian?"

"I didn't contact them, they contacted me," Dr. Rob replied. "They came to my office unannounced and asked for my help. They needed a brain expert to help them figure out how to get the professor's brain working again, so he can tell them who attacked him, and what they were after.

"I helped the FBI director's son a few years back and have consulted on a few of their brain cases. He remembered me and gave them my contact info. Then, they told me that the professor was at Bellevue, and that they had assembled a group of neurologists to examine and evaluate the chances of recovery.

"I went with them to Bellevue, and we all examined him together. I was the only one who thought he could be helped. As of now, they have dismissed the other neurologists, and I'm in charge of putting together a treatment plan."

"That's great!" exclaimed Peter. "Now you'll be able to help him and keep anything he says quiet, right?"

"I'm afraid it's not that simple," replied Dr. Mills. "I'll have to report back to them regularly. This is a very high-profile case, so I'm sure I'll be monitored closely. The agents said it has national security implications.

"You know what that means; the spotlight now falls on me. I must be very careful not to reveal my involvement in all of this. One slip, and they'll be all over it. If they find out about my past connection with Ian, they'll ask lots of questions. So, we must work fast and under the radar. Limit your cell phone calls, avoid using credit cards, and be very judicious about your internet use. These guys have eyes everywhere."

"Did they say anything more about the case? Do they have any clues as to who attacked the professor?" asked Roger.

"It seems they have some video of that night from a neighbor's home security camera," Dr. Mills replied. "It shows a black SUV in front of the professor's home before he was attacked, and two men getting out of the vehicle and entering the house. Then, later, the same two men are seen fleeing the scene just before a police cruiser, which had been called to the scene of the Einstein house break-in, passes by. They must have been spooked by the sirens. Then, that same video shows Ian and Peter entering the house and running out ten minutes later."

"They don't think that the boys are responsible for the attack on the professor, do they?" asked Carol, the worry evident in her voice.

"No," said Dr. Mills firmly, "the timing doesn't work. But they also have campus security video showing Ian and Peter entering the building where the professor's office is and then running out of there with Ian holding a violin and a piece of paper, which we know was the letter."

Roger and Carol looked at each other and then Peter.

"Ian had that violin with him when we dropped him off at the airport. He said it was Einstein's violin. What in the world was he doing with Einstein's violin, Peter?" Carol asked.

Peter replied, "When we broke into Einstein's home to examine the desk, Ian was having a hard time visualizing where Einstein might have hidden the documents. He said that if he had his violin, he would be able to visualize better. I found two violins that were part of the exhibit, so I gave him one to use.

"He started playing while sitting at Einstein's desk, and that was when he figured it all out. He shouted to me, and I got startled, fell, and broke the window. The alarms went off, and we ran out of there to go back to the professor's house. Ian never realized he was still holding the violin. We couldn't go back there and return it, so we just kept it. I am sure he plans to return it after this is all over."

"Great, breaking and entering, fleeing the scene, and theft. Not to mention fleeing the country. This just gets worse and worse," said Carol, shaking her head. "Is the FBI looking for Ian?" she asked Dr. Rob.

"They have his picture and the video. I'm sure they'll be watching his cell phone and maybe even run some facial recognition on security cameras from the train stations, bus stations, and airports. But that will take time. They definitely want to find him and Peter, but they're also trying to find the two guys who attacked the professor, so their focus will be divided. I'm sure they perceive the two men who attacked the professor as the greater threat. Who knows what the professor told those two guys before his brain went dark? They could already know more than we do. I hope the FBI finds them before they find Ian."

CHAPTER TEN

Zagreb, Croatia

Ian arrived at a private airport outside Zagreb. He was physically tired but still emotionally energized by the adventure. He'd been able to get through a lot of the information in the documents, and his head was spinning. He was starting to understand the outline and concepts that the two great men had been working on, but he still had a long way to go before he'd have a workable understanding or any actionable protocols.

What surprised him most was that he was actually understanding all of it. Nothing in the documents, formulas, or diagrams was outside of his capabilities. He struggled a little bit with the Tesla stuff, but not the stuff that Einstein had been working on. He had never worked with such challenging problems before, but somehow, he was able to keep up with it.

This encouraged him greatly. It gave him confidence that he could succeed, that he could make it all work. He just had to find that key and then the rest of the information that Tesla had left for them to find in the post office box. Then, he would have everything he needed.

Well, except for the professor. Ian still felt that he needed his mentor's input and perspective as he had actually worked with Einstein on much of it. With his help, maybe they could come up with a solution. He hoped that Dr. Mills was able to find out where the professor was and would be able to help him recover.

Ian gathered his bag and the violin case, then headed to the private car which would take him to his hotel. He arrived at the Hotel Esplanade and tried to move nonchalantly to the check-in desk, his heart pounding all the while. He introduced himself as Dr. Robert Mills, surreptitiously sliding a few bills across the desk toward the clerk. Without looking down, the clerk covered the money with his palm, slid it off the desk and into his vest pocket.

"Welcome, Dr. Mills," the man said politely.

Ian was grateful, he didn't ask for ID. Dr. Mills had said he'd chosen this hotel because he knew that for a few dollars, no questions would be asked. Additionally, they would take American cash as payment.

After he settled in, he took a shower and then checked the television for information about the conference. It said that the laying of the wreath ceremony was starting in a few minutes, and that after that, the celebration would begin in one of the ballrooms.

Ian dressed quickly and headed out to the plaza where the wreath-laying ceremony was taking place. He wanted to see it, but more than that, he hoped to spot Angelina. He believed that she would easily stand out in the crowd.

Ian arrived at the plaza and approached the statue of Tesla. He examined it closely, noticing that it was a pretty good representation of the man, although slightly stylized. It showed him in a sitting position with his legs crossed at the ankles.

A large statue, it gave the impression of a man with a powerful mind deep in thought. A melancholy energy emanated from it, as well as a sense of dreaminess. As if the image of the man had been captured as he sat reflecting on the lost opportunities of his life and thinking about all that might have been.

Tearing himself away from his observations, Ian scanned the crowd for Angelina. He searched all during the wreath-laying but did not spot her. The crowd was now starting to disperse, and many of them were making their way back to the hotel for the festive celebration. Ian decided he would try to encounter her there. Then, as he was walking by the statue, he saw her. She was standing quietly by herself, looking up at the statue.

Wow, Ian thought, she's even more beautiful in person, and I haven't even seen her face yet. He approached her and stood next to her looking at the statue. He gathered up every ounce of courage he had and spoke.

"Great man, Tesla. This is a fitting tribute to him, I think," offered Ian. Angelina said nothing. Ian continued. "I get a sense of melancholy from this statue. It is said that he died a broken man who was disappointed that none of his greatest dreams were realized."

Angelina turned and stared at Ian. She was amazing! His heart began to race, and his mouth went dry.

"Really?" she said sarcastically with a Croatian accent. "What could you possibly know about his dreams? You have no idea what you are talking about. You're just another American frat boy who gets all his information from *People* magazine and the nonsense on the internet. Get a life!"

Then, she turned and headed toward the hotel.

Ian ran after her. "I'm sorry," he said as he caught up with her. "I just meant that he was greater than anyone realized. I'm an admirer. I think he could have changed the world, if people had just listened to him and taken his concepts seriously. I didn't mean any offence. May I walk with you to the hotel?"

Angelina gave him a sideways glance, then looked him up and down, but she continued to walk. "I suppose so, as long as you keep your mouth shut and your hands to yourself."

Ian smiled. "I can do that," he said and thought to himself, so you're saying I might have a chance?

They arrived at the hotel, and as Ian held the door open for Angelina, she stopped walking. "I can do that myself," she said, then waited for Ian to release the door. When he stepped aside, she reopened the door for herself, and Ian followed her in.

"Are you going to the reception?" he asked her.

"I thought we agreed that you weren't going to talk," responded Angelina.

"I'm not talking," he said. "I just communicated with you telepathically, and you heard me. That says that we are on the same wavelength. It's a good sign!"

Angelina stopped walking and looked at Ian again with a quirk of a smile blossoming on her lips. "Okay, Telepathic Boy, can you read my thoughts now?"

Ian scrunched up his face in a display of concentration. "Yes, you are thinking that you want me to join you at the reception, and that you will pay for all my drinks. Am I close?"

"Not even in the vicinity," Angelina replied. "But, hey, I want to find out about all of your other powers, so I guess I could stand to be with you for a while. It might help to alleviate the boredom."

Ian smiled as they walked together into the reception. Before they entered, Ian was asked for his ticket. He said he left it in his hotel room.

Angelina stepped in and said to the ticket taker, "He's with me."

The man bowed his head and said, "Very well, Miss Novak. Welcome!"

"I guess you must be some kind of big deal around here," Ian remarked as they entered, knowing full well who she was, but hoping she wouldn't realize that. "That person knew who you were. Why is that?"

"Read my mind, and you will find out," Angelina

responded.

Ian laughed, "No, seriously, why are you here?"

"I've been nominated for a stupid award, and I have to be here. What's your excuse?" she replied.

"I'm here doing research for one of my professors," Ian replied. "He wants to know more than is generally available about Tesla, and he felt this was a good starting point for that research. Do you know a lot about Tesla?"

"Yes, more than is generally available," she replied in a snarky tone.

"Well," replied Ian, "that is very fortunate for me! I can start my research right now. But first, can I buy you a drink?"

Angelina nodded, and Ian quickly found the bar. He came back with two glasses of red wine, and they found a table.

"So," he started, "how is it that you know more than is generally available about Tesla?"

Angelina took a sip of her wine, then responded, "I am Tesla's great-grandniece. I've grown up hearing about him since I was born. I know all the family stories, history, and all the stuff that never makes it into *People* magazine or the internet."

"Really?" Ian replied, hoping he sounded innocent. "That's wonderful. I'm honored to make your acquaintance and to have the opportunity to have you share those stories with me."

"What makes you think I would share any of that with you?" Angelina shot back. "I don't know you, and I am not even sure I like you. For you to even have a shot at me trusting you, you'll have to prove that you're smarter than I am. I have to tell you first, though, that no other guy has ever passed my test."

"Really? That's interesting," replied Ian. "Maybe we

should test each other? I also have a test, and no one has ever been able to answer it as quickly as I did. So, it is agreed, let the mutual testing begin!"

"No," said Angelina, "I will take your test and prove to you just how lowbrow you really are. I already know that you would not pass mine. Have at it, frat boy."

Ian asked the waiter for a pen. He then grabbed a napkin and drew the same grid of dots that the professor had drawn on the blackboard on his first day of class. He showed it to Angelina.

"You have to figure out how to connect all of the dots with one single straight line. You cannot lift your pen from the paper, you cannot use curved lines, and you cannot phone a friend. You have twenty-four hours. Begin."

From the information in the FBI file, and from his understanding of the brain from his years working with Dr. Mills on his own issues, Ian knew that this girl had a very strong left hemisphere. That meant that she had incredible left-brain skills, like memory, an aptitude for numbers, and a very high IQ, but she did not have the right brain abilities that he knew were related to visual and spatial skills. She would never solve the problem.

She looked at it and said, "Piece of cake. Is this all you got, a polka dot matrix? I have to go get my award, but by the time the ceremony is over I will have solved this problem, and then you can kiss my butt goodbye."

Angelina stood from the table, patted Ian on the head, and left him there as she walked toward the front to the room for the start of the presentation ceremony. Ian smiled. This is going to be fun, he thought. He watched her as she walked away. Again, he thought, she's unbelievable. She was tall and thin, like Tesla. Even at this formal affair, she wore a black leather jacket and an old

Ramones rock T-shirt. She had tight, black jeans with rips on the knees, and short motorcycle boots. She walked like a model on the runway with an attitude to match. This girl was badass for sure!

Then he realized something. Her attitude was more than independent. It was more challenging, or rebellious, maybe even taunting. Whatever it was, however he described it, he wanted more of it. She was like no one he had ever met.

Once she reached the front, he allowed his gaze to wander, scanning the room. Everyone was dressed more or less formally and very conventionally. Everyone except him and Angelina. Ian was wearing a pair of clean blue jeans and a button-up casual shirt his mom had put in his bag.

Her long hair was dark brown and highlighted with streaks of blue and purple. She had multiple piercings around the perimeter of her beautiful ears and another in her nose. It was obvious that she was not into conformity. Either that or she was trying to disguise her intelligence by distracting people with the way she dressed. It seemed to Ian that maybe she liked letting people make foolish assumptions about her and humiliating them when she proved them wrong.

The award ceremony began, and they called the candidates to the stage. The presenter started by telling the audience all about the award.

"First," he began, "we wish to say a big thank you to the genius, Nikola Tesla, whose inventions marked, undoubtedly, the turning point of our civilization. The goal of our project is to strengthen the role of civil society as the catalyst for positive social change. Knowledge and innovation are the best promoter of each country and the foundation of their future.

"This annual award, the 'Nikola Tesla - Genius of the Future Award' is a unique project, which involves science, innovation, creativity, and art through the work of Nikola Tesla, the most famous inventor of all time. The award will be granted to individuals which rate as the best in three categories.

"First, a challenging quiz in physics and general knowledge about Tesla.

"Second, developing a creative and innovative product inspired by Tesla's inventions or a replica of one of Tesla's inventions, which distinguishes itself with unique functionality, quality, and acceptability in the market.

"And finally, a project from the field of Tesla's extended activities focused on a clean planet, protection of the environment, the use of renewable sources of energy, or educative projects regarding how to awaken the innovation and creativity naturally resident in each individual.

"May I have the envelope, please? The winner of this year's Nikola Tesla – Genius of the Future award goes to… Angelina Novak! Angelina achieved a record score on the physics quiz part of this competition, created a working model of one of Tesla's most imaginative theoretical devices, the thought camera, and completed a very well received treatise on the role of renewable energy in promoting peace between nations. I present to you, Angelina Novak!"

Angelina approached the presenter, accepted her award, stepped up to the microphone and said, "I usually hate this kind of attention, and tonight is no exception, so I'll just say thank you."

She then turned and left the stage to a hearty round of applause. She hustled to the table in the back of the room where Ian was, grabbed his hand, and dragged him out of the ballroom.

As Ian was being dragged away by the newly crowned Genius of the Future, he asked, "So where are we going?"

She replied, "I'm not sure; anywhere but here."

They ended up sitting on the edge of a large fountain in the plaza across from the hotel. From their position, they could clearly see the statue of Tesla.

After a few moments of silence, Ian asked, "What was all that about? Why the quick exit? Those people loved you and wanted more time with you. This is a big deal; an amazing accomplishment."

She replied, "I felt like I was drowning, like I couldn't breathe. I can only take so much of being around people. Being around lots of people is torture for me. Add to that the stress of actually trying to act civilized, and I lose it. If you want to go back and enjoy the festivities, go right ahead. I can't go back in there."

Ian realized that she was still holding his hand, and that her hand was shaking in his. "Angelina, I get it. I don't want to back in there, either. Truthfully, I only came here tonight so I could meet you. Let's just sit here for a while and decompress, then we can go somewhere and talk, if you are up for it."

Angelina agreed and then said, "Wait, what do you mean you only came here tonight to meet me? I thought you were here on a research assignment?"

Ian smiled. "I have a confession to make. Back in the U.S., I read about you. A friend showed me your picture, and knowing that I was coming here this week, he told me about the award ceremony. I realized it was taking place on my first night here, so I made meeting you my first objective."

"Really? So that is what I am, an objective? Well,

mission accomplished, frat boy. Now you can check that one off your list." She stood to leave.

"You can't leave yet," Ian said, "you owe me an answer."

Angelina looked at him and asked, "What answer? Oh, you mean the polka dots?"

She took the napkin out of the back pocket of her skin-tight black jeans, crumpled it up, and tossed it into the fountain. "That is your answer." Then, she turned and walked away.

Ian felt devastated. How could he have been so stupid?

CHAPTER ELEVEN

Manhattan

After more discussion about their situation, and the implications of Dr. Mills's work with the FBI, Roger, Carol, Peter, and Dr. Mills had a simple, quiet dinner and retired for the evening. The doctor showed them to their rooms, made sure everyone had what they needed, said goodnight, then headed back down to his study to work on the treatment plan for the professor.

Just as he sat down at his desk and fired up the computer, he heard a loud crash upstairs and a thump. He called out, "Roger? Carol? Everything all right up there?"

Peter appeared at the top of the stairs and said, "It wasn't me, doc."

Dr. Mills replied, "Okay, Peter, do me a favor and check on the Petries? See if everything is okay and if they need help with anything."

Peter responded, "Will do, doc!"

Just as Peter was about to knock on the door, a shot rang out. It was quickly followed by another, and the door to the bedroom where the Petries were staying burst open. Peter heard Carol screaming and Roger moaning in pain. Carol knocked Peter down as she bolted from the room, holding a gun.

By this time, Dr. Mills was at the top of the stairs and made a quick decision. He grabbed Carol as she ran by him and called out to Peter.

"Peter, the safe room, quickly!"

Dr. Mills and Carol disappeared into his bedroom, then ducked into the safe room. They heard Peter in the other room scrambling to his feet, then a loud thump.

"Doc!" Peter yelled. "Close the door!"

Dr. Mills, recognizing that they didn't have time to delay, closed the door to the safe room. As it was closing, he saw a huge man enter the bedroom, dragging an unconscious Peter behind him by the collar. As the door slammed shut, it was peppered by bullets.

"Carol, what happened in there?" Dr. Mills gasped as he grabbed the still-smoking gun from her hand. Carol, distraught and crying, took a moment to gather herself, then replied. "Two men broke in through the doors on the balcony. They burst into the room and grabbed Roger. I took Roger's gun from his bag and shot the one coming at me. That startled the man holding Roger, and as Roger struggled to break free, the man shot him! He shot Roger!" She shuddered, then continued. "I ran from the room, and he followed me. We must get back out there to help Roger! Please, Dr. Mills, let's go help him!"

Dr. Mills held Carol tightly, trying to calm her, but she would not be calmed. He knew they were safe in the room, so he said, "Carol, let me call the ambulance, and we can get out of here as soon as they come." He helped her lay down on the cot, then picked up the phone and dialed 911.

"Please send the police and an ambulance to 7733 Madison Avenue, a man has been shot. Quickly! This is

Dr. Robert Mills." He waited for confirmation and hung up.

"Carol, they'll be here in ten minutes. Stay calm," he said.

Then, looking at the security video monitors, he saw the huge man drag Peter to the garage, open the garage door from the inside and leave.

After a while, he returned and headed back upstairs. Just then, they heard sirens and urgent pounding on the front door. The man bolted back down to the garage and slipped away in the darkness.

Dr. Mills activated the code, and the safe room door slid open. He ran downstairs and let the emergency medical people in. He led them up to the bedroom where Roger was. What he saw horrified him.

Roger had been shot in the lower abdomen and was bleeding profusely. Face down on the bed was another man, apparently dead from a gunshot to the chest. The emergency medical team began to assess the scene, pronounced the man on the bed dead, and started emergency care on Roger.

Dr. Mills ran back to the safe room and got Carol. He told her that Roger would be okay and that the paramedics were working on him. He shepherded her downstairs to the living room and made her sit. She was in shock. He covered her shoulders with a blanket and sat next to her with his arm around her, trying to comfort her.

The police soon arrived and began asking questions. Dr. Mills told them that it was apparently a break-in, and that they were the victims of a seemingly random attack. He shared that Carol had shot one attacker with Roger's gun. He didn't tell them about Peter, the safe room, or the fact that he had video of the incident. By then, the paramedics were bringing Roger down from upstairs. Before leaving the house, Dr. Mills told them to bring Roger to Bellevue, and that he and Carol would be there after they dressed.

When the house was finally empty and things had calmed down, Dr. Rob spoke to Carol.

"Carol, we have to get to Bellevue. Everything will be okay. Do you understand?"

She looked at him with a faraway expression and nodded her head. He helped her to his bedroom, then went to the other bedroom and got her bag. He helped her pick out her clothes and laid them on the bed. Before leaving the room, he grabbed some clothes for himself, Roger's gun, some cash, and his passport. He went back to the other bedroom and found the box of ammunition. After reloading the gun, he put it in his overnight bag.

They would not be coming back here tonight. Maybe not for a while. Whoever those two guys were and whomever they worked for, they knew where he lived and may very well know about Ian. Things were going to get a lot more complicated from this point on.

He gathered up Roger's things and headed back to his bedroom. Carol was dressed and waiting.

"Carol, do you have everything you need? Make sure, because we won't be coming back here for a while."

She nodded, and he grabbed all the bags and Carol's hand, then headed to the garage. Jumping in the car, he pulled out, looking for the black SUV. Thankfully, he didn't see it, so he drove straight to Bellevue.

The black SUV was speeding over the George Washington Bridge, driven by a very angry man. He had just lost one of his best friends in the world. He and Rolf had worked as a team for the past twenty years, and he'd been like a brother to Axel. In fact, his father and Rolf's father had worked for Hitler back in the old days. He looked into the back seat where the college punk was bound and gagged. As soon as I get to the motel, this kid will pay, he thought.

He imagined all the fun he was going to have using the thought camera on him. It would not be quick. He was going to take his time and find out everything he knew, even if it took days. Maybe I need to buy some popcorn, he thought. This could be a fun show. Then, he picked up his cell phone and dialed the number for headquarters to report in and ask for another agent or two to replace Rolf.

Dr. Mills and Carol arrived at Bellevue and headed for the admissions area. They found out where Roger was and went directly there. Dr. Mills talked with the attending doctor, while Carol went to Roger and held his hand. When Dr. Mills finished talking with the doctor, he joined Carol at Roger's bedside.

"Carol," he said softly, "they've stabilized him, but he's still in critical condition. They're going to take him to surgery right away. They're not yet sure of the extent of the damage, but they feel they can help him. He's strong and in great shape, so I am very optimistic."

Carol's eyes never left Roger's face. "Dr. Rob, I can't lose him. We've been together so long, and he is my life. All my dreams are wrapped up in him, in us. Please, make sure they do everything they can for him."

"I will, Carol," Dr. Mills replied. "I know all the

doctors here, and they're great. I'll be here every day to make sure he's getting everything he needs."

The surgical team arrived just then and took Roger to surgery. Carol and Dr. Mills headed to the surgical waiting room. She settled into a chair as Dr. Mills took out his cell phone.

"Carol, I have to make a call, and then I'll be back."

She nodded her understanding and he moved out into the hallway. He took a business card from his coat and called the number.

"Agent Armstrong, this is Dr. Mills. We need to talk. Meet me at Bellevue hospital as quickly as you can."

Armstrong agreed and replied that he would be there in thirty minutes. Dr. Mills hung up. He wasn't sure he had done the right thing, but he also felt that he had no choice. They needed help, and he was going to have to trust the FBI, as frightening as that was. Peter and Ian's lives were on the line, and he was not going to take any more chances. He pocketed the phone, took a deep breath, and headed into the waiting room to fill Carol in on the plan.

Hotel Esplanade, Zagreb, Croatia

Ian was sitting in his hotel room thinking about Angelina. *How could I have been so stupid?* he wondered. *I just needed to go slow, and everything would have been fine. Instead, I go and tell her that I was trying to meet her. She must think I am a stalker or something. I may be intelligent, but I sure am stupid.*

Just then the phone rang, and Ian answered.

"Hello, who is this?" he asked.

"Dr. Mills, this is the front desk. There's a young lady here asking for you. She described you exactly but keeps using a different name. She insisted we call you. We told her that she was describing Dr. Mills, but she still insisted. Would you come down and help us sort this out. So sorry for the trouble."

"I'll be right down," replied Ian, hanging up and heading out the door.

As he exited the elevator, he saw three security people surrounding Angelina. She was standing there with her arms crossed and an irritated expression on her face. Ian hustled over and spoke to the security staff.

"I know this lady. Please let me speak with her in private. There's nothing to worry about. She's a friend." With curt nods, they left, and he and Angelina found a quiet part of the lobby to talk.

"What's going on, Angelina?" Ian asked.

"Why are you registered under a different name?" she asked without preamble.

"Excuse me, Angelina," he replied, "but I don't recall telling you my name. You never asked, and I was following your lead."

"How stupid to do you think I am?" she asked rhetorically. "I know who you are. I knew it from the moment you spoke to me in the plaza. You are Ian Petrie. You won the Intel award and sold your PhotoEx application to Google. I saw it in a magazine once, and I remember everything I read. I never forget a name or a face."

"So," said Ian, "I guess I'm not the only one that reads *People* magazine!" That made Angelina crack a whisper of a smile.

"You still haven't answered my question," she shot back.

"And you have still not answered mine!" replied Ian. "Why don't we go up to my room so we can answer each other's questions? We have a lot to talk about."

Angelina looked at him with a bit of surprise and said, "I don't like you yet, you know."

"I know," replied Ian, "but you will. Remember, I can read your mind." Angelina actually laughed, and they headed to the elevators.

When they got to his room, Ian called room service and ordered a bottle of Croatian red wine and two glasses. When he hung up, he turned to Angelina, who was sitting in the armchair with one leg slung over its arm.

"Have you solved the problem I gave you yet?"

She replied, "I am not going to answer your stupid question. You saw me throw it into the fountain. That was my answer."

"So, you can't solve it, can you?" said Ian. "You said that you have a great memory and never forget anything. You don't need to have the napkin; you have it memorized. The truth is, you can't figure it out." He knew he was taking a chance talking to her like this. She could very easily bolt out of the room, and he would never see her again, but he also knew that she was tough. He knew she was extremely intelligent, and he hoped she would respond to someone as smart and tough as her.

"It does not have a reasonable answer," Angelina replied. "There is no formula that fits. There's no physical way to connect all the dots that fits the parameters of the challenge. It was a red herring. Just a way for you to try and embarrass me."

Ian replied, "I would never do that, Angelina, let me explain."

He then went on to tell her all about the problem, about Einstein's response, and his own response on his first day of class.

Angelina nodded her understanding. "So, this problem needs 'outside the box' thinking. I could never have solved it without discarding the self-imposed limitations of traditional thought processes. I have to admit that this is the first time I've ever lost a brain challenge. I find it most disorienting."

"Don't take it too hard," Ian tried to comfort her. "If I'd tried to answer your challenge, I probably would have lost, too. Our brains work differently, that's all."

"I can live with that," Angelina replied. "When you were talking about right- and left-brain skills, you mentioned Dr. Mills. That's the name you're using here. Why? Is that who you're doing the research for?"

There was a knock on the door. Ian was glad for the interruption, so he had time to think of a way to answer Angelina's question. He opened the door and let the room service waiter in. He paid cash for the wine and escorted the waiter to the door. Opening the wine, he poured two glasses and handed one to Angelina. He sat down across from her on the chair he had pulled over from the desk and raised his glass.

"To answers and friendships, may they always be true." They clinked glasses and drank.

Ian took a deep breath and began. "Dr. Mills is not who I am doing research for. Well, not the primary person, anyway. He was the functional neurologist that helped me unlock my potential. As a kid, I was diagnosed with a pervasive developmental disorder not otherwise specified, generally known as PDD/NOS. It's a mild form of autism. Dr. Mills was the only doctor who understood enough about the brain to help me. He has become a real friend and mentor over the years. He's the one who made the reservation for the hotel. That's why it's under his name."

Angelina, looking more at ease, told him that she, too, did not speak for a long time when she was young, and that she had been labeled with Asperger's syndrome. She admitted that she had difficulty reading people and their emotions. She had seen some therapists as a kid, but no one was able to help her like Dr. Mills had helped Ian.

"So that answers one part of the question, but not the other. You didn't change the reservation when you got here, and you still have not said who you are doing research for, or what it has to do with Tesla," Angelina said.

"Well, that's where things get a little complicated," replied Ian. "Before I answer, I need to know if you like me yet."

"Can't you read my mind, Telepathic Boy?" Angelina laughed.

Ian scrunched up his face in concentration and said, "The answer is not clear, ask again later."

They both laughed, then Ian sobered. "Seriously, what I am doing is very sensitive and dangerous. I can tell you some of it, but I want to be careful. The more I tell you, the more danger you're in. Are you okay with me holding a little back from you for a while?"

"Not really," replied Angelina, "but tell me what you can, and after that, I will let you read my mind again and you can decide. Deal?"

Ian stuck out his hand and said, "Deal! I'm here to locate some information that Tesla left for Albert Einstein to find. Tesla had sent a letter and documents to Einstein before he died in 1943. Tesla felt that he was being watched and needed to send his discovery to someone he could trust.

"Einstein got the information only a day or so before

Tesla died, so he could never follow up with him for clarification. He spent over a decade trying to understand the information Tesla sent and eventually was able to combine Tesla's discoveries with his own work and solve the Unified Field Theory question.

"In the documents Tesla sent to Einstein, he included a strange metal key. He said the key would lead to more information and answer the question about 'how to close the door'. We don't know what that means.

"Apparently, the discovery that Einstein made was so astounding that it scared him. In a letter Einstein wrote to his friend, Clarence, he said that 'Nikola was right' and that the world was not ready for the revelation, whatever it was.

"He said that he had to find a way to close the door that his discovery had opened before he could reveal it to the world. Einstein died before he could finish the work. I've been sent here to find the key and the rest of the information, and then solve the whole problem."

Angelina was silent.

Ian looked over to find her staring at him with her mouth open. "Angelina, are you still with me?"

She closed her mouth, swallowed hard, and said, "I have a few questions. How do you know Einstein solved the Unified Field Theory question? Did he tell anyone that?"

"No," replied Ian, "but he alluded to it in the letter he wrote. While Clarence was on vacation, Einstein apparently finished the work. He as much as said so in the letter. He also said that he was going to make a copy of his work, then conceal it 'where it was born' and destroy all his original work. He planned to show him where it was when he returned from vacation, but Einstein died before he returned. So, the information has been lost all these years. Clarence has quietly tried to piece it together for the past sixty years but has not been successful. That's where I came in."

"How did you get involved in this, and how can you possibly figure out what no one else has in sixty years?" asked Angelina.

"Because," responded Ian, "I have a 'greater mind'!"

He laughed and then went on to tell Angelina about being obsessed with Einstein as a kid, going to Princeton, Professor Kearney, the nine-dot problem, and the reference to him in Einstein's letter. He did not tell her about the break-in, the hacking, the attack on the professor, or the fact that he was on the run from the FBI and some other unnamed group.

When he finished, he asked Angelina, "Are we good? Do you have a clear picture of what I am up to, and why I am here?"

Angelina finished her glass of wine, stood up, retrieved the bottle from the table, and refilled both their glasses.

She sat back down and put her face close to Ian's and said, "You tell me, Telepathic Boy."

Ian's face flushed, being so close to her. Tasting her breath on his lips. Feeling his heart pounding in his chest. He just wanted to grab her and kiss her. Hard.

Instead, he scrunched up his face in fake concentration and said, "My sources say no."

"Sounds like your sources are correct," replied Angelina as she sat back in her chair and sipped her wine. "But, I definitely have enough for tonight. This is a lot to absorb, even for a left-brained person. We can talk about it more tomorrow. For now, how about a little music? I see you have a violin. Can you play it?"

"Definitely," replied Ian. He stood up and got the

violin and bow, which were lying on his bed. "I usually play when I am trying to solve a problem. It helps me visualize the problem and the answers just come."

"May I hold it?" she asked.

"Sure," said Ian and handed her the violin.

She looked it over and asked, "Why is one of the pegs different from the others?"

"What do you mean?" Ian asked.

She showed him the tuning pegs, pointing to one near the top, "Here, this one is made of brass and is a little bigger, and the others are made of laminated wood."

Puzzled, Ian looked at it. He'd never really examined the violin. When they'd taken it, it had been dark, and they'd been on the run since then. He hadn't really had a chance to play it since he'd arrived at Dr. Mills's house and had been so focused on everything else that it he never picked up on it.

Of course, it would take a left-brained, "detail-oriented" person to notice a small difference in this violin, he thought to himself. He examined it closely and saw that the peg had the number three-six-nine engraved on it! He looked at Angelina and grinned.

"Angelina, you have just completed my second objective. Thank you."

"What do you mean?" she asked.

"As I told you earlier tonight, meeting you was my first objective. Finding the key that Tesla sent to Einstein was the second objective. You have just found the key! This is not a peg; it's the key to closing the door that Einstein was afraid to open. Angelina, if you are in, I think we're going to make an amazing team. Will you help me?"

She just smiled and said, "Read my mind."

He scrunched up his face one more time and said, "It is decidedly so."

His cell phone rang. He grabbed it and looked. He didn't recognize the number, but on a hunch, he answered it.

"Hello?"

"Ian, it's Dr. Mills, we have to talk."

New York City

Axel had finished using the thought camera on the kid, and now had everything he needed to complete the mission. Well, almost everything.

He knew where Ian Petrie had gone, and that he had all the concealed documents. He knew that the professor was at Bellevue, and he knew that Dr. Mills was working with the FBI.

What he did not know was what was in the concealed documents, or if the information he had been sent to obtain was really in them. He would have to find Ian Petrie and get the information out of him. Ian's brain was really going to be fun to watch on the television screen.

Then he remembered something else that he had seen in the kid's brain; Angelina Novak. How could he forget that one? Her picture had been in the FBI file. Even if she wasn't involved in all this, he was going to make a special effort to visit with her.

He picked up his phone and called headquarters. "This is Axel. I know the location of Ian Petrie. Send a team to Hotel Esplanade in Zagreb, Croatia. He's staying there under the name of Dr. Robert Mills. I will catch the first plane and meet you there. Don't kill him before I get there. I need to use the thought camera on him first."

He hung up, grabbed his gear, and left for Newark

airport, leaving Peter handcuffed to a chair, shaking, babbling, and drooling.

Zagreb, Croatia

Ian listened carefully to all Dr. Mills had to say, and it was not good. Dr. Mills was using a disposable cell phone, so his call could not be traced. His dad had been critically injured, his mom was a wreck, Peter had been kidnapped, and Dr. Mills was now working with the FBI. *How could all of this have happened in the short time I've been gone?* he wondered.

Dr. Mills finished the conversation by telling Ian to leave the hotel without checking out. "Just leave money on the dresser to pay for the stay and leave. Don't tell anyone where you're going."

He was worried that Peter might reveal information if they tortured him like they did the professor. Ian told Dr. Mills that he'd found the key and would start working on it tomorrow. He asked him to give his mom a kiss, tell her that he loved her, and that he would be home as soon as possible. Then he hung up and sat silently looking at the floor.

After a few moments, Angelina broke the silence. "Well, that didn't sound good."

"It wasn't," replied Ian. "We have to get out of here. Do you know anywhere we can go where no one can find me?"

"Sure," she said, "we can go to my apartment. No one will look for you there. You're not my type."

"Great," said Ian, "I'll fill you in on the way. Looks like the time for holding back information has passed.

There are things you need to know. It may change your decision to help me."

"I doubt it," said Angelina, "but I'll let you read my mind after you tell me."

They packed up Ian's stuff and the violin, placed a few hundred dollars on the dresser, put the DO NOT DISTURB sign on the door, and left the hotel.

Dr. Mills's office

Dr. Mills received a text on his phone informing him that the FBI agents had arrived to speak with him. He excused himself and told Carol that he had to go speak with someone about the professor. He got her another cup of coffee before leaving the waiting room. As he exited, he saw the agents waiting for him near the elevators.

They greeted each other, and Agent Armstrong asked, "So, what is so urgent that it couldn't wait until tomorrow? We were going to meet at ten o'clock in your office, remember? Why here, and why now? Has something happened to the professor?"

Dr. Mills replied, "No, nothing to do with the professor, but it does have to do with the case you're working on."

As he was saying the words, he realized that he was about to make an irreversible decision, and he needed assurances before he went any further. And they needed privacy for this conversation.

He led them down the hall to a small conference room. As they entered, he sat facing the door so he could keep an eye on the window. He looked at the agents, took a deep breath, and began.

"Before I get into the details, I need your assurances that you will listen to all I say before reacting, and that you will let me take the lead on the personal part of it. Secrecy and patience are critical. There is a lot going on, and the lives of people I care about are at risk. Do I have your word?"

"Doctor, I cannot give you my word based on that, I need more. But I can tell you that giving us as much information as you have will be nothing but helpful to all of us. I can't imagine what you could tell us that would be more dangerous than what we already know. Tell us what you know, and you will be treated fairly and with consideration. Unless you implicate yourself in some way, we have flexibility," said Armstrong.

Dr. Mills sighed. "That depends on your definition of implicate. I have involvements with this case which you are unaware of. I intend to lay it all out for you, but how much I tell you will depend on how much I can trust you. I expect no charges to be filed against me or anyone I name for anything I tell you. Without that assurance, I will keep it to myself and will excuse myself from working on the professor for you. Can I get those assurances?"

"You understand that I could just leave here, pull all your cell phone, credit card, and even tollbooth records, and arrest you if I see anything suspicious related to this case, without your cooperation? Based on what you just told me, I can bring you in as a material witness right now, for your own protection, of course. Why should I agree?" asked Armstrong.

"Because I know more than you think I do, and I won't reveal what I know if you do what you're planning. Time is critical right now. Every second we spend talking about this, the greater the possibility is that we will all fail.

And failure in this instance, gentlemen, could very well mean a worldwide disaster. Time is ticking, agent. Decide."

Agent Armstrong did not look happy. "I have to tell you, doctor, I do not like negotiations, especially when I feel you are backing me into a corner. I need more information, and I need it quick." He stopped and looked thoughtful.

Dr. Mills was silent.

Finally, Armstrong spoke. "The professor won't be able to give us anything for a while. We haven't had any hits on the facial recognition of the two men on the video yet, and the FBI director is breathing down my neck. All right, tell me what you know, and we'll work this out together. But if I feel that you are being anything but fully forthcoming, I will arrest you in a heartbeat and personally escort you to Guantanamo."

He stuck his hand out, and Dr. Mills shook it. "First of all, the same men who attacked the professor broke into my home tonight and shot Ian Petrie's father. Ian's mom shot and killed one of them. The other one kidnapped Ian's roommate Peter Wu, who was the one that hacked your file on Einstein and Tesla. Roger Petrie is in surgery right now, and we don't know if he's going to make it. The police have the body of the attacker that Carol killed. I am sure that if you go to the morgue, you'll be able to start the identification process and figure out who he is and who he works for. How's that for starters?"

"It's a decent start. Why were Ian Petrie's parents and the roommate at your home? What's the connection, and where is Ian?" asked Armstrong.

"I am a longtime family friend of the Petries," said Dr. Mills. "I've worked with Ian since he was seven years old, helping him develop his brain. When Ian and Peter had their trouble at Princeton, they came to me. With the professor out of action, and knowing they were being hunted by the FBI and whoever attacked the professor, they felt it was too dangerous to go to Ian's house or involve his parents."

He then went on to fill them in on the break-ins at the Einstein's home and at the Petrie's house, the hidden documents, and the need for Ian to flee the country.

When he was finished, Armstrong nodded. "I think I understand. So, where is the kid?"

"I can say with all honesty that as of this moment, I don't have any idea where he is," replied Dr. Mills. "I may know more tomorrow. If he contacts me, I will fill you in. Right now, our priorities are finding Peter Wu and the attacker that kidnapped him. We must stop them. We also have to get the professor's brain working again. I'll begin the treatment plan on him tomorrow.

"I suggest you guys pull the tollbooth records or whatever other magic tricks you have at your disposal and find out where he took Peter. Whatever they did to the professor, they will most certainly do to him. You're looking for a black SUV headed out of Manhattan tonight. How hard can that be for the FBI?"

Armstrong just shook his head. "Just stick to your voodoo brain work, doctor, and let us handle the investigative stuff, okay?"

Just then, Dr. Mills saw the lead surgeon heading into the waiting room. "I have to go," he said. "I'll see you here tomorrow in the professor's room." Then he headed into the waiting room to join Carol and to hear what he hoped was good news.

When he entered the waiting room and saw Carol standing next to her chair with her hand over her mouth, his heart sank.

Then, he heard the doctor say, "It was a very close call, and it was touch and go for a while, but we have stabilized him, and he is now resting in the intensive care unit. The gunshot he suffered severed a small artery near the stomach. We repaired that, and don't see any permanent damage. I suggest that you go home and come back tomorrow. We'll call you if there are any changes."

Dr. Mills crossed to Carol and put his arm around her, holding her up. He said, "Thank you, doctor, we'll be here in the morning."

He then turned and spoke to Carol, "I've made reservations for both of us at the Carlyle Hotel. It's not too far, and we can walk or take a cab in the morning. They have great security, and our rooms will be adjoining, so I can keep watch. I'll go with you to visit Roger in the morning, and then I will make a visit to the professor to check on his progress."

He still did not want to worry her with the revelation that he was going to be cooperating with the FBI, or that Ian was on the run. That would all come in time. Right now, he had to make sure she was taken care of and safe.

He was so focused on Carol that he didn't notice the FBI agents approaching the elevators and did not hear Armstrong's cell phone ring.

Armstrong listened to the message and then pounded on the elevator button.

"What's up?" his partner asked.

"They found the roommate in a motel on the Jersey Turnpike. He's in the same condition as the professor, shaking and babbling. Let's go!"

CHAPTER TWELVE

Zagreb, Croatia

When Ian woke up, he saw Angelina in the kitchen making coffee. As he looked around the living room, where he had slept on a couch with his feet hanging off the end, he saw that she'd decorated it like a 1980s dance club, with posters on the walls of the Ramones, Joan Jett, the Sex Pistols, and Dead Kennedys. The walls held pictures of Tesla, Einstein, and the other greats of physics. Ian could see that she also had bookshelves filled with books by Kafka, Nietzsche, and Tolstoy, as well as books on neuroscience, physics, art history, and ancient aliens.

Man, this girl is serious and intense, he thought. He smiled as he realized that he really liked her. She was sexy, cool, mysterious, and smart. Crazy smart, and she had tattoos! She wasn't like any girl he'd ever met.

"Everything happens for a reason, isn't that right, Professor Einstein?" he said aloud to the framed photograph of the scientist as he rolled off the couch onto the floor.

"Good morning, sunshine, what's cooking?" he

greeted Angelina, playfully.

"Just coffee," Angelina replied, a bit testily. "I don't do cooking."

"I see we are in a special mood this morning," said Ian.

"No," said Angelina. "This is my everyday mood, get used to it."

"Thanks for letting me crash here last night," said Ian. "I honestly don't know where I would have gone if you hadn't offered. We really have to keep a low profile from this point on; we need to stay off the grid."

"No worries, I can go underground as fast as anyone. I don't have any credit cards, and I don't have to go back to my job since I won the prize money. I can live off that for a long time. I pay cash for my apartment, and it's a month-to-month lease. So you see, I am practically invisible already," Angelina explained.

"Except for the fact that you just won that amazing award, and it will be in all the scientific journals, and maybe even *People* magazine," Ian replied with a wry smile as he poured two cups of coffee.

"Well, there is that. But I am still *practically* invisible," she replied.

"What about the address the FBI had for you in the file?" asked Ian.

"That was two apartments ago, and I never leave a forwarding address. I don't get any mail worth forwarding," she answered.

"Good," said Ian. "Then we can start right away. Let's be careful, though. They know what we look like, and facial recognition technology is everywhere these days. If they're going to find us, let's make them work for it. Can you figure out how to 'punk me up' a little?"

"Not sure I can hide the preppy frat boy look enough,

but it'll be fun trying!" said Angelina with a grin.

She got out her makeup kit, jewelry, and colored hair spray. When she was done with Ian, he didn't even recognize himself. His hair was highlighted with purple and blue streaks. He had a clip-on nose ring and earrings, and black velvet eyeliner.

She gave him a new shirt that fit the look, and a funky hat. Angelina stepped back and gave a rare smile as she surveyed her work.

"Now you finally look acceptable; more my type. All you need is a few tattoos."

Ian replied, "This will work for now. If we survive this, I'll get a tattoo of your name. You are a genius!"

She agreed with his assessment, and they prepared to leave the apartment. As they were heading out the door, Angelina turned to him.

"I want you to get three tattoos of my name when this is over."

Ian looked at her, puzzled. "That's cool, but why three?"

"That's my favorite number," she said with a shrug, "and that's the deal for me helping you."

Ian couldn't argue with that, so he didn't even try.

"So," said Ian, "do we agree on the plan?"

"Yes," said Angelina, "we're going to the General Post Office on Jurišićeva Street. We'll show them the key and ask if they know the location of the box that the key fits, or if it even still exists."

They had examined the key last night after arriving at Angelina's apartment. With some searching on the internet, they verified that it was a mailbox key for one of the post offices in Zagreb. They couldn't tell which post office, so they decided to start with the biggest and oldest one in the country. The main post office had been there for over one hundred years and hadn't undergone any renovations since it was designated as a historical landmark. They were hoping that the boxes that were there in 1943, when Tesla may have mailed or hidden whatever it was he referred to in the letter to Einstein, were still there. It was a long shot, but they had to start somewhere.

They headed out on foot and began the ten-block walk to the main post office.

"This is really nice," said Ian. "I haven't been this relaxed in a week. Right now, I feel like I'm on vacation or something, and finally excited that I might be able to solve everything. Knowing I have your help is a huge positive. Thanks, Angelina, I really appreciate it."

Angelina turned to Ian and punched him in the shoulder. "Don't go soft on me now, Ian, and don't go letting your guard down. Stay alert and always watch your back."

"Got it," he replied, "we'll watch each other's backs."

They arrived at the General Post Office and carefully searched to see if there were security cameras. There were, so they evaluated which line would make them the least visible. They stepped into that line and kept their backs to the nearest cameras. When they were called, they approached the worker at the counter. Angelina spoke in Croatian.

The worker looked at the key, then looked up, amused, replying quickly in Croatian.

"I told him that I have a key that belonged to my grandmother, and I would like to look in this box if it's still here. I said it was stated in her will that there is something in it for me. He said this is a very old key," Angelina translated. "The ones they have today look different, but they work the same way. He's going to look up the box number and try to locate it for us."

The clerk took out a logbook and began searching. He found a box number and slid his finger over to the end of the paper. Frowning, he shook his head and spoke to Angelina. When he was finished, she turned to Ian.

"He says he's sorry, but that box has an overdue rental payment. It was rented with a one-time prepaid rental payment for seventy years. That prepaid rent ran out in 2013. He says before he returns the key, we have to pay the outstanding balance."

Angelina turned back to the postal worker and asked something in Croatian.

The worker did some quick calculations in a piece of paper, then answered her.

She frowned. "He says the past due balance is about thirty-five hundred kuna."

"What!" Ian gasped. "Did he say thirty-five hundred dollars?"

"No," she replied, shaking her head. "Thirty-five hundred Croatian kuna."

"How much is that in U.S. dollars?"

"Just give me five hundred dollars and that should cover it," she replied. "I don't know the exchange rate right now, but we should be close."

Ian counted off five one-hundred-dollar bills and handed them to Angelina who gave them to the clerk.

Angelina turned to the clerk and asked him something in Croatian. He counted the bills, looked up at her, and mumbled something, ducking his head so only Angelina could hear. She winked at him, mumbled something back, and held up her hand.

"What was that all about?" Ian whispered as he watched the clerk pocket a couple of hundred-dollar bills.

"He says we gave him two hundred too much. I told

him to keep the change and thanked him for his help. Hopefully, that will ensure his silence should anyone come around asking questions."

The clerk motioned for them to follow him. He led them to a vast array of mailboxes. He found number 369 and inserted the key. It still worked. Looking at Angelina with a mixture of pride and surprise he spoke to her.

Again, Angelina replied in Croatian. He nodded and handed her the key and left.

"He said he is glad I can get what my grandmother left for me," she interpreted for Ian, "but I should really turn the key in for a new one. I asked if I could keep it for a while for sentimental reasons."

"Good thinking," Ian said, grinning.

Angelina looked at him. "You should do the honors."

Ian smiled and reached into the old mailbox. In it was a large, thick envelope addressed to "The Man of Integrity" with the post office box address. At the top left, it had N. Tesla and the return address for the New Yorker hotel. He was ecstatic.

Angelina glanced over her shoulder, then looked back at the envelope. "Let's not open it here," she said quietly. "Too many eyes. Let's just get out of here and read it back at my apartment."

Ian agreed, and they headed out of the building, nodding their thanks to the clerk as they left. They hailed a cab and headed back to the apartment, paying the cabbie with cash, plus a generous tip.

"Well, that was unexpectedly easy," said Ian as they reached Angelina's door. "I really thought we were going to have to traipse all over Croatia to find the mailbox, but it makes sense that it would be at the oldest and most central one."

"I was always taught that Uncle Nikola was a very

logical person," replied Angelina. "He was an excellent chess player and always thought things out ten steps ahead. He would have foreseen that anyone trying to follow the trail of the key would start at the most central point. I hope this bodes well for the rest of the search."

As they sat down at the kitchen table, Ian took a deep breath and opened the envelope. He carefully withdrew the top document and unfolded it. It was written on New Yorker hotel stationery, dated January 4, 1943 and was addressed to "Albert". He began to read it out loud.

Albert,

If you are reading this communication, it is apparent that you have received my previous package, have begun to analyze the information, and have figured out the meaning of the key. I hope you have not delayed in retrieving this letter, since it will be critical to the complete understanding of the information. I assumed it would take you a while before you traveled to Croatia, so I rented the mailbox for as long as they would allow.

Remember, the information I sent you in the initial package was only the first of my secrets. They will enable you to understand how to combine my theories with your own and resolve the problems that caused us such significant conflict in our early collaboration on Project Rainbow.

The rest of the information that the key led you to is critical, because it will help you understand how to close the door that our discovery will open. As you will see and come to understand, this discovery will lead to a new golden age for mankind, where many of the ancient dreams can be realized.

If it is used for the benefit of all people, we will have opened the door to unlimited free energy, be able to feed and clothe every human being, travel easily throughout time, and teleport people and materials anywhere in the universe. Even instant communications throughout the universe will be possible.

However, if this discovery falls into the wrong hands, it will result in the enslavement of all mankind. This information must not fall into the hands of evil men or be given to just one government. You must ensure that it is given only into the hands of men like yourself, who will use it for the benefit of all civilization.

This is why I chose you as the keeper of my dreams. You are a man of utmost integrity, and I know you will protect this information with your life. I very well may lose my life in the next few days for the same reason. I am at the end of my road, so it will be no great loss to humanity. The Nazis are circling around, and I needed to delay the inevitable until I could ensure that my greatest work was in your hands. I can now walk into the light knowing I have done my best.

Below is the first half of the "door closing" formula, and a clue that will lead you to the third part of what you need to complete the work.

The second page of the document had a complex formula which neither Ian nor Angelina comprehended. They realized it would take time to understand, so they moved on to reading the last paragraph.

The third part is with the dead. Consciousness and death are manifested in light. Find the bright light of my life, and you will find the answers resting in peace, waiting for our lights to be joined.

Nikola

They put the letter down on the table and just stared at each other for a while. Ian tried to digest what they'd just read, but there was so much to take in, and his mind was racing.

Finally, Ian spoke. "In all the years that you have been told stories about your great granduncle, did anyone ever mention Nazis? And do you have any idea who or what the 'bright light of his life' could be?"

Angelina nodded. "Yes, in fact, that was a big part of what the family talked about. They could never understand why the FBI never fully investigated the allegations that Tesla was killed by the Nazis. I was so intrigued by it all that I've spent much of my teenage years hacking into various databases to gather my own files on the subject." She stood and went into her bedroom and came out with a huge file. She laid it on the table and began to explain.

"What you don't yet know about me is that this is what I do for a living. I get hired by different groups and organizations to hack into databases. It is one of the reasons I stay so far off the grid and out of the limelight. It allows me the flexibility to disappear at a moment's notice and still earn a decent living. I can get into any database in existence.

"Over the years, I have accessed information from Soviet Union files, information which was stolen from the Nazis after the fall of Berlin, along with secret black ops files from the U.S. and England, among others. Let me show you some of the stuff I've uncovered."

She opened the file. "These files contain declassified

and classified documents that seem to prove that Tesla was murdered by the Nazis for what he knew and for what he would not give them. The Nazis knew they were losing the war and were grabbing at various straws to come up with an 'ultimate weapon'.

"They even sent the *Ahnenerbe* out to find and gather mythical objects of great power, such as the Ark of the Covenant, the Spear of Longinus, also known as the Spear of Destiny, and other relics and mystical items that they thought would ensure their victory. At the same time, their scientists were trying to develop atomic weapons and other devices that would help them save the reich.

"Although the Germans were successful in developing V2 rockets and were able to use them effectively, they had not gotten to the point where they could combine the rocket delivery system with the atomic bomb. The FBI records show there was a Dr. Ronald Richter working on an atomic bomb that would have been bigger than any that the United States had, and they were very close. If they had developed the bomb, Germany would have won the war. The OSS, which later became the FBI, was even making plans to assassinate Richter. Apparently, after the war, he and many other Nazis escaped."

She put those documents aside and picked up the next set. "These indicate that Richter also worked on something he called 'the bell'. Apparently, they were attempting to create an antigravity and time travel device. They might have gotten some of this info from Tesla's notes and from what they believed was a UFO the Nazis recovered. The information in the hacked file indicated that they may have had some level of success but had not worked out all the problems before the war came to an end.

"Much of the information they used to create and try

to perfect this device came from past research they stole from Tesla. They needed the final piece, and that's what they were trying to obtain from him before he was murdered. He must have refused to give it to them, and they were so desperate at that point that they killed him and took all the documents from the safe in his room. That's why there was nothing for the FBI to find when they discovered him the next day.

"I've also found that one of the big prizes they sought from Tesla's work was the final plans to what he called his death ray. It's not known if they were successful in getting this information from his safe, but all indications are that they did not find a workable design.

"There are rumors of other inventions, however, which may have been developed from his stolen information and combined with advances in modern technology and physics to create workable weapons. The one mentioned most often one in the hacked files is the thought camera."

Ian stopped her there. "So, a number of questions come to mind. First, who are the people developing this stuff? If the Nazis had all this stolen info, and they are no longer around, who is utilizing this information? And second, can you fill me in on what this thought camera is? Didn't you say you'd created a working model of the device? Wasn't that one of the reasons you won the Genius of the Future award? At least, they said so at the ceremony."

Angelina nodded. "In regard to your second question, the thought camera is a concept that Tesla had. He believed he could create a device that could project the thoughts and memories of any person onto a screen for that person or any other person to watch like a movie. He believed that the electrical impulses in the brain could be interpreted and then be made visible. Just like we can interpret radio waves and television signals. Of course, television had not been invented at the time, so he envisioned it as a movie, which was his best frame of reference. If you think about the current advances in computers, quantum physics, and television, you can see how this might be a workable concept now. The working model I submitted to the Tesla committee really didn't interpret actual brain waves or impulses. I just created a computer program to simulate it, then I interpolate how it might be a viable concept."

Ian thought for a moment, then said, "I think that the attack on the professor may have included the actual use of this device. The professor had strange markings on his face and head and was found handcuffed to a chair facing the television in his office. If they used a working device on him, they may very well now know all he knew about me, Einstein, and Tesla."

Angelina frowned. "If that's the case, it could very well give me the answer to your first question. The Nazis are still around and may have been the ones that attacked the professor. There is evidence in my files that show that back in 1955 they were trying to get to Einstein. They thought he could give them the information they needed to complete the bell and the other devices they'd developed from the stolen Tesla research.

"They were monitoring him and closing in when Einstein suddenly died of a brain aneurism. I believe they've been monitoring a friend of his since that time to see if he would be successful in understanding and developing Einstein's theories. If he showed any signs of success, I am sure they would have taken action. Maybe they felt it was time?"

"So, you're saying that the Nazis are responsible for

the attack on the professor and are the ones after me?" asked Ian.

"It's very likely," responded Angelina.

"Come on, Angelina!" exclaimed Ian. "How is it possible that there are still Nazis around at this point in history? How can they have the organization and power to do all the things you suggest? Weren't they destroyed after the war?"

Angelina pulled out another set of documents. "I recently recovered these documents that detail how Hitler, Bormann, and others escaped Germany in those last days of World War II. There was an elaborate flow of events that shaped how Hitler and many of his senior staff escaped from Germany. As I mentioned before, according to FBI documents released in 2014, it's clear that Hitler did not die in a bunker at the end of the war. The FBI knew this and were tracking him and other Nazis for years."

"How could it be that no one knew that for this long?" Ian asked, incredulous.

"C'mon, Ian," Angelina chided, "this is the government we are talking about. Stalin insisted until the day he died that Hitler escaped to Spain or Argentina. Franklin Delano Roosevelt even formed a special division of the FBI to investigate Hitler's whereabouts.

"Declassified documents and testimony at the Nuremburg trials confirmed that the last time anyone saw Hitler was on his birthday, April 20, 1945, and was the date on the last documents he ever signed. No one saw him after that. Bormann signed all official documents from that date on.

"Nazi Admiral Karl-Jesko Von Puttkamer testified at Nuremberg that on April 21, 1945 there was a mass exodus of planes carrying high level Nazis, including

Hitler, from Templehoff Airport. According to Puttkamer, Hitler personally flew one of the planes. Additionally, there has been recent confirmation that there were tunnels leading directly from a spot near Hitler's bunker to Templehoff Airport."

Angelina began to speak faster, and one by one, slid papers from her file onto the stack in front of Ian.

"An official log of the first plane to take off that day had listed all the personal belongings of Adolf Hitler on that plane. From there, Hitler went to Spain. Eyewitnesses have testified that they saw his plane land in a potato field in Spain near a Catholic monastery in Samos. Nazis at the end of the war were aided in their escape through 'ratlines' established by the Red Cross and the Catholic Church. Apparently, they felt Nazis were preferable to Stalin.

"Hitler was protected by Francisco Franco, who owed Hitler for helping him win his revolution. From there, Hitler went on a U-boat, which stopped in the Canary Islands to refuel and then went directly to Argentina. The whole thing took two to three months.

"On May 2, 1945, the Germans surrendered, and the Nazi command told all ships and U-boats to surrender. All but forty-six did surrender, and two of those U-boats resurfaced three months later when they surrendered off the coast of Argentina. Soon after that, J. Edgar Hoover received two letters from people who claimed that Hitler was alive and well and living in Argentina.

"It seems Hitler moved around a lot, and over the next several years, he was aided by many powerful, rich German sympathizers, and Nazis in Argentina. Juan Peron and his wife were Nazi agents and helped him. He was obviously trying to train soldiers, as well as make artillery and other weapons. He also actively continued to try and develop a nuclear bomb. Later, he apparently tried to develop other weapons of mass destruction.

"What is clear is that Hitler was never going to give up. He was determined to raise a Fourth Reich, and he believed that Tesla and Einstein held the key to that somehow. Hitler had big plans, but they needed one big weapon to wipe out Manhattan in order to strike fear in the world and resurrect and unite the enemies of America.

"FBI records say they believed there were over fifty million young boys and girls worldwide that were part of the Nazi youth programs. They had schools all over the world, which were like terrorist cells that they believed they could activate with a major blow to the USA.

"They started working on different contingencies and strategies, secretly building a nuclear facility. Juan Peron himself gave Dr. Richter a blank check, and he was known to have been developing a nuclear facility in Argentina.

"Juan Peron was overthrown in Argentina in 1955, and the Nazis were no longer protected, so they had to move. There is good evidence and eyewitness accounts that Bormann and Hitler made their way to Chile and then Peru.

"Eventually, it's believed they ended up at a facility known as Colonia Dignidad, which was like a Nazi cult. They were training children to be Nazis. Documents showed this continued until the 1970s at least, and many believe it still continues to this day. The facility was a military compound with state-of-the-art communications and weapons.

"It's also thought they were producing weapons of mass destruction at this facility, which included sarin gas and other chemical weapons. They also were trying to use genetic engineering to create super humans that could be made into super weapons and super soldiers.

"There is a town in Argentina, Candido Godoi, where there are an unusual number of twin births. As many as one in five pregnancies there have resulted in twins. Most of them were blue-eyed with blond hair, perfect Aryans. It was later learned that Josef Mengele, the 'Angel of Death' from Auschwitz, had visited the town many times until he died in 1979. He escaped after the war and was never captured. He spent the rest of his life conducting human experiments and trying to raise the Fourth Reich. He may also have gone to Colonia Dignidad to work on very special cloning projects.

"But most of all, the Nazis wanted to complete Tesla's work on the time machine and the death ray. Hitler really thought that the ultimate weapon was time travel, and if they could go back in time, they could change the outcome of the war.

"In the late 1940s and early and mid-1950s, they pursued Einstein, hoping to have the final piece of the puzzle. They were ultimately unsuccessful, but they never gave up. The Nazis never went away. Even after Hitler died, apparently, there was chatter that the FBI heard of a 'new Hitler' that was going to lead them to victory.

"These are all government documents, and I'm just giving you the main points. Believe me, the Nazis are alive and well, and up to something bad! They've been monitoring anyone connected with Einstein over the years. That includes Professor Kearney, and now, apparently you, Ian," Angelina finished.

"How come the world is not aware of all of this?" asked Ian. "If they are still around and this powerful and active, and we know where they are, why hasn't someone taken them out? Sent a SEAL team in there or something?"

Angelina looked at Ian with a pitying look. "Ian, you are so naïve!" she exclaimed. "Many of the governments in the world collaborate with them. They benefit from all the devices and inventions that come from there. They're like some secret, nefarious weapons developer for the world. They sell their information to governments, and in exchange, they get gold, protection, and anonymity. It's a very symbiotic relationship."

"Well, that's hard to believe," replied Ian. "There is no way Hitler, Bormann, or any of the other original Nazis are still around. How do they continue the effort?"

"They have tried to clone Hitler many times, according to the reports I have seen," Angelina replied. "It's really horrific what they have done with genetic engineering and cloning. They were the ones that developed the process, and they sold it to the rest of the world. It's rumored that the current clone of Hitler is the most highly developed version. Vast intellectual capacity, extremely personable, influential, and revered as a god.

Their worldwide power and influence are extensive. It would seem this person has decided that the time is right to capture whatever it is that you now possess and use it to establish the Fourth Reich. This is a critical time, and you, my friend, seem to possess the key to a Nazi tomorrow. We have to keep you and your information safe and out of their hands."

"If that's the case, and both the FBI and the Nazis are on our trail, then I think we need to keep moving," suggested Ian. "We can't assume we're safe, even here. Think about where we can go next. Do you know anyone else in the country we can stay with?"

"I have a lot of friends that can help us," Angelina replied. "They do the same kind of work I do and know how to stay off the grid. But before we decide which one is best, don't you think we need to figure out where the third part of the secret is?"

"Yes, sorry," said Ian. "You're right. Let's look at that again."

CHAPTER THIRTEEN

Bellevue Hospital

Dr. Mills and Carol arrived at Bellevue to visit with Roger in ICU. They found him still in critical condition, but he was improving. Dr. Mills got Carol comfortable and told her that he needed to go and check on the professor. He headed up to the professor's room and found the two FBI agents already there waiting for him.

"Good morning, gentleman," he greeted them, then moved to the computer in the corner of the room.

After inputting his security code, he pulled up the professor's vitals. He clicked through a couple of screens, then signed out of the program.

"How's he doing, doc?" Agent Armstrong asked.

"He's stable," Dr. Mills replied as he moved to the bed to look into the professor's eyes.

"Well, that's good, isn't it?" Armstrong asked.

"Not necessarily. It's good that he's not deteriorating, but I'm not seeing much improvement, either." After looking in both eyes, Dr. Mills stood and faced the agents again. "Although, he does seem less agitated now, which is a good sign."

"Do you know how he got this way?" Armstrong asked again, looking at the bed. "It seems so strange to me."

Dr. Mills nodded. "I believe the device used on the professor was a way of attempting to look at someone's memories without their consent. A long time ago, I read that Nikola Tesla had come up with an invention that he called the thought camera. The theory behind this device was to use electricity to access and project someone's memories onto a screen so they could be viewed by others. I don't know if that's what we are looking at, but this certainly reminds me of it.

"It's possible that someone has devised a machine that can create hyper-connectivity of cells in a network. A thought is basically a pattern of brain cells firing together emulating reality in our brain, so what we see in our head matches as closely as possible what happens outside of our brain. This is what we perceive as reality. If what we see in our head does not match reality, we develop psychosis. Memories are really just a pattern of particular brain cells in particular networks firing together in the same space and moment in time.

"Each time we recreate that pattern and the cells all fire together as one, we recreate that memory, and it becomes stronger. If we don't recall the memory, then it eventually fades. The more emotionally significant the memory is, the more powerfully we remember it, so that one moment can be frozen in our brain forever.

"But during severe trauma, we have something called the 'freeze response'. According to the polyvagal theory, this is a very old response that developed in reptiles, but remnants of it remain in our brain today. The freeze response occurs when we feel like our life is in danger.

"Normally, a memory is made up of both sides of the

brain and both memory systems. We have the detail aspect of the left brain along with the experiences, feelings, and emotions of the right brain. But when we are traumatized as in war, during a rape, or when we feel our life is in danger, this freeze response kicks in, and it literally causes a split between our right brain and our left brain so as to prevent us from forming a conscious memory of the event. This is why most rape victims don't remember the actual event, but they carry with them subconsciously the pain, bodily sensations, and the fear for the rest of their lives. This is also what actually happens in the brain with PTSD."

Dr. Mills stopped and looked at the agents intently. "I believe that the device they used on the professor is having this type of effect on his brain, only a hundred times more intensely. I believe the device can lock onto a pattern of brain cells that make up a memory to cause a hyper-connection between these cells, intensifying the memory so that it can be projected onto a screen for viewing. It then links a series of these memories together to see what has happened in the past to the person.

"Each of these hyper-connected memories is like one image in a moving picture. When linked together and projected, they appear as one flowing, continuous event. This hyper-connectivity usually only happens when connected to extremely strong emotions. So, when this is done to someone, the body reacts as if it's under severe trauma.

"Being subjected to this device is more intense than anything anyone would experience in real life. This hyper-excitability combined with the stress response of the body and massive release of stress hormones like cortisol, literally causes a massive and powerful functional disconnection between the right and left hemispheres of the brain.

"Normally, even after severe trauma, the hemispheres reconnect and move forward normally for the most part. Some people end up psychotic because they cannot spontaneously reconnect, and they remain in a virtual world. But the professor's case is so severe that he's not only in a psychotic state but has sunk into an almost catatonic state. The massive release of stress hormones has literally affected his body so significantly that it caused early degeneration of the lens in his eyes. I'm sure you've noticed they've turned white. This is just like you would normally see in the process of advanced aging. We call them cataracts, and normally, they progress rather slowly, but in this case, it happened in only a few minutes.

"The good news is that there is no actual damage to the brain. I've previously been successful helping many trauma victims recover from their psychoses back to a normal state. So, I think it's possible I can do the same for the professor. His case is much more severe, however, so it will take longer. We need to reconnect his hemispheres functionally, and we need to reconnect the conscious and unconscious memory systems. To that end, I have worked out a treatment plan."

He pulled a file out of his briefcase and opened it on a nearby table. The two FBI agents stepped to the table to look at it. Pointing to the first page, Dr. Mills continued.

"I will be implementing some cognitive and sensory motor protocols that I believe will allow us to create new pathways in the brain. If this is successful, the professor should come back to reality and access his memory. Because this is a normally developed brain, we can also use trans-magnetic cranial stimulation in combination with sensory motor and cognitive activities to reconnect these networks more quickly.

"Obviously, we're dealing with significant disruption here, and I've never dealt with this type of injury to this degree, but I believe the theories I have will work to access his memories. We'll reconnect the networks on either side of the brain and create new neural connections.

"I'll call the other doctors in and show them the protocols. They need to complete the exercises every four hours. We can check back in with them daily to assess the progress. Every brain is different, so I can't predict when the professor will be able to answer your questions, but I am hopeful it will be in a week or so."

"That's fine, Dr. Mills," said Agent Armstrong, "but at this point, it may be irrelevant. Last night, we were called to the scene of another attack at a motel on the New Jersey Turnpike. It seems that Ian's roommate Peter was subjected to the same device used on the professor. He was found handcuffed to a chair facing the television. By the time we got there, he was in the same condition; babbling, shaking, and drooling. Completely incoherent."

"Where is he?" asked Dr. Mills with immediate concern.

"We had him brought here to Bellevue," said Agent Armstrong. "He's in a room a few doors down. He seems to be in worse shape than the professor. It may be that they used the device longer, or at a higher intensity. Is that possible? Do you think you can help him utilizing the same protocols you are planning for the professor?"

"Again, every brain is different," replied Dr. Mills, "but I would say that it is our only hope. Fortunately, younger brains are more resilient, so if it works with the professor, we can assume it will help Peter, as well. We will be implementing the exercises much sooner than we have with the professor, so that's a definite plus. Let me inform the doctors they'll be working with both of them. Then, we can talk some more."

Dr. Mills gathered the doctors and nurses and showed them the exercises they were to perform on Peter and the professor. When he was comfortable that they understood, he went back to the agents.

"Have you been able to view the second attacker's body yet?" he asked.

"Yes," Agent Armstrong answered. "After Peter was brought here, we went to the morgue. They're doing fingerprints, DNA, and facial recognition work as we speak. The body had some identification on it, but we're still not sure where it will lead. We believe we'll be able to connect the dots soon. In the meantime, we have alerted all New York area airports to be looking for the man you described to us. If you can tell us where Ian went, we can narrow the search to anyone looking to go to that same destination. Do you have anything further to share with us about that Dr. Mills?"

"I've not heard from Ian since you and I last spoke," replied Dr. Mills.

"Look, Dr. Mills," said a visibly tired and annoyed Agent Armstrong, "we have been up all night, and I need you to understand that you are withholding critical information. We are not the bad guys here. As I see it, we are your only hope. Without our help and protection, your kid is a sitting duck. Whoever these guys are, they have networks all over the globe, and they're very bad people, with worse intentions. They will find him, and they will fry his brain just like they did the others. Tell us where he is, and we will pick him up and take him into protective custody. Stop playing secret agent and come clean!"

Dr. Mills was at the end of his rope. He had Carol to

consider, Roger was in critical condition, and Peter and the professor were out of action and in big trouble. He made the tough decision. He was going to have to tell them where Ian was and hope that Ian could stay off the grid long enough to finish his assignment.

"Ian is in Croatia," he confessed, "but again, I have no idea where at this point. I suggest you pull all the records from all the airlines that fly there from any New York area airport, since that's where the people hunting him will go."

"Don't tell us how to do our job," said Armstrong crossly. Then he turned to his partner. "Cuff him. I'll get the mother, and we'll bring them both in for their own protection."

"You can't do that!" shouted Dr. Mills. "I need to be here working on the professor and Peter. You agreed not to arrest us."

"We'll bring you here every day," growled Armstrong. "You can do your work. You are not under arrest; you're being protected. We can't afford to have you become an easy target for these guys. I still think you know more than you're telling us, and I don't like being played. From now on, we're doing this my way."

Then, he led Dr. Mills away and his partner went to collect Carol.

On the way down in the elevator, Dr. Mills felt defeated. Now Ian had no support, and he would have no way to communicate with the boy. He felt as if his entire world was crashing down. He was going to have to figure out a way to get a message to Ian, and he was going to have to explain all of this to Carol. That was going to be a painful discussion.

Zagreb, Croatia

Axel was really annoyed. The late-night flight to Croatia was overbooked, and he'd had to wait until morning to get the next one. While waiting for takeoff, he was still seething about Rolf's death and was itching to take his revenge on the kid at the center of it all.

From the information he got from the roommate's brain, he knew that Ian was working on unraveling the Einstein and Tesla information. The roommate had seen the documents and heard all the conversations, but he must have some form of ADHD, because the images were all spotty and unfocused. The kid had real concentration issues. The images were not helpful in understanding the formulas and data that was there. He would need to get to Ian Petrie if they were going to gather the information they needed to complete the bell and the death ray.

The *Führerin* was not going to be happy with this delay. They had waited for decades to move in on the professor. To have been so close and to lose it all now would be a fatal blow.

They were risking exposure, but the *Führerin* was not one to wait. Although she was young, she was impressive. Brash, commanding, intelligent, and much more brutal than her previous incarnations, she also had an impatient streak. That may be her fatal flaw, but only time would tell.

He remembered when she was younger, and she had not yet been chosen as the next leader. She was scheduled to face the other clone candidates in the arena. This was a brutal test, where the physical skills and resourcefulness of the clone candidates would be tested against each other. She'd been impatient then, too. He recalled that she did not wait for the contest the next morning. Instead, she had brutally murdered her competition in their beds the night before.

When the sun rose the next morning, only she stood in the arena, holding the severed heads of her now-defeated competitors. She was immediately and unanimously named *Führerin*.

Regardless, Axel vowed he would not fail. He would find that kid and get what they needed. He knew the kid was out there on his own with no support. He knew he was staying at the Esplanade Hotel, and his first objective was to find information about the key.

He had seen a picture of it on the television screen when he scanned the roommate's brain, and he knew what the key was. He had seen them many times in Europe. It was a mailbox key with the number 369. He would start at the main post office and track them from there. This was going to be easy.

He smiled to himself for the first time since frying the roommate's brain, then settled in for the fourteen-hour flight.

Ian and Angelina were busy trying to decipher the meaning of the last paragraph of Tesla's letter to Einstein. They read it again.

The third part is with the dead. Consciousness and death are manifested in light. Find the bright light of my life, and you will find the answers resting in peace, waiting for our lights to be joined.

Ian asked Angelina, "Any idea what he might mean by 'find the bright light of my life'? You know all the stories about Tesla. Did you ever hear anyone mention anything about his bright light?"

Angelina thought about it, reviewing all the stories and conversations she'd heard during the time with her relatives.

"I have a few ideas," she replied. "The first thing that comes to mind is that in the last years of his life, he was very lonely. He had no female relationships. But he had said in an interview how he fell in love with a white female pigeon with violet eyes, whom he loved as much as any man loved a woman. He also said that when she died in his hands, he'd seen rays of light emanating from her eyes. That may qualify as a bright light. But the pigeon died, so we would have to look for the grave of pigeon or something, which seems silly and impossible."

Ian agreed. "What is the next idea?" he asked.

"He loved his mother very much and idolized her, as many Croatians do. I remember reading letters that he sent to his mother before she died. They were respectful and asked for her prayers. He never referred to her as a bright light, but he definitely confided in her. I remember a quote from one of the letters. He wrote, 'I realized that I had missed something big in my life. As if I had left an aspect of light unrecognized completely. Some formula has been within the grasp of my understanding, and I have failed or didn't want to clarify it. That has to be connected to that Moorish lament, I am sure of it now'."

"Wow," said Ian. "That's very interesting. We're going to have to remember that and figure out what it's all about. He referred to a formula that he connected to some 'Moorish lament'. What does that mean?"

"A Moorish lament refers to Arabic poems or songs

from the 1200s to 1300s," replied Angelina. "Many of them were written in Spain when the Moors ruled. They were songs lamenting the loss of a son or a husband or some highly valued possession. They are haunting, and if you ever heard one, it would stay with you forever. Even if you don't understand the words, the emotions seep into you and tell the story to your soul."

"Okay, got it. What is your next idea?" asked Ian.

"The only other thought I have is that Tesla lost his brother, Dane, when he was killed by a fall from his horse. Tesla was the younger brother and loved Dane more than any other person in the world. He was everything to Tesla. He always blamed himself for Dane's death, because it was Tesla who hurled a rock at the horse.

"Apparently, he was upset that his brother wouldn't let him ride it. The rock struck the horse, causing it to throw Dane to the ground. His brother later died from those injuries. He never forgave himself.

"Throughout his life, he always told everyone that Dane was considerably smarter than he was and would have outdone him in every way. He was tortured by his death, and had said that when Dane died, a bright light had gone out of his life."

"That's it!" exclaimed Ian. "He has to be referring to his brother, Dane. It makes sense. He must have put the third part of the secret with his brother's body. All we have to do is figure out where Dane is buried, and we will find the information."

"Seriously?" said Angelina. "All we have to do is dig up a dead body? You say that like it's going to be easy. I hack computer databases for a living. I dig up information, not bodies!"

Ian didn't hear her response. He was already searching the internet for information on Dane. He soon found references to him and where he was buried.

"Do you have any friends in Smiljan?" He asked with a smile.

Angelina just nodded her head and moved to start packing. "I do, and I'll call on our way to the train station," she said. "But I have to warn you, Bruno is stranger than me and you combined. Get off your butt and start packing. Don't leave anything important behind. We leave in ten minutes."

At a private airstrip outside of Zagreb, a private plane touched down. A beautiful and commanding young woman emerged, accompanied by four huge men. They deplaned and gathered their equipment, threw it in the trunk of the waiting black SUV, and took their seats.

"What is our destination, *mien Führerin*?" the driver asked.

"Hotel Esplanade," she commanded, and the SUV took off.

As they drove, the young woman contemplated all that was at stake. She recalled all the stories about past triumphs and failures. She was groomed for this opportunity. It was the whole point of her existence. It was never really a choice for her. Her fate, her destiny, was decided before she was born. All she had to do was survive and rise to the top. She was truly born for this; or should she say "cloned" for this.

She did not know for certain that the boy had the exact information she needed to complete the work, but she was sure that whatever he had would result in victory. Destiny could not be denied forever.

Carol and Dr. Mills were being held in an FBI safe house on the lower east side of Manhattan. It may have been "safe", but it certainly wasn't clean. It was filled with old furniture and smelled sour, like old convenience store hot dogs. Carol was not happy with the surroundings or the situation.

"Carol," said Dr. Mills, trying to calm her, "we didn't have a choice. I had to cooperate to get their help. We both have Ian's best interests at heart, and he needs backup. You and I can't be that for him now. The professor is out of action, and so are Roger and Peter. You and I both need to be here for them. When Ian figures this all out, he's going to need his parents and the professor to help him deal with whatever he finds. I will cure the professor and Peter. Roger's getting better, and I want to keep an eye on him. The best way for us to stay safe and contribute is to focus on them. Can you understand that?"

"Don't patronize me, Dr. Rob!" spat Carol. "I'm no dummy. You know my IQ is every bit as high as yours. What I am most upset about is that you did this on your own. You never consulted with me on any of it. We agreed that we would all do this together and keep Ian's best interests as a priority. I don't care what happens to me, and frankly right now, I don't care what happens to you. All I care about is Ian and making sure Roger recovers. To hell with the professor! He got Ian involved in all of this, and that is unforgiveable.

"Those FBI guys don't care about him, either. All they want is to solve a case and be done with it. National security! That's just an excuse to be brutal. They throw that out there, then the Constitution goes out the window.

They've imprisoned us without due process and call it protection. I am so mad at you right now! What do you think they'll do to my son if they catch him and realize that he has found the answer to the greatest mystery of the universe? Do you think they'll just let him go back to college? No! They will use him to make weapons for them and prevent Ian from ever living a normal life."

"Carol, believe me, I am mad at me, too," replied Dr. Mills, "but you know that the police are going to start asking questions. They want to know more about what happened at my house. They're suspicious. While we're here, they can't interrogate us. Let the FBI deal with the NYPD.

"When this is all over, and Ian is back home, all of this will make sense. Then, we can go on with our lives. Right now, this may very well be the best place we can be. I can work on the professor and Peter, you can see Roger every day, and we'll be safe while doing it. The only thing I need to figure out… sorry, that *we* need to figure out, is how to get a message to Ian. He needs to keep moving and stay off the grid long enough to solve everything he's working on. We need to buy him the time to do that and to have the professor in good shape by the time he gets back. Can I count on you?"

Carol was still seething and glaring at Dr. Rob. "You know I will do everything in my power to help him. But I warn you, if you keep anything from me, I will cut you out of our lives from that moment on. Understood?"

"Understood," said Dr. Rob. "Let's talk about getting a message to Ian. I threw away the disposable phone I used to call him the other day. We need to get another one or use someone else's phone. Keep your eyes open for any opportunities when you're with Roger or in a waiting room or the cafeteria. I'll do the same. Agreed?"

Carol agreed and moved to another part of the filthy and uncomfortable room to be alone with her thoughts.

Zagreb, Croatia

Angelina and Ian had finished packing, making sure that there was no evidence of Ian having been there, or any hints as to where they were headed. Angelina called her friend Bruno on the way to the train station to inform him of their arrival and make sure they could stay with him for a short while. He agreed and said that he would pick them up at the train station in Smiljan when they arrived. They purchased their tickets with cash and settled in for the three-hour trip.

"We have a few hours," Ian said to Angelina, "so why don't we start digging into all the information we have. We can at least figure out how much we already know and what else we need to figure out. When we get the third piece of the secret, it would be great to know where it fits into all of this."

Angelina agreed. She was actually itching to see it all and to start using her brainpower to fill in the gaps in Ian's thought processes.

Ian pulled up the initial letter from Tesla to Einstein, highlighting the section that he needed Angelina's help with.

"Here's the part where I believe Tesla is giving us hints to what he found. I know you know all about Project Rainbow from the databases you have accessed throughout the years. Einstein and Tesla's collaboration seems to have been a devastating experience for both men. It had a chance of pulling them together if they succeeded, but instead, the failures and frustrations just pushed them further apart. Tesla seems to be saying that using Einstein's foundational equations regarding the relationship of matter, energy, and the velocity of light were not the right ones for what they were trying to accomplish. What do you think he means?"

Angelina shrugged. Together, they bent over the paper and read through it again, more carefully.

I am now at the end of my life, and I am seeing things in a different light, you might say.

I know that our early collaboration on Project Rainbow was a low point for both of us and may have poisoned the water for future collaborations, but it made me more determined than ever to perfect my understanding of what we were working to accomplish. You moved on to other secret projects with Von Neumann, so I know that you have probably wiped the dust of Project Rainbow from your shoes. But I must tell you now that we were not completely wrong!

I have done the follow-up work, and I have understood where we went wrong. We had everything right except one thing, and unfortunately, it was foundational. We started with a flawed premise. We were working with the foundational formulas you had developed and then built from there. But I have found that the formulas did not apply to what we were trying to accomplish.

We assumed that the forces we were trying to unleash would behave like all other matter, and that seemed to be a reasonable assumption at the time. But we needed to go back further, back to the beginning. We needed a primal, more ancient understanding of matter. I will stop there.

I want you to look at the work I have sent you and draw

your own conclusions.

Angelina thought about it and said, "Einstein started with the premise of the equivalence of energy and mass. When you boil it all down, that is as foundational as it gets. What Tesla seems to be implying is that they needed an even more foundational starting point. He says that they needed a 'more primal, ancient' understanding of matter. That is the crux of the matter. What is more primal, more ancient, than energy and matter?"

"You mean like where energy and matter came from?" asked Ian.

"Yes," replied Angelina, "something like that. What was at the beginning of Einstein's work? Wasn't the Theory of Relativity the beginning?"

"Wow," said Ian, "that's going to take some thought. You don't think he was referring to subatomic particles or quantum theory, do you? That stuff was already out there and gaining support at the time. The same thing with string theory. But that wasn't the beginning for Einstein, that came much later for him."

Angelina thought about that and said, "I think it is even more foundational than that. Those theories refer to the building blocks of matter. Tesla said the understanding they needed was 'more primal, ancient', I don't think he meant just a deeper understanding of what was already understood. I think he meant an understanding of something that has been forgotten or overlooked."

"Okay," said Ian, "let's work under that premise. But also, let's think about all we know of what they were trying to accomplish with Project Rainbow. I have read up on it, but I'm sure you've seen documents that I have not regarding the project. What have you been able to piece together from your hacking?"

"From what I have read of the Philadelphia Experiment," began Angelina, "they were supposed to be looking for a cloaking device. Something that would prevent ships from being picked up by radar. They hoped a portable Tesla field of electricity would cloak the ships.

"But the real purpose of the work was to create a combined time and teleport device. They were trying to find a way to warp space-time to relocate ships to alternate locations and alternate times. Think about it. If they had a fleet ready to deploy and sitting at the Philadelphia Naval Shipyard, they could use this concept to teleport the ships and crews to any point on the globe instantly *and* even send them back in time to a point where their presence could either surprise the enemy or be in position before the enemy arrived.

"For example, think about Pearl Harbor. If they could go back in time and teleport the ships sitting there to another location before the attack happened, it would have changed the course of the war and of history. What a huge advantage that would have been!

"From the classified reports I've seen, the results were mixed. They had some marginal success in that the ship did disappear from one location and briefly appeared at another location, but the end result was horrific. It did not appear that they were able to incorporate the time travel aspect, and the teleport aspect was greatly flawed. Have you heard the stories about the crew being found embedded in the walls, floors, and superstructure of the ship?"

Ian nodded.

"That's all verified in what I've seen," Angelina continued. "So, I believe we should be focusing on understanding how this all relates to time travel and teleportation.

"But I must tell you that this experiment did not go unnoticed by Hitler. Earlier, I hinted in my apartment that I have seen documents that indicate that he was still alive at the time of the Philadelphia Experiment and in South America trying to raise the Fourth Reich. He needed a powerful weapon, one powerful enough to plunge the world into another war. He was trying to develop a nuclear bomb with the help of Juan Peron in Argentina.

"But then his spies found out about Project Rainbow. He'd known that the U.S. was trying to use Tesla's knowledge and technology, and that they were working with the German traitor, Einstein. When Hitler got word of how the ship had vanished and reappeared, he believed he'd found the weapon that would not only change the world, but could change history. He knew if he could control time, he could control the past and the future, and he could therefore control the whole world. He realized the ultimate weapon was time travel. He believed that the technology that allowed for time travel was in the mind of Tesla, Einstein, or both, and he had to have it.

"Near the end of his life, it is said he became even more obsessed and more determined to ensure success. It is believed that Hitler died in 1962 in Argentina or Peru, but what is also clear is that his operations did not die with him. If anything, they have grown in power and complexity. The Nazi influence in various parts of the world is as strong as it has been since World War II. Something is happening, and someone is directing all of this. Things like this don't happen on their own organically.

"The question is, who is now directing this renewed interest? Have they created a clone to be as equally charismatic to their followers as Hitler was? If so, how does the world not know about any of it?" finished Angelina.

"That's scary stuff, and very interesting," said Ian, "but let's go back to the physics. As you were reviewing all the information about a more ancient and a more primal understanding of matter, I had images in my head. So much of physics is about duality. Einstein proved that space and time were not two separate entities. Instead he proved that they were an interwoven continuum. The same can be said for matter and energy.

"Then there is the duality of electricity and magnetism and the wave/particle duality of light. Everything is yin and yang. Everything has its opposite half, or more accurately, the other side of the same coin. Duality is the most basic principle of the universe. Even the most ancient religious texts refer to this duality in the relationships between good and evil, light and darkness, mind and body, spirit and flesh. There is a greater truth here than we are seeing. Maybe that was the thing that Einstein and Tesla had not incorporated into their early collaboration work on Project Rainbow? What is the first duality, the prime duality?"

"If we could answer that, we would have a good starting point," replied Angelina. "What else have you gotten from reviewing all of the documentation on the microdot? Anything that would help us figure that all out?"

"In my review of Einstein's work, it appears that he had boiled all of his previous work down into a set of equations I am trying to understand. There is a gravity equation that's puzzling. There is some connection between gravity, matter, and dimensional membranes. I am running it through my head constantly to try and sort it all out, but I can't see it all yet. Maybe I need to apply duality thinking to this equation, also.

"It will take time. But right now, I think Einstein was heading toward gravity waves that may have influence beyond our own dimension. It's possible that these gravity waves are interdimensional in their influence."

"That's astounding!" said Angelina. "That would definitely have the potential to be the bridge concept he needed to solve the problems of the Unified Field Theory. If there are other universes around us, and they all have a form of gravity, then a nearby universe would have an invisible effect on the universe that we could not account for because we could not see or measure it. This may have been the universal constant that Einstein had put in his original calculations that he thought was a huge mistake, but later he realized was they were correct. However, he never understood where it came from. Perhaps he figured that out at the end.

"This would also answer the question of dark matter. No one understands how there can be this powerful force throughout our universe that can affect us but is beyond measurement and detection. It does not seem to have any mass to it, yet it creates a powerful force. If we're bordering multiple universes, then perhaps this force could be so strong that our gravity is partially supplemented by gravity from other universes. This may be why Einstein had trouble figuring out how gravity works, how such an apparently weak force could have such an effect on time and space.

"Ian, it sounds like it is all coming together," said Angelina. "When we get to Smiljan, let's go to Dane Tesla's grave as soon as possible. We have no idea how long it will take for us to get what Tesla left there, and the sooner we have it the better."

Ian agreed and pulled up what he could about the

location of the grave.

"Dane is buried at the Nikola Tesla Memorial Center in the cemetery near Tesla's birth house and the Serbian Orthodox Church where his father, Milutin Tesla, was a priest. The church and the grounds have been renovated, and it's now all run as a memorial to Tesla. It sounds like we might have a crowd of visitors, and possibly some security people to work around," Ian observed.

"We can have Bruno create some sort of diversion or somehow keep the memorial staff occupied at another part of the site while we explore the gravesite," suggested Angelina. "And it's obvious that we need to wait until nightfall."

"Great, digging up graves at night. That can't get us into *any* trouble," he said sarcastically.

"I've been thinking about that," replied Angelina. "There's no way that Tesla would have buried the information with Dane. For one, he would not have desecrated the remains that way. Also, he wouldn't have wanted anyone else to do that, either. He would have made it hidden, but still accessible. It would have to have been able to survive the ravages of time and the elements. Let's not have any preconceived notions. Let's just get there and see what we find."

CHAPTER FOURTEEN

Zagreb, Croatia

The *Führerin* was not happy. She and her team had arrived at the Hotel Esplanade and discovered that Ian had evacuated his room a day or so before. When they had asked for Dr. Mills's room, which they knew was the name Ian was using, they had been told that he'd left the hotel unannounced and had not checked out upon leaving. His room bill had been paid in cash that the maid had found on the dresser.

When pressed for more information, the management told them that he had been seen in the company of a beautiful girl. They got a description of the girl and began asking questions. One of the workers suggested that she'd been seen at the hotel during the award festivities and had been the recipient of the Nikola Tesla - Genius of the Future award.

The *Führerin* knew she was the young relative of Tesla that Axel had described. So, she was involved in this, too. What a wonderful revelation! Not only would they capture the kid from Princeton, but they would get the girl in the bargain. She would then have two of the brightest minds on the planet working for her. With them under her control, she knew that victory was certain. She did not usually get involved in this sort of mission, but this one was different. They were so close, and she wanted to make sure there were no mistakes.

"Send a message to Axel," the *Führerin* commanded. "Tell him that when he arrives, he is to meet me here. Meanwhile, go to the General Post Office and show them the picture of the key that we obtained from the brain of the roommate and pictures of Ian Petrie and Angelina Novak. Find out where the mailbox may be, and if it is there, make them open it for you. I want what is in that box. Also, find out where the boy and the girl are. I want them found immediately!" She retired to her suite, while her men headed out to the General Post Office.

When they arrived at the post office, they confronted a clerk who told them that he was not the one who served the two kids but had noticed them when they arrived. More accurately, he had noticed the girl, as she was very beautiful. He brought them to the clerk who had helped them. That clerk told them that he recognized the girl, but that she was with a different young man. He described him. Blue and purple spiky hair, nose ring and earrings, and eyeliner. He told them they had a key to box 369, and that he helped them get access to it.

When asked if he had seen what was taken from the box, and he told them that he did not. Frustrated, they left the post office. Before leaving, one of the men suggested that the kids may have taken a taxi.

They approached one of the cabs at the front of the building, showed him a picture of Angelina and Ian, and asked the cabbie if he had seen the couple. He had not. They did the same with every cab lined up there. Eventually, they found the cab that had taken the kids to

Angelina's apartment. He recalled the address.

They got into the cab and had the man take them there. They broke in and searched the apartment and found nothing that would indicate where they had gone. The *Führerin* was going to be angry. They could not return without something tangible.

The four men decided to split up. Two would go to the train station, and two would stay at the apartment building, in case they returned.

Two agents arrived at the train station and started showing the pictures to the men in the ticket booth. They finally found one that recognized Angelina and indicated that they had bought tickets to Smiljan about six hours earlier. The two agents called their partners, filled them in, and then headed back to the Esplanade Hotel to report to the *Führerin* and wait for Axel's arrival.

Smiljan, Croatia

Three hours before, Ian and Angelina had arrived in Smiljan and had been met by Bruno. Angelina was right, Ian thought. Bruno was a unique character. Standing six foot, three inches tall, with the body of a middle linebacker, he was intense, brooding, and completely dressed in black.

Despite his intimidating physical appearance, Bruno had an incredible mind. Angelina had told Ian that he had been a previous winner of the Nikola Tesla - Genius of the Future award ten years ago, but he'd been working as a mercenary in Afghanistan for the past five years. They had met when she called him for some help with a project she was working on for the Tesla award. He'd taken a liking to her, and they remained friends.

He picked them up in a car that was far too small for him. Ian, of course, had to squeeze into what was generously called the back seat. Angelina asked Bruno to take them to the Tesla Memorial Center so that they could scout it out while it was still light. On the way, they discussed the outline of what they needed to do.

"So, you intend to rob a grave?" asked Bruno. "I've been involved in almost every shady type of deal you can imagine, but I draw the line at grave robbing."

"We are not going to actually rob the grave or desecrate it in any way," replied Angelina, shooting a warning glance at Ian. "We're just going to check it out and see if we can find the clue that Tesla may have left. All you have to do is be a distraction for the staff, if needed. Can you do that?"

"That I can do," replied Bruno. "I've been itching for some action for a while now. Things have been slow lately."

Angelina turned to him and said, "Bruno, no explosives, do you hear me? Just a simple diversion. We are not looking to call attention to this."

Bruno smiled and said, "We'll see."

They arrived at the Memorial Center, and Ian kept a lookout for signs of the cemetery. They found it about fifty yards behind the old Serbian Orthodox Church. In ten minutes, they located the grave of Dane Tesla, which was a simple grave surrounded by two-foot-high, wrought-iron fencing.

The grave monument was about four feet high in an elongated, pyramidal, column shape with an orthodox cross carved at the top. Weather-worn and listing slightly to the right, it seemed like a sad and dim memorial to such a bright light, who was maybe the only man smarter than

Tesla himself.

Angelina, Ian, and Bruno leaned over the fencing to get a closer look. Other than the basic information about the occupant and the dates of his birth and death, nothing else seemed to suggest the secret they were looking for. Of course, Ian knew they would need to examine it more closely, but with the other visitors present, they couldn't do that now.

They returned to their vehicle and decided to return after closing. Bruno took them back to his modest apartment to wait until the time was right.

"It seems like you two are in trouble, if you ask me," said Bruno as he opened a couple of bottles of Ožujsko beer and handed one to Angelina and one to Ian. "Who are you running from?"

Ian was startled by the observation. He looked at Angelina, who obviously was not. Ian thought about it for a moment. Angelina had told him Bruno was sharp, and that he knew how to read people. He had survived over the past five years by being cautious and aware, and he could smell trouble.

"*And* don't lie to me," Bruno warned, interrupting Ian's musings.

Angelina answered, "No one you need to worry about, just the FBI and the Nazis."

Bruno spit out his beer. When he recovered, he asked, "Seriously? How is that possible? What are you two into? Did you hack into something you shouldn't have, Angelina? I warned you about that. Nothing is untraceable. It was only a matter of time before they tracked you down."

"That's just part of it, and I was not the one that did the hacking," replied Angelina. "Ian here is an Einstein-level genius. He's obtained some very dangerous information, and both the FBI and the Nazis are after him. If they get their hands on it, we're all in trouble. We can't tell you too much, or you'll be in danger, too. Just trust us. What Ian has in his iPad and in his head will change the world. We're looking for the last piece of the puzzle that Tesla left. It has something to do with Dane Tesla's gravesite. Just help us find it, and we'll be gone. You won't have to be involved any further, okay?"

Bruno drained his beer, stood up, got another from the refrigerator, then turned to look at them. "You kids need protection. You can't do this by yourselves. Stick with me, and I'll get you through this. I can handle the FBI and the Nazis, but I need to know how close they are. Have you been followed?"

"We really have no idea," Ian ventured. "We haven't spotted anyone, but we know they're both in play. I had a call two days ago and was told that my mentor back home was working with the FBI. They probably know where I am by now. We also assume that a Nazi-based group has already kidnapped my roommate and shot my dad. They've probably already gotten information about my whereabouts from my roommate with the use of a torture device. We must assume that they know I am in Croatia, but we're hoping that's all they know. We've been careful not to leave a trail."

"Really?" said Bruno. "You've been in public, right? You have purchased train tickets and been to the General Post Office. With all the security cameras and as noticeable as you two are," he said, gesturing toward Ian's blue and purple hair, "someone is going to be able to identify you. Believe me, the FBI and the Nazis have the scent already. At best, you have a few hours' head start. From this point on, we're going to assume we are being watched and take appropriate precautions. We are going to the gravesite tonight fully armed and with an escape plan. As soon as you have what you need, we are out of here. What's the next destination?"

Ian and Angelina looked at each other with bewilderment. Angelina said, "We haven't thought about that yet."

Bruno put his head in his hands. "So, what were you going to do, just sit here in Smiljan and wait for them to catch up with you? You must keep moving. Your next move has to be somewhere unexpected. We should assume that they know you're here looking for Tesla information. You need to go somewhere unrelated to Tesla. Any ideas?"

"I need to find a place where I can have enough time to put this all together," Ian replied. "I don't want to go home without resolving all the questions. I need somewhere to get some inspiration. The reason I went to Princeton was to be where Einstein did much of his work. It was great, I had so much inspiration there. The only place which would be better would be the town of Bern. I have always thought about how great it would be to go to where Einstein first had all his great ideas. There is a museum there with all his major papers, and they've even fixed up his old apartment as a memorial to him. Would that work?"

Bruno said, "Maybe. Do you think the Nazis will be looking in Einstein-related places, as well as Tesla-related ones?"

"Probably," Ian replied. "But I'll be able to think clearer, and faster, if I have Einstein's surroundings to inspire me."

"All right, then. We can drive there in ten hours, and we only have to deal with one EU border entry point. I have friends in Bern. Angelina, any objections?"

"Other than the one you brought up? Not that I can think of, except the size of your car. Ten hours in that thing will kill us," Angelina replied, half-smirking.

"I'll rent another vehicle," said Bruno. "I will drive my car to the memorial and park in the main lot. You will drive the rental. Use the back entrance to the memorial site. It's closer to the grave. At some point, I'll torch my car, causing a great diversion. I will head to where you are, and we'll leave through the back entrance after you have the info you need. Then, we can head right for the border. Make sure you put everything you need in the rental car before you go to the gravesite. Sound like a plan?"

"A crazy plan," said Angelina, "but then, I would expect nothing else from you, Bruno. Crazy is good. I knew you would have to blow something up eventually. Just make it as small as possible, please?"

"We'll see," said Bruno with a smile on his face. Then, he went into his bedroom and came out with a collection of guns. He stepped over to Angelina and held them out to her. "Lady's choice," he said.

Zagreb, Croatia

Axel had arrived at the Esplanade Hotel and met with the *Führerin*. She reviewed with him the information the four agents had gotten from their search for Ian and Angelina. They knew the kids were headed for Smiljan. The *Führerin* decided to wait at the hotel for the team to return to Zagreb.

She told Axel that he was to wait with her while the others went to Smiljan. As soon as they had word that the kids were in the hands of the agents, they would fly back to Argentina and prepare for their arrival. Then the really fun stuff could begin. Axel was not happy to miss the capture, but he was pleased that the *Führerin* would let him have first shot at Ian and the girl. He had a lot of anger to work out.

Bellevue Hospital

Dr. Mills had just finished his work on the professor and Peter for the day. They were both responding well, and it should only be a few more days before their memory functions would be working well enough that they could be questioned. Before he left Peter's room, Agent Armstrong entered.

"Dr. Mills, we have a positive ID on the dead attacker," said Armstrong. "His name is Rolf Eisenstaedt. He has a long and dark background. He apparently worked for the *Bundesnachrichtendienst*, the Federal Intelligence Service of Germany for a while. Since then, he has been connected with some shadow organizations working out of Argentina. He's a really brutal guy. If he was involved, we can assume that the rest of his crew is just as bad. We need to find Ian quickly, get him to a safe house in Europe, and then bring him back here. Tell us where he is."

Dr. Mills looked at Armstrong with amazement and disgust.

"You really are stupid," he said. "You have had us in custody and took our phones, how am I supposed to know where he is? I have been honest this whole time, unlike you. If you want to know where he is, give me a phone and some privacy, and I'll see if I can find out.

Otherwise, use your own methods."

Armstrong looked thoughtful, then nodded. "Okay, let's all go back to the safe house, and I will let you use a phone there. I don't want your conversation overheard." They went downstairs and got Carol, then they headed back to the safe house.

Smiljan, Croatia

Ian, Angelina, and Bruno drove to the Tesla Memorial as soon as it was dark. It was nearly closing time, so the main parking lot was empty. Bruno parked his car and waited. Angelina and Ian drove around to the back entrance and found a spot to park the rental car not far from the cemetery.

They had agreed that when they had the information they were looking for, they would text Bruno. He would set the timer on the incendiary device, then meet them at the grave. Ian hoped that they wouldn't be disturbed before that.

Angelina and Ian exited the vehicle, grabbed their flashlights and shovels, then made their way to the grave. Ian's heart raced, and he prayed that no digging would be necessary, but they were prepared for the worst.

Arriving at the grave, Ian looked up at the huge tree overhanging the plot. The thick foliage hid the stars.

"Quit star-gazing," Angelina said. "We have work to do."

They jumped over the wrought-iron fencing and started to examine the headstone. Angelina could read the Croatian inscriptions, but she didn't find anything unusual written there.

"Ian, shine your flashlight on the headstone while I take some pictures with my phone. I want to capture every surface so we can examine it later. Maybe your PhotoEx app will help us find any hidden symbols." She took her pictures while Ian held the flashlight. After a few minutes, she was done.

"Did you see anything we could use?" Ian asked.

"Nothing," said Angelina, "but we can look more closely at the pictures later. Right now, I think our only option is to start digging."

They turned off the flashlights and reached for their shovels. Before they could put the first spade into the ground, Ian noticed something odd out of the corner of his eye.

"Angelina, look at the headstone!" he whispered.

She looked up at the strange symbols glowing in the dark below the cross engraved at the top.

Ian grabbed his flashlight and shone it on the spot where they had seen the writing. It disappeared. He shut off the flashlight and the symbols re-appeared, even brighter.

"Fascinating!" Ian whispered. "Tesla must have used some sort of photo-phosphorescent substance to create the symbols." He looked back up at the tree. "The tree must have shaded it during the day. Otherwise, someone would have found this years ago!"

"In that case," Angelina responded, "I'm grateful for trees right now. Let me get a few shots of this." She took out her phone again, shut off the flash, then took a series of pictures.

"Do you think that's what we are looking for?" asked Ian.

"I don't know," said Angelina, "but if it isn't, I'd be really surprised. How often do you find glowing symbols on a dead Croatian's headstone? It all fits with the light references in Tesla's letter. Anyway, it saves us from digging up the dead body of one of my own relatives. Let me make sure the pictures are clear, then we can text Bruno." She checked the pictures, texted Bruno, then they headed back to the car.

Ian heard the explosion in the distance just as Bruno arrived at their car. He leaped into the backseat and shouted, "GO!" They headed out the back entrance and in the direction of the highway headed north for the ten-and-a-half-hour drive to Bern.

They'd been on the road for about an hour when Ian's phone rang.

"Why is your phone on?!" Bruno exclaimed. "Anyone could be tracking us with GPS!"

"I didn't think about it," Ian replied, chagrined.

"Well, don't answer it unless you know who it is," Bruno advised. "Even if you do, don't say your name, and make it short!"

Ian looked at the number and did not recognize it. He let it ring.

"It could be Dr. Mills," Ian said. "Last time he called, he was using a disposable phone. He might have purchased another one."

"If it's him, he'll leave a message, right?" suggested Bruno. "If he does, and you're confident it was him, you can call him back. After that, we're going to dump your phones so we can't be tracked. I'll keep mine for emergencies."

Ian let the call go to voicemail and waited. When he saw the voicemail notification pop up, he played the message on speaker.

"Ian, this is Dr. Rob. I need to know where you are. It's been confirmed that one of the men who attacked your parents, the professor, and Peter, was connected with an organization out of Argentina with Nazi ties. The one that escaped used the brain device on Peter and knows everything. You are in great danger. The FBI has your mom and me at a safe house. Your dad is recovering well. I've been working on the professor and Peter, and they're improving. The FBI wants to contact you to bring you to a safe house somewhere in Europe. I think it may be the best thing right now. Call me back and let us know where you are. Call back at the number I called you from; it's an encrypted satellite phone, so it can't be traced."

Ian hung up and shook his head. "This is getting out of control. Everyone involved in this is either in the hospital or in FBI custody. I think I'd better call them back and give myself up. I have all the information, and even if they get it, they'll need me to understand it. It would be a bargaining chip, right?"

"You are being naïve, Ian," Bruno said, shaking his head. "You have no idea what the FBI is capable of. There may be some in the FBI who have proper intentions, but I can assure you that there are others that have the same intentions as these Nazis and may even be working with them."

Ian was shocked. "You mean to say that people in the FBI want to see a Fourth Reich or see Hitler resurrected?"

"No," replied Bruno, "but they want to gain power over the world just as the Nazis do. They may believe that they're acting for the benefit of national security, but it's all to gain power and control. America would become a de facto Fourth Reich, if these people have their way.

"As Angelina has told me, over the years, the U.S. government got access to some of Tesla's research after he died. You may ask yourself, how is this possible since nothing was found in his hotel room when he was found dead? The answer is that in 1999, a man named Otto Skorzeny confessed on his deathbed that he and another one of Hitler's bodyguards killed Tesla and stole his papers. Guess who they went to work for after World War II?"

"I don't know," Ian replied. "I assumed they were either charged with war crimes or possibly punished in their own country."

"No, Ian, they went to work for the FBI. They were documented FBI agents and are listed by the FBI as two of their ex-agents," revealed Bruno. "They were never charged with a crime because they brought with them much of what they had stolen from Tesla. That was the deal."

"How do you know this?" asked Ian.

"Because I'm a freaking awesome hacker!" proclaimed Bruno.

Bruno then had Angelina pull up the documents on Ian's iPad and show them to Ian.

"The documents recount an eyewitness testimony by a guy named Eric Berman," she read aloud. "He tells how he discovered that his former girlfriend was the daughter of ex-Nazi SS Commando Otto Skorzeny. He met the elderly Skorzeny, who'd been living for years in the U.S., working as a carpenter with a new identity supplied by the FBI after World War II, through his former girlfriend. Berman heard a full confession from Skorzeny, who was nearing the end of his life, and was given a shoebox full of more than a hundred photographs to substantiate his claims.

"Among a number of other highly significant revelations, Berman heard from Skorzeny that he had personally suffocated Nikola Tesla on January 6, 1943, assisted by fellow Nazi, Reinhard Gehlen. Tesla was then eighty-six years old. According to Skorzeny, he and Gehlen had been working on Tesla for months trying to get him to reveal the full details of his most important discoveries.

"They thought they had an agreement, but at the last minute, Tesla reneged. They'd been at dinner with him earlier in the evening, and after he told them that he would not follow through on the deal, they decided that he must die. They followed him into his room, suffocated him, and then positioned him on the bed to appear as if he had died in his sleep.

"After the murder, they stole the contents of Tesla's safe, all the other devices and drawings in his room, and delivered it all to Hitler. Otto Skorzeny was Hitler's bodyguard and assassin, one of the many Nazis who exfiltrated to the USA after World War II, as part of Project Paperclip. Many of these Nazi scientists ended up working for NASA, the FBI, and other U.S. secret services.

"Although he supposedly died in 1975 in Spain, Skorzeny resurfaced in 1999. Otto Skorzeny described how, contrary to the FBI-written history books, he helped Hitler escape to Spain in a plane flown by a female pilot, Hanna Reitsch. 'Hitler did not commit suicide,' Skorzeny recounted. 'His double was shot between the eyes, and the dental records proved he was not Hitler. The Americans kept it a secret, worried the truth might anger the Russians'."

Bruno took over the history lesson from Angelina. "Ask yourself why the FBI would take two of Hitler's bodyguards into the agency after the war if they didn't have something to bargain with? They became agents because they brought with them Tesla's research. Combined with what they already knew about Tesla and his research, they hoped it would be enough to give them the whole picture. But it wasn't. There wasn't anyone alive that could figure out what Tesla was thinking. It was way beyond anyone, and it still is. They didn't make the connection to Einstein until right at the end of his life, but it was too late. They've been watching and paying attention ever since.

"Then you pop up, and once again, the race for information is on. So, before you go turning yourself in, you'd better think twice and realize you might be putting yourself and everyone else into the worst possible position. If they get their hands on this information, you will never see the light of day again. Neither will your parents, or any of the others. You will all just disappear. Your best bet is to work through all the information and stay free. At that point, you'll hold all the cards. If you choose, you can trade it for the freedom of the others or go public with it. But if you go in now, you will lose it all."

"I agree with Bruno," Angelina said quietly. "But I do think you should call them back. Just tell them you are going to Argentina to give the information to the Nazis. Maybe then they'll stop trying to kill you. Tell them that the Nazis almost blew you up in the parking lot of the Tesla Memorial Center in Smiljan. They will verify that and believe it. Tell them you're flying out of Zagreb in a day or so. That will give us time to get to Bern and figure this all out. After that, we can head to New York."

Bruno said to Ian, "I like that. That can work. Not sure about the New York part, though, and we still need to avoid the Nazis. If we can keep you alive for another forty-eight hours, do you think you can have this all worked out?"

"Maybe," said Ian. "I have a pretty good picture of where this all heading, but there is still the final piece.

Let's work on that before I make the call."

They agreed, pulled up the pictures of the grave on Angelina's cell phone, and transferred them to Ian's iPad. They looked at the symbols.

(سفر التكوين 3:1)

"The numbers are clear, but these don't look like letters," Ian observed.

"I agree," Angelina said. "They look like a code. To break the code, we'll need a code key. Something we can compare the symbols to."

"What kind of code key would Tesla have used?" Ian wondered aloud.

"It would probably be a document, a formula, or a book that Einstein would be familiar with, and be able to easily access." Angelina offered. "It would have to be something common to both of them."

They started discussing the characteristics of the two men to find commonalities. Tesla was Croatian, Einstein was German. Tesla was left-brained. Einstein was right-brained. Einstein was working on the visible aspects and material aspects of the universe. Tesla loved dealing with the invisible and immaterial aspects of the universe. Einstein was a Jew. Tesla was a Christian. In almost every way, they seemed opposite. What could have been common to these two impressive men?

Ian observed that both Jews and Christians have the Bible in common. At least the Old Testament, and definitely the first five books of the Bible, the Torah. It was also something that Tesla knew the Jews were meticulous about translating, so it was the same in any language and had not changed much over time. Could he have used the Bible for a key to break the code? Einstein, although not religious at the end of his life, was brought up in the Jewish faith, and Ian had seen a Bible in is home at Princeton. Tesla's father, Milutin Tesla, was a priest in the Serbian Orthodox Church and Tesla would have been very familiar with the Bible. He, too, always had a Bible handy. They agreed that the Bible might be a good starting point.

Suddenly, Ian grabbed the phone and stared at the picture again. After a moment, he slapped his forehead. "I'm such an idiot! It's so obvious!"

"What's obvious?" Angelina asked, confused.

"Arabic!" he responded. "These aren't a coded message. At least, not in the traditional sense. They're Arabic letters."

"Don't tell me you can read Arabic," she said, doubt filling her voice.

"No, but what if we enter them into Google and see what comes up?" Ian offered, already typing on his iPad.

To Ian's surprise, the Arabic letters and numbers in English said, "Genesis 1:3."

He looked up that verse, and read, "'And God said, "Let there be light"; and there was light'."

Ian was ecstatic! They'd found the third part of the message!

"But how do we put it all together?" Angelina asked, bursting his bubble.

"Well," Ian replied thoughtfully, "now we know that the symbols we saw on the grave were not symbols, but letters in a different language. We have the verse that Tesla wanted Einstein to read. We need to figure out how this relates to the rest of the information I have. Any ideas?"

Angelina recited the passage Tesla left in his letter in the mailbox, which had the clue to finding the third part.

"'The third part is with the dead. Consciousness and death are manifested in light. Find the bright light of my life, and you will find the answers resting in peace, waiting for our lights to be joined'."

Then, she recited from memory the quote that she had told Ian about, the one that Tesla had written in one of his last letters to his mother.

"'I realized that I had missed something big in my life. As if I had left an aspect of light unrecognized completely. Some formula has been within the grasp of my understanding, and I have failed or didn't want to clarify it. That has to be connected to that Moorish lament, I am sure of it now'."

She put it all together for Ian and Bruno. "Moorish refers to the Arabic language, and the symbols we have just translated are in Arabic. Why would he have used Arabic? It wasn't his own language. He had to be pointing to some other reference. I believe the quote I just gave you could be that reference. In both instances, he talked about light and finding answers. In the second one, he referred to hearing a Moorish or Arabic voice in his dreams. I believe what he was telling us is that the Moorish voice in his dreams led him to his final understanding of the problem. The answer might be summarized by the Genesis verse, 'And God said, 'Let there be light'; and there was light'.

"All of this has something to do with light. Light is the common denominator. Ian, you have to focus on what all the information has to do with light!" Angelina exclaimed.

"That's a great starting point, Angelina!" said Ian with just as much enthusiasm. "It also reminds me about the very beginning of Einstein's career. His first paper published in his miracle year of 1905 was on the photoelectric effect. He was trying to understand the nature of light. That's the main reason I called my application PhotoEx, because it was the first thing I developed. So, I named it in honor of Einstein's first great paper that year. It was literally the very beginning of his remarkable career. Right from the beginning of his career, he must have realized the primacy of light.

"This will all help me have a better idea about how to put it all into context. I can already see how much of what I have reviewed references, or incorporates, the speed of light and its relationship and interaction with matter. I'll review all the documents and formulas with the assumption that they are all pointing toward some aspect of light. Well done, Angelina!"

Then, Ian pulled out his cell phone and made the return call to Dr. Mills.

When Dr. Mills answered, Ian said, "I can't talk long, so just listen. I am going to Argentina to give all the information I have to the Nazis. It's my only choice. They are hot on my trail, are closing in, and have already tried to kill me. They blew up the car I was using in the parking lot of the Tesla Memorial Center in Smiljan, where I was searching for a clue. They almost got me at that point. If I go to Argentina, all this madness can stop. Tell the FBI that if they want the information, they'll have to go after the Nazis. I'm done. Some of them are still here in Croatia, so tell the FBI to try to get them while they are still here. Tell my mother I love her."

Then he hung up and handed his phone to Bruno, who was driving. Angelina did the same. Bruno removed the batteries, rolled down the window and threw them out over a cliff at the side of the road.

"Well," said Ian, "we really are on our own now."

CHAPTER FOURTEEN

FBI safehouse

Agent Armstrong stood stunned as Dr. Mills hung up the speaker phone. His and Carol's faces showed total shock. Armstrong couldn't believe what he'd just heard. Ian must not understand how devastating this would be to national and worldwide security. Giving that information to the Nazis would be handing them the keys to the future of every nation on earth. He didn't waste any time. He called Director Simmons.

"Armstrong here, sir. We just got a call from Ian Petrie. He told us he's taking a plane out of Zagreb to Argentina in the next day or so. He plans to hand over all the information to the Nazis. They tried to kill him by blowing up his car, and he's tired of running. We need to alert the teams in Croatia and Argentina to check every commercial and private flight out of Croatia to Argentina. Tell them to detain Ian and anyone with any connection to the Nazis. Also, check the hotel registries in Zagreb, and all the border check points out of Croatia. Sounds like we have a short window of time, so make it an urgent priority." The director agreed and hung up to put out the order.

Zagreb, Croatia

The *Führerin* hung up the phone. She had just received news that she did not want to hear. She turned to Axel.

"That was the team following the kids. They were headed to the Tesla Memorial Center in Smiljan. We believed that they'd go to that spot. It's the place in Smiljan most related to Tesla. They may have been after some information that was hidden there.

"Before our agents arrived, there was a car bombing in the parking lot of the Memorial Center. The place was overrun with firetrucks and police, so they couldn't search for them. They're waiting for any information regarding the owner of the car and if there were any victims. They must make sure that the kids were not in the vehicle. Right now, we have lost their trail. They will also check the train station and see if anyone remembers them buying a ticket.

"They must be found! We cannot let them slip through our hands when we are so close. I want the border check points monitored. I want the airports monitored. Find them, Axel, do you hear me?"

"I hear you, *mein Führerin*!" replied Axel. "I will oversee it myself. Trust me, they will not escape." He picked up his phone and relayed the orders she'd given.

CHAPTER FIFTEEN

Ian, Angelina, and Bruno were approaching the Slovenian border. They stopped at a rest stop before the crossing to discuss the plan. Bruno explained the problem.

"The Schengen Agreement abolished many of the EU's internal borders, enabling passport-free movement across most of the bloc. But Croatia, although an EU member, has not ratified the agreement. In order to continue our trip, we need to cross the border into Slovenia before we can go on into Italy and Switzerland.

"Fortunately, I've had many interactions with Slovenian border security because of the work I do and have greased their palms many times. When we arrive, I'll stop the car, get out, and talk with my friend who runs the crossing. You two will stay in the car. Say nothing. Just sit here and be quiet. Do not draw attention to yourselves. I will arrange for a sticker to be placed on the windshield which will identify us as EU citizens and allow us to cross the remaining borders without having to stop. This crossing is the critical one. How much cash do you guys have on you?"

Ian took out his cash and counted. "I have about three

thousand U.S. dollars."

Angelina laughed and said, "I have about three hundred and fifty kuna."

Bruno reached back and took a thousand dollars from Ian. "This should do it," he said and pocketed the money. "Remember, when we get to the crossing, just shut up and let me handle it all."

They started the car and pulled back onto the highway. As they approached the border, they avoided the long line of cars by heading straight toward the administrative building. Bruno parked the vehicle and walked into the building to speak with his friend. Angelina and Ian sat quietly in the car for a while.

Soon, Ian regretted not using the restroom at the last stop, and asked Angelina if she thought it would be okay for him to run inside to use the restroom before Bruno got back.

"That sounds like a really stupid idea," said Angelina. "Not only will you make Bruno mad, but it could expose us. Just hold it until we are well into Slovenia."

"It's not that easy, Angelina," replied Ian. "I'm not sure I can. I'm going to just run, and in three minutes, I'll be back."

He heard Angelina take a deep breath as he jumped out of the car and ran inside. Ian knew if Bruno came back before he returned, he was going to be livid. Still, he simply couldn't wait!

When Ian returned, Angelina just glared at him.

"See, no worries," he said as he climbed into the back seat, slightly breathless from rushing.

Angelina exhaled like she'd been holding her breath the whole time he'd been gone. Feeling a bit embarrassed, Ian sat in silence. After a few minutes, Bruno returned with a sticker and without Ian's thousand U.S. dollars. He put the sticker on the windshield, got into the car, and said nothing as he headed for the express lane. They crossed the border without incident.

When they were a few miles away, Bruno spoke up. "That was really stupid, Ian. When I was in the supervisor's office, I saw you enter the building on the security monitors. I told you to stay in the car."

Ian responded, "Seriously? I just went to the bathroom. How could that raise any alarms for border security?"

"Every border point has the most advanced facial recognition technology available today. Every face that appears on a security camera is analyzed and sent to every international security organization, including Interpol and the FBI. You just advertised our whereabouts. Assuming the FBI and the Nazis are looking for us at border crossings, they'll have the information soon. Nice job."

Ian paled. He hadn't thought about that. "Why didn't you tell us that when we were at the rest stop?" Ian asked.

"You're supposed to be a smart guy," Bruno responded. "And I usually don't have people I'm protecting disobey my orders. Make it the last time, or you'll be on your own. It's a long walk to Bern."

They sat in silence for a long time after that. Ian spent the time analyzing all the documents on his iPad. He reviewed it all from the beginning. Einstein apparently had the answers to his Unified Field Theory in 1955, but he realized it was too dangerous to release, so he hid it. Tesla also had an amazing discovery that meshed with Einstein's previous work. Together, the two discoveries apparently led to the ultimate understanding of the visible and invisible universe.

The symbols on Dane Tesla's tomb were the key to blending them together and revealing the final answers.

Those symbols pointed them to the Bible and toward a new, or perhaps ancient, understanding of the nature of light.

Tesla had said that the initial collaboration on Project Rainbow would have been more successful if they had had a more ancient and primal understanding of matter. The Bible quote referred to the beginning of time. What could be more ancient and primal than that?

During the early phases of Project Rainbow, Einstein and Tesla had been working on a combination of time travel and teleportation. Tesla said they failed because they were working with the wrong foundational assumptions.

Ian thought about his discussion with Angelina on the way to Smiljan. He remembered telling her about the equations that Einstein had used to summarize his findings and that the gravity equation which related to the mysterious relationship between gravity, matter, and interdimensional membranes was puzzling.

But there was also another set of equations Ian had not yet understood. Could those relate to a relationship between light and something else? He was still convinced that incorporating the duality principles would be the right way to go. So, he started to review all the equations with a focus on light and duality. He felt certain he was getting closer to the truth. Ian reached over next to him and grabbed Einstein's violin.

"Anyone mind if I play the violin for a while?" he asked.

Bruno responded, "No, as long as you stay in the car while you do it."

While it was very difficult to do in a moving car with so little space, Ian played Einstein's violin and visualized all the equations and the Bible verse.

FBI safehouse

Agent Armstrong entered the room of the safe house where Dr. Mills and Carol Petrie were deep in conversation.

"Sorry to interrupt," he said. "I've gotten a call from the FBI director. He has been informed that they just received a facial recognition hit on Ian. Apparently, he was seen at the Slovenian border about six hours ago in the company of two other people.

"One is Angelina Novak, a relative of Tesla, and we don't know who the other man is. We don't know if he is a friend or a foe. He could be connected with the Nazis and may have captured the kids, but it's too soon to make that call. We must assume that Ian still intends to fly to Argentina with the information. He just may be doing it in the company of the other two or under the control of the Nazis. We'll expand our surveillance to include all airports in Europe and continue to monitor all EU border crossings."

"That's it?" said Carol incredulously. "You have to do more! You must go get him. Don't let him go to Argentina. If he gives them the information, they won't let him go. They'll imprison him until he gives them what they want, and then they'll kill him!"

"We have teams in various locations right now," replied Armstrong. "They'll track them on the ground, if they can figure out where they are going, and will call ahead to other teams located near wherever they are headed. We've alerted all borders in the EU to report the passing of the vehicle. We'll figure out their destination soon, whether it's an airport or some other location. Until he's in the air, we still have a shot to defuse this."

Carol put her head on Dr. Mills's shoulder and wept.

Zagreb, Croatia

Axel got a call on his cell phone. He listened, hung up, and went to the *Führerin's* suite to inform her.

"*Führerin*, I have received information from our people inside the FBI. Apparently, they have a facial recognition hit on Ian Petrie. He was spotted using a restroom at the Slovenian border about seven hours ago. We've accessed the external security cameras and have video of him entering a vehicle parked at the administrative building. The video shows one other female passenger and a male driver. We must assume the female passenger is Angelina Novak. We're running facial recognition on the driver and should have his identity soon. What are your orders, *mein Führerin*?"

"Thank our moles inside the FBI for their help," she replied curtly, "and tell them to continue the monitoring of Interpol communications. Tell the jet crew to prepare for takeoff. As soon as we are certain of Ian Petrie's final destination, we will go there."

Switzerland

Ian breathed a sigh of relief. He, Angelina, and Bruno had crossed the border into Switzerland an hour ago. They had encountered no issues during the crossings from Slovenia into Italy, or from Italy into Switzerland.

They had about two hours left before reaching Bern, and Ian was finally feeling safe. It was time to discuss plans.

Bruno spoke first. "When we get to Bern, we'll need a safe place to stay. I have a contact there who did some work for me a few years ago, and during the operation I saved his life. I'll check with him. Do either of you have any personal contacts there that we can depend on?"

"I don't," said Ian.

"I've never been to Switzerland," Angelina replied. "I have done some work for a few Swiss-based organizations regarding bank accounts and money transfers, but that's about it."

Bruno dialed his phone. "Luca, this is Bruno, just listen. I'm calling in a favor. I'll be arriving in a couple of hours with two people who need protection. Call a few of your men, and we'll meet you at the warehouse on Rathausgasse. This is serious international security stuff, and we're actually on the right side this time. We need serious firepower and absolute secrecy. Can you handle it?"

"Absolutely," was Luca's reply, "Sounds like old times, my friend. We will be ready when you arrive."

Bruno hung up, placed the phone in his pocket, and floored the accelerator. Time was a valuable asset when you were being hunted.

FBI safehouse

"They crossed into Switzerland three hours ago, heading north," said Agent Armstrong. "We have alerted the Federal Office of Police in Switzerland with the description of the vehicle. They have agreed to stop them and hold them until our men get there. They'll be monitoring all traffic and security cameras on the highways, in all the cities, and at the airports, in case they're flying to Argentina from Switzerland. Let's just hope they haven't ditched the car or gotten on a plane yet."

Dr. Mills kept quiet, but he wondered to himself. If they're not flying to Argentina, why would Ian go to Switzerland? What if what he told us was a ruse? What if his real plan all along was to go to Switzerland for more information, or could he be following another clue? What's in Switzerland that would be valuable in all of this? Then it hit him; Bern.

That's where Einstein did his most impressive work. While he lived in Bern, he was prolific. He completed an astonishing range of theoretical physics publications. All of his most impressive foundational work was done there. Ian must be going there to verify and validate his findings or to get inspiration like he did when he broke into the Einstein home exhibit at Princeton. If that was true, then he knew where Ian was headed.

He decided to keep this all to himself. He still had trust issues with the FBI.

Zagreb, Croatia

Axel ran to the *Führerin's* suite. He knocked vigorously and entered. "*Führerin*, they've been spotted crossing into Switzerland headed north. We believe they are headed for Bern. It's the only place that has a strong relationship to the information the boy has. I suggest we board the plane and get there as soon as possible. The trail has grown warm once again. I will alert the teams to converge on Bern."

The *Führerin* smiled for the first time in hours. But it was not a smile of joy. It was a serpent's smile. The involuntary one serpents get when they have sensed prey, and they know that they will be devouring it momentarily.

Switzerland

While they were still twenty minutes from the warehouse on Rathausgasse, Bruno spoke up. "I've been thinking about all the information you two have been discussing, and I think you're missing something. I listened when you read the letters from Tesla, the information on the tombstone, and what Tesla wrote to his mother." He quoted the part he was referencing.

"'Consciousness and death are manifested in light'. Neither of you have taken into consideration the references to consciousness. On the surface, that seems outside of the realm of physics and seems out of place in all of this, but it must be there for a reason. Remember, Angelina, I received my Genius of the Future award for showing the similarities between Tesla's work and the nature and function of consciousness. I see relevance here."

He began to tell them about the most current understanding of consciousness, the functioning of the brain, and memory. He talked about the three-fold nature of the brain: matter, thought in the form of electrical impulses resulting in thoughts and memories, and consciousness. From matter comes thought, and from thought comes consciousness. He reminded them that the word enlightenment referred to new understanding or a higher level of consciousness. There was a definite additional connection to light.

"Brilliant observation!" Ian jumped in. "Dr. Mills and I have discussed some of this. It's one of his areas of research, as well. There's another way of looking at that triad of matter, thought, and consciousness. One way is that consciousness emerges from the brain and that thought creates consciousness. But Dr. Mills thinks there is another possibility.

"He believes that as the brain is developing, we get to a point where the brain is able to tap into consciousness. That as the brain gets more and more connected, and as areas of the brain start firing in a more coherent rhythm, there is a threshold that is reached. When that threshold is crossed, something happens and consciousness emerges from a convergence of space and time in the brain. He said that his research shows that whatever is happening to create consciousness is happening at the quantum level.

"If it is at the quantum level that consciousness emerges from in the brain, then perhaps it's always there at the quantum level, everywhere in the universe, waiting for something to be able to tap in to it.

"This would mean that consciousness may not come *from* the brain, but that it arises based on physical and biological properties that allow the brain to access it. The brain may not be creating it, but rather allowing the neurons to tap in and channel consciousness from the universe itself.

"This may explain why during a seizure, people can lose all consciousness, yet still be doing normal life support activities. Consciousness disappears and then suddenly, when the seizure is over, it comes back. During this time, there is no actual damage or physical change to the brain at all. The only change is the firing pattern of neurons, where the normal timing and rhythm of firing in the brain is disrupted. During these dysrhythmias in the brain, access to consciousness is lost, and when rhythm comes back into the brain, consciousness returns. The only change is in the temporal-spatial relationships in the brain. Therefore, it may not be a physical structure in the brain that creates consciousness. Rather, it may be the connectivity and timing of the brain.

"Perhaps that consciousness is always there waiting for us to tap into it when our brains are in a similar frequency or vibrational resonance with the quantum consciousness of the universe. This could explain why psychic viewing, telepathy, meditation, astral projection, and prayer may have such powerful effects. They may all tap into the same frequency and collective consciousness. This is the theory of the extended mind Dr. Mills discussed with me. He explained how it may allow us to access information if we can resonate at the proper frequency with the universe.

"Maybe this is how I seem able tap into Einstein's thoughts as if they are my own when I do my visualization exercises. It usually happens when I practice the same pieces from Mozart or Bach that I know he used to play on his violin. Perhaps the music, resonance, and vibrations allow me to synchronize my neurons with what Einstein was thinking. Somehow, all of this is connected. I can feel it. I just have to figure out how, just like Einstein and Tesla did."

"We need to examine what we know about light, and take the nature of consciousness into consideration," Angelina said. "Let's focus on that as we look at the documents again. Maybe we can discover what light and consciousness have to do with it all."

With this inspiration, Ian and Angelina became newly energized. Ian's point of view fed into Angelina's point of view, and together, they made progress. He came to understand that what they had before them was a breakthrough understanding of the nature of light and maybe consciousness. They just needed more time to put it all together.

He felt in his heart that they had something that would change the world. But would it be for better or worse? He didn't yet know, but he was determined to have it all resolved after they visited the Einstein House and Museum in Bern. He was hopeful they'd find some final insight and perspective there.

They arrived at the warehouse on Rathausgasse and drove into the waiting open bay door, which closed behind them. They exited the vehicle and Bruno greeted Luca and his crew, filling them in on the situation. While they were talking, Ian and Angelina found a place to stretch out and talk.

"Are you sure you'll find what you need here?" asked Angelina. "We already have all the information and clues from Einstein and Tesla. What could you possibly find here that would add anything to what we already have?"

Ian reached over and grabbed her hand. "Inspiration, Angelina," he said. "Inspiration and perspective. I have it all in my head, but I need to find that final bit of perspective that will help me put it all into the right boxes. I finally understand all the equations. That's been relatively easy for me. I see the connections between them, too, but what I don't have yet is the correct order. These equations have a flow, a progression, and I don't have the right sequence yet.

"I'm hoping that being in the same environment that

inspired Einstein to do his greatest work will spark a thought. Some outside-the-box concept that will help me put it all together. Trust me, this is the best thing for me. It's the way my brain works."

"Let's just make sure you stay alive long enough for your brain to do its work," said Angelina. "No more random bathroom breaks, okay?"

Then, she leaned in and kissed him. Hard.

Bern, Switzerland

After finishing the briefing with Luca and his crew of four, Bruno returned to where Ian and Angelina were sitting.

"We're going to rest here for a while. Luca has food and drink for us, and we can discuss the plan together. Come, let's get something to eat."

He led them to an office where there was a spread of food. Surprisingly for the morning, it included pasta and pizza, along with a collection of quiches. Ian realized how hungry he was and grabbed some pizza before sitting at the table. When they all had filled their plates, they sat down to discuss the plan.

"Luca has agreed to help me protect you both while we're here," started Bruno. "He and his men are some of the best mercenaries I've ever worked with. They'll do their jobs, but you both have to do yours. We'll be going into very public places, which will make it challenging to keep you safe and incognito.

"So, when you go to the Einstein House and Museum, do your work fast. Don't do anything to call attention to yourselves. Be aware of your surroundings, and don't separate from each other. Don't go walking down any dark hallways alone, and don't go to the bathroom, Ian. All those places are ambushes waiting to happen. One of us will always have eyes on you, but we will stay out of sight.

"Each of you will have an earpiece to stay in communication with the rest of us. If you feel in danger at any point, say the safe word, which is 'violin', and we'll immediately converge on where you are, understood?"

Ian and Angelina nodded their understanding.

"The Einstein House exhibit opens in one hour," Bruno continued. "You will be the first ones there, so don't linger. Get what you need and get out. The museum will be the real problem. By the time you get there, it will be crowded. Same thing. Only spend as much time as you have to, and then get out. I estimate, at best, you have two hours. Then, we'll all come back here to debrief. Everyone in agreement?" asked Bruno.

Everyone agreed, and they focused on finishing their meal. Ian was nervous. For one thing, he didn't like being rushed when he was trying to visualize solutions. He needed calm and quiet. The other thing was that he was going to be watched. He knew Luca's crew and Bruno were going to be watching him, but he also knew it was possible the FBI and Nazis were also going to be nearby, and that made him nervous for Angelina. He leaned close to her.

"You don't have to go with me, you know," he said. "I can do this part on my own. You'll be safer staying here."

Angelina looked at him, took another bite of pizza, chewed slowly and swallowed, then replied, "Read my mind. What's my answer?"

Ian scrunched up his face in concentration and said,

"The answer is no."

"Almost right, Telepathic Boy. The correct answer is HELL NO!" Then, nonchalantly, she continued to devour her pizza.

When they finished eating, Bruno and Luca went off to a corner of the room and talked quietly, apparently refining the coverage plans. They shook hands and Bruno came back to Ian.

"Give me another thousand in cash and don't ask any questions."

Ian took out the money, counted off a thousand, and handed it to him. "I thought these guys owed you a favor. Some friends. Where I come from, favors are free."

"You're in my world now, Ian," Bruno said as he took the money, "and here, nothing is free."

Bruno returned to Luca, handed him the money, and again they shook hands.

"All right, everyone, time to saddle up," Bruno announced, looking back at them.

They entered two small, white, work vans that looked like they'd seen better days. Inside, Ian observed a collection of handguns, Uzis, and even some grenades. He was shocked by the amount of firepower they were bringing, but he was oddly comforted by it. If they went down, it was not going to be without a fight.

At a private airport outside of Bern, the *Führerin's* jet touched down and rolled to a stop. She and Axel were met by the local crew, and they all piled into two black SUVs. She directed the driver to drive to the center of town, specifically the Zytglogge, the historic clock tower near the central point of the city. From there, they would have a good view of all the major tourist attractions and restaurants. It was a great place to wait and watch for those kids. She knew they were in Bern for a reason, and she knew it had something to do with Einstein. When her prey came for what they were looking for, she would tighten her coils around them and make sure they did not escape.

FBI safehouse

Dr. Mills had still not discussed his thoughts about Ian's intentions with Carol or Armstrong. He knew it was imperative that the FBI not get their hands on Ian before he was able to finish his work. He was tortured by the prospect of Ian falling into Nazi hands, but also confident in Ian's reasoning ability and adaptability. Ian had always been able to see the big picture and think outside the box. He could do this. Ian could figure it out.

Dr. Mills just had to plan ahead for Ian's return to the U.S. He needed to figure out a way to keep him out of the FBI's reach long enough to decide what to do with Ian's discovery. To do that, he needed to be free. Somehow, he would have to escape from the clutches of the FBI.

CHAPTER SIXTEEN

Einstein Museum, Bern, Switzerland

Ian, Angelina, and Bruno were the first in line to buy tickets and enter the Einstein House exhibit. It was in the upstairs apartment at Number 49 Kramgasse Street, where Einstein lived from 1903 to 1905. When they entered, they saw that it was furnished authentically in the style that would have been prevalent at the time.

While he was living there, Einstein published five of his most important papers, which he referred to as his "*Annus Mirabilis*", a miracle year which included his breakthrough on his theory of relativity. Einstein was twenty-six years old at the time and had recently married his sweetheart and fellow physics student Mileva. He'd taken a job at the Bern patent office and moved into this two-room apartment on the historic main street of Bern. It was just a short walk from the town's famous medieval clock, the Zytglogge, with its hourly movements of human and animal figures.

Ian found it incredibly inspirational. He felt especially overwhelmed with the feeling of the presence of Einstein. He looked out of the windows and saw the same views

Einstein saw while living here. He looked out of the closest window and focused on the medieval clock tower. He remembered the story he'd read about how Einstein used the clock to visualize the impact on a person's perception of time if one were to be aboard a vehicle moving at the speed of light.

From that very window, looking at that very same clock, Einstein had done a thought experiment where he visualized moving away from the clock at the speed of light. What would he experience? What would he see?

He realized that if he were moving away from the clock at the same speed as the light reflecting off it, then it would appear to him that the hands of the clock would never move. If he receded from the clock at half the speed of light, the hands of the clock would appear to move, but at only half the speed they would if he were standing still.

Then, he asked himself, what if I were to be able to move away from the clock at twice the speed of light? Would I be able to see the light from the past reflections off the face of the clock? Would the hands of the clock appear to move backward? Ian felt that this must have been one of the ways Einstein used his visualization skills to understand the relationship of light and velocity on the perception of time.

Then, Ian focused on the tram running down the middle of Kramgasse Street. He remembered that Einstein's breakthrough theory of relativity resulted from his riding one of the town's tram cars, contemplating time, travel, and space. Ian's mind started to kick into high gear. He could feel the same thought processes that Einstein felt and started to visualize all the information from the documents, formulas, and letters he'd been working on. It finally started to come together for him.

He then noticed that in the apartment was a desk with

replicas of Einstein's notes. He asked for permission to sit at the desk, and they allowed it. He started his visualization technique. Angelina cringed. Ian was drawing attention to himself, but she said nothing.

After a minute or two of sitting at the desk, he opened his eyes, looked at the notes, and had a breakthrough. A flood of images filled his mind like a movie; space, time, light, and consciousness. He could feel it all blending together. This is what Einstein had referred to as "thought experiments". He didn't think in numbers; he thought in images and intuition.

Ian shook himself out of his visions and told Angelina and Bruno that they needed to go to the Einstein Museum right away. They left immediately and took the short walk to the museum.

As they exited the Einstein House, a black SUV pulled up and parked next to the clock tower. The second SUV did the same. The *Führerin* smiled her serpent's smile. Her prey had appeared. She watched with glee as they walked into the Einstein Museum, unaware of her lethal presence.

Dr. Mills and Carol were at Bellevue making their daily visit to Roger, the professor, and Peter. All of them were recovering well. Roger was out of ICU and was communicative. Carol had not filled Roger in on Ian's situation. All she had told him was that Ian was still away and close to finding the solution.

Dr. Mills was with the professor, who was now moderately communicative and starting to remember things. He had not shared that information with Agent Armstrong. Dr. Mills decided that it was time for the professor to help in the cause. He filled the professor in on the plan he and Carol had devised. He told him that in fifteen minutes, he was to act as if he was having a major seizure. He was to make as much noise as possible, thrashing about and pulling out all the tubes in his arms.

He would then call Agent Armstrong into the room for help in holding the professor down. When the agent was engaged in the effort, Dr. Mills would tell him he was going to get a sedative shot to calm him down. He would go and get two syringes of the most powerful, fast-acting sedative they had. When he returned, he would inject the sedative into Agent Armstrong.

By then, Carol and the other agent would be in the waiting room where he would meet them and inject the second syringe into the other agent. They would then leave the hospital by the basement entrance and disappear.

The professor smiled. "I can do that," he said. "Thanks for letting me feel useful again. Just promise me you won't waste this. Make sure Ian stays safe and that you keep that secret out of the FBI's hands."

Dr. Mills gave the professor a wink. "You can count on it, Clarence."

Einstein Museum

Albert Einstein's life and work had been turned into a permanent exhibit known as the Einstein Museum. The exhibit, which was first assembled in 2005 on the hundredth anniversary of Einstein's most important year, took up two floors of the museum.

Ian was thrilled to be there. He'd read all about it and

had dreamed of visiting with his parents someday.

The exhibits of the Einstein Museum explored his life in Bern at the beginning of the twentieth century, his Jewish heritage, and the nature and meaning of his work and theories. They were composed of film documentaries, audio, animation, papers, and memorabilia. The exhibit used photos, original documents, and instruments of Einstein, as well as contemporary items and multimedia, to explain not only the work and theories of Einstein but also the human being behind the science.

They entered the museum and headed up a surrealistic stairway of mirrors and pictures, which gave Ian the feeling of flying through the cosmos, or perhaps through the mind of Einstein himself. He was transported immediately.

As he climbed the stairway of mirrors, Ian felt as if he was progressing deeper and deeper into the depths of genius, and he was entranced. Thoughts, images, visions, and equations were all running through his head at the same time. He saw it all through the eyes of Einstein and could even feel his struggles with certain concepts. He heard the sweet sound of Einstein's violin playing in his head and understood that he was accessing the "music of the spheres" to help him visualize his greatest theories.

They reached the top of the stairway of mirrors and entered the museum exhibit to listen to some of the explanations of Einstein's work. To Ian, it felt and sounded as if he was being fed the information by Einstein himself, and it was all working together to illuminate his mind. Finally, he heard a recording of Einstein's actual voice while looking at a replica of his original paper on the photoelectric effect.

That was when he had his final breakthrough. He now

understood! He could see it all clearly! The formulas and equations all made sense and had fallen into the right progression. He now knew what it all meant, and it shook him to his core.

"Angelina! Bruno!" he shouted. "I have it! I understand!"

Everyone in the museum went quiet and looked at Ian. Security men started to converge on the disturbance. Bruno appeared from behind one of the exhibits. He grabbed Ian and Angelina by their arms and started running for the stairway as he shouted "Violin!" to alert the rest of the team to the trouble. Halfway down the stairway of mirrors, they were confronted by two armed Nazi thugs running up the stairs.

Bruno nailed the first one with a kick to the throat, while Angelina and Ian dove onto the second one from above. They all tumbled to the bottom of the stairwell. Bruno quickly took out his handgun and shot the first Nazi in the chest. Blood sprayed across the mirrored walls of the stairway like the spiral arms of the Milky Way galaxy. He then headed to the bottom of the stairwell where Ian and Angelina were wrestling with the second Nazi. Bruno stomped on the man's throat with his size-thirteen boot, and the man stopped struggling.

Again, he grabbed the kids' arms and headed for the exit. Before they ran out into the street, he stopped and scanned the area. Ian followed his gaze and saw a black SUV where three more thugs with guns drawn were starting to cross the street.

Bruno shouted into his microphone. "Three armed incoming, crossing the street!"

Just then, the two white vans, which had started toward the museum at the first sound of trouble, rounded the corner with tires squealing. The first one slammed into two of the Nazis, sending them flying. The other van pulled up in front of the entrance to the museum with the side door open.

"Get in!" yelled Bruno as he shoved the kids into the back of the van. He dove on top of them and slammed the door, shouting "Go! Plan B!"

Ian heard gunfire. Bullets peppered the side of the van as they passed by the black SUV parked in front of the clock tower. They didn't see the enraged young woman sitting in the rear seat, nor the Nazi thug climbing into the driver's seat after they passed.

Luca was driving the van carrying Ian, Angelina, and Bruno. He yelled back, "Everyone all right?"

"Yes, thanks to you, Luca," Bruno answered.

"Are we even yet?" asked Luca.

"Not yet, my friend," replied Bruno. "Get them on that plane and in the air in one piece and maybe then we will be even."

"Plane?" asked Ian, "What plane?"

"That was what the thousand dollars was for. I have another friend with a private jet who owes me big time," explained Bruno as he moved off of Ian and Angelina.

"Do all of your friends need money to do you favors?" asked Ian, sitting up.

"The money was to bribe another buddy in the flight tower to let us file a fake flight plan to Argentina. You are headed to a private airport outside of Albany, New York. And yes, I have another friend there, too. Mercenaries and their patrons are everywhere."

Bellevue Hospital

Dr. Mills's plan had worked perfectly. The professor's performance was masterful. The blood spurting from the places where he had pulled out the IVs added legitimacy to the faked crisis. Agent Armstrong had entered the room without Dr. Mills even having to call for him.

The sedative worked on Armstrong quickly and effectively. When the nurse got to the room, Dr. Mills pointed to the agent on the floor and asked her to help him.

Then he'd gone to the waiting room where Carol and the other agent were. Carol also performed well. She improvised a fainting spell, falling into the agent's arms, making it very easy for Dr. Mills to inject the sedative unchallenged. They sat him in a chair and positioned him as if he were asleep. Then, taking the stairs to the basement, they left the building.

Carol was ecstatic to be free.

"Where are we going now?" she asked Dr. Mills. "What's the next phase of the plan?"

Dr. Mills pulled Agent Armstrong's satellite phone from his pocket. "We disappear and wait to hear from Ian."

"How is Ian going to call us if he's on a flight to Argentina?" Carol asked.

"I don't think he's going to Argentina," revealed Dr. Mills. "I think he always intended to go to Bern, and just told us that to throw the FBI off his trail. I'm not sure about it, but that's my suspicion. Let's just hope he remembers the number for this phone, or that he leaves a message for us on my home phone or my office phone. I'll keep checking them. I'm sure glad this phone is untraceable."

CHAPTER SIXTEEN

Bern, Switzerland

Luca screeched the van to a halt next to the waiting Citation X, looked in his rear-view mirror, and said, "We have company."

Bruno looked out the back window and saw the first of two black SUVs closing in. "Get the kids into the plane and tell the pilot to start the engine!" He grabbed an Uzi and shattered the back glass with the butt of the gun.

"Go!" he yelled to Ian and Angelina. "Get out to the plane now!"

Angelina gave him a quick farewell hug, then she and Ian hustled out of the van.

As they entered the plane, Ian heard the shots. Bruno was firing everything he had at the fast-approaching SUV, and they were firing back. Ian and Angelina climbed aboard the plane and the pilot started to taxi.

They looked out of the windows just in time to see the second white van come out of nowhere and ram into the driver's side of the first black SUV seconds before it would have slammed into the van Bruno was firing from. The black SUV tumbled over three times and came to rest upside down, then burst into flame.

By then, the Citation X was reaching takeoff speed, and, in a moment, they were airborne and free. The smoke rising from the tarmac partially obscured their view of Bruno and Luca. Ian thought he could just make out Bruno with his fist in the air hugging Luca.

They watched as long as they could and then took seats next to each other. When the plane reached cruising altitude, the cabin door opened, and they were approached by a short, stocky man dressed in jeans and a crisp, white, button-down shirt. He took the seat across from them and introduced himself.

"I am Mario Ducati, and you must be the amazing physics twins," he said and smiled. "Bruno and Luca told me that you two have in your heads the secrets of the universe, and that I am to protect you with my life. Is it true?"

"Which part?" asked Angelina. "The part about being twins or the part about the secrets of the universe?"

"I can see that you're not twins, so I assume that is a nickname," Mario replied. "I mean the part about the secrets of the universe, of course."

"I can't say right now," said Angelina. "My twin over here is the one with it all in his head, and he hasn't told me what he's discovered yet. You need to ask him."

Mario looked at Ian who was staring out the window. Angelina nudged him with her elbow.

"Earth to Ian, come in Ian," she joked.

Ian snapped out of his reverie. "Sorry, I was just thinking about what I realized back there in the museum. It's pretty overwhelming."

"What did you realize?" asked Mario.

Ian looked at Angelina and Mario and said, "That I hold the key to the future and the past, life and death, and freedom or enslavement for all mankind. And that I can never tell anyone, or at least anyone in a position of power. How's that for starters?"

"That sounds like a lot of information for one head to hold," said Mario, "and it sounds like a rash decision to me. What I hear you saying is that you cannot give the information to anyone who will not use it wisely for the ultimate benefit of all mankind. Think about it differently, son. Ask yourself, if you could give this information to anyone, who would you give it to?"

Ian thought about that. It was a very good question.

"Well," he began, "the first two that come to mind are dead, Einstein and Tesla. They were the ones who originally figured it all out and were both men of integrity. They would know how to handle it and how to control it. But that's not going to help me now."

"No, I suppose not," said Mario, "but are there any Einsteins or Teslas around today? Men or women of integrity and goodwill who would make certain the use of this information is only for beneficial purposes?"

"I can't think of anyone right now," replied Ian. "The only people I trust in the world right now are my parents, Angelina, Professor Kearney, and Dr. Mills. My dad is in critical condition, Professor Kearney has a brain injury, and Dr. Mills and my mom are in FBI custody. That leaves only Angelina and me."

"I see," said Mario. "It seems to me that you two will have to depend on each other and commit to keeping the secret safe until the others you mentioned are well enough or free enough to help you. Let me tell you about myself and make a suggestion. The first reason Bruno and Luca called me was because they knew I was in Bern and had a plane ready that could get you out of there safely. The second reason is because they have worked with and for me, in the past, so they trust me.

"I own a company called Light Wave Resources. You've probably never heard of us, but we are one of the most well-respected technical research companies in the world. We've worked with almost every government on the planet to aid in the development of special technologies. All, not some, but *all* of which must be kept absolutely secret. That's where Bruno and Luca come in. They've helped me enforce that secrecy. They are the best in the world at it.

"Most of what we work on does not result in workable applications to the degree that the governments desire. But it always leads to new understandings and advancements. We test theories. We develop ideas. We push the envelope. We search for the next great technological advancement. Governments love that stuff."

"What kind of stuff do you work on? Can you give us examples?" asked Angelina.

"If I tell you, I'll have to have Bruno and Luca kill you," said Mario, looking very serious. Then he smiled. "Seriously, yes, I can give you some examples. Recently, I've been working with an unnamed entity to try and develop antimatter weapons. We have also been involved with research regarding the potential of using dark matter for energy generation."

"Seriously?" exclaimed Ian. "Explain that one to us!"

Mario replied, "I am sure you two are well aware that the most abundant and efficient source of energy in the universe is nuclear fusion, such as what goes on in our Sun. Nuclear fusion is about 0.7 percent efficient; for every kilogram of hydrogen that you fuse, 0.7 percent of that mass becomes pure energy. Is there anything more efficient than that? Sure, if you collide a proton with its anti-matter counterpart, an antiproton, that is *one hundred percent* efficient!

"Well, this happens to all particles and antiparticles. You run them into one another, and what you get out is one hundred percent pure energy. There's very little anti-matter in the universe, and most of it would be very detrimental to a spaceship or a reactor, as it would annihilate whatever it encountered first!

"But dark matter, which we know doesn't interact with, and certainly doesn't annihilate, normal matter, is very special. All the most accurate models of dark matter that we've developed show that dark matter contains a very special property. Dark matter is its own antiparticle!

"The universe is full of dark matter. If we could figure out how to collect and collide dark matter particles, we would have a one hundred percent efficient source of energy that would be virtually unlimited. Why? Because there is five times more dark matter than normal matter in the universe. Does that answer your question?"

Ian was astounded. He looked at Angelina and saw amazement reflected in her expression, as well. If Mario was telling the truth, he was working on some of the most cutting-edge research in the world.

"Let me give you some advice," Mario continued. "I have found that the best way to keep a discovery out of the wrong hands is either to destroy it, or to develop it and keep it for yourself. If you can develop it yourself, you can control the outcome, the devices that come from it, and the distribution of those devices. You can build in the limitations and safeguards. You can control access, and most importantly, you can control the proper use of it.

"Think about the atomic bomb, and all nuclear weapons for that matter. After seventy years, wouldn't you think that every country on the planet would have a nuclear weapon? There are instructions for building them available on the internet, for goodness' sake. Every scientist worth his salt knows the components and process. Why isn't there a massive proliferation of nuclear weapons? Why hasn't there been more use of them? It's because when they were developed and demonstrated, the world was horrified by the power. Enlightened self-interest and mutually assured destruction. Regulation, enforcement, and oversight. Those are the reasons.

"If the information you have is as dangerous as that, then you need to follow that same path, but it will take time. You must develop the beneficial aspects while understanding the destructive capabilities. Tie one to the other. Give the technology for the benefit of all while assuring the users that if they violate the beneficial use policy, it will result in absolute annihilation for the user.

"Just as the world allows the building of nuclear reactors for peaceful energy uses, but it will punish the misuse of that same technology for aggressive purposes. That is the only way. That must then be enforced by a worldwide legislative body, with all nations agreeing to the terms. Do you understand?"

"I do," said Ian, "but it's so overwhelming. I don't even know where to begin. I've just come to understand all of this and can already see hundreds of applications. Half of them are amazing and beneficial, while the other half are a nightmare. Where do I start?"

Mario put his hand on Ian's shoulder. "You start with the best of the best," he said. "You start with the highest good. I have observed that when people have full bellies and their families are safe, they rarely go out looking for trouble. If you can show the world that there will be benefit for everyone and ensure their safety, you will have already won more than half the battle. Throw in some entertainment and freedom from worry and no one will look to cause trouble. That is a simple man's advice for achieving world peace. What do you think? Can your discovery provide those things?"

"I believe so," said Ian, "and I think I know the right thing to start with. I just need to find a safe place to work for a while and develop it."

"That's the final reason Bruno and Luca sent you my way," said Mario. "We're going to Albany because I have a facility in the Catskill Mountains where you will not only be safe and can work in secret for as long as you need, but I have everything you will need to develop your concepts. How does that sound?"

"It sounds amazing," said Ian, looking at Angelina.

She nodded. "It sounds great," she said.

"Wonderful! It's settled then," said Mario, clapping his hands together. "Though I must ask that you refrain from all communications until we have you safely at the facility. Then, if you choose, you can contact whomever you need or want to. Bruno would hunt me down if I failed to keep you safe. Now *that* would be a nightmare!" He rose from his seat and disappeared back into the cockpit.

"Do you think we can trust him?" Ian whispered to Angelina.

"I don't think we have a choice," she replied. "I trust Bruno, and therefore, I trust Mario, I'm simple that way." Then she reached over and grabbed his hand. "And I trust you. We can do this, even if we have to do it alone."

CHAPTER SEVENTEEN

After escaping from the FBI and leaving Bellevue, Dr. Mills and Carol hailed a cab and took it north to Westchester County Airport in White Plains, New York, a small regional airport. Dr. Mills thought that it would not be unusual for a couple from the city to fly from there, and hopefully, they would not set off any alarms if they were being watched.

Once at the airport, they would let themselves be seen by security cameras. Then, they would immediately take another cab to Newburgh Airport seventy miles further north and let themselves be seen again. After that, they would walk to one of the small, local, budget motels and pay with cash for a room.

Hopefully, this would confuse whoever might be looking for them via security video. Why would they be at two different regional airports in such a short period of time? Had they booked flights under different names? Where did they fly to? It would take the FBI days, if not weeks, to find them here in upstate New York. That would give them time to wait for word from Ian and figure out their next move.

"You look very tired, Carol. Why don't you just go to

sleep, and I'll stay awake and keep watch. It's been a very long day, and at least one of us needs to get some rest," suggested Dr. Mills.

"I will, Dr. Rob," replied Carol. "It's just so hard to shut my brain off. I'm worried about Ian, and I'm worried about Roger and what they will do to him, knowing we escaped. The same goes for the professor and Peter. I feel like we abandoned them in their time of need."

"I know, but we can help them more if we're free," he replied. "If we can connect with Ian, find out where he is and what he has accomplished, we'll have leverage. We can also be free to tell our story to the world and shine a light on what the FBI is trying to do. With that kind of publicity out there turning the spotlight on them, they can't hurt us or the others. We need to stay free and available to help Ian."

"I know you're right," said Carol, "but still, I worry. After all, I'm a mother. It's my right and my duty to worry. Before I go to bed, can you check the messages to see if there's any word from Ian?"

"Sure," said Dr. Mills. He took out Armstrong's satellite phone and checked his messages. There was a new message. He played it and wished he hadn't. It was from Agent Armstrong.

"You think you're very clever, Dr. Mills, don't you?" growled Agent Armstrong. "That was a neat trick, but it will do you no good. I'm sure you are smart enough to stay hidden for a while, but not forever. Sooner or later, you will make a mistake, and when that happens, you will be mine.

"Also, tell Carol Petrie to remember that I have Roger, and his life is literally in my hands. If he were to get an infection, or if his oxygen were accidentally cut off, the poor man might not make it. I suggest you use that satellite phone to call the Manhattan bureau and tell us where you can be picked up. It would be best for all involved." The message ended.

"Anything from Ian?" asked Carol.

"No, nothing from Ian," Dr. Mills replied truthfully, but keeping Armstrong's message to himself.

He then went to the window to begin his watch. It was going to be a long night.

Mario reappeared in the cabin and woke Ian and Angelina. "We are two hours from landing," he said. "I thought you might like some refreshments and a chance to be fully awake when we land. From that point on, we'll be moving fast.

"I have two identical vehicles waiting for us at the private airport. They even have the same license plates. One will take us to my facility, and the other will drive south to New York City. If anyone is trying to track the vehicle, they'll be confused.

"We'll also be met by another friend of mine and Bruno's. He will oversee your security while you're with me. You can trust him with your life." He left them and came back with coffee and two sandwiches, then returned to the cockpit.

Ian was thankful for the refreshments, since it had been many hours since they had eaten. They'd been so exhausted that shortly after takeoff, they'd fallen asleep and had not even spoken about the breakthrough Ian had at the Einstein Museum.

"We have a couple of hours before landing," Angelina said between bites of her sandwich. "I think this is a good time to tell me what you know. Once we hit the ground, we'll be on the move and someone will always be around. You need to tell me everything while we have the chance, especially the stuff that no one else can know. You and I need to know it all, but anyone else should only have bits and pieces on a need-to-know basis. That way, if anything happens to either of us, the other will have the whole picture and be able to carry on with the work."

Ian finished his coffee, then replied, "Agreed. I was thinking the same thing. It's just that I don't know where to begin. It is all so complex, yet so simple. We all should have seen it from the start."

"Can you summarize the most important concept? What have you discovered that's so earth-shattering?"

Ian thought for a moment. "What I have come to realize," he finally replied, "and what Einstein and Tesla found through their combined effort, is that everything is made of light! *Everything*!"

"I don't understand," said Angelina. "What do you mean when you say *everything*, and what do you mean when you say *light*?"

"I mean that all matter, right down to the smallest quantum building block of matter is made up of protophotons," Ian explained. "Everything in the visible and invisible universe is made from the very first light, photon particles, and waves that emanated from the Big Bang. Einstein, in his first paper, was studying the nature of light and trying to understand what photons were!"

"How can that be?" asked Angelina. "There are many different forms of matter. Many different forces that derive from the differences and interactions within and between them. How can all matter be derived from the same singular particle which wasn't even a particle at the first moment of creation?"

"The Bible verse that Tesla pointed us to, with the

comment, 'a more primal and ancient understanding' reads, 'God said let there be light, and there was light'," responded Ian. "God did not create the sun or any stars at that point, so where did the light come from?

"It was just protophotons, *but* there was also vibration. The Bible says that 'God said' or 'God spoke' and it was so. The vibration and frequency of 'his voice'. In other words, the sound of the big bang at the beginning interacted with the protophotons and created vibratory activity in the protophoton waves. They began to vibrate at what we know as the speed of light. Some of them traveled linearly and some rotationally. Eventually, some of them traveled circularly. The ones that moved circularly became particles.

"Think of something moving so fast in a circle that it catches up with itself, like a snake swallowing its tail. These were the first particles. Light is *the* fundamental particle, which would make it the fundamental constituent of all matter. Protophotons are the elementary wave-particle. Remember that light is a very simple electromagnetic wave. It seems evident that light is the basic building block of everything. I know it sounds too simple to be true, and it turns everything upside down, but it's logical and beautiful and Einstein's formulas prove it," Ian finished.

"Are you saying that matter can be converted into light, and light into matter?" asked Angelina.

"Yes, I am," replied Ian. "I believe that's the thing that Tesla struggled with for so many years. He felt it was within his grasp, but he couldn't or was afraid to articulate it. When he mentioned the Moorish lament, I think he meant that was the moment when he realized it. It took so long because, deep inside, he was afraid of the implications."

Angelina looked thoughtful. "As far as I know, there is nothing to date in the standard model which suggests the universe appeared in a flood of protophotons. To say that the protophoton is fundamental is like saying a quark-gluon sea did not occur. It's tit for tat between the two ideas. Personally, I have always believed there was a phase transition from photons into matter post Big Bang, but you're saying that there was no phase transition and protophotons turned in on themselves and became matter? That a protophoton can loop on itself, forming all particles, including quarks, that we see and don't see? That it can loop on itself because of space-time curvature and that curvature itself can self-generate, depending on its frequency?"

"Yes!" exclaimed Ian. "If a photon wave enters a highly curved space-time region, it could catch its tail, and the wave could close on itself. It would stop moving at the speed of light, according to outside observers, and it would appear to them as a particle. It would even create a gravitational field. You just need curving space-time and light.

"Every different type of particle and force is just a variant of energy density and relativistic movement, or vibration and frequency, with only some quantum states possible, which arise from the specific electromagnetic field. The same way the magnetic field is a relativistic effect of the electric field, the weak and nuclear forces could be relativistic effects of the electromagnetic field. Remember that Einstein said that *any* energy momentum will produce a space-time curvature.

"Light possesses an electromagnetic field, but no mass, and yet, it curves space-time. This means that the electromagnetic field equals gravity. C, or the speed of light, in Einstein's equation is the link between light and space-time in the equation $E=MC^2$. It explains the dichotomy of quantum theory and relativity theory, which was such a stumbling block for Einstein. Quantum theory is ultimately a theory about light, and relativity is a theory about gravity or curved space-time. They are both linked with the constant C, or the speed of light, but otherwise, they are independent, because the universe is made of two things; light and curved space-time. More specifically, space-time that curves in the vicinity of light.

"What I've found is that Einstein was able to integrate the curvature of space-time into the quantum theory general equations. He determined that the protophoton is the elementary foundational wave-particle!"

"Okay, so matter is made of light and matter can be converted into light, have I got it right?" asked Angelina.

"Yes, and yes," said Ian. "What's more, it's done without the violent release of energy. When mass is converted into another form, energy is released violently, but when light is transformed, there is no violent release of energy, just light and sound. Remember, the verse said God spoke and there was light."

"Okay, so tell me the implications of this, and why is it all so frightening?" she asked.

"It's frightening when combined with the other aspects of what Einstein and Tesla discovered," replied Ian, "that time and gravity are two sides of the same coin. They found that time appears only from photon interactions, and they also discovered that for decades, everyone has been searching for the gravitational waves, but they are really time itself!"

"Oh," said Angelina, "you're really going to have to break that one down for me."

"Time rate, as gravitation," Ian excitedly continued, "comes from the acceleration of the energy momentum of photons rotating and spinning as a particle. If you accelerate in space, you accelerate all the photon energy momentum you are made of, so you'll have a slower local time rate, and you'll feel gravity, or acceleration. Relativity and m=infinity at V=C, which I know you are familiar with, is actually a proof that everything is made of light.

"The rotational light waves produce time waves, but they are not time waves. You measure the effect of time waves by measuring time! When you measure the relative time rate of two localities, you measure their difference in gravity and acceleration. Acceleration of the energy momentum of a massive particle produces a deceleration of time just like gravity does. Gravity is produced by the radial acceleration of photons in a closed form, a massive particle form, get it? Can you see it now?" asked Ian excitedly.

"I think so," said Angelina, hesitating a little. "Let me restate it. Time should propagate at the speed of light. The time rate you experience is the sum of all time waves at every specific locality of every massive elementary particle of your body. The sum is the effective gravitational field. So, every particle has its own relative time rate. Time is totally localized, thus the existence of relativity. Did I say that right?"

"YES!" cried Ian. "Don't you see what that means? All matter is made of light, and all time information is in the light itself. Convert anything into light, and it can go anywhere in space and time. *Anywhere*! *Anytime*!"

"So, this is only about time travel and teleportation? Or are there other implications?" she asked.

"There are tons of other implications. If everything is made from light, then anything can be made *from* light! Think about that, *anything* can be made from light! What would that mean to the world? We can relieve hunger and energy issues, no starvation or pollution, no one dying of the cold or heat. Clothing can be made on the spot for people. Water can be made from light. All the basic essentials of life, freely available for next to nothing.

"Once we figure out a way to determine each object's photonic vibrational frequency, it would be as simple as turning a radio dial to that particular vibrational frequency, and we can turn light/photons into that specific object. You could even convert one form of matter into another. Rocks into food, saltwater into drinkable water, plastic into fabric… stuff like that."

"Lead into gold?" said Angelina skeptically. "Sounds like alchemy to me."

"It does, doesn't it?" replied Ian, chuckling a little. "I think mankind has always had an inkling of this. I think the ancients knew it. Think about all the unexplainable things we see in the world. We wonder how ancient man created huge megalithic structures like Stonehenge and the pyramids. Even the legends about Atlantis and how their power came from the use of crystals and light.

"All of it may just be genetic memories of an actual scientific truth; that everything is made of light and vibration, and we can manipulate it to create whatever we want or transport anything to where we want it to be.

"Einstein and Tesla were able to rediscover this truth and translate it into the language of mathematics and physics. Remember what Arthur C. Clarke wrote, 'Any sufficiently advanced technology is indistinguishable from magic'. I think that about sums this up."

"I can see why this frightened both Einstein and Tesla," said Angelina. "Anyone or any government who controls this knowledge would have absolute power to control the world, and as we know, 'Power tends to corrupt, and absolute power corrupts absolutely', to quote John Dalberg-Acton. What we have here is the key to absolute power. How in the world are we going to control this?"

"I think Mario has the answer," replied Ian. "We need to develop an application of this power and demonstrate it to some unaffiliated world body. A worldwide demonstration that will amaze them, but also frighten them and catalyze them into immediate action. Only by some overarching method of regulation and control can we hope to avoid this falling into the hands of one government or controlling entity. It must be available to everyone or no one. That's the only way."

"How are we going to quickly develop a practical application of this before we are hunted down by the FBI or the Nazis or some other government?" Angelina asked. "Do you have any ideas?"

"I do!" Ian replied excitedly. "You won't believe how easy it will be. Think about the PhotoEx app. I unknowingly utilized some of these basic concepts. It really was, at the core, a manipulation of the properties of light. The ability I built into it to be able to see hidden objects or documents beneath layers of other things has to do with refraction concepts and inference algorithms. When those algorithms are combined with the right hardware modifications, similar to the ones I made to my iPad, it can use minuscule vibrational resonance patterns to interpret light waves in such a way as to either increase clarity or to see beneath objects, depending on the mode it's in.

"I can expand and modify the concept to interpret the vibrational frequency of an object, and then feed that information to a device I will create to transfer the vibrational frequency to another object. When they are resonating in sync, the one will become the other in form and function."

"Okay," said Angelina, "I'll have to trust you on that for now. You can help me understand more later. I get that you can turn one thing into another, but what about the time travel and teleportation part of it? Have you got that figured out, too?"

"Kind of," replied Ian. "I just have to work on how to modify the concept so we can determine the frequency of any specific place in space-time. Each moment of space-time has a frequency signature or address. Time itself started at the absolute highest frequency at the beginning of space-time. I need to figure out to what degree that frequency has diminished over time and apply a declining, sliding scale of sorts.

"I will be able, over time, to calculate the exact frequency of each point in space-time and send anyone or any object to that moment with incredible accuracy. We would apply the same transfer of resonating frequency pattern to the photons in the object or person we are sending, and they would, in effect, just be there. There is no actual transportation taking place. No actual movement. Just being or not being there. Understand?

"That's what we've gotten wrong all these years. Everyone thought that in order to travel back in time, you had to make something move faster than the speed of light, and that is impossible. You can't move faster than light, because you *are* light. But because you *are* light and light is everywhere and has always been everywhere and never did not exist, you can be anywhere at any time, as long as the photons in you are resonating at the same frequency as the time and place you want to be!

"Dr. Mills taught me about the ten-hertz rhythm in all our muscles, known as the physiologic tremor? This means that around ten times per second, our muscles are turning on and off. This provides a timing mechanism to coordinate all our muscles to work together. The timing mechanism in the thalamus and the rest of the brain is the same, but it's actually much faster.

"It's built on top of and emerges from this ten-hertz rhythm, but it's transformed through something called superharmonic frequency transformation into a forty- to sixty-hertz rhythm in the cortex. I think this also has a relationship to all of that and is involved with consciousness and the body's ability to move through time. Can you see it? Can you visualize it? It's just transferring from one part of space-time to another without any linear movement. So, just like matter cannot be created or destroyed, time is never destroyed; it just exists at a different frequency."

"WOW!" exclaimed Angelina, "I do see it. I get it! It's so simple and elegant. How much power is needed to effect the resonance?"

"That's what's so cool. Right now, I think I can do it with something as small as a large car battery!" said Ian. "Think about the effect of a person being shocked with twelve volts or eight hundred amps. Contrary to what you see in movies, you won't die from it. You'll get a very strong tingling sensation with the possibility of disruption to some of the electrical impulses to the heart or brain. At moderately higher levels, it could kill you. Tesla was actually very close to this revelation when he worked with his Tesla coil.

"Remember that the Tesla coil was an electrical resonant transformer coil designed as a power supply for his system of electric lighting. It was used to produce high-voltage, low-current, and high-frequency alternating current electricity. Tesla experimented with several different configurations consisting of two, or sometimes three, coupled resonant electric currents. It was, in its simplest form, a radio frequency oscillator. Tesla coils can produce output voltages from fifty kilovolts to several million volts for large coils. But, it's all variable and controllable, and we can get what we need by creating a miniaturized version, increasing the yield and efficiency, and powering it with nothing more than a large car battery."

"That makes sense," said Angelina, "and it's all coming together. I remember being told a story by my family. They always said that he had a brush with time travel, but no one ever knew if it was true. The story goes that in 1895 while conducting research with his transformer, he had his first indications that time and space could be influenced by using highly charged, rotating magnetic fields.

"This revelation came about from experimentation with radio frequencies and the transmission of electrical energy through the atmosphere. Based on the hacked information I've gathered over the years, it seems that this simple discovery would, years later, lead to the infamous Philadelphia Experiment and the Montauk time travel projects.

"With these experiments in high-voltage electricity and magnetic fields, Tesla supposedly discovered that time and space could be breached, or warped, creating a doorway that could lead to other time frames. But with this monumental discovery, Tesla also discovered, through personal experience, the very real dangers inherent with time travel.

"Tesla's first brush with time travel came in March 1895. A reporter for the New York Herald wrote on March 13, that he came across the inventor in a small café, looking shaken after being hit by three and a half million volts, 'I am afraid,' said Tesla, 'that you won't find me a pleasant companion tonight. The fact is, I was almost killed today. A spark from my experimental coil jumped three feet through the air and struck me here on the right shoulder. If my assistant had not turned off the current instantly, it might have been the end of me.'

"Tesla, on contact with the resonating electromagnetic charge, found himself outside his time-frame reference. He reported that he could see the immediate past, present, and future, all at once. But he was paralyzed within the electromagnetic field, unable to help himself. His assistant, by turning off the current, released Tesla before any permanent damage was done.

"A repeat of this very incident would occur years later during the Philadelphia Experiment. Unfortunately, the sailors involved were left outside their time-frame reference for too long, with disastrous results. From that point on, he was worried that his secret time travel experiments would continue on in the hands of others who were not as concerned with humanity as he was."

"Exactly!" said Ian. "That's a perfect illustration of what I'm saying. He basically had it. It was just that the power was too great, and the frequency and resonance were too wide. His photons were experiencing the past, present, and future all at once. Too much power and not enough focus. We'll utilize the right power with precisely tuned frequency and resonance and basically recreate what Tesla had already proven.

"We can do this, Angelina! We can accomplish everything that both Einstein and Tesla dreamed of. We just have to stay alive and free."

Mario returned to the cabin and announced that they would be landing in thirty minutes, and they should gather their things and prepare to move quickly. Ian and

Angelina gathered their backpacks and Einstein's violin, then returned to their seats. Ian took out the violin and began to play. He had much to visualize and work through in his head before they landed.

Luca woke up with a pounding head. He felt incredible pain in his arms and shoulders. As he gained consciousness, he realized his hands were tied and connected by a long chain to the ceiling. His feet were bound together, barely touching the ground. He was in his boxer briefs and was freezing cold.

As he blinked and squinted in the dim light, he determined that he was in some sort of warehouse. It must be close to an airport, because he heard jets flying close overhead.

He struggled against his bonds and began to remember the battle at the airport where he and Bruno were trying to get Ian and Angelina to safety. He recalled the other white van ramming into the side of the Nazi SUV and then flames and smoke. That's where his memory ended.

He could feel a gash throbbing on the back of his head. They must have hit him over the head. He had no recollection of being brought to this place or by whom. Nor did he know what they wanted, but he assumed it had to do with Ian and Angelina.

As he struggled to remember, a door opened, and light flooded the room briefly. For a moment, he could see Bruno about ten feet from him, unconscious. He was also hung by chains attached to the rafters above. The door closed, and the room was once again plunged into darkness. He heard heavy footsteps approaching in the distance. The footfalls came closer, and a gas lantern was lit. In the lantern light, he saw the face of the Nazi referred to as Axel.

"What do you want with us?" Luca asked as he approached.

"It is not what I want," Axel replied, "it is what the *Führerin* wants, and what the *Führerin* wants, she gets. Always."

At that point, a couple of floodlights came on, exploding in Luca's eyes, and he was momentarily blinded. When he could see again, standing next to Axel was a stunning woman. Luca immediately recognized her as the *Führerin*. He had only seen her once before and only very briefly during a mission for Mario. As she came closer and he got a good look at her, he was overwhelmed by her beauty.

She was almost six feet tall and wore what looked like a military uniform, but more stylized. She had over-the-knee riding boots, a fitted skirt and blouse, all in black. Over the blouse was a short, military-style jacket. He watched as she smoothed out the wrinkles in her skirt. Her hands were enveloped by black leather gloves. Her hair was platinum blond and pulled back in a severe ponytail. As she stood before him, he was mesmerized by her crystal blue eyes and exquisite features.

A stray thought entered his mind; she is the perfect embodiment of the Aryan race that Hitler had always hoped to create.

His thought was interrupted when she spoke. "You look very familiar to me. Have we met before?"

Luca was startled for a moment. "We have not officially met, but I have seen you from a distance, and I know who you are."

She sneered. "Luca, there are many ways to torture

someone, so many different implements, but I am a traditionalist and basically an old-fashioned girl. I like to keep things simple and effective."

Luca watched as she reached for a ten-foot bullwhip, which looked incredibly wicked. From the way she handled it, Luca knew she had used this whip many times before.

"This one is my favorite," she cooed. "I love using it more than any other implement, and I have to say, nothing gives me more satisfaction than hearing the crack of the whip followed by the scream of a man. I know I don't seem like the sentimental type, but it really goes back to one of the first times I experienced torturing a boy."

The woman strode toward Luca and started to stroke his body with her gloved hand, gently caressing his chest. She strode around him like a tigress circling her prey. Her expressions and movements gained energy and animation, and it was obvious to Luca that she was invigorated by all of this.

"As a young girl," she continued, "I was raised in a very controlled and competitive environment. We had to compete to prove ourselves worthy to continue our education and progression. Each week, our instructors would pit us against each other in hand-to-hand combat. I grew tired of the constant challenges from my male peers.

"One day, I decided I was not going to hold back. I would unleash the full fury of my rage on whoever was chosen as my opponent that day. The boy chosen stepped into the arena with a smug expression. He seemed pleased to know that I was his opponent. I'm sure that since I was a young woman, he felt confident in his victory.

"When the signal was given to begin, I held back,

feigning concern and wariness, which drew him in. As soon as he was within range, I snapped. I landed a roundhouse kick to the side of his head. As he lay semi-conscious on the floor, I attacked and unleashed my fury. The instructors had to pull me off him, or I would have killed him right there in the arena in front of all my peers.

"But his humiliation was not complete. Because he begged for mercy when I defeated him so completely and so quickly, he was dismissed from the program, and I was given the right to dispatch him with my choice of weapons. I chose the bullwhip. My instructor, also a female, helped me with the preparations.

"The instructor told the boy to take off his shirt, then bound his hands with rope, threw the rope over a rafter, and pulled him up so his toes barely touched the ground. She bound his ankles very tightly and then secured them to the ground so that the boy could not move or twist. His body was beautiful and seeing him bound like that was one of the most satisfying things I had ever witnessed. I felt this overwhelming need to hurt him. My instructor took time to guide me on the proper use of a bullwhip. I was always very athletic and a quick study.

"At that age, I was already the height I am now, and I was stronger and faster than almost all of the boys in Colonia Dignidad where I was raised and trained. Pretty soon, as the boy struggled and dangled in anticipation, I mastered the use of this beautiful weapon. All I could think of was how badly I wanted to torture this boy who thought he would humiliate me in front of the others.

"My instructor told me to get on with it. It did not take me long to get into a perfect rhythm lashing the boy on his back. He began developing red welts, and he was screaming. His screams motivated me even more. It was as though someone had unleashed a monster in me.

"Finally, one lash of my whip broke his skin and blood flowed. I felt an overwhelming feeling of power. I felt I had finally gotten in touch with my true self and my true destiny, to rule others and make the world do my bidding.

"From that moment on, I've had a fondness for the bullwhip and its effects on men. You, Luca, are my next lucky victim."

The *Führerin* paced and stalked her victim as she told her story. Luca felt himself becoming more and more mesmerized by her energy, but he knew that if he submitted to this truly evil woman, he would be done for. If this woman gets hold of the powerful secret that Ian and Angelina have, he thought, the world is doomed. She will be as ruthless a dictator as the world has ever seen, and the world will not be able to resist bowing down to her.

At that moment, she stopped in front of him with her back to him, standing completely still, allowing him to drink in her beauty and power, and think about what she was about to do to him.

"Very well, then," she said, "enough pleasantries. Let the torture begin."

She was true to her word, lashing out with her whip again and again. The *Führerin* seemed tireless. The longer it went on, the more intense she became. She truly did seem to get incredible pleasure out of inflicting pain, and the more she enjoyed it, the more aggressive she became. There was a point when Luca realized she was never going to stop. So, after two hours of intense interrogation and torture, Luca finally cracked.

"Yes, yes," moaned Luca, "I will tell you where they were taken. Just stop the torture and I will tell you."

"No!" shouted Bruno, now fully awake and being subjected to the violent ministrations of Axel and the

Führerin. "You can't do it, Luca, you know how important their safety is. Don't sell out now! Stay strong."

Luca's back was once again sliced open with the expert strike of the *Führerin's* bullwhip. His body jerked in pain. She smiled her serpent's smile at the sight of the blood flowing down his now-shredded back.

"Tell me where you sent them, Luca, and your pain will end. Although I may keep your friend over there around for a while for future entertainment."

Luca broke down and began to talk. "They have been sent to a facility outside of New York, in the Catskill Mountains. That's all I know."

"Well, then," sneered the *Führerin*, "you have told me enough. There is only one facility that I know of in that location which would have the equipment and capacity to enable their research. I am very familiar with it and its owner. Very familiar. I am interested to know how you arranged for them to go to that particular location. There are not many people who are even aware of its existence."

Once again, the bullwhip cracked, and another gash was sliced into Luca's already scourged back.

"I sent them with a man I worked for," groaned Luca. "I had just completed an assignment for him and knew he had not yet left for New York. I contacted him and asked for his help. After I told him about the kids, he agreed. We bribed the flight controller to file a false flight plan to Argentina and then got the kids on the plane."

The *Führerin* backed away from Luca and stood next to Axel. She said to him, "It looks as if we have uncovered a serious betrayal. Someone has broken ranks. Finish with these two, and when you've had your fun, throw them both in the underground storage locker. After we've secured the kids, we can use these two for leverage with them. They seem to have become very fond of one another. Then, meet me back at the hotel. We have plans to make. No one betrays the *Führerin* and lives."

CHAPTER EIGHTEEN

Upstate New York, Light Wave Resources

The Citation X landed at a private airstrip outside of Albany, New York. As the jet rolled to a halt, two identical vehicles pulled up to the plane. Ian, Angelina, and Mario Ducati climbed into the closest one. Ian looked into the other vehicle next to them and saw that, besides the driver, there were three passengers already in it, an older man, a young man, and a young woman.

Mario glanced at Ian. "Those are our body doubles. They will head north while we head south. Can't be too careful. We don't know who is watching. Right, Carl?" he addressed the driver of their vehicle.

"Absolutely right, Mr. Ducati," replied the driver. "I'm Carl Brush. I'll be your shadow while you are with us. Bruno would be very unhappy if I let anything happen to you two." Then, he put the car in gear and headed south toward the Light Wave Resources research facility.

On the way to the facility, Mario filled them in on what to expect. "As I told you, I have the most up-to-date private research facilities in the world, and we are one of the most secure places in the country. Because we work on the most highly sensitive projects, security and secrecy are paramount. When we arrive, you will each have your retinas, fingerprints, and faces scanned for biometric analysis and security clearance. There's no need to carry ID cards, because our entire facility is monitored by biometric scanners twenty-four hours a day.

"Everywhere you go in the facility, you will be tracked and constantly authorized. If a door does not open for you, that means you do not have the proper clearance. That shouldn't happen often, unless you try to enter a project area unrelated to your work. Carl will accompany you everywhere. He knows everything about the facility and will be your shepherd and protector. Give him your complete trust and allow him to help you. Any questions?"

"Yes," said Ian. "I'll need access to information and equipment specific to the device I intend to produce. How can I be sure you have what I need?"

"Believe me, son," said Mario, "if it exists and is relevant to scientific research, we either have it or can manufacture it in very short order. We have multiple state-of-the-art 3D printers, which can make objects the size of a house. That's what we do every day. If you have a list of what you need, you can give it to me now or after we arrive, and it will all be ready and waiting for you tomorrow."

"Have you heard from Bruno?" Angelina asked. "I'm worried about him and wanted to thank him."

"I left a message for him during our flight," said Mario. "I told him that if he can avoid the Swiss police long enough to join us, I'd send a plane for him." He turned to look out the window.

Although Mario hadn't sounded worried, Ian sensed there was more that he wasn't telling them. Before he had a chance to question him further, however, they arrived at their destination.

The Light Wave facility gates opened onto a bucolic scene. As they proceeded up the long drive, Ian observed what appeared to be a working dairy farm with pastures, cows, and a few enormous modern barns.

"I assume you're not going to make us milk the cows as repayment for your generosity, are you, Mario?" Ian joked.

Mario chuckled. "Be patient, and you'll understand."

They rounded a bend in the dirt road and entered the largest barn. When the bay doors closed behind them, they exited the vehicle and walked through a set of metal sliding doors into a well-lit open room. The doors closed, and the room started to slowly descend.

The descent continued for two minutes, then the doors opened, revealing a vast underground facility.

"Welcome to Light Wave Resources!" announced Mario, obviously proud and enjoying the surprised look on his guests' faces.

"So, everything here is underground?" inquired Angelina. "I guess that makes sense from a security and secrecy standpoint. Very cool. I already feel much safer."

"Excellent," said Mario, "that's the intent. You can work here in complete safety and with complete support. Let me show you to your living quarters."

He brought them to a wing of the underground facility that was fitted out like a luxury hotel, and quite different than the rest of what they had seen passing through. The rest of the facility was scientific, sterile, and obviously made for research. This wing, however, was homey, warm, and inviting.

He showed them to their rooms and suggested that they relax for an hour or so before dinner. He informed them that they would be dining with him in the chairman's dining room and that dress was obviously casual, given that they had a limited wardrobe with them.

When he was finished with the pleasantries, Ian asked, "I would like to make a call to let my parents and Dr. Mills know where I am and that I am safe. What's the security protocol for that?"

"Every call to and from this facility is monitored and recorded and is run through a voice recognition and analysis program," said Mario. "We can instantly recognize the voice of the internal person receiving or making the call, and in short order, also evaluate the level of stress in the voices on the line. It's a sort of lie detector system, so we can review and evaluate the veracity of the information being exchanged. I'll receive a call after you hang up from a technician with the results of the data. If all is well, then it's over. If they detect any issues, I will be notified, and security protocols kick in based on the findings. As you can imagine, we need to be extremely cautious with the communications coming in or going out of here."

"That's fine," said Ian. "I'm just going to leave a couple of voicemail messages. I don't know where they are or what phone they might be using. Is that all right?"

"It is, but I caution you," responded Mario, "do not leave any detailed information. Just tell them to call you back at the number on the phone in your room. We'll be monitoring that call. Do not tell them where you are. If they call you back, and you decide that you want them here, find out where they are. My men that will pick them up and bring them. Understood?"

"Got it," said Ian.

"Good," Mario replied. "Dinner in one hour."

Ian went to his room, and Angelina went to hers. Ian

unpacked his small assortment of belongings. His room was appointed with all the toiletries they would need, along with a well-stocked, full-sized refrigerator and microwave. It had a separate bedroom area and a spacious living room area.

The lack of actual windows was disguised by sheer curtains in front of false windows with holographic displays behind them showing images of the countryside above, synchronized to the correct time of day.

Ian went over to the desk and thought about what he was going to say before he picked up the phone. He definitely wanted Dr. Mills and his parents here, but he was afraid of what he might hear when he spoke with them.

The last he had heard was that Peter had been subjected to the same torture as the professor, the FBI was holding Dr. Mills and his mom in a safe house, and that his dad was recovering well from the shooting. He hoped that things had improved since then, but he had to be prepared if they had not. He took a deep breath and dialed the number for Dr. Mills's office, thinking that would be the safest place to leave a message.

The phone rang, and he listened to the message, then spoke at the beep. "Dr. Mills, this is Ian. I need you to call me back at this number as soon as possible." Then, he hung up.

He dialed the number for Dr. Mills's home. Same process and same message. Finally, he dialed the number that Dr. Mills had used the last time they spoke. Angelina had remembered it, written it down, and had given it to Ian. He dialed the number. It rang and Dr. Mills answered.

"Hello, this is Dr. Mills," the man said rather formally.

"Dr. Mills!" Ian said excitedly, glad to hear his voice.

"It's Ian, what's with the formality? Have you forgotten the sound of my voice already?"

Dr. Mills replied, "No, I've just been through a lot recently. Where are you? Are you safe?"

Ian responded, "I can't tell you that, but if you tell me where you are, I can have someone meet you and bring you to me. Are you with my parents?"

"I'm with your mother. Your father is going to be okay, but he's still in the hospital, as are Peter and the professor," Dr. Mills reported. "Just tell us where you are, and we will come there. No need to have someone come and get us. We're anxious to see you."

"I can't do that, Dr. Mills," replied Ian. "There are rules where I am. Just tell me your location, and we can be together soon."

There was a slight delay, and then Dr. Mills said, "Okay, we are at the Newburgh Comfort Inn off the New York Thruway in Newburgh, room 333. Call us back before our ride arrives, so we can be ready. Okay?"

"You got it, Dr. Mills. Can't wait to see you both and tell you all about this. Bye!" said Ian, and he hung up.

He was so charged up he pumped his fist in the air. "Yes!" he shouted.

Angelina appeared in the open door to his room. "What going on?" she asked.

"I just hung up with Dr. Mills," he said. "They're going to come here, and they're only about an hour and a half away! I can't wait for you to meet them. We have so much to tell them, and all of it good."

Then the phone in the room rang. Ian picked up. It was Mario. "Ian, we have a problem."

Dr. Mills hung up the phone and turned to look at Carol. She was frightened, with good cause. The FBI agent standing next to her holding his gun to her head made sure of it.

"I did what you wanted," Dr. Mills said to Agent Armstrong, who stood next to him with his gun aimed at him. "Put the guns away and have a little respect for American citizens."

Agent Armstrong laughed. "Respect? Is that what you showed me and my partner when you drugged us and made us use valuable government resources to track you down? That's funny. I told you this was a matter of national security. If you really cared anything at all about your American citizenship, you would have helped us. Instead, all you did was hinder our investigation. From now on, you are going to be treated like hostiles. I think you're really going to like Guantanamo Bay. The weather is lovely this time of year."

"What's the problem, Mario?" Ian asked, shooting a worried look at Angelina.

"The voice analysis came back from your call to Dr. Mills, and it's bad. He's either lying to you, or he was under some intense duress," said Mario.

"He said that he'd been dealing with a lot recently, and I know that he is or was in FBI custody. Would that account for it?" asked Ian.

"No," responded Mario, "what we picked up was fear and anger. Ian, I think they're in trouble."

"So, what do we do?" asked Ian.

Mario replied, "We could do nothing, stay safe here, and let them keep their trouble to themselves. Or we could go and get them, armed for bear. That could cause more issues than we want to deal with and could expose your work here. Remember, I have done work for a number of agencies of the government, and although it is all part of the black ops budget, someone could know something. I'll let you make the call on this situation. What do you want us to do?"

"I want you to go get them!" shouted Ian without hesitation. "Go get them and bring them here. That's what I want!"

"Okay," said Mario, "I'll send my best team. Just make sure you understand that could mean you'll have a lot less time and possibly a lot more trouble. I have the recording and know where they are. I'll tell you when to place the return call with the time of the pickup. Obviously, when you call, we'll already be there, ready to go. Surprise will be our friend. We have no idea how many people we may be dealing with, or how armed they might be. This could get ugly, so prepare yourself, understood?"

Ian replied, "Understood," then hung up and slumped into the desk chair. He looked up at Angelina's worried face. "This is just too hard."

She stepped over to Ian and put her arms around him. "Just stay strong and focus on your work. Let Mario deal with this. He's proven to be a good friend and extremely competent so far. Trust him and be patient. They'll be here soon." Then, she kissed the top of his head and sat on his lap. "I'm going to take a shower, and you definitely need to do the same," she said wrinkling up her nose. "Then, we'll have a nice dinner and feel human again. Mario will fill us in on the plan and keep us informed. Let's not worry before there is anything to worry about, okay?"

"Okay," said Ian, and kissed her. "Thanks. I'm just so

afraid for them."

"I know, and I think that's great," she said. "Not a selfish or self-centered bone in your body. You know what? I'm starting to like you, Ian Petrie!"

Just then, there was a knock on the door.

"You two okay in there?" Carl's muffled voice asked. "It got quiet."

"We're fine," Ian replied. "Can't two kids be quiet for two minutes without everyone thinking we're dying or something?"

"Just doing my job," said Carl.

They both laughed and Angelina gave Ian another kiss before heading to her room for a shower.

The satellite phone rang. Dr. Mills answered very formally and hit the speaker button. "It's Ian, Dr. Mills. Stop with the formalities already. I've been told that your ride will be there in thirty minutes. It will be a black Lincoln Town Car and the driver's name is Fred. Speak up when you talk with him, because he's old and can't hear so well. Also, put your own bags in the car, because he has a bad back. See you when you get here! Tell Mom I love her!"

Dr. Mills hung up and spoke to Agent Armstrong. "Are you going to kill Fred when he gets here? It's what you do, right? All in the name of national security, right?"

The FBI agent smirked. "Of course, we won't kill him; at least not right away. We need him to tell us where he came from. After that, we will see."

Thirty minutes later, Agent Armstrong stood and peeked through the draperies at the window. After a moment, he nodded and stepped away from the window, looking satisfied.

"Okay, I just saw a black Town Car drive up and park in front of the room. The driver fits the description Ian gave. Wait until he knocks on the door and enters to get your bags. Then, close the door behind him. Got it?" he said looking at Dr. Mills.

When Dr. Mills nodded, Armstrong turned to his partner. "Let's put the guns away. We don't want to scare him off. We need him in one piece." Then, he went back to the window and pulled aside the curtain to observe the elderly, frail-looking driver.

Fred got out of the car, stretched, and held his back as if in pain. He walked slowly to the door and put on his glasses to read the room number.

Then, he knocked softly and called, "Mrs. Petrie! Dr. Mills! Your ride is here!"

Agent Armstrong nodded to Dr. Mills and motioned for him to open the door. When he did, all hell broke loose. Fred charged into the room and tackled Agent Armstrong. Four heavily armed and armored security agents followed him. They quickly subdued Armstrong and his partner and hustled Dr. Mills and Carol out of the room to a van parked at the back of the motel.

"Who are you?" shouted Dr. Mills.

"Ian sent us," the security agent replied as he slammed the door shut and climbed into the back.

"What are you going to do with those FBI agents?" Carol asked.

"Don't worry about that, Mrs. Petrie, just know that they won't be bothering you anymore. What's more, they will not remember any of this tomorrow. They'll be found in an embarrassing state of undress and in a compromising position with some very incriminating pictures. They'll not even want to remember any of this.

All is well!" finished the security agent with a smile.

Dr. Mills put his arm around Carol and said, "Just think about seeing Ian in a little while and forget all of this happened. We have a reunion to look forward to."

Mario hung up the phone and turned to Ian and Angelina. "Mission accomplished!" he said. "One hundred percent success, and they are on their way. Now, lift your glasses for a toast. Tomorrow is the first day of a new dawn for humanity. It will be remembered forever!"

They raised their glasses and drank.

"No pressure on me, I guess," Ian said, laughing.

As they finished their dinner, they discussed the plan for tomorrow. Up at dawn, breakfast, and then the work would really begin. Ian described the equipment he would need, and Mario described the workspace.

This is going to be fun, Ian thought. He couldn't wait to begin.

CHAPTER NINETEEN

Later that evening, Ian received a call in his room that his mom and Dr. Mills had arrived. He ran to the elevator area to meet them. Spotting his mom first, he grabbed her in a huge bear hug, lifting her off her feet.

"Mom!" he exclaimed. "It's so good to see you! I've been so worried about you and Dad. Are you okay?"

His mom held on for a while longer, took a deep breath, and said, "Much better, now that I see you are well. Talk about worry! Telling us you were going to Argentina to tell the Nazis everything! You scared us half to death!"

"I know," Ian replied sheepishly. "I really didn't have another choice. We had to disappear, and if I told the FBI where I was, they would've ruined everything. I had to throw them off my trail."

"Well, let's not have any more of that!" commanded his mother. "Have you had any success with all of this? Was it all worth it?"

"Definitely, it's incredible! Let's get you settled in, and I'll fill you in on what I've come to understand." He took his mom's arm and led her over to Angelina, who'd just arrived.

"Mom, this is Angelina Novak. She's a genius and also Nikola Tesla's great-grandniece. Without her help and brainpower, none of this would've happened."

His mom started to shake Angelina's hand, then chuckled and said, "Oh, come here, and give me a hug."

When they finished their introductory hug, Ian took Angelina over to Dr. Mills, who was still speaking with Mario. At a break in their conversation, he introduced her to Dr. Mills.

"Come!" said Mario to the group. "Let's head to the library for some after dinner drinks. We can catch up and discuss the next few days. There will be a fresh change of clothes waiting for you in your rooms, and anything else you need will be provided upon your request. Consider this your home for the foreseeable future."

As they followed Mario to the library, Dr. Mills put his arm around Ian and slowed his pace a bit, so they could talk without the others hearing. "So, Ian, what do you know about Mario? Why is he being so generous and helpful?"

"He's a friend of a friend of Angelina's," Ian replied. "He helped us escape from the Nazis, and so far, has been very helpful and has given us some great advice. He has experience in working on top secret projects and knows all about secrecy and security. I believe he'll be a great asset in helping us complete our work in peace. Look at this place! He has everything I need to create a working device from the Einstein and Tesla information."

"Okay," said Dr. Mills, "but it's just going to take me a while to get as comfortable as you. After what your mom and I have been through, I'm just a little wary. Just don't tell him or anyone else too much, and if he starts prying, let me know. Powerful men like Mario don't usually do anything out of the goodness of their hearts.

He didn't create all of this for charity. So, be careful."

"You got it, doc!" said Ian as he slapped him on the back and hustled him along to the library.

The library was a beautifully furnished room with a huge fireplace. Antique furniture was artfully placed around the roaring fire. The walls were filled with an incredible collection of literary works, maps, and even some ancient-looking scrolls.

Ian and Angelina took a seat on the plush couch, and Ian's mother chose a comfortable armchair next to the fire. While Mario poured them all glasses of his best cognac, Dr. Mills explored the room. After a few moments, he chose a seat and accepted his drink from Mario.

"You have a very eclectic collection of books here, Mr. Ducati," he observed. I see first editions by many famous authors from the eighteenth through the twentieth centuries, rare volumes on the history of Rome, and a variety of scientific books on physics, neurology, robotics, and artificial intelligence. I would love to spend some time examining it all while I'm here, if you would allow me that privilege."

"Why certainly, Dr. Mills!" responded Mario. "I am pleased to have a guest who appreciates literature. This is but a small sample of my total collection, but it contains many of my favorite acquisitions."

"I notice you have a large section devoted to World War II," said Dr. Mills. "Is that of special interest to you?"

Mario put his drink down and replied, "Absolutely. The whole dynamic of the war was fascinating. It was the last time the whole world was actually on the brink of disaster. I believe that we can learn a lot about human nature and the way small incidents can cause vast, unforeseen repercussions. I feel that we must learn from the past.

"That's one of the reasons I am so grateful for the opportunity to help Ian with his current challenge. I've observed that the most impactful discoveries of science have had both negative and positive implications. As a student of history, I believe that I've come to understand how to control these advances in science so as to limit the negative or destructive applications, while maximizing the positive and beneficial aspects for all mankind.

"In fact, Ian, Angelina, and I have discussed this already, and I think they can attest to the soundness of my advice. Isn't that so, Ian?" he asked as he looked over at Ian.

Ian looked a little surprised that all eyes were now on him. He'd been only partially listening to the conversation between Dr. Mills and Mario. In fact, he'd been significantly distracted by Angelina sitting so close to him on the couch.

"Y-yes," he stammered, "I would say that's true. Mario has pointed out that the best way for us to retain control over our discovery is to complete a working version, which will demonstrate to the world the power of the concept, while illustrating clearly the need for worldwide cooperation and control. He likened it to the way the world has been able to regulate and limit the proliferation of nuclear weapons. After that, we can continue to develop the beneficial aspects and limit or completely control any negative outcomes. Have I restated it correctly, Mario?" finished Ian.

"Yes, Ian, in a nutshell," Mario said.

Dr. Mills took a sip of his cognac, before replying. "Sounds elegantly simple, but I fear that the devil is in the details. It may be that Ian needs to work quickly to create a working prototype of whatever the most beneficial aspect of his discovery is, but while he is doing that, we all need to put our heads together to decide what worldwide body or organization can be trusted to do the right thing with the information. In my opinion, it may be a scientific organization, not one connected with any government of any sort. Can we all agree on that?"

Mario smiled. "Certainly. In fact, I have some ideas about that myself! We can discuss that all over the next few days. Right now, let's drink a toast to Ian and Angelina, and to the dawning of a new age for mankind!"

Everyone but Dr. Mills lifted their glasses and drank; Ian could see he was going to need more convincing.

As they sat around the roaring fire, Ian gave them an overview of the larger concepts of his discovery. He kept the details and the formulas between himself and Angelina. He spoke to the benefits of the discovery and painted a beautiful picture of what it could mean for humanity. By the time he was finished, almost everyone looked convinced that not only could he do it, but that it must be done immediately. Dr. Mills, however, still looked unsure.

"Ian, I hear you," he said quietly, "and I'm extremely proud of everything you've accomplished, but I still have one burning question which I don't believe you've answered sufficiently."

Ian, looked surprised and a little hurt. "What's the question, Dr. Mills?"

"If Einstein and Tesla felt that this information was too dangerous to reveal to the world," Dr. Mills responded, "why is it that you believe it's safe to do so now? What has changed since 1955 to make you think that the world is ready? From my perspective, the world is a much more dangerous place now than in 1955. I think we should all take a step back and think about this before we proceed."

Mario, looking amused, replied to Dr. Mills's question. "It is as I said, Dr. Mills, having learned from the past, we can avoid the pitfalls. I believe that with the rise of globalized economies, increased international cooperation and oversight, and the lessons learned from World War II and the Cold War, the world now has the collective will and ability to utilize this incredible gift in the right way. Where is your trust in your fellow man, Dr. Mills? Why such skepticism?"

Dr. Mills finished his drink, then stood from his chair and faced Mario. "I suppose the FBI has taught me a few things recently that has soured my opinion of my fellow man. I've seen a side of things that I hadn't seen before." He hesitated. "Or maybe I was choosing not to see. Either way, I would advise caution and patience. Now, if you will all excuse me, I am very tired and would like to retire to my room."

"Certainly," said Mario. "Your room is three doors down on the left. Breakfast will be served in the dining hall at 7 a.m. Good night, Dr. Mills."

As he left the rest of the group chatting happily in the library, Dr. Mills could not shake the feeling that they were all making a huge mistake. He hoped it was just the experiences of the past few days giving him that cold, sick feeling in the pit of his stomach. Still, this was all moving way too fast. He needed some time alone to sort through it, but mostly, he needed time alone with Ian away from Mario. They had a lot to discuss.

For Ian, the morning brought with it the feeling of Christmas. Today was the day he would unwrap all the presents that the last few weeks had laid under his tree.

He hadn't slept much last night, with everything running through his head; visions of the big bang and its reverberations of time, space, light, and matter. He felt as though he was able to witness thirteen billion years of creation in one night.

Ian remembered being in his bedroom as a child. He could recall seeing the picture of Einstein's desk. He remembered an old photograph of Einstein with a goofy smile, sticking his tongue out like a kid. He wondered what was so funny, and what this funny-looking man was thinking.

Although he didn't sleep, Ian woke full of energy and had so many thoughts running through his head, it almost hurt. He felt like the only way he could get it all out and make complete sense of it was to get in the lab and get to work. Today, he hoped, was the day that he would take his place alongside the greatest minds of science. It was the first day of a new tomorrow, and he couldn't wait to get started.

He shot out of bed and dressed quickly, not even bothering to shower. Before he headed for the door, he heard a knock. He opened the door and found Dr. Mills standing there, holding two mugs of coffee, and looking tired and worn.

"Ian, we need to talk," was all he said as he handed him a mug, then walked past him into the room.

"What's wrong, Dr. Rob?" Ian asked as he closed the door.

Dr. Mills put his coffee on a table, then went to the door and locked it. He took a deep breath, then took a seat at the desk. Ian sat on the bed facing him.

"Ian, I have been up all night thinking about this," Dr. Mills whispered. "This is all too 'convenient' and I don't like any of it. We need to figure out how to get out of here and find a place where no one can find us."

Ian looked at his mentor as if he'd lost his mind.

"'Too convenient?' What do you mean? This is the greatest thing that has happened to us in like… *ever*! Not only do I finally have all the answers, but I have a place with all the equipment and resources I need to create maybe the single greatest device the world has ever seen! And we are safe and protected. What could be bad about any of that? I don't understand."

"First of all, please, keep your voice down," Dr. Mills replied. "We have no idea what kind of listening devices Mario has in these rooms. Second, I have you and your mother to think about, not to mention your father, Peter, and the professor. I don't believe they would do it, but the FBI has actually threatened to do something to your father if we don't turn ourselves in."

Ian suddenly had a sick feeling in his stomach, which quickly turned into anger.

"We really know nothing about Mario Ducati," Dr. Mills pointed out. "I believe it's way too early to trust him completely and give him access to all you know. From what I've gathered, he has connections with governments and organizations all around the globe. We don't know whether he's a good guy or a bad guy. Anyone who works for everyone is, at best, amoral.

"As I said, a guy like Mario doesn't usually do anything out of the goodness of his heart. He wants something, and I think we can both guess what that may be. Maybe I am wrong about him, but I think we need to go very slowly and test the waters. Spend a few days gathering and testing the equipment you'll use and setting yourself up in the lab. Meanwhile, I'll evaluate his willingness to let us have our freedom if we ask for it. I'll do some research on him and his intentions.

"I suggest that when you meet with him this morning, insist that the only two people allowed in the lab with you will be Angelina and me. See how he reacts. Also, insist on having no monitoring or recording devices of any sort in the lab. My guess is that he won't agree, or if he does, he won't be happy about it.

"Above all else, do *not* tell him or any of his people what you're creating. That needs to stay between you, me, Angelina, and your mom. Understood?"

"What I understand, Dr. Rob, is that you are paranoid," whispered Ian loudly. "The man saved our lives. He has been nothing but accommodating, and he even rescued you and my mom. I think that you've spent too many years analyzing other people's brains, when you should have been examining your own. Don't ruin this for me. Let me do this my own way and just support me. Okay? Can you do that?"

Dr. Mills looked Ian in the eye and shook his head. "No, I can't. I'm sorry. There's way too much at stake. Trust me, Ian. You've known me most of your life, and in all that time, have I ever once given you bad advice or ever given you any indication that I had anything but your best interests at heart? Promise me you'll go slowly at first and insist on the precautions I suggested. If you do that, I promise that as soon as I am comfortable, I will be all in. One hundred percent. Can you do that? For me?"

In that moment, Ian once again saw the man who had been there for him during his toughest times, who helped him to maximize his potential and believed in him when everyone else just saw a damaged and struggling young boy. He remembered the encouragement. He remembered the effort. He remembered the love and care that Dr. Mills had poured into his life, and he felt ashamed.

"I can do that," Ian whispered. "For you." He reached across and hugged his mentor. "Just get comfortable quickly, please, because this is going to go fast. I already have it all worked out in my head, and if I have to wait too long, my head may explode!"

"You got it, Ian," replied Dr. Mills. "Now, let's head down there and see what the day holds for us."

They left the room and headed to the dining hall. Angelina and Ian's mother were at a table in deep conversation. They approached the pair, and Dr. Mills asked, "May we join you two lovely ladies, or are you waiting for your dates?"

Ian's mom responded, "I think we've been stood up, so you two will have to do."

As they took their seats, Ian asked, "So, what have you two been talking about?"

The ladies looked at each other and smiled.

"Your mom has just been filling me in on your checkered past," Angelina offered. "You are much more interesting than I imagined."

"Don't believe anything she tells you," Ian replied with a chuckle. "She only knows the safe stuff. I don't tell her any of the really bad stuff."

They were laughing as Mario approached the group. "I see everyone is in a good mood this morning, and well you should be! This is a *big* day! Is everyone ready to go to work?"

"Absolutely!" Ian exclaimed. "Can't wait to get started. What's the plan?"

"First, I'll take you and Angelina to the lab you'll be working in. Dr. Mills and your mom are free to spend the day doing whatever they like. I'll introduce you to your staff of researchers and technicians, and you can fill them in on your objectives and timeline. After that, you will begin to create a new tomorrow for the world! How does that sound?" Mario asked.

"Most of that sounds great," said Ian, "but I have a few requests to make before I begin. Can I talk to you in private?"

"Certainly," said Mario looking a little crestfallen and puzzled. "Can we talk as we walk to the lab?"

"Sure," replied Ian. "Angelina, come on, you need to hear this, too." Then, he leaned down and kissed his mom. "Have fun today!" he said as he, Angelina, and Mario headed off to the lab.

Carol looked at Dr. Mills. "Okay, so now what? What is there to do in this place?"

Dr. Mills leaned in close to her and whispered, "First, we need to go to the library and talk. After that, we can decide on the agenda for the rest of the week."

"Okay," replied Carol quietly, "but I have to tell you that doesn't sound like a lot of fun."

Dr. Mills looked at her with a serious expression. "Fun is not high on my agenda right now. Come on, let's get started." They got up from the table and headed to the library.

"So, what's on your mind, Ian?" Mario asked as they walked down the long, sterile hallway toward the research section of the facility.

"I have a few small requests to make regarding the work environment," Ian responded, glancing quickly at Angelina for support. "First of all, I'll gladly meet with the staff, but I do not want them in the lab while I am working. Most of the time, I want only me and Angelina in the lab. Occasionally, I will need Dr. Mills's assistance, but beyond that, Angelina and I are perfectly capable of doing all the work ourselves. Second, I do not want any of what I do in the lab monitored or recorded in any way. Do you have an issue with any of that?"

Mario abruptly stopped walking and stared at Ian. "Yes, I have a problem with that," he said curtly. "You are inexperienced with the workings of this billion-dollar facility, and it's critical that you have seasoned technicians guiding you on the workings of the instruments and systems. I don't want you blowing this place up on the first day.

"Additionally, the work you're doing needs to be recorded for posterity. If you're successful in your endeavors, what you do from this point on will be historic. Not only that, we need, I mean *you* need, to be able to replicate it. I've been involved with many projects, and you'd be surprised how difficult it can be to replicate the steps of even a very simple procedure. Meticulous recording of every step in the process is a basic rule of scientific research. I cannot agree to forego it."

Angelina spoke up. "Mario, I have an eidetic memory. I remember everything I see, hear, and read in minute detail. I am the recording device. You have no need for another. Problem solved."

Mario looked taken aback. "That will need to be proven to me, Angelina. I will allow this first day to go unmonitored or recorded, and if at the end of the day, you can repeat it exactly to me step by step and answer all my questions, then I will consider it going forward. But I cannot let you work unattended in the lab."

"Then, we have no deal," stated Ian firmly. "Angelina, let's go get our things, and tell Dr. Mills and Mom that we'll be leaving shortly."

He stuck out his hand to shake Mario's, saying, "Thanks so much for the hospitality, Mario, you really have been a friend. Send me the bill for the ride from Bern, and I'll have my accountant reimburse you for the expense."

Then, he and Angelina turned to head back the way they had come. As they walked away, Angelina shot him a look like she thought he had lost his mind.

"Just keep walking," he whispered to her, "and don't look back."

"Just a minute, young man!" shouted Mario. "Who said we had any *deal*?" Ian and Angelina kept walking as Mario continued. "What we have here is an *offer*, not a deal. An offer which gives you free access to the most sophisticated technology and research facility on the planet and could make you the richest man in history! All I'm asking in return is to follow some simple rules. Are you willing to walk away from such a generous offer because of your own immaturity and overconfidence?"

Ian stopped walking, turned around, and walked back to face Mario. "I am. Unless you let me do this my way, then I will have to regretfully decline your 'offer' and find another benefactor, or I'll just do it myself. I created the PhotoEx app in my *bedroom* after school, in five weeks. I added an X-ray component in two weeks in my spare time. I have thirty-three million dollars sitting in my bank account. Trust me when I say I can do this without your help or interference.

"My offer to you is that after I create the device I have in my head, you'll have a seat at the table to help determine the proper deployment and a piece of any profits. Are you willing to walk away from such a generous offer because of *your* own inflexibility?"

Mario and Ian stood staring at each other for what felt

like an eternity, neither one moving or saying anything. Then Mario blinked. "All right, have it your way. Make it more difficult on yourself than it needs to be. I'm sure that eventually you'll see the wisdom in my 'inflexibility'. Just make sure you don't blow this place up, or send us all to another galaxy, or back to the Stone Age. Understood?"

Ian smiled. "I agree to your offer. Now, do we have a deal?" He stuck out his hand, and Mario shook it.

"Deal," Mario said with a slight chuckle. "Now can we get this thing moving?"

"Absolutely," said Ian. "Let's go!"

Dr. Mills and Carol sat across from each other in front of the softly burning fire in the library. They were leaning forward, talking in hushed tones.

"Do you really think that we have reason to be suspicious of Mario's intentions?" asked Carol.

"I believe that we need to be wary of anyone who seems to be giving Ian something for nothing," replied Dr. Mills. "A man of his ilk may seem affable and generous, but you don't get to his level of success in a dangerous business like weapons development and secret research without having some larceny in your heart. I just don't think we've seen the real Mario Ducati yet.

"We need to keep observing, and testing the waters, and planning for the worst. If I'm wrong, then all will be well, and we can ask the church to canonize him after this is over. Until then, I say we plan for trouble.

"The first thing I want you to do is ask Mario if we can put a call in to Bellevue to get an update on Roger, the professor, and Peter. Let's see how flexible he is about that. It's a reasonable request, since you're Roger's wife, and they are all my patients. After that, we'll test his willingness to let us leave for a short while for an outing or a shopping trip or something. My guess is that there is no way he wants us to leave. In the meantime, I'll be gathering research on him, his background, and connections. Beyond that, keep your eyes and ears open and don't say anything that you don't want recorded. I believe this whole place may be full of listening devices. Agreed?"

"You make it sound like we're prisoners here," said Carol. "I really want to believe that Mario just wants what is best for Ian and wants to use his experience and resources to help him succeed. But I trust your instincts and agree that caution is the best approach. After lunch, I'll ask him to let me call Roger. Will that work?"

"Perfect," said Dr. Mills, "but don't let any doubt or worry seep into your voice. Confidence and positivity are key."

"Got it," said Carol. "Confidence!"

CHAPTER TWENTY

When Ian, Angelina, and Mario arrived at the lab, they saw Carl waiting for them by the door.

"Nice to see you again, Carl," said Ian. "I thought we lost you!"

"Not a chance," Carl replied. "I always have my eyes on both of you. Can't let Bruno down, you know."

Mario unlocked the door and motioned for Ian and Angelina to enter. As they entered, the lights came on, and Ian saw a magnificent room filled with every piece of equipment he had requested the day before.

Mario spoke to Carl. "Tell the staff to join us in Laboratory Three, please."

In two minutes, five stern-looking technicians appeared in long white lab coats and joined them in the room. When they were gathered, Mario addressed them.

"This is Ian Petrie and Angelina Novak. They will be in charge of the project you'll be working on. They've requested that they be left to work in solitude. If they require your assistance, they'll leave the lab to request it. You are not to enter the room unless you are summoned by one of them. You'll stay at your cubicles outside the room and wait to be contacted.

"I understand that each of you is familiar with the workings of every device and piece of equipment in this lab, and I expect you to be ready to explain their operation if your assistance is required. Do you understand?"

The technicians nodded their understanding.

"Thank you. You are dismissed," said Mario. They left the room and closed the door behind them.

Mario turned to Ian and smiled. "Well then, Dr. Petrie, I suppose it's all up to you now. Let's see what wonders you can create from light!"

With a final nod, he left them alone in the lab.

Angelina looked at Ian and asked, "Do you know how to use any of this stuff?"

"Of course. It's all intuitive," replied Ian. "They make these instruments basically idiot-proof. Besides, I really don't need it all, anyway. I just asked for anything I *might* need. I wanted it all to look more difficult than it is. All I really need to do is expand on the concepts I used when I developed the PhotoEx app.

"After realizing what Einstein and Tesla had discovered, and examining the formulas and theories, I immediately saw that I had unknowingly incorporated a lot of the concepts into that application already. The whole photonic vibration and frequency concept was what I used to 'see' beneath the documents on Einstein's desk. I was thinking of it differently, but, in essence, it was a very similar concept."

"So, what exactly are we going to build here? What aspect of it are we going to focus on first?" asked Angelina.

Ian smiled a huge smile. "Time travel! Believe it or not, it's the simplest device to build. The energy requirements are manageable, and I believe I've identified the formula that Einstein already created for understanding the initial frequency of the light and sound that emanated from the Big Bang to then calculate the diminishing multivariable resonances throughout space-time.

"That means we are already more than halfway there. We just have to do the math to understand the frequency and resonance factors of any moment of time and place that we want to visit."

He pulled out his iPad and pulled up the formula he was referring to. As they looked at it, and Ian explained it to Angelina. She understood it right away.

"I can do this," she said. "Piece of cake." Then she noticed that there was a very long string of handwritten numbers under the formula. It almost appeared as if Einstein had tried a sample calculation using the formula. "What are those numbers?" she asked.

"Not sure," he replied. "Just use the formula to calculate the starting point, and as we go along, maybe we can figure out what they refer to."

"I can't wait to get started," Angelina said, grinning. "I love working with multivariable equations, and this is a brand new one with huge implications." With that, she dove right in.

Using his iPad, Ian began to create a schematic of the device he wanted to develop. Before they knew it, it was lunch time, but neither of them wanted to stop. They were in "the zone," working on the problems of their dreams. By evening, they had made significant progress. All without the help of a technician or any of the equipment in the room. They heard a knock at the door. It was Carl.

"Everything okay in there?" he asked. "It's dinner time, and I'm getting hungry. You two ever gonna take a break?"

Ian laughed. "Yes, Carl, we're fine. We'll be out in a

few minutes."

They packed up their things and headed toward the door. Before leaving the room, Ian reminded Angelina that she was going to have to tell Mario what they had worked on in detail. They had to figure out what she would tell him.

"I don't want him knowing that we are working on a time travel device," Ian said. "When you describe our work, just tell him we spent the day doing calculations and working on the engineering schematics. Just pre-work stuff. If he really presses you, tell him we're working on a small teleportation device. Something that will move an object from one location to another and then back. Okay? Can you do that convincingly?"

"Read my mind," she said.

Ian scrunched up his face in mock concentration, then said, "It is decidedly so."

She smiled and kissed him on the forehead. "You're really getting good at this."

They opened the door, and Carl led them down the hall to the dining room.

Ian and Angelina joined Dr. Mills and his mother for dinner. None of them talked in too much detail about the work that Angelina and Ian had done that day, for fear of being overheard. Ian said vaguely that they had begun the calculations and engineering, and they'd worked on understanding the equipment. Dr. Mills was pleased with that, and that Ian had negotiated the privacy rights that he had suggested.

They agreed that Dr. Mills would join them in the lab tomorrow so that he would be able to observe what they were working on and get up to speed. They would then have the privacy they needed to discuss the plan and what Dr. Mills had found out about Mario.

The next day, they arrived in the lab bright and early and locked the door behind them. Before Ian and Angelina dove into their work, Dr. Mills huddled them up for a conversation.

"Okay, let's talk about what you two have worked on so far, and exactly what it is you're building," he began. "Then, I'll tell you what Carol and I have been working on."

Ian spoke first. "I've decided to focus on building a time travel device. I believe that based on the work I have already done in building the PhotoEx application and the fact that Dr. Einstein has already provided us with the multivariable regression analysis formula for determining the resonance frequencies for any coordinate in space-time, it will be the easiest and most impactful device to build first. Angelina is working out all the calculations, and I've worked on the engineering schematics. We're almost there."

"Have you shared this information with Mario?" Dr. Mills asked, his expression serious.

"No," replied Angelina, "not fully. He grilled me last night after dinner about what we'd worked on yesterday because he only agreed to let us work without recording and monitoring if I could prove to him that I had an eidetic memory. So, I told him that we were only at the beginning stages, and it would take some time before we finish the calculations and engineering work. Ian suggested that we not disclose that we were building a time travel device, so I told him that we were working on a teleportation device instead. He actually seemed very pleased with that and accepted my review."

"Excellent!" said Dr. Mills. "That's perfect. Well done.

I want you two to continue to work on the time travel device and do it quickly. Don't tell Mario how you're progressing. If you're questioned again, tell him it will be at least a week before you'll finish the groundwork calculations and schematics. We want him to feel a little complacent. We don't want him to know how far along you actually are."

"Why is that, Dr. Rob?" asked Ian. "Have you found something that confirms your suspicions?"

"Not exactly, Ian," replied Dr. Mills. "Yesterday, your mom asked him if it was possible for us to contact Bellevue regarding the status of your father, the professor, and Peter. He refused. He said it was too dangerous, because the FBI is probably still looking for us, and any contact could lead them here.

"It sounds reasonable on the surface, but given all the safeguards and security he has built into this place, I would think there would be ways around it. So, I'm not really sure his response tells us anything about his willingness to let us have our freedom now or after your work is complete."

"What about his background?" asked Angelina. "Did you find anything that would cast doubt as to his intentions?"

"I have to be a little careful in my searches while using the computer system, since it's tied into the facilities network," Dr. Mills admitted, "but so far, I haven't really found much on him, which I find a little troubling. There is really no information about him prior to 1980. Anything I have found is really just fluff. Casual mentions of financial contributions to charitable organizations and educational institutions and such. He's basically invisible out there on the internet. To me, that's a red flag."

"I agree," said Ian, "but for a man involved with secret

research for various governments and who knows who else, it's not all that unexpected. Even so, I agree that we need to keep this all as close to the vest as possible. Make him earn our trust going forward."

When they'd all agreed, the kids turned back to their work, while Dr. Mills spent the first part of the day searching for listening devices. When he was satisfied their work was secure, he assisted the kids in any way he could. A genius in his own right, his understanding of the workings of the brain and the nature of consciousness were invaluable.

By the end of the day, Angelina had finished her calculations and loaded the regression analysis into Ian's iPad. Ian showed her the finished engineering and schematics for the device.

"With an appropriate power source and a few magnetic and photonic components," he told her proudly, "I can create a prototype device ready by the end of the day tomorrow."

"Does your iPad have enough computational capacity to run the program?" she asked.

"Assuming your calculations are correct, we should be able to run a live experiment tomorrow," he replied.

"Are you sure?" Angelina sounded doubtful.

"Oh yes, I'm sure," Ian said. "The Apollo 11 mission to land astronauts on the moon used computers with thirteen hundred times *less* processing power than this iPhone. This baby has more than enough power."

"That's amazing!" she replied, shaking her head in wonder.

They agreed that the following morning, they would run the analysis of the numbers that Dr. Einstein had handwritten under the formula to see if it would validate Angelina's work.

They packed up their belongings and notes and headed to the dining room. As they were walking down the hall, Ian noticed that none of the technicians were at their desks.

"Where is everyone?" he asked Carl. "Did they take the day off?"

"No," Carl responded. "About an hour ago, Mr. Ducati called them away for a meeting. He seemed very excited and nervous. Not sure what it's all about, but I have never seen him in such a state."

"What do you know about Mario, Carl?" Dr. Mills asked. "How well do you know him?"

"Not very well," Carl replied. "I just started working for him a year ago. Bruno contacted me and said that one of his frequent employers was looking to add to their internal security force and that he had recommended me. Since I lived here in upstate New York, it was a natural fit. So far, it's been great. No real issues, and he's been very fair with me. But that's as far as our relationship goes."

"Have you seen a lot of government types in here? You know, high ranking officials and such?" asked Dr. Mills.

"I can't really talk about specifics" replied Carl, "but I'm always asked to protect the people who visit, and there are a lot of them, foreigners mostly, but that's to be expected when you work for an international company. We have satellite centers in a few countries like England, Germany, South Africa, and Argentina. But I guess that they all want to visit the world headquarters here in New York."

"Very interesting," replied Dr. Mills. "Sounds like a fun job. Thanks for the perspective, Carl."

"No worries, doc," Carl said. "Just don't tell him we

had this discussion, or it could cost me my job. Sometimes it's just nice to have an actual conversation with someone, you know?"

They arrived at the dining room, and Carl went off to join the security team for dinner. Ian, Angelina, and Dr. Mills joined Carol at their regular table. For the first time, Ian felt relaxed. His mind was filled with visions of what they would accomplish over the next two days and the incredible things they might experience.

Carol cocked her head as she studied her son. "You look excited. I take it things are going well? Are you making progress?"

"Absolutely, Mom," replied Ian. "I'm hoping that soon we will all have something great to share with the world."

As they were finishing their dinner, Ian saw Mario enter the room and walk over to Carl's table. He spoke in Carl's ear and then they left the room together.

After a few minutes, Carl returned. He came directly to their table and announced, "I'm being taken off your security detail for a few days. Apparently, someone more important is arriving tomorrow, and Mario needs me pick them up and deliver them here. You're going to be assigned to another member of the security team. I'm sure after the dignitaries leave, I'll be back on your detail." Then he said goodnight and left the dining room.

"Well, that's certainly strange timing," said Dr. Mills. "I hope it has nothing to with the conversation we had with Carl on the way here."

"I hope not," replied Ian, "I was fairly confident that we weren't overheard, but who knows? With all the tech in this place, there could be listening devices everywhere. What amazes me is that given how much Mario knows about our work and the level of secrecy, why would he agree to a visit here when he could easily meet them somewhere else?"

Everyone nodded.

"Perhaps it's just a commitment he couldn't get out of, or had scheduled for a while," Carol suggested. "It must be very hard to manage schedules when you are dealing with so many high-ranking officials."

"You may be right," Dr. Mills agreed. "There's nothing we can do about it, though, so try not to worry. I suggest we focus on finishing the work as soon as possible. Meanwhile, let's retire for the night. Tomorrow's a big day!"

The following morning, Ian woke up to an urgent knocking at his door. He roused himself and answered it. It was Angelina.

"What's going on?" asked Ian.

"I've been thinking about the calculations I did…"

Ian frowned and signaled her to hush, then motioned for her to follow him. He led her into the bathroom, where he closed the door and turned on the water to both the shower and the sink.

Finally, he leaned in and whispered, "I'm sure my room is bugged, but if we whisper in here, I think the water will mask what we say."

Angelina nodded her understanding.

"I think I figured out what the numbers are that Einstein had written down below his equation!" Angelina whispered excitedly.

"Oh. Couldn't this have waited until we were in the lab, or at least until breakfast?" asked Ian, yawning.

"No," replied Angelina, "it's too cool to wait. When I

ran the regression of the frequency and resonance patterns over time, I began to understand how it all plays out. The sound and frequency patterns, or signatures of each moment of time, have a code. Basically, the bottom line is that it's kind of like a very long phone number."

"Okay," whispered Ian, "we kind of knew that already. Why is that so amazing?"

"Because," Angelina replied, "I think that the number Einstein left us was his own space-time phone number! I ran some calculations, trying to validate the equations. I ran my birth date and location, and it came out correctly. Then, I tried plugging in a random number close to it, and that worked, too. So, I plugged in the number Einstein wrote down and guess what! It came out to be April 13, 1955, in Princeton! Einstein must have been doing the same sort of validation I was, so I was able to calculate the date that he probably finished the equation. How cool is that?"

"Very cool," responded Ian, impressed. "That was only five days before he died, and possibly a day or two before he wrote the letter to Clarence and hid the documents. I think we have the space-time address for our first experimental journey! I can't think of anything more exciting than to make a visit to Einstein on my first trip back in time. I really have to think about what I'll ask him."

"*Your* first trip?" asked Angelina, sounding hurt. "Why you? Why not me? Or some lab rat? Don't you think it will be a little dangerous for you to do this? What if something goes wrong? You're the one with all the information. How will I get you back if you can't do it yourself?"

"Angelina," replied Ian, "you know it all already. We've worked together in the lab; you've seen the engineering plans and schematics. With your eidetic memory, you could recreate all of it, including the Einstein and Tesla documents you've read. You're like a walking hard drive. That's why it makes sense for me to do it. Plus, I can give firsthand analysis of the experience, unlike some lab rat. Believe me, we got this. Let me get dressed, and I'll meet you at breakfast. Don't tell anyone else about this yet. We can tell Dr. Mills when we're in the lab, and he can help us plan it all out."

After breakfast, Ian, Angelina, and Dr. Mills headed to the lab, accompanied by their new security agent. The man was huge, intimidating, and very quiet. He said nothing as he led them to the lab, unlocked the door, and shut them in.

"Well, he's certainly a lot less fun than Carl," Angelina remarked.

"Yeah, compared to him, Carl was a party animal," agreed Ian.

Dr. Mills frowned at the closed door. "He seems familiar somehow, but I can't place him." After a moment, he shook his head and shrugged. "Maybe it'll come back to me. So, what's on the agenda today?"

"Angelina validated the calculations of the space-time addresses last night," replied Ian, "so, all I have to do is put the device together and run some systems checks. Then, we should be good to go for a trial run. We could do it this evening before dinner, if it all checks out."

"Wow!" exclaimed Dr. Mills. "You guys are really working fast. I like that. How do you plan to test it?"

Ian answered, "Angelina has verified that the number that Dr. Einstein wrote below the formula was his way of validating that his formula was correct. She's determined that the number is actually Einstein's very own space-time address. I'll be traveling back in time to that address, which is the point in space-time when he verified the formula, five days before he died."

"What?!" exclaimed Dr. Mills. "You? *You* are going to be the guinea pig in this experiment? I would advise against it. We have no idea how this will work, or if it's safe! Figure out something else."

"We can't, Dr. Rob. We need firsthand observations," replied Ian. "I need to experience it. Then, if I need to make any adjustments, I'll understand how to do it. Remember, all we're doing is changing the resonance and frequency of the photons in my body. I am not really traveling anywhere. I will just 'be' somewhere else. No crash landings or traveling faster than the speed of light. It's just a gentle transition. Very calm and very peaceful.

"I'll carry a smaller mobile time travel device and a power source with me, so that I can make my own return. I feel like Einstein knew that if someone who thought like him ever figured it out, they would want to come back to meet him in the past. He must have had a reason. I feel like Einstein has something to tell me. It's as if he predicted it in his letter. Remember, he said there would be someone in the future who had 'the greater mind'. I need to speak with him in person. It has to be me. Besides, you'll have the original here as a backup. I'll go visit with Dr. Einstein and then return to the exact same point in time. It'll be like I never left."

"That sounds confusing," said Angelina. "I think you should return to a point a few minutes later, so it will be clear that the experiment worked, and that you can change the return point from the past."

"Great idea, Angelina!" said Ian. "That way, we can test another aspect of the portable device."

"No!" Dr. Mills objected. "*None* of this is a great idea! We can't chance you getting hurt. Send me. I'll do it. I can make the observations. If we lose me, it's no big deal. You two are the key. You're too valuable."

"Dr. Mills, I appreciate your concern," replied Ian, "but I have to do this, and I *want* to do this. I really want to meet Dr. Einstein and tell him all we have accomplished. I want to let him know that his efforts were not in vain. Please, you have to let me do this."

Dr. Mills was quiet for a while, then he sighed. "All right, but we need to have rules and a backup plan. Messing around with time is tricky and dangerous. We have theories about the implications of time travel, but obviously, we have no firsthand experimental data. You will go, meet with Einstein, if this is really an address for him, and then come back here to a point in time five minutes after you left. Don't tell him about when he will die. If you change that, you'll change everything. Understood?"

"Got it, doc, now can I get to work?" asked Ian.

Dr. Mills just shook his head and gestured towards the desk where Ian had been working the day before. "Have at it."

In Mario's office, a meeting was taking place with his guests, who'd arrived late the night before. Carl had met Mario's private plane at the same airport where he'd picked up Ian and Angelina. Mario was there to greet the guests when they arrived at the facility and had met with them in secret until just a few hours ago.

"Why are we changing the plan now?" asked Mario. "When we spoke a few weeks back, you said you were after a complete package. No half-finished work. They haven't even finished their calculations or designs."

His guest responded, "That was before you decided to take action on your own without informing me. Your ill-advised decisions have caused the death of several my best men. I'm not used to people I cooperate with taking matters into their own hands and keeping me in the dark. I could easily assume that you never intended to tell me about this until after you had the secrets for yourself. That would certainly have put you in a very enviable negotiating position."

"I would never do that, I assure you," replied Mario. "I just wanted to have a clear picture of what they know before bothering you. I know how you hate incomplete work."

"Yes," agreed the guest, "I am sure it was all about *my* convenience. If I thought otherwise, you would be dead at this moment. I must say, I did quite enjoy torturing your friends in Bern for the information. However, my trust in you would have been enhanced by a quick communication before you took off for New York.

"Since I now have trust issues, and after hearing from you all that they have discovered and the true impact, I've decided not to wait. I changed my mind last night, and I want them put into my custody now. We have them all together in one place, and we can't take a chance that they might escape or communicate with anyone on the outside."

"But you know this place is secure," argued Mario. "It's one of the most secure places in the world. Every niche is monitored, and no one can leave here unless I let them, not even you! Why don't you just show some patience, let them finish the work here, and then make your move?"

"After all the years that we have been together, don't you know that patience is not a quality I possess?" replied the guest. "Besides, this is now personal. They humiliated me and my team. No one gets away with that. Not even you!"

"Touché," said Mario with a nervous laugh, "and I do know you and your love of pain. It won't be any fun for you to have the device without it having cost them something other than embarrassment and humiliation. A little physical agony will add to the fun, am I right?"

The guest smiled a serpent's smile. "Exactly. Have you put my man in place?"

"Certainly," responded Mario.

"He has replaced my man, Carl, as their security agent. He is outside their door as we speak. They cannot leave without him knowing and escorting them."

"Good, then we make our move tonight, after the day's work is complete," the *Führerin* said with menace. "Then the *real* fun will begin!"

CHAPTER TWENTY-ONE

Ian had finished assembling the prototype devices. It had been as easy as he had believed it would be. Using off-the-shelf components and lithium batteries taken from the other scientific instruments in the room, he'd created two almost identical units. One was slightly larger than the other. He'd used some of the smaller batteries and components for the wearable device he would take with him.

They had run some tests on the units and were confident that everything was in working order. Of course, having two of the brightest minds on the planet helping him made it much easier, and massively increased his confidence level. Angelina had used components from the satellite phone Dr. Mills had taken from Armstrong to create a mobile "space-time dialing device" for the wearable unit so that Ian could easily calculate and input the space-time address for the point in time and location that he chose to return to. It appeared everything was set for what would, hopefully, be history's first documented and successful journey through time.

Ian attached the wearable device components to his belt and stood. "How do I look?" he asked his partners.

"Am I presentable enough for my meeting with Dr. Einstein?"

"No," said Angelina frankly, "but there's nothing we can do about it now. We'll just have to go with it as is. You should have at least shaved this morning."

"Who knew today would be the day?" said Ian.

"You did," Angelina replied, slugging him lightly on the shoulder. "You said so this morning."

"Stop fooling around, you two," said Dr. Mills a bit testily. "We need focus here. Ian, are you seriously ready to do this?"

"I am," said Ian. "Let's light this candle!"

Dr. Mills rolled the larger time travel unit over to where Ian was standing and began the initiation and calibration protocols. When the unit was ready, he announced, "Go time."

Angelina went to Ian and gave him a huge hug, then kissed him hard. "Make sure you come back in one piece, please? I'm starting to like you. And don't think about what happened to those sailors."

"What sailors?" asked Ian, confused.

"The ones from Project Rainbow," Angelina answered. "I'm sure we will have much better results than Einstein and Tesla had. After all, we've used the right concept of matter!"

"Nice, thanks for that parting image," said Ian. "Just what I needed to hear."

"Are you ready?" asked Dr. Mills.

"Ready, doc. Push the button," replied Ian, excitement and a few nerves churning in his stomach.

Dr. Mills pushed the button, and Ian was bathed in a bright, white light and a wave of variable resonant sound waves. Arcs of blue lightning surrounded him, and in an instant, he was gone from their view.

Dr. Mills and Angelina stood there looking at the empty space where Ian had stood just moments before. They'd experienced a slight tingling sensation in their own bodies and felt a slight pulling or tugging feeling when Ian departed.

They would have to figure out what that was after Ian returned. They noted the time of Ian's departure and the time of his expected return. All they could do now was wait anxiously for his return five minutes from now.

As they began to examine the device for any signs of damage from the initial experiment, the door of the lab burst open.

Einstein's home, 1955

Ian experienced a sensation of being pulled in reverse. It was almost as if he had been sucked backward off a very high cliff, but there was no real sensation of gravity. It was as if his insides were moving but his outsides were not. It seemed to last for several minutes.

Then, suddenly, the sensation stopped, and he found himself standing in a darkened room. When his eyes adjusted to the darkness, he recognized the place. He was in the kitchen of the Einstein house near the Princeton campus, the very same one he and Peter had been in not long ago. He turned around slowly and saw that a light was on in the adjoining room.

He tiptoed toward the light and slowly pushed the door open enough to look in. What he saw made his heart leap in his chest. There, sitting at his desk, was Albert Einstein, deep in thought.

I did it, he thought. I really did it! This is crazy.

He was so excited that he pumped his fist in the air in silent exultation. Unfortunately, in doing so he hit a potted plant on a nearby shelf causing it to fall.

"Who is there?" asked Dr. Einstein, startled out of his deep thoughts.

Ian knew that this was the time to make his entrance, so he opened the door fully. "Dr. Einstein, I am Ian Petrie. Clarence sent me."

"Is that so?" said Einstein, removing his spectacles and examining Ian. "Are you one of his roommates sent to tell me that he is extending his ill-timed vacation?"

"No, sir," replied Ian. "He's my physics professor."

"Really?" chuckled Einstein. "He told you he is a professor? That is amusing. He is barely qualified to be a student, no less a professor. What is this about, and how did you get in here?"

"Sir, I don't really know the right way to tell you this, but I came here by following the space-time address you wrote down under your formula," said Ian.

"The space-time address?" asked Einstein.

"Yes," Ian replied. "That's what I've called it. May I write it down for you so you can recognize it?"

Einstein motioned for Ian to approach the desk and take a seat.

Ian sat, took a pen, and wrote down the very long number. Einstein's eyes grew wide with recognition.

"Why, that is the number I just wrote down a moment ago in my notes. It was the result of a validation calculation I did for my frequency and resonance regression formula! How did you know that number?" Einstein asked.

"It's a very long story, Dr. Einstein," Ian replied. "May I tell it to you? Do you have the time?"

"Young man, if what I believe you are going to tell me

is true, it would appear that even if I do not have the time, you have all the time in the universe. You may begin."

Light Wave Resources, 2018

"Dr. Mills, Miss Novak," said Mario. "I need you to step away from the device and put your hands in the air where I can see them."

He was not alone. Angelina saw two people standing next to him. The one to his left was the security agent that had just been assigned to them that morning as Carl's replacement. He had a very large and lethal-looking gun pointed directly at them. The other person to his left was a severe but beautiful woman with platinum blond hair pulled back in a ponytail, with a very satisfied smile on her face.

"I'm sorry to have to interrupt your work, but this matter cannot wait," finished Mario. Looking around the room, he frowned. "Where is Ian Petrie?" he asked, panic beginning to rise in his voice.

Thinking quickly, Dr. Mills replied, "He left. He was tired and asked us to clean up before we finished for the evening."

Mario shot an angry look at the security agent and said, "How is that possible? You were supposed to stand guard and not let anyone enter or leave this room. Did you see him leave?"

"Of course not," answered the security agent. "I've been here all day. I left my post for only a few minutes to relieve myself a while ago, but otherwise, I have been here continually."

"Axel, if you have let him escape again, I will have

your head!" shouted the woman. Then, she turned to Angelina. "Where did he go?"

That's when Angelina's eidetic memory finally kicked in. She recognized the woman and Axel as part of the Nazi team that had attacked them in Bern. She'd thought that they had all been killed in the explosion of the SUV at the airport. Apparently, these two survived somehow.

She realized that it was now a life or death situation and checked her watch. Only four minutes until Ian's scheduled return. She could not have these people in the room when he arrived.

Unexpectedly, she bolted for the door shouting, "Follow me, I know where that coward has run off to! If he set us up for this, I will kill him with my own two hands!"

Axel grabbed her. "Let me go! He's going to get away!" Angelina cried.

The *Führerin* said, "Axel, let her go and follow her. Mario, grab the doctor. I'll take the device. Meet us in Mario's office as soon as you find the boy. Go!"

Angelina took off, with Axel in hot pursuit. Mario took out his own weapon and grabbed Dr. Mills by the arm, leading him to the door, while the *Führerin* rolled the device out of the room. There were still two minutes left before Ian's scheduled return.

Einstein's home, 1955

Ian could not believe that he was sitting across from Albert Einstein, about to tell him that his greatest accomplishment had been validated and realized, and that his wildest dream had come true. He started at the beginning and did not leave out any details. He told Einstein everything; about the picture of his desk, Dr. Mills, Princeton, the professor, the letter to Clarence, the break-in, his violin, finding Tesla's clues, the FBI, the Nazis, and Bern.

He explained how he put all the information and formulas together and what he had concluded from it all. Finally, he told him what he had built with the information and what else could be developed from the work he and Tesla had left for him and Clarence to find.

It all had come out in a rush, a firehose blast of information. All the while, Einstein sat quietly with his hands folded in front of him on his desk, leaning slightly forward, listening intently.

"And that, Dr. Einstein, is how I came to be in your kitchen and sitting at your desk at this moment in time," Ian finished, feeling exhausted from the effort and excitement. He added, "Your violin is amazing."

Einstein said nothing for a while. He just sat there, focusing all his attention on Ian, who felt as if he was being examined from the inside out. Einstein's intense, but sad, blue eyes peering into his own, searching, evaluating, and weighing Ian's truthfulness in the balance of his own understanding and intellect.

"So, you are the one that I knew would come," he said to Ian at last, "the one destined to finish my work. We shall see if that is a good thing or not for both of us. Tell me about my death."

Ian was startled by the question. Einstein did not ask about time travel or the nature of light, or about the world Ian came from, and that surprised him.

"Dr. Einstein, I'm sure that you understand that I cannot discuss that. You, above all people, should understand the impact that would have on the timeline. I would love to answer any other questions you have for me, but I must respectfully refuse to answer that one," Ian replied hesitantly.

"I have other secrets to reveal to you that will make you a very rich man and will ensure your place among the greats of science," offered Einstein. "All I ask is that you tell me the date and manner of my death. A very simple question to be answered for a very handsome reward, if you are truly who you say you are and know what you say you know."

Ian began to squirm in his chair. He needed Einstein's trust and confidence, but he knew this was the one thing he could not do.

"Dr. Einstein, all I have told you is true," said Ian. "I beg your pardon, but I cannot meet your demands. Please understand and take what I have told you at face value. If you're not convinced, then I will simply return to my time and place, and I'll thank you for the opportunity to have met with you."

Einstein smiled a huge, bright smile. "Well done, Ian Petrie! Your refusal to reveal that information is the one thing I was looking for. It shows me that you understand the seriousness and danger inherent in your work. It tells me you are an honorable man of integrity, and that you will protect the information you have and make certain that it is not misused, no matter the personal cost or benefit. Now, tell me about your plans for the device and others that may come from the work."

Ian was massively relieved to hear those words coming from the man whom he had idolized. It was the greatest moment of his life.

"I'm really not sure what to do with it, Dr. Einstein, and I'm hoping that you can help me decide." Ian then went on to describe their rescue by Mario Ducati, all about Light Wave Resources, and the working environment. He told him about Dr. Mills's concerns and all they knew about Mario and the advice he had given them.

When he had told Einstein everything he could think of, he added, "So, you see my dilemma. If I trust Mario and follow his suggested path, we might be able to control the worldwide dissemination of the information and the technologies. I will be protected from the FBI and the Nazis. If I don't trust him, I am left to my own resources and connections, which are not enough to build the foundation needed to develop and control the discovery of time travel and teleportation.

"Finally, I need to stay out of the hands of the FBI and the Nazis and anyone else who might want to get their hands on this information. If I strike out on my own, I will be a sitting duck, without the ability, resources, experience, or know-how to protect myself, Angelina, Dr. Mills, or my family. What should I do?"

"Ian, before I give you my opinion," began Einstein, "let me ask you, do you believe the world of your time is ready for this information?"

Ian responded immediately. "Yes! No! Well, I really don't know. Sorry, but I've been trying to work it all out. Most of my energy has been focused on creating the device and staying out of the hands of the Nazis and the FBI. I guess I've spent so much energy trying to figure out what I *could* do, that I have neglected thinking about whether or not it *should* be done.

"Mario believes the world has learned great lessons from the experience with nuclear weapons. The planet is much more interconnected and interdependent than ever before, and he believes that bodes well for international cooperation. But on the other hand, Dr. Mills is advising caution. He feels it's all moving way too fast, and that Mario's help and support has been far too 'convenient' for his liking."

Einstein nodded his head, as if understanding Ian's confusion. "Let me ask you another very important question, Ian, and this one may very well give us our answer. Between the time we are in now and your time, has the nature of man changed? Has mankind become more generous, peaceful, and cooperative, or has the opposite taken place?"

Ian thought for a while. He thought back on all that he was taught about the world of 1955 and the history between then and 2016. He thought about terrorism, globalization, and the fragmentation of society into niches of self-interest groups. He thought about the fall of the Soviet Union and the federation that took its place. He reflected on the general lack of kindness and civility in politics and society in general. He thought about the internet and the opportunity and danger that all that connectivity and access to information had fostered.

Finally, he sighed and answered Einstein's question. "Mankind has become more connected, but we have also grown further apart in many ways. We have access to more information but are less classically well-educated.

"There is much less civic and personal virtue. There is much more rhetoric and demagoguery, and less statesmanship. Our technology is mind-boggling, but instead of relieving the existential problems of the world, it's all focused on entertainment and some economic efficiencies.

"There is still poverty, and hunger, and war. We are building walls instead of bridges. The income gap between the richest and the poorest on the planet has gotten wider. Africa, for example, is still enveloped in poverty and despotism. The Middle East is worse than ever, and terrorism is at an all-time high. I would say that overall, Dr. Einstein, mankind has not progressed to the extent that you would have hoped for. The nature of man has neither changed nor improved."

A forlorn expression crossed Einstein's face. It was as if the light of hope had faded from his eyes and was replaced by disillusionment and disappointment. He leaned back in his chair and looked up at the ceiling in contemplation. Then, he slowly leaned forward and spoke.

"Young man, it appears that I must regretfully give you the same advice that my friend Nikola gave to me. The world is still not ready for these revelations. I know this is a hard message to hear. I understand your youthful enthusiasm and drive are pushing you to develop all you can.

"You desire to get it out there in the world for all the wonderful benefits it could bring, and all the suffering it could alleviate, but apparently, it is not yet time to do so. There is too great a probability that it will fall into the wrong hands and be utilized for destructive, selfish, or authoritarian purposes. This cannot happen.

"My initial response is that you must go back and destroy the device you have created, along with any hard evidence of the documents or the process. You and your friend, Angelina, have the information and understanding inside of you. Keep it there for now."

Ian was stunned. "Destroy it all? Then what, Dr. Einstein? Am I supposed to just live the rest of my life knowing that we have the knowledge and ability to change the world and never do anything to make the world a better place? Isn't that the greater sin?"

"No," said Einstein, "it is not. I am not saying that you

can never reveal it. What I am proposing is that you are putting the cart before the horse. You have told me that you are a wealthy young man. Use those resources to try and create, over time, the kind of world or organization through which you can ensure the proper utilization of this information. Build the outlet for the dissemination of the information before releasing the power. Build the distribution and control mechanisms first. Lay the foundation before building upon it. That is all I am saying.

"My second option for you is that in lieu of destroying the device, you keep it secret. Since you apparently can build a time travel device anytime you desire, and you can travel anywhere in time, you can always return to me, and we can discuss what you have accomplished. Together, we can, over time, determine the right place and time to reveal this. Do the work you must do. Be patient. Build wisely. You have all the time in the world."

"So, you think it would be all right to keep this portable device instead of destroying it? It would be a great way for me to continue to work secretly and improve upon what I have developed," asked Ian.

Einstein chuckled a bit and replied, "I assume, as a well-educated young man, you have heard of the book that was written in 1937 by my friend J.R.R. Tolkien titled *The Hobbit*. If it is still required reading in your day, it could serve as a parable for your situation. Remember when Bilbo Baggins found the 'One Ring'?"

Ian nodded.

"He found that it had amazing powers, and that power could be used for wonderful things. But soon, he became dependent on it. It started to influence him and ultimately became a malevolent influence. He was in danger of losing himself to it. The only thing that saved him from destruction by the ring was his innate goodness and virtue. This device could very well be your, 'One Ring'. I would say that you seem virtuous to me, but you are still young. If you choose to the keep the device, I advise vigilance, caution, and wisdom."

Ian replied, "I will be vigilant, Dr. Einstein, I promise. But I still have a dilemma. If we are assuming that Mario does not have our best interests at heart, and he's helping us for selfish or nefarious reasons, then how can I keep the device secret and escape while still ensuring the freedom of my mother and the others? We are all still their 'guests' and I'm not sure they'll just let us leave.

"Also, Mario knows much about what we have discovered, and that I have the knowledge to utilize it and build devices based on the discoveries. He will never just let me leave and keep it quiet. Can you help me work out a plan of action?"

"Of course, Ian," said Einstein, "let's put our heads together. I am sure we can come up with a workable plan."

They worked for the next hour on a step-by-step plan to escape with the devices while ensuring freedom for Ian and the others.

When they were finished, Einstein cautioned, "Remember, Ian, no plan is foolproof. Be prepared to improvise, but always keep the main objectives in mind. Use your intellect and be flexible. You have no idea what you may find when you return. Be prepared to act quickly and decisively. No doubt. Remember that. Have the proper addresses imbedded in your mind so you can input them when it is time. Then, just act."

"Thank you, Dr. Einstein," replied Ian. "I will follow the plan and will return to you if and when I can, to inform you of our progress. Thank you for all your help."

"It was truly my pleasure to meet you, Ian," said

Einstein. "Now, go and make the world a better and safer place, and you will be fulfilling all my dreams."

Ian stood from his chair at Einstein's desk and prepared the portable time travel device for his return. He input the address to return five minutes after he had left, just as they had agreed.

Before he pushed the button, he said, "See you soon, Dr. Einstein. Wish me luck!" and then he disappeared.

Dr. Einstein sat at his desk and contemplated all that had transpired. He knew he had to follow through with everything he had intended to do before Ian's arrival. Everything had to take place just as Ian described it, or there would be significant disruption to the timeline.

Light Wave Resources, 2018

Ian started to breathe again. He was back in the lab. He checked the clock on the wall. It was exactly five minutes after he had left, even though he had been at Einstein's desk for more than three hours. He was ecstatic. It worked! It all worked perfectly. Then, he realized that he was alone.

Where were Dr. Mills and Angelina? His heart began pounding, and he got a sick feeling in his stomach. Had something gone wrong? Had something unexpected happened when they activated the time travel device? He looked around the room for the device, but it was gone, too.

He went to the door of the lab and opened it, hoping maybe they had just stepped outside the room for a minute. No one was there, not even the security detail. He knew something was seriously wrong.

Then he heard Angelina yelling. "Let me go, you big ape! I told you I need to find Ian. He's here somewhere, and I have to find him!"

Ian hid behind the door and saw Angelina being dragged through the hallway by the new security agent who'd been assigned to them that morning.

"Shut up, you little brat!" said the security agent to Angelina. "You had your chance. You said you knew where he escaped to, but obviously you were just leading us on a wild goose chase. Now *we* will do the looking, and you will stay with Dr. Mills and the others until he is found. Then, the *Führerin* will have all of you together and finally have her victory. The Fourth Reich will begin tonight!"

Ian watched until they disappeared into Mario's office. Ian closed the door quietly, locked it, and hid behind the equipment. He needed time to think.

Apparently, Dr. Mills and Angelina had been taken from the lab under duress. What had initiated the capture? How had the Nazis infiltrated Light Wave, and how did they know they were here? The realization hit him like a ton of bricks.

It was Mario. It had to be. He must have been working with them all along, and when he realized they were close to finishing the device, he must have brought them in. Anger flared up in Ian. It was just as Dr. Mills had feared; they were being played. Mario never intended to be their mentor and protector; he was just using them for his own purposes.

Ian fought hard to remember the plan that he and Einstein had put together and adapt it to this new reality. The original plan was to go back, gather Angelina, Dr. Mills, and his mom in the lab. When they were all together, Ian would use the larger device to send them back to a safe location and a time just before all of this started.

After that, he would use the portable device to send himself and the larger time travel device to where the others were. That way, the past weeks would not have happened. They could start over, still knowing all they now knew but without Mario, the Nazis, or the FBI on their trail. In effect, Ian would reset their timelines and be working from a fresh start. He was glad he had Einstein to help him work through all the timeline implications. He wasn't sure he could have done that on his own.

But now, the plan had to be modified. How was he going to get all of them together in the lab alone, now that they were in the hands of the Nazis? It was just as Einstein had said, be prepared for changes.

Quickly, Ian did some calculations and programmed a few space-time addresses into the portable device. He was going to have to time this all perfectly, if he was going to have any chance of success. After working out the order and the process, Ian steeled himself for what was coming. All their futures were in his hands, and he was determined not to fail.

He took a deep breath, highlighted the first space-time address on his device, and pressed the button.

Dr. Mills, cuffed to a chair in Mario's office, looked up when Axel entered Mario's office with Angelina in tow.

"This one knows nothing," he said. "She just ran all over the place and had no idea where the boy went. I'll take some men and find him myself." He threw Angelina at Mario, who grabbed her and handcuffed her to a chair next to Dr. Mills.

"Have you found the mother yet?" asked Mario.

"Yes," said Axel, "she'll be joining you shortly."

"Excellent," said the *Führerin*. "With all his loved ones in our hands, he will come to us willingly. Just find him quickly. Everything is falling into place nicely."

When Axel left to gather his men and search for Ian, Mario walked over to the *Führerin*. "Didn't I tell you my scheme would make you happy, my love? Now all our plans to rule the world together will be fulfilled. After all these years of planning and preparing, we will finally see our dream realized. We will see the rise of the Fourth Reich, control the most powerful technology ever created, and build a new world in our own image. What could be better?" He grabbed her in his arms and tried to kiss her.

She pushed him away harshly. "Mario, now is not the time. We still have one piece of the puzzle missing. No celebrating until the boy is here in this room with us. Understood?"

Mario smiled and said, "Soon, my love, very soon."

Dr. Mills jumped when alarms started blaring. The monitors in Mario's office came to life just as his phone rang. Still staring at the monitors, an incredulous expression on his face, Mario picked it up.

"What's happening?" he shouted into the phone.

The voice on the other end was loud and panicky. "There has been a breach in security. We have seen the boy on Security Camera 13. He just exited in the elevators in the large barn and is making his escape. All security details are being sent to intercept him now."

"Excellent, he must not escape. Capture him immediately and bring him here! Send everyone you have. Axel and his men will join the search."

He hung up the phone and turned to Angelina and Dr. Mills. "I don't know what you and your friend had planned, but it ends now. Very soon, you will all be working for us at your new home in Argentina."

The office door burst open and Carol Petrie was shoved into the room.

"Here is the mother, Mr. Ducati."

"Good," said Mario. "Now, Mrs. Petrie, you can watch with the rest of us as we enjoy the capture of your son. Please take a seat next to Miss Novak."

He handcuffed her to her chair and turned to the *Führerin*. "My love, I must excuse myself for a few minutes. I'm needed at the security center to coordinate the efforts of my men. Please enjoy the company of these lovely people while I gather the last piece of the puzzle." He bowed to the *Führerin* and left.

"You won't find him," Dr. Mills spoke up. "Ian is much too smart for you, and even if you do, he will never give you what you want."

"Is that so?" said the *Führerin*. "I think you underestimate my power and strength. I have broken many men. Breaking Ian will be child's play, I assure you. After all, no boy wants to see his mother and his girlfriend 'mistreated', now do they? Axel has had his eye on both of them, and after all his years of service, I believe he deserves a reward. If Ian does not comply, he shall have it." Then she smiled that serpent's smile of hers and took a seat across from them.

As she sat down, Ian appeared behind her in a flash of blue electricity. He grabbed her, pushed the button on his portable time travel device, and disappeared in another flashing crackle of blue electricity. The others were dumbstruck. It had all happened so fast.

"Dr. Mills," said Angelina, "did you see that? What's

going on?"

"I think Ian has a plan, and we'd better be ready when he returns!" Dr. Mills replied, hoping he was right.

At that moment, Ian returned without the *Führerin*.

"Listen closely; we don't have a lot of time. I am going to use the device to send you all to a safe place. When you get there, just stay put, and I will join you shortly. Don't ask any questions, just follow my instructions."

He took out the handcuff keys he'd taken from the *Führerin*, unlocked their cuffs, and gathered them together near the larger time travel device. He punched in the space-time address and booted it up.

"Mom, you first. Stand in front of the device." She complied, and he pushed the button. Carol Petrie disappeared.

"Angelina, you next, quickly!"

"No!" said Angelina, "I want to stay with you. You need help. Let me help!"

"Angelina, please, don't argue," pleaded Ian. "I have it all worked out, and you need to go now. You have all the information. Trust me, we'll all be together soon. Just do what I say. Now!"

Looking hurt and annoyed, Angelina complied and stepped in front of the device. Ian pushed the button, and Angelina departed.

"Now you, Dr. Mills," said Ian.

Dr. Mills complied but asked, "Ian, please, tell me where you are sending us. I need to be prepared."

Ian smiled. "The safest place I know," he said as he pushed the button.

After they were all gone, Ian looked at the monitor in Mario's office and saw the *Führerin* and all the security men heading into the elevator in the large barn on their way back to Mario's office. He wished he'd had time to transport her to the Himalayas or somewhere farther away, but without those particular coordinates in his device, well, at least he'd bought them some time.

Calmly, he grabbed the larger time travel device in his arms, lifted it off the ground, and pushed the button on the portable mechanism. He disappeared in the now familiar flash of crackling, blue electricity.

The *Führerin*, Mario, and Axel all burst into the office expecting to find Ian, Angelina, Dr. Mills, and Carol Petrie waiting for them. What they found was an empty office, no captives, and no device.

With deadly calm, the *Führerin* turned to Mario, smiled, and shot him in the heart.

Ian materialized in a now-familiar kitchen. He saw the potted plant he'd knocked over still lying on the floor, and saw the same light shining from under the door. He put down the device he was carrying, walked to the door, and opened it, wishing with all his strength that he would see what he hoped to see.

He stepped into the light and started to breathe again. Sitting there around Einstein's desk were his mom, Angelina, and Dr. Mills.

"Won't you join us, Ian?" said Einstein, with a huge, bright smile on his face. "It appears the first phase of our little plan has succeeded. Now, we must implement phase two!"

CHAPTER TWENTY-TWO

Einstein's home, 1955

Ian took a seat by Einstein's desk and addressed the group. "I'm sorry for the urgency and the secrecy. It was critical that we initiated the process quickly. Dr. Einstein and I had worked out a plan for escaping from the facility when I was here the first time. When I got back to the lab and saw that you all were being held in Mario's office, I had to adjust to avoid further complications."

"It all happened so quickly, and I was so confused," said Carol. "After you got back to the lab, what happened?"

"After I got back, I decided that, with all of you in Mario's office together, I could still carry out the first phase of the plan, but I needed to try to get you there alone. So, I used the portable device to relocate myself to the elevator in the large barn; the one we had used to enter the facility.

"I knew there were security cameras there and that my presence would set off the alarms. I wanted to draw them all outside the building, and I counted on them sending all the security force after me. I was hoping that at least one of your captors would join them. That way, I would have a chance to reappear in the room and teleport the remaining one back outside the facility. Then, I would return to the Mario's office and send you all here, where it was safe.

"After that, I could use the portable device to send myself back here with the larger device so that neither Mario nor the Nazi woman would have it. I know it was convoluted and clumsy, but it was all I could figure out in such a short time. By just teleporting the woman outside the facility, all they could ever assume was that we had constructed something for teleportation. They would have no way of knowing that we had actually constructed a time travel device."

"I get it," said Dr. Mills. "This can be used to either travel in time or just change locations if you keep the temporal variable the same. Ingenious, Ian, well done!"

"Yes," said Einstein, "well done. Very creative! I can see why Clarence had such faith in you. Now, we must discuss phase two. As I understand it, there are still three of your group that need to be freed from captivity. We need to choose between two options for affecting a change in their circumstances.

"The first one would be similar to the last rescue. It would entail having Ian travel to where they are, use the larger device to send them to a safe place, and then use the portable device to bring himself and the larger device to where they are.

"The second choice is more complex. It would require that all of you return to the starting point of this grand adventure and subtly and carefully manipulate events going forward from that point in time so that none of this ever happened. You will be living in a world where there will be two of each of you for a while. You must avoid contact with your past selves while working as a team to manipulate the actions of each other's past selves to create a new timeline in which none of this occurred. That way, your friends will never have been captured, and neither the FBI nor the Nazis would ever be aware of your discoveries. Do you understand?"

Angelina spoke up, "Dr. Einstein, wouldn't that mean that we would then have changed things so as to erase our memory of all of this? If we manipulate events so that it never happened, will we forget what we know now?"

"Excellent question, young lady," said Einstein. "I understand your concern, but my answer is no, you will not forget. You will be creating a new timeline, and therefore, the past versions of yourselves will never experience the things you have experienced. However, the 'present' versions of yourselves have experienced it, and that cannot be changed. You are, and always will be, the 'present' version of yourselves working outside of time. Therefore, you will retain all of what you know and have experienced.

"Once you have permanently changed the past, you can return to your proper place in time, which is right after you left Mario's office. Remember, there are no versions of yourselves living in that timeline now, as you have vacated it by traveling here. There, you will assume your proper roles and continue to move forward through time with your current understanding, but you will be free from the past you had created in the other timeline. Can you see that now?"

"I do," replied Angelina. "You have made it much clearer for me. As long as we avoid contact with our past selves, we can change the past and then rejoin the new version of it in progress at the proper point in time. Wonderful! I vote for that option. It seems much cleaner and simpler to do it with just the four of us than trying to do it with the three others involved. Fewer people wandering around in the past potentially messing up the timeline more than we intend to. Fewer people, more control of the outcome. Right?"

"Exactly," replied Einstein, "you will be creating a clean slate. Are you all in agreement?"

Dr. Mills seemed a little concerned and raised a question.

"The only concern I have is that the others, Roger Petrie, Dr. Kearney, and Peter will have no knowledge of any of this in the new timeline. They will be in the dark as to what we know. How should we handle that? Can we ever tell them?"

"Again, an excellent observation, Dr. Mills," said Einstein. "You have pointed out a natural consequence of our plan. I would say that you could, over time, bring the critical members into the loop. It will be difficult for them to accept, and it will require proof, but it can and should be done. I would suggest, however, that you leave the roommate out of it. He does not seem to have a critical role going forward. Of course, if you choose to include him in future plans because of his skillset, that is up to you."

Ian raised another question. "Dr. Einstein, it seems to me that trying to change every event in the past that led up to these current circumstances is going to be very difficult and unwieldy. There are so many variables. I would think that we would have to identify one or two critical points in time to change so that we create a different future, but we can't mess around too much with the past. The consequences could be very unpredictable. What would you suggest?"

"You have identified a key point, Ian, one I was going

to address," replied Einstein. "We might as well discuss it now. We have in this room one of Ian's parents, his mentor, and his partner in this. All of you have different perspectives on what may be the critical turning points in Ian's life which could have created the current undesirable situation. I would like for you to think about what could be changed to ensure a different future in that timeline."

"If we never took Ian to Dr. Mills, none of this would have happened," said Carol Petrie. "That was the critical decision Roger and I made that set all of this in motion. If we change that, then we will create a vastly different outcome."

Einstein thought about that. He was very quiet for a while, then responded. "Remember that when you join the timeline already in progress, you will have to reassume the identities you have set in motion. Let's say that you do not take Ian to Dr. Mills, what would have been the consequences of that action?"

"Ian would not have gotten the help he needed to maximize his potential," Dr. Mills replied. "He would have continued to struggle in school. He may have become convinced that he could not do the things he was capable of and given up in frustration. He would not have created the PhotoEx application, he would not have sold it for such a tidy sum, and he would not have attended Princeton.

"Those are just some of the obvious changes. If we change that, we will be severely limiting our options when we rejoin the timeline. Ian will have a much harder time building the foundation of support he will need to safely reintroduce the discoveries you have left for him. He will not have the standing, recognition, or resources he will need."

"Correct," said Einstein. "So, we will have to choose some point in time after Ian has finished his work with Dr. Mills, and after he creates the PhotoEx application. What happened afterwards that would have a significant impact if changed?"

Dr. Mills responded again. "If I never encouraged him to explore his interest and connection to you, maybe he would have taken up a different interest. He would never have become so obsessed with the picture of your desk, and that would have changed his history and trajectory. But it would have also, once again, negated his development of the PhotoEx application and the subsequent outcomes of that, so I guess that won't work, either," he conceded.

"Once again, you are correct," said Einstein. "Let's continue. What are some other ideas?"

This time, Ian spoke up. "What if I decided to go to some other school besides Princeton?'

"What would have been the result of that?" asked Einstein."

"I would have never met the professor," replied Ian. "Since he was the one with the most significant connection to you and had the letter you wrote to him, if I never met, him none of this would have transpired as it did. Is that an option?"

The group seemed excited about this observation. It would require some hard work, but it could be done. It would definitely result in a different timeline and maybe solve their problems. Ian would still have created the PhotoEx app and have the thirty-three million dollars to build upon.

The downside would be that he would have no relationship with Professor Kearney. It seemed to Ian that he would need the professor's help and counsel going forward in the new timeline, if they were going to be successful in creating a safe world in which to share the information.

"Dr. Einstein," Angelina asked, "if we choose this option where Ian never went to Princeton and never met or developed a relationship with the professor, is that a big deal? Is that something that would cause problems or complications when we return to our place in time?"

Einstein responded quickly. "As I see it, it is not a reason to avoid this option. From what Ian told me, Clarence was already under observation by either the Nazis, or the FBI, or both, perhaps. His interaction with Ian and the subsequent events, including the hacking of the FBI files and the break-in at this residence, were critical in forcing their hands.

"So, if Ian were not to attend Princeton, then these events would be negated. The only thing that any of you would have to make sure of is that Clarence did not subsequently discover the secrets and let them fall into the hands of the FBI or the Nazis. If you could do this, then all will be well.

"Should you need Clarence after your return to your timeline you could always meet with him and fill him in to the extent that you feel is necessary. He will still have all the knowledge, perspective, and position in the scientific community that you may require, but he will not be in danger to the same extent, because the Nazis and the FBI will not have been alerted.

Additionally, with this option, you are only dealing with changing the events of the past few months, not years. That is very helpful. The fewer changes, the better. I think that this is the best option. Leave Clarence out of this for now."

"That's all well and good," said Carol, "but it will be

up to me to convince the past version of Ian not to attend Princeton. That won't be easy, since there will be the past versions of myself and Ian's dad encouraging him to go and live out his dream. How am I going to do that? This is all so crazy. I can't do that alone while trying to avoid contact with my past self. I'm afraid I'm not cut out for all this time travel and timeline stuff. I am going to need help."

"And you will have it," said Dr. Mills. "Remember that I will still have a relationship with Ian's past self. You and I can meet with him, and together, we can try to influence him, or I can do it alone. He trusts both of us. Together we may be able to get the job done."

"And if your influence doesn't work," said Angelina, "I have a feeling that going to school where an attractive and interested female Croatian Genius of the Future will be going may add to his incentive to go somewhere other than Princeton. I am certainly willing to help in any way that I can!"

Ian smiled and said to Angelina, "That would work! Any version of myself in the past would definitely take that incentive into consideration. I can vouch for that! With the three of you influencing the past Ian, I'm sure we can do this. Let's give it a try. I always struggled a bit with the fact that Princeton is only the ninth best global university for physics.

"I was fixated on it because I wanted to emulate you, Dr. Einstein, but I could have gone to MIT, which is widely regarded as the number one school in the study of physics, matter, and energy. I had applied there and was accepted. Let's convince my past self to go there. I can still make all the high-level connections in the world of physics I will need and won't draw as much attention to myself. When the time comes for the timelines to converge, I can just pick up where my past self left off. What do you think?"

"I think we have determined a respectable outline of phase two," said Einstein. "You will all return to a point in time before Ian made the decision to go to Princeton and work together to convince him to attend MIT instead. Once that is accomplished and you have done something to ensure that the secrets I left for Clarence to find are safe, you will return here, and we can discuss phase three. Agreed?"

"Agreed," they replied, nearly in unison.

Carol had one final question. "So, we'll decide on a time, but what about the place? If I understand all of this correctly, there will be past versions of ourselves floating around out there. We can't go back to our homes, because the past versions of ourselves live there, yet we must interact with the past Ian. We need a place to work from. A base of operations. Any suggestions?"

"Very observant, Carol," said Dr. Mills. "You're correct. I suggest that we pick a hotel in Manhattan to work from. It can be near my office and home, so I can get things I need from those places when my past self is away. We can arrange for a meeting with Ian in the city, which won't be suspicious, since that's where my office is. When we involve Angelina, it will also not be suspicious that a nice Croatian girl is visiting the city before starting school in the U.S. What do you all think? Any suggestions as to which hotel?"

Angelina responded. "I would like to stay where my great-granduncle, Nikola Tesla, stayed all those years, the New Yorker. I think that would be fun and help me feel closer to him. Can we do that?"

"Absolutely," Dr. Mills agreed. "I think that's appropriate, and it rounds this all out very nicely. Very poetic, you might say, since that's where all of this started."

"Then, it is agreed," said Einstein. "You will together decide on a space-time address to return to and carry out the plan. Remember to guard the devices carefully. Always keep them fully charged. Other than that, be meticulous in your calculations, and the next time I see you all, I am sure we will be able to celebrate the success of phase two. Do not forget that you also need to ensure that Clarence will not divulge the secrets unknowingly. Do what you must to make certain of that. I wish you luck!"

"Thank you once again, Dr. Einstein," said Ian. "We appreciate your help and insight. If you could keep thinking about phase three while we're gone, that would be very helpful."

They rolled the larger device into the office from the kitchen and stood around it. Ian punched in the space-time address they'd calculated and agreed to and began the process. One by one, Ian sent them to a secluded spot in Central Park. There, they would gather and then head to the Hotel New Yorker to settle in for their assignment.

When the others were all safely transported, Ian gathered the larger device in his arms and input the address into his portable unit. He pushed the button to leave, and nothing happened. There was no sound, no vibrational resonance, no crackling, blue electricity... *nothing*. He turned to Einstein.

"Something is seriously wrong. Nothing happened. I need your help, Dr. Einstein, can you help me do a diagnostic examination to figure out how to make it work again?"

"Certainly, Ian, but before we get too upset, let's think about this. You have used this smaller device several times now. Is it possible that the batteries need to be recharged?"

Ian laughed. "Of course. That's probably it. All I need to do is recharge them. But how are we going to recharge lithium batteries in 1955?"

Einstein stood and approached Ian, who opened the case holding the batteries. Einstein examined the unit, stroked his chin, then nodded. "Let's crosswire the larger unit's power source with the smaller one. I have some wire and tools in the garage, and we can have this done in no time. It will drain the larger unit, but you can recharge that one when you get back to your time." He left Ian alone in the office and returned soon with all he needed.

They worked together to crosswire the units, and when they felt they had accomplished their objective, Ian started the portable device.

"Looks like all systems are go, Dr. Einstein," said Ian. "Once again, thanks for the help. Disaster averted!"

He hung the components back on his belt, pushed the button, and departed. He arrived in Central Park and found all three of his party waiting for him.

"Sorry for the delay," he said to them. "The batteries died on me, and I had to get Dr. Einstein to help me figure out how to recharge them. Thank goodness he's a genius, or I might have been stuck back in 1955."

"What are you talking about, Ian? There was no delay," said Angelina. "We all just got here at the exact same time."

Ian thought for a second and then laughed. Even though it had taken thirty minutes for he and Einstein to recharge the batteries, he had used the exact same space-time address as the others. Thus, he appeared at the exact same moment in time as they did. No time would have appeared to have elapsed.

"Sorry, I forgot," said Ian sheepishly. "It took me thirty minutes back there to recharge, but no time elapsed here. It's hard keeping this time travel stuff in order. Let's head to the hotel and settle in. We have a lot to accomplish."

They gathered up the larger device and headed out of the park. They knew it was about a half mile to the hotel, and the most direct route would be down 5th Avenue to 34th Street. However, they wanted to avoid the more crowded areas, so they headed to 8th Avenue and walked south to 34th.

"Should we stop and get some cash?" Angelina asked.

"No need," Dr. Mills reassured her. "I have enough on me for a hotel and other short-term needs."

When they arrived at the hotel, Dr. Mills got two rooms, and checked in. After everyone had found their rooms, they gathered in Ian and Dr. Mills's room to discuss the plan for the next few days.

"So," said Dr. Mills, "it's decided. I'll call the Ian of this timeline and set up an appointment for a dinner meeting. Angelina will join us there. I will introduce her as the daughter of a friend of mine and tell Ian that she will be attending MIT in the fall to study physics. I'll suggest that they get to know one another and hope that with a little luck and a slight romantic spark, that Ian will make his decision for MIT instead of Princeton."

It all seemed simple enough, but they knew none of this was going to be easy. It also had the advantage of not getting Carol involved, since anything she did could be mentioned to the past Carol, and that could cause problems. They agreed, and Dr. Mills made the call. He got Ian's voicemail.

"Ian, this is Dr. Mills calling. I would like for you to meet me tonight at the Waldorf Hotel for dinner. I have some important things to discuss with you, and a special person I'd like you to meet. No need to call me back. Just be there tonight around 7 p.m. See you then."

Petrie home, 2018

The past Ian had been busy at school and had the ringer of his cell phone turned off. After school, he checked his messages and heard the voicemail from Dr. Mills. It sounded like fun. He always liked talking with Dr. Mills, and it had been a while since their last long talk. He immediately called his mom at home.

"Mom, I got a call from Dr. Mills. He wants me to meet him tonight for dinner at the Waldorf Hotel. He wants to talk with me about something important."

"Okay," said the Carol from the past, "that sounds nice. Do you need your car?"

"No," said Ian. "I'm just going to walk to the LIRR station and take the train in from there. I'll see you tonight when I get home."

"Okay," replied Carol. "Have fun and tell him we said hello!"

Ian arrived right on time and found Dr. Mills waiting in the lobby with an amazingly beautiful girl. She was stunning, in a punk rock sort of way. Not normally his type, but *wow*, she was gorgeous.

"Dr. Mills!" Ian called. He quickened his step and closed the gap in no time. "So good to see you. What has it been, two months or so, at least, since we last talked? Thanks for the invitation." Then, he looked at Angelina and stuck out his hand. "Hi, I'm Ian Petrie. Glad to make your acquaintance."

"Nice to meet you, Ian," Angelina said as she took his hand. "I've heard a lot about you from Dr. Mills. He can't stop talking about you. I feel as if I already know everything about you."

Ian blushed and felt his heart racing. He stammered, "Well, then you are way ahead of me. I have to catch up. Why don't we sit, and I can learn more about you. I'm sorry, but I didn't catch your name."

"Angelina Novak," she replied. "I'm from Croatia."

"Angelina," Ian repeated. "Such a beautiful name."

They followed Dr. Mills into the restaurant and took their seats. The waiter arrived with water and the menus, told them the specials, and departed.

Dr. Mills spoke. "Ian, before we get too involved with our dinner, I wanted to tell you why I asked you here tonight. The last time we spoke, you indicated that you were leaning toward attending Princeton in the fall. I know you haven't made your final decision, and I wanted to give you some perspective. Would you be offended if I speak my mind?"

"Not at all, Dr. Mills," replied Ian. "You know I have always respected your opinion, and you have never given me anything but great advice. I'd be glad to know what you think about it. It's all so confusing, and I could sure use someone else's perspective right now."

"Wonderful," said Dr. Mills. "If I may ask, what are your main reasons for attending Princeton over all the other universities who have accepted you?"

"Well, the main reason is that I want to be where Einstein was. I want to see what he saw and be in the same environment where he did much of his work. I know it is only the ninth-ranked physics program in the world, but my affinity for Einstein is outweighing that at the moment," Ian replied.

"I understand all of that," Dr. Mills responded, "and I take some responsibility for it. I always pushed you to study everything you could about Einstein. I did that when you were young so that you would have a role model to emulate, someone who started with the same challenges as you, and yet accomplished great things. It was never intended to become a lifetime obsession for you. Your parents have filled me in on your study of the picture of Einstein's desk. While I applaud your tenacity, I feel that it's time for you to broaden your horizons. Maybe focus now on other great people. Expand your vision. Add to your perspective."

"I don't know, Dr. Mills," said Ian hesitantly. "I feel like I'm very close to a greater understanding of Einstein's work; a real breakthrough. I'm trying to develop a supplemental program for my PhotoEx app that would help me to be able to see everything that was on Einstein's desk in that picture I'm studying. Right now, I can only see what is visible. If I'm successful, I'll be able to read even the documents that are covered up. I am so close. Being at Princeton might help."

The waiter returned and took their orders. After he left, Dr. Mills continued. "I understand how you might think that, but I believe that other diverse experiences might actually be beneficial. We know that in science, the wider our understanding of the universe, the better the probability that we will find the right answers.

"I would like to propose that you 'up your game' by taking the challenge and accepting the offer to attend MIT. It *is* ranked as the number one physics program in the world, and you might actually be challenged there. I'm not sure that Princeton will provide the same growth opportunity for you. What do you think?"

Ian replied, "I understand how you might think that,

Dr. Mills, but isn't it better to become an expert in one specific field of study or one focus? I don't want to waste all that I understand about Einstein by losing my focus. I want to take this all to completion and figure out what Einstein was working on at the time of his death in 1955. It could change the world!"

"I believe," said Dr. Mills, "that your research and perspective will be rewarded by going to MIT. You still have all the knowledge about Einstein in your head, and that's not going anywhere. You will add a new perspective to what you already know, and I guarantee that before your first year is done, you will have all your answers. I also believe that it's time for you to become your own man, not just a shadow or imitation of Einstein. I truly believe that over time, the world will be talking about Einstein, Tesla, and Ian Petrie in the same breath. Of this, I am certain."

Ian considered this for a while. "That all sounds logical and prudent. But my heart is drawing me to Princeton."

At that point Angelina joined the discussion. "Well then, *my* heart will very, very sad," she said in a sincere tone.

Ian turned to her and asked, "Why is that, Angelina? Why will your heart be sad if I choose Princeton over MIT?"

"Because," she replied, looking down, "then I won't have you there with me. We will not be able to get to know each other better and become friends. I was so excited when Dr. Mills told me that we would be having dinner with you. I have read all about you in magazines, and now meeting you in person, I see that none of the articles have fully captured your true character. I would love the opportunity to get to know you better and study alongside you."

Ian was completely flushed at this point. He was definitely smitten with this girl, and now she was flattering him and telling him that she would like to get to know him better. This was a very interesting development indeed.

"So, you will be attending MIT in the fall?" Ian asked.

"Yes," replied Angelina, "and as of now, I know no one there. It would be so great to have a familiar face to help me adapt to school and the culture here in the United States. But if you are determined to go to Princeton, then I suppose I will have to do it alone."

From that point on, all Ian could see was Angelina. Everything else disappeared from view. She told him all about her relationship to Tesla, about her nomination for the Genius of the Future award, and the research that got her the nomination. Ian realized that sitting next to him was an amazing girl. Beauty, brains, and talent, all in one incredible Croatian package. Ian felt that he could not pass up the opportunity to explore this further.

What's the big deal about Princeton anyway, he wondered. I could still accomplish everything I need to at MIT, and I could do it with Angelina by my side.

Dr. Mills interrupted his thoughts. "Ian, what are you thinking? Will you consider MIT instead of Princeton?"

Ian looked at Angelina and said, "Read my mind, Angelina. What do you say the answer is?"

Angelina scrunched up her face in mock concentration. "It is decidedly so!"

They laughed together and Ian said, "Wow, you are really good at that. I thought I was the only one around that knew all those crazy Magic 8-Ball answers. Well done, Angelina." Then, he turned to Dr. Mills. "Doc, looks like I will be heading to MIT in the fall! How could I pass up an opportunity to study with the great-grandniece of Nikola Tesla? After all, wasn't Einstein quoted as saying that Tesla was the smartest man in the world? Time to expand my horizons and focus on what Tesla can teach me!"

"Excellent!" said Dr. Mills. "Now, all you have to do is convince your parents."

"That won't be hard, doc, they've always said that they want me to make the choice that is right for me. They'll go along. I'll let you know when I've completed the paperwork. In the meantime, maybe Angelina and I can get to know each other better before we head to school. Will you be in New York City for a while, Angelina?"

Angelina shot a questioning look at Dr. Mills and hesitated. Dr. Mills answered for her. "She'll be here only for the next day or so, and then she has to leave. In fact, she may be leaving as soon as tomorrow evening."

Although disappointed, Ian accepted that. "Well, this has certainly been a great meeting. A new direction, a new school, and a new friend. Amazing how life can change in one day!"

"Yes, it is," agreed Dr. Mills. "Life is funny that way."

Ian pulled a pen and scrap of paper out of his pocket, wrote down his phone number, and gave it to Angelina.

"Please call me. I'd love to talk with you more before we meet again at MIT. Will you do that?" he asked her.

"Certainly, Ian, I'll call you as soon as I can." Then, she leaned over and gave him a gentle kiss on the cheek, sealing the deal.

They finished dinner, and Ian headed for the train station. Angelina and Dr. Mills headed back to the hotel to share the good news with the rest of the group.

The New Yorker hotel, 2018

"By the end of the meal, Ian had agreed to everything we proposed," said Dr. Mills as he finished his review of the meeting.

"Well, that sounds way too easy," said Ian. "I can't believe I caved in so quickly. I mean, I *really* wanted to go to Princeton."

"I know," said Dr. Mills, "but Angelina really did a number on you. She played it perfectly. It was pretty obvious you were smitten with her from the start."

"Oh, really?" replied Ian. "Where were the 'mental challenges'? The 'I don't know if I like you yet'? All the stuff you put *me* through?"

"No need for that," replied Angelina. "I've already gotten past all that with you, and past Ian seemed different; more innocent, and more vulnerable. I really liked him. Maybe more than you!" Then she laughed. "Are you jealous of your own past self? Now *that* is something that is going to cost you thousands of dollars in therapy, if you don't get over it."

They all laughed and settled in to discuss the next steps.

"So, with Ian firmly on the path to MIT, the only thing left is for us to ensure that the secret does not fall into the hands of the FBI or the Nazis. Any ideas?" asked Dr. Mills.

"I have an idea," replied Ian. "If we can get the letter from Professor Kearney's office and then remove the microdot from it without him knowing, there would be no way it could fall into their hands, right? Without that, there's no secret to find. They could never put it all together without that information."

"That seems pretty clear," replied Angelina. "That is

definitely the critical item."

"Agreed," said Dr. Mills. "So, what's the plan? If we use the teleportation device, Ian could slip in, grab the letter, and be gone without raising suspicion or tipping off the FBI or the Nazis who are watching the professor."

"But," Ian interjected, "what if the letter has been moved from where I last saw it? I believe we'll be better off to once again rely on the skills of our Croatian genius. With her physics background and connection to Tesla, she could ask for a meeting with the professor. She can tell him that the family has told her stories about some Einstein and Tesla connection, and since he knew Einstein, she thought he might be the best person to verify the information. I'm sure he will take the bait.

"With a little prodding and the right questions, Angelina will be able to convince him to show her the letter. When he does, she can just secretly remove the microdot, which he has no idea is there, and we're good. Sound like a plan?"

"Surprisingly, yes! I think it could work," replied Dr. Mills. "It's simple and doesn't have too many moving parts, as long as he actually shows her the letter. I'm not one hundred percent certain he will do that. At least not at first, but we'll see. If she has the same impact on him that she had on the past Ian, this will be a piece of cake. If not, it could take multiple attempts. We'd better start as soon as possible."

"Let's wait until morning to call him, so Angelina can have a better chance of talking to the professor live. I don't think leaving a voicemail message is a smart thing to do right now," said Ian. "The professor is in his office every day at 9 a.m. sharp. He stays there for at least an hour. Let's call him then and ask for a meeting later in the day. It's only about an hour's drive from here, so if he agrees, we can make it work. Agreed?"

They agreed to make the call in the morning and then all retired to bed.

The following morning after breakfast, they once again gathered in Dr. Mills's room and rehearsed the call with Angelina. When she was fully ready, Ian dialed the number for her and handed her the phone. After three rings, the professor answered.

"Hello, Professor Kearney here. Who is this, please?"

"Good morning, Professor Kearney, my name is Angelina Novak. I am a visiting physics student from Croatia, and I would like to meet with you to discuss a few things. Would you have any time today to do that?"

"I don't know, young lady. Can you tell me what this in reference to and why you need to speak specifically with me?" Professor Kearney asked.

"Certainly, professor. I am the great-grandniece of Nikola Tesla. Over the years, I've been told many tales of him by my family. One of them involves a secret connection with Albert Einstein. In my research, I've discovered that you knew Dr. Einstein at the time of his death. I believe that you can give me some valuable insight that will help me in my research about my great-granduncle.

"I would very much appreciate it if you could give me an hour or two of your time later today. I need to return to Croatia soon, and I would hate to miss such an amazing opportunity to speak with someone who knew Dr. Einstein as well as you did. Could you possibly accommodate my request?" asked Angelina.

"Well, that is very interesting," replied Professor Kearney. "I, too, have some interest in Nikola Tesla, and I'd actually welcome the opportunity to hear some of your family tales about him. Would it be possible for you to meet me here at my office around 4 p.m.?"

"Absolutely, professor. I can do that," replied Angelina. "May I have the address to your office?"

The professor gave her the directions to his office on the Princeton campus and hung up.

The group was thrilled. The first step was complete, and they were on their way.

They decided that Ian and his mom would stay at the hotel to protect the devices, while Angelina and Dr. Mills would make the trip to Princeton. They spent the afternoon role-playing the meeting with Angelina and the professor to account for every possible scenario.

By 2 p.m., she felt ready. Dr. Mills ordered a car, then he and Angelina headed down to the lobby. If all went well, they could return to Einstein's desk to discuss phase three by this evening.

CHAPTER TWENTY-THREE

Professor Kearney's office, 2018

Angelina and Dr. Mills arrived at the Princeton campus at 3:45 p.m. Dr. Mills asked the cab to wait for them to return and to keep the meter running. Since they had some time, they took a leisurely stroll through campus, Angelina thinking all the while about how much this place meant to Ian.

When they found the building where Professor Kearney's office was located, they took a seat on a bench nearby to wait until it was time to go in. Angelina looked around to see if she could spot any FBI or Nazi types staking out the professor, Dr. Mills doing the same next to her. She didn't spot anyone that made her feel suspicious, so when the time came, Angelina headed into the building for her meeting. Dr. Mills stayed outside on the bench to keep watch.

Angelina found Professor Kearney's office and knocked on the door. She heard shuffling, and then the door opened very quickly. The professor grabbed her by the elbow and hustled her into the room.

"Welcome, my dear, so glad you are on time. I was so

anxious for our meeting! I've been thinking about it all day! Here, sit, sit, we have much to discuss."

Angelina felt as if she had opened the door to a whirlwind of activity. What energy and enthusiasm the professor had! She sat down and waited, giving the professor a minute to settle himself in his own seat. When she sensed he was settled, she began with one of the conversations she'd rehearsed earlier with Ian.

"Thank you, professor, for agreeing to see me on such short notice. We do have a lot to share. Where would you like me to begin?"

"Why, at the beginning of course!" replied the professor. "Tell me about your relationship with Nikola Tesla. You said he was your great-granduncle?"

"Yes, professor," replied Angelina, "that's what I'm told. His sister was my great-grandmother. As you can imagine, our family is very proud of him, and we discuss him and his achievements often when we get together.

"They tell me I was very much like him as a child, and as it turns out, I am the only one in my family that has taken up his mantle in the realm of physics. I've studied it since I was small, and have recently been nominated for the Tesla Society of Croatia's Genius of the Future Award for my model of one of Tesla's most imaginative theoretical devices, the thought camera, and for having completed a well-received treatise on the role of renewable energy in promoting peace between nations."

"Very interesting," said the professor. "It would seem that you are an accomplished young woman. Are you as familiar with all of the other work that he did?"

"Yes, I am, professor, as well as many of his lesser known, and even secret theories," replied Angelina, hoping to pique the professor's curiosity. "In fact, that's one of my main reasons for contacting you."

"I see," said the professor. "Why don't you tell me what you would like to discuss regarding this topic. I know a few secrets myself," he said with a chuckle. "Maybe we can share secrets."

Angelina knew this was her opening. "One of my family's most interesting stories is about a letter that Tesla was supposed to have written and mailed just days before he died. It's said that Tesla was being hounded by the Nazis to give them plans for several of his theoretical devices. Among these were the death ray, the thought camera, and anything he had that could help them complete the bell, which was their failed attempt to build a time travel device.

"They felt that these weapons could help them to win World War II and would ensure the dominance of the Third Reich over the world for the next thousand years. He initially agreed to work with them, then he had second thoughts.

"In his last days, he destroyed many of his models of the devices and gathered all his documentation, formulas, and theories and sent them to the only man he felt he could trust. A few days later, he was dead. The FBI said it was a natural death, but my family believes otherwise."

"And who does your family believe the documents and the letter were sent to, Angelina?" asked the professor.

"I've been told that the letter was sent to none other than Albert Einstein," Angelina replied.

The professor looked shocked. "Is that so? Interesting. I have always wondered about their relationship. On the surface, it seemed quite adversarial, but in many casual comments, they are quoted as speaking very highly of one another. I know that they worked together on Project Rainbow. Are you familiar with it?"

"Yes, I am," responded Angelina. "I have actually seen many documents on the project, and the rumors are accurate. They did work together on the early phases of that project. In fact, it's my family's understanding that Tesla eventually figured out the reason their early efforts failed.

"Of course, he was never aware of the eventual total disaster that befell the project, but when he discovered the underlying cause for the failure of the initial collaboration and realized the truth, the information shook him to the core. I believe that is when he decided to share the information with Einstein, so they could incorporate his knowledge into Einstein's theories of the universe, and hopefully, use it to complete his Unified Field Theory.

"He knew Einstein was a man of integrity, and that only he would have the ability to see the truth and safeguard the secret until the time was right. It is said that he told Einstein at the time of his death that the world was still not ready for the revelations. Apparently, he hoped that by the time Einstein had put it all together, that the world would be ready. None of my family knows what happened after that. I hope you can help me fill in the blanks."

The professor looked enthralled. His expression turned thoughtful for a moment, then asked, "My dear, do you mind if I ask you a question; a riddle of sorts? Just to fulfill an old man's curiosity?"

"Not at all," replied Angelina.

"Good!" said the professor and he took out a pad of paper and grabbed a pen. He drew a square grid of nine dots on the paper. He turned the paper so Angelina could see it.

"The problem is this: how can you connect all nine

dots with just one straight line? You cannot lift your pen off the paper, you cannot go back over a line. Can you tell me the answer to this riddle, Angelina?"

Angelina fought hard to prevent a huge smile from blossoming on her face. It was the same problem Ian had presented to her when they met in Croatia. She pretended to think for a minute and then said casually, "One big, fat line."

The professor shot out of his chair. "Would you repeat that, please?"

Angelina repeated, "One big, fat line. That's not the only way to solve this problem, but it's the easiest."

"My dear young woman, do you realize that you have solved this problem just as fast as Einstein did, and that he was the only other person to ever solve it as quickly? That tells me that you are a very unique and special young woman. It has also helped me make a decision. I will share with you something I have never shared with anyone else. I said earlier that maybe we could share secrets. You have shared yours, and now I will share mine."

He sat back down in his chair and lifted the blotter on his desk, removing an old, yellowed document. He reverently placed it on the desk and slid it in her direction.

"This is the letter that may confirm the story your family has told for years. I have had it since shortly after it was written in 1955. The information in it, combined with what you have shared with me today, confirms that Tesla did send Einstein all the information he had, and that Einstein used that information to help him complete his work on the Unified Field Theory. Please, read it and tell me your opinion."

Angelina carefully lifted the paper from the desk and began to read. She was already familiar with the letter, having read it multiple times during her and Ian's research. So, she focused on locating the microdot. She finally found it right where Ian said it would be, at the end of the last sentence, next to Einstein's signature. Angelina carefully placed her right thumb on the microdot and increased the pressure slowly. When she felt the dot release, she lifted her thumb and the microdot came along with it. She handed the document back to the professor with her left hand while palming the microdot in her right hand.

"Thank you for sharing that with me, professor," Angelina said. "I agree, it seems to confirm that the two of them did have a working relationship of sorts, and Tesla very well may have given Einstein his information. Have you ever found the hidden documents? The ones that were 'left where they were born'?"

"Sadly, no, Angelina, I have not. That is one of the greatest disappointments of my life," the professor confessed. "I have felt like a total failure in this regard. But since meeting you, I feel that there is hope! It may be that you and I together could figure that out. Would you be willing to work with me to that end?"

Angelina reached across the desk and grabbed his hand. "Professor, I wish I could, but that's not possible right now. I'll be attending MIT in the fall, and for now, I must return to my home. Maybe someday soon we can work on this together and solve all the mysteries of the universe. But for now, it must wait. I hope you can understand."

The professor looked crestfallen. It was as if his old hope had died a new death. He sighed. "I understand, my dear, it's just that I do not have much time left, and I was hoping to complete this work before my death. It seems we never have as much time as we plan or hope to have."

Angelina smiled and said, "Professor, who knows, you

might just have more time than you could possibly imagine! Be strong and stay positive. This will all work out the way it's supposed to, I'm sure of it."

Then she stood, gave the professor a parting hug, and left the office to go meet Dr. Mills with the microdot safely in her right hand. Phase two was complete!

She met Dr. Mills at the bench where he was still sitting and gave him a big smile and a thumbs up. Without saying a word, he rose from his seat and joined her as they walked to the other side of campus to meet their waiting cab.

When they were safely in the cab and headed back to New York City, Angelina opened her right hand and showed the microdot to Dr. Mills. He took it from her and placed it into a small plastic bag he had brought. He sealed it, put it into his pocket, and sighed a great big sigh of relief.

"Did you enjoy your meeting?" he asked. Angelina could tell he was trying to keep his conversation as generic as possible.

"Yes, I did," she replied. "He's a very sweet and energetic man. It's so sad that he has not been able to see his dreams fulfilled. I'm hopeful that we can remedy that in the near future."

"I agree, but let's just take one thing at a time," advised Dr. Mills. "We still have a long way to go."

They arrived an hour later at the New Yorker hotel, paid the cab, and joined Ian and Carol in Dr. Mills's room. They showed them the microdot, and Angelina filled them all in on her conversation with the professor.

"And then he pulled out a piece of paper and drew the nine-dot matrix!" said Angelina, describing the problem that Professor Kearney gave her. "Of *course,* I recognized it immediately. Thank goodness you told me the answer in Croatia, Ian, because that was the thing that convinced him that he could share his secret with me! He trusted me and respected me from that point on. I think he's convinced that I am the one with the 'greater mind' that's destined to solve all the problems!"

"Just great," said Ian. "Not only do I have my past self hitting on you, but now the professor thinks that *you* are the next Einstein. Wonderful! I am quickly becoming irrelevant. Let's get back to Einstein's desk before I become completely expendable!"

They all laughed.

"Okay," Dr. Mills spoke as the laughter died down, "let's review. Ian is on his way to MIT. That's done. We have the microdot and that should ensure that Einstein's and Tesla's secrets will be safe from the FBI and the Nazis for the time being. What else remains to be done for phase two?"

"Nothing!" said Ian. "I've been recharging both devices since we arrived, so they're good to go. I suggest that we just head back to visit with Dr. Einstein to discuss phase three."

Everyone agreed. Dr. Mills went downstairs and paid their bills, then returned to the room. By that time, Ian had already sent Angelina and Carol back to the past. Dr. Mills gathered his things and made sure he had the microdot. Then, Ian sent him back, too.

Finally, Ian searched the room and made sure there was no evidence that could be connected with them, and then sent himself back to meet with Dr. Einstein once again.

Einstein's home, 1955

Everyone arrived in the kitchen of Einstein's home at the same time. Ian saw the light still on in his office, so he entered, and the others followed behind him.

"Don't you ever sleep, Dr. Einstein?" asked Carol as she came in. Einstein looked up from his work and answered, "Why, yes, my dear, a few hours a night, but it is still not time for bed for me. You only left a few minutes ago, and I have a few more hours of work before bedtime."

Carol looked confused, but Ian jumped in to explain.

"Mom, each time we return here, I only advance the time coordinates of the space-time address a few minutes. We can't keep returning here at the same point in time, because then Dr. Einstein would not remember the last meeting we had. So, I advance the time by ten minutes each time, so that he will remember, and he has time to work on the next phase of our plan, understand?"

"Sort of," said Carol, still looking perplexed.

"Look at it this way, Mom," said Ian, "if we returned before that last meeting, how would Dr. Einstein remember anything if we hadn't had the meeting yet, according to his timeline? We can all remember things because we are the ones traveling through time, so it's all sequential to us, but for Dr. Einstein, being stationary in time, it would be out of sequence. We have to keep things in order for him, if we are going to have him remember and work with us, get it?"

"Yes," replied Carol, "I get it now. It's just so hard to keep it all straight. It's the same reason that your father and the professor don't remember anything about the other timeline. It hasn't happened to them yet, and now never will, because of the changes we made, right?"

"Exactly," said Ian. "You've got it now!"

They took seats around Einstein's desk and reviewed with him all that took place during the trip to their past for phase two.

Einstein seemed pleased but asked a question. "How do you propose to deal with the fact that Angelina is supposed to be attending MIT in the fall? She will obviously need to fulfill her commitment to Ian to ensure he stays at school there and does not become discouraged and transfer to Princeton. That could undo all you have done."

"I've been thinking about that, sir," Ian replied, "and I believe we can address that after we complete phase three. We can send Angelina back to the point in time where she would need to apply to MIT, then send her to the point in time where she would receive the acceptance letter, and she would accept. Finally, we send her there for the first day of school, which I will pay for, by the way.

"From that point on, she would have to attend school normally and interact with the past Ian for a few months until she reaches the point where we first traveled back in time from Mario's office. At that point, my timeline, Angelina's timeline, and our past selves' timelines will once again converge and be in sync. I will take over for the past Ian, who will, in effect, no longer exist. Angelina will take over for her past self. Easy."

Einstein looked at Ian for a long moment. "It is not easy. You have miscalculated, my dear boy. No one has ever done this before. It is not certain that when the timelines of your lives converge, that you will remember anything of your 'present past'. You will now be merging into the new timeline reality, and it is possible that you may not remember anything about all you have been through recently. You will be assuming a new timeline reality, and it is unknown whether *your* experiences or the *past* Ian's and Angelina's experiences will dominate. It could also be that you will remember for a while, but that over time, the memory will fade as if it were all a dream. We need to prepare for that possibility."

"Are you saying, Dr. Einstein, that all of this could be for nothing?" asked Ian incredulously. "That all we have been through, all that we have discovered and invented will just be lost to us? That would be horrible! How can we ensure that none of what we have accomplished will be lost or forgotten?"

"I will need to think about that for a while," replied Einstein. "I am certain I can craft a solution. In fact, I have some thoughts about that already, but we can deal with that later. For now, let's just deal with phase three.

"You have been to the past. Now, you will be required to go into the future. You have set new events into motion, and you must understand the impact of those changes if you are to manipulate events so that you can eventually reveal all you know to the world. As we discussed previously, Ian, you must build a solid foundation before you can build a secure future for the world.

"By traveling to the future, you can become aware of who the influencers in the halls of power are at that time. Who are the dominant personalities that shape the world's opinions? Where will you invest your fortune to maximize your resources so that you have the financial ability to be independent enough to make your own decisions and influence the world to your point of view? You also need to assess the life trajectory of yourself and Angelina. By going to MIT, you have significantly altered both of your lives. By observing your future selves, you can go back and make the adjustments you may need to make to accomplish what we all desire. Do you understand?"

Ian felt a little overwhelmed. "Maybe it would have been easier to leave things the way they were. Hiding from the FBI and Nazis for the rest of my life might almost be simpler. This seems too hard and seems like it could require a lot of timeline adjustments. Do you really think we can do this, Dr. Einstein?"

Dr. Mills answered Ian. "Ian, first of all, we have the time travel devices. Those will allow us to react quickly to any changes that need to be made. Second, nothing is permanent. Since we can go back and forth through time, we can always change whatever the stimulus was for a problem that may arise in the future and then examine the result or repercussions immediately. As long as you keep those devices in working order, we have all the time and opportunities we need to get it right. Is there anything else that you could imagine that would be more worthwhile? Is there anything else you would rather spend your life doing?"

"And," said Angelina, "we will all be doing it together. Together, we are all smart enough and resourceful enough to get this right. We are free of the Nazis, we are free of the FBI, and, most importantly, we have Dr. Einstein at the height of his abilities and experience. Not only that, but we actually have access to all of the greatest minds of history, since we can travel to any point in time for a consultation with them. That is, of course, if we don't do anything to alter the past significantly in talking with them. We can do this, Ian."

"I agree with your observant young friend, Ian," said Einstein. "It will just take time, patience, and a plan. All of which I can help you with… except the patience, of course. That one is up to you. Are you up for the challenge?"

"I am," replied Ian, feeling boosted by everyone's support. "One hundred percent."

"Very well," said Einstein, "let us begin. We will start by mapping out the points in time that Angelina needs to return to in order to fulfill her obligation to attend MIT.

"Then, we will map out the final phase. It will need to be done in a series of excursions into the future to make observations, and then back to the past to make adjustments. Some of these excursions into the future and past may take considerable time, as you experience it. Some changes and observations could require only minutes, some hours, some days, weeks, maybe even years.

"This brings up another point of which you must be aware. While I sit here at my desk waiting for your intermittent returns, I will only be aging by minutes, you on the other hand, will be experiencing time as it flows. You will age. If you go into the future or the past for any length of time, you will age that amount of time. For example, if you go into the past when you are twenty years old and stay there for a year, when you return to me here, you will be a year older, but I will only be ten minutes older. The same goes for the future. Do you understand?"

Ian looked at the others. He hadn't thought about that, and it took a minute to absorb it all. Finally, his gaze rested on Einstein again.

"So, you are saying, Dr. Einstein," replied Ian, "that we don't have all the time in the world to get this done. We are limited by our natural life spans. We can't take a hundred years of our time to get it done. We still need to do things quickly and efficiently while traveling through time, making observations and adjustments, if we are going to be young enough to enjoy the future we are trying to create. Correct?"

"That is correct," replied Einstein, "and there is one more consideration. I will use this case to illustrate. If, for example, we were to wait twenty years as you experience it before sending Angelina back in time to attend MIT with Ian, she would in fact be, and look, twenty years older.

"The Ian of the past would have remembered meeting an eighteen-year-old girl at the dinner with Dr. Mills a few months ago. How could he reconcile the fact that she was now thirty-eight years old only a few months later? This is an aspect we need to consider.

"You will need to try and be, or appear to be, close to the appropriate ages that you are trying to portray in the times you will be trying to effect change in. If you don't, it will raise suspicions and may render your efforts ineffective.

"Another example could be that you travel to the future, and you are trying to get a meeting with a very powerful leader of some nation. You tell him you are Ian Petrie from New York and MIT, they will do a background check on you. If you are supposed to be fifty years old, but you only appear to be twenty years old, that will obviously cause problems. There are many other examples I can use, but I think you get the picture."

"So, how are we going to deal with that one, Dr. Einstein?" asked Angelina. "We can't age ourselves for the times we are traveling to in the future, so what can we do?"

"We must look at this as a multivariable equation!" exclaimed Einstein. "We must map it out very carefully, taking into account how long each part will take you, the order in which things need to be dealt with, what ages you can reasonably pass for, and which of you is the appropriate age for the task at hand. This we can and will do. After all, we have some of the greatest minds in the world here in this room, and access to many others from the past. Now that you understand the circumstances fully, let us begin."

They put their heads together, all contributing to the analysis and input, utilizing their varied skills, understanding, knowledge, and experience. Carol had a surprising amount of perspective that she shared, and the others found her insights valuable. Dr. Mills's understanding of how the human brain works and how to influence people based on their neurological strengths and weaknesses was also invaluable.

Of course, the big picture skills of Ian and the detail-oriented skills of Angelina, combined with her eidetic memory, complemented each other perfectly. Finally, the vast knowledge and worldly experience of Einstein, and his historical understanding of classical physics and mathematics combined with Ian and Angelina's current understanding of new physics and quantum physics enabled them all to maximize the time. In short order, they had put together an outline for the final phase.

As they sat reviewing the plan, Ian felt tired and hungry, but energized at the same time. If they could accomplish all that they had outlined, within the next year or two, they would be able to enjoy the fruits of their labors and give the world a brand new start.

They would have succeeded in implementing Einstein and Tesla's greatest dream; a world free from want and disease, a peaceful world where everyone's physical needs were met, giving them time to enjoy the life they were given with their family, friends, and neighbors. Truly a new beginning.

"Dr. Einstein," Ian said, "do you really believe that we

can do all of this in the timeframe we've outlined? Are you certain that we can travel to the future just as easily as we have gone into the past?"

Einstein responded, "Ian, I have always maintained that the difference between the past, present, and future is only a stubbornly persistent illusion. Now that I understand that everything is made of light, and that light, vibration, and resonance frequencies were the building blocks of all matter in the universe, I am even more convinced. It is said in the Bible that God is light and that he spoke all things into existence. Whether that is a metaphor or not, you have proved it to be true.

"So, it is my current belief that all things, past, present, and future, were created at that point in time. The complete equation was spoken at the beginning of time and the past, present, and future came into existence simultaneously.

"However, the smaller details are constantly changing based on free will. Even though everything exists, and the future is determined by God, none of it is determinable by us, as there are too many variables. Our task will be to change just enough variables to impact the larger issues that will influence the generalized outcome we desire. That is what our plan will accomplish. The smaller variables will not be enough to outweigh the larger, more impactful things we will set in motion. None of what we do will impact the future that God has outlined.

"All of that is to convey that I have high confidence that we can and will accomplish all that we have set before us today. Does that make sense?"

"It does. When should we begin, Dr. Einstein?" asked Angelina.

"Given that I am a very old man, and my time could come soon," replied Einstein, "I suggest you begin immediately. Who knows how many more sessions we will have here at my desk? Even though you can return here to this exact point in time no matter how many years you spend in the future or past, fate is a cruel master, and we must assume nothing. Always prepare for the unexpected and be ready to alter your plan accordingly."

Ian sat, knowing the exact time and place of Einstein's death and that he had just a matter of days. It took every ounce of self-control he possessed to avoid blurting out the information. He understood the dangerous impact it could have on all they had accomplished and all they were trying to do.

Still, there sat his hero, his guiding star, just days from his death, and it tortured him to know that he could possibly prevent it, and yet, he should do nothing about it. It crystallized his resolve. He would do this. He would complete the final phase, and he would do it quickly and efficiently so that Einstein could see the fruits of his labors and dreams. One day, he would sit here once again at Einstein's desk and announce that the mission had been completed.

"Time to go," announced Dr. Mills. "We'd better get started. We have a lot to accomplish." They stood from their chairs and lined up to say their goodbyes to Dr. Einstein. Carol was first.

"Dr. Einstein, I have always felt as if you were a part of our family. There were pictures and posters of you everywhere in our home, so I rarely went a day without seeing your face. Now, I have had the incredible pleasure to have met you in person. I am so grateful that our son chose such a good man to model his life after. Thank you for everything."

Dr. Einstein took her hand and kissed it gently. "My dear lady, thank you for your kind words. I am honored by them."

Next was Dr. Mills. "Dr. Einstein, as a man of science, I have always had a sense of your greatness. But now, I know that all we understood about you was nothing compared to your actual magnitude. You, sir, are a giant, and I've been honored and changed by our time together. There will never be another like you. Thank you for all your help and guidance." He stuck out his hand, and the two men shook hands firmly.

Dr. Einstein responded. "Dr. Mills, I am honored by your tribute, but I must say that you have proven yourself to be a man of great insight and integrity. I am grateful to have met you and to know that whatever the world you come from is like, science can still produce men such as you. You are a credit to science, and I know you will be a worthy mentor to Ian in the years to come."

Angelina was next and rushed to Dr. Einstein to hug him. She was teary-eyed and had trouble speaking for a moment. When she had composed herself, she said, "Dr. Einstein, although we have only spent a short while together, I feel as if I have found a long lost relative. You are like the grandfather I never had. You are such a good man, and I truly appreciate all you've done for us. Please take care of yourself when we're gone. We all want you here as long as possible, so we can visit many more times. Please, promise me you will."

Dr. Einstein had a slight smile on his face. It had been a long time since he'd felt the loving embrace of a child. He was not an overtly emotional man, and the relationships with his own sons had been very challenging, but he did have a tender heart.

"My dear child," he said, taking her face in his hands, "I shall do my best. I, too, think of you all as family. I have lived alone now for many years and forgot how wonderful it is to have family. Now, I ask the same of you. Be very careful in all you do. Remember, although you possess the ability to travel throughout time, you are not invincible, and you are not immortal. I would be very sad if any of you were lost to me. Will you promise me that you will be careful and protect yourself and the others?"

"I do promise, Dr. Einstein, with all my heart," said Angelina as she released him from her embrace.

Finally, it was Ian's turn. He stepped up, stood before Dr. Einstein, and looked him directly in the eye. "Dr. Einstein, words can never describe fully the impact and influence you've had on my life. Everything the others have said goes for me, too. You are my mentor, you are my hero, you are my inspiration, and you are now my family. I've been honored to sit at your desk and work side by side with you. It's a dream come true. I promise, sir, that I will make you proud. I *will* sit here with you one day and present to you the keys to a new world. A world you will have created. A world we will see together."

"Ian, it has been my honor," Einstein said. "Working with you has given me a new purpose, new hope, and a new dream. For that, I am eternally grateful to you. When a man enters into his final season, he reflects on all he has done.

"For all I accomplished, I still had a gnawing sense of despair. I knew in my heart I could have done more, but the answer came too late, and at a time when the world was not ready to receive it.

"The despair is now gone. The disappointment has fled. Even if I am not around to witness the end of your adventure, I will die knowing that the torch has been passed, and the dream will be accomplished. Thank you, Ian Petrie! Thank you for completing my life's work.

Now, make for me a brand new world full of hope and dreams. Then return to me, if you can. Who knows what new dreams we may imagine together someday? Now, go and send the others on ahead. I have one more task for you before you join them."

The others gathered around the larger time travel device and Ian sent them on ahead into the selected point in the future. Then, he turned to Einstein. "So, what is the task I have to perform before I join them?"

Einstein sat back in his chair and said, "Remember when we were discussing whether or not you would remember your 'present past' once your timeline converged with 'past Ian's' timeline?"

Ian replied, "Yes, sir, I remember."

"Well," said Einstein, "I have determined a way that we can have a failsafe in the event that the worst happens. Here is what I need you to do."

When he told Ian about his idea, Ian was ecstatic.

"What a great idea, Dr. Einstein!" Ian exclaimed. "It is so right and so poetic. This will close the circle and fulfill one more dream. I'm on it."

Ian input the space-time address into the portable device, pushed the button, and disappeared in a flash of blue lightning and resonant sound. He reappeared a moment later with a man who looked much disheveled and completely confused.

Einstein stood from his desk in greeting and said, "Welcome, Clarence! So good of you to have finally returned from your ill-timed vacation. Can we now get back to work? We have a lot to do and not much time to do it. We have a whole new world to create!"

The professor stood before Einstein, obviously in shock, looking back and forth between Ian and Einstein, trying to understand.

"Professor," Ian said, "I know this is astounding, and none of what I said to you back in your office makes any sense right now, but you are truly standing before Albert Einstein once again. I promise, he will make all things clear."

The professor, with tears in his eyes, said, "Dr. Einstein, is it really you? I have missed you so much these past sixty-one years. How is all this possible?"

Standing from his desk and approaching Clarence, Einstein put his arm around his friend and paraphrased Shakespeare.

"'There are more things in heaven and earth, Clarence, than are dreamt of in your philosophy!' Come, my friend, let us talk, and all will become clear. I am going to make you the repository of the information that will change the world. Here, you will be safe from those who would harm you. Here, you will be part of creating the future we always wanted. All of our mutual dreams will be fulfilled."

The professor took a seat at Einstein's desk, still looking bewildered and astonished.

Ian went to Dr. Einstein and the two hugged. "Although we will be traveling through time," he whispered in the old man's ear, "we will not forget. We'll see you soon, Dr. Einstein. Be waiting for us!"

"I will, Ian," said Einstein. "I will be waiting right here at my desk with Clarence, dreaming new dreams and thinking of you all. Godspeed."

Ian re-entered the proper space-time address and departed from Einstein's presence into an unknown future.

A future he was determined to create according to the hopes and dreams of a giant of a man of utmost intelligence and integrity.

ABOUT THE AUTHORS

Domenic Melillo, the author of the groundbreaking *Swords of Valor* trilogy, is a husband, father, son, and brother living in Wake Forest, North Carolina. His passion for writing and poetry was inspired by his father, Joseph Melillo, who read to his children many of his favorite poems by the classic poets.

All of Domenic's writings take inspiration from real-life events and personal experiences. In each novel, he strives to reveal the "what if" questions we all have, highlight and contrast the light and dark sides of life, and explore unseen worlds, historical secrets, and possible scientific breakthroughs. The themes of family, faith, heritage, loss, and redemption have always fascinated him.

He is an avid student of history, has a passion for reading, and enjoys delving into physics and classic literature. Domenic strives to embody many of the characteristics of one of his heroes, Don Quixote, in that he longs to see things as they should be, not as they are.

Described as a soul living out of his time, Domenic yearns for the days of chivalry, virtue, valor, and honor. He writes with the hope that his words will inspire families and society to return to these foundational qualities.

Dr. Robert Melillo is a successful author with five bestselling books, which he's written over the past ten years. *Disconnected Kids* is his biggest seller, and it has been translated into twelve languages thus far. These books focus on brain development, neurobehavioral disorders in children and adults, as well as cutting edge neuroscience. He has also published a widely read textbook, *Neurobehavioral Disorders of Childhood, An Evolutionary Perspective*, which discusses the evolution and emergence of the human brain and mind. He has also co-written and published more than fifty peer reviewed scientific articles and twenty chapters in other books on neuroscience, brain development, functional neurology, neuropsychology, and education.

Dr. Melillo is the creator of the Brain Balance Program and The Melillo Method. These are the most cutting-edge approaches available today for changing the brain. The information presented can help improve, or even correct, many developmental neurological disorders, which previously have been believed impossible to change. He is one of the most knowledgeable people in the world about the development and inner workings of the brain and the mind. He heads up a brain research lab and is well versed in evolution, psychics, and neuroscience. He is a student of history and historical figures, such as Einstein, Tesla, Newton, Darwin, etc.

Einstein's Desk is Dr. Melillo's first work of fiction, but his love of creative writing goes back to early childhood. His father, an amateur poet himself, inspired his children to love literature and to write. Robert's love of history, science, science fiction, superheroes, mythology, UFOs, time travel, and the brain also go back to childhood. He and his brother, Domenic, would lay in their beds at night, discussing all these fascinating topics and books, dreaming of someday writing about such things. Teaming up with his brother to write this thrilling novel based on all their favorite subjects and figures is truly a dream come true for Robert.